ArtScroll Series®

Rabbi Nosson Scherman / Rabbi Meir Zlotowitz

General Editors

by Yair Weinstock

translated by
Libby Lazewnik

Published by
Mesorah Publications, ltd

for the Soul

A famous novelist retells holiday stories with passion and spirit

FIRST EDITION
First Impression ... August 2002

Published and Distributed by
MESORAH PUBLICATIONS, LTD.
4401 Second Avenue / Brooklyn, N.Y 11232

Distributed in Europe by
LEHMANNS
Unit E, Viking Industrial Park
Rolling Mill Road
Jarow, Tyne & Wear, NE32 3DP
England

Distributed in Australia and New Zealand by
GOLDS WORLDS OF JUDAICA
3-13 William Street
Balaclava, Melbourne 3183
Victoria, Australia

Distributed in Israel by
SIFRIATI / A. GITLER — BOOKS
6 Hayarkon Street
Bnei Brak 51127

Distributed in South Africa by
KOLLEL BOOKSHOP
Shop 8A Norwood Hypermarket
Norwood 2196, Johannesburg, South Africa

ARTSCROLL SERIES®
HOLIDAY TALES FOR THE SOUL
© *Copyright 2002,* by MESORAH PUBLICATIONS, Ltd.
4401 Second Avenue / Brooklyn, N.Y. 11232 / (718) 921-9000

Typography by CompuScribe at ArtScroll Studios, Ltd.
Printed in the United States of America by Noble Book Press Corp.
Bound by Sefercraft, Quality Bookbinders, Ltd., Brooklyn N.Y. 11232

Table of Contents

Rosh Hashanah

JOURNEY OF A SHOFAR

T HE SMALL TOWN LAY IN THE GRIP OF A PEACEFUL AFTERNOON stillness. The only sound to be heard was the rustling of leaves in the gentle breeze.

A gang of non-Jews, barefoot and red-faced from the sun, wandered down the main street in the direction of the river.

"Hey, guys, what's this awful quiet? Where are all the Jews?" one youth demanded.

"Don't you know?" another answered. "This is the Jews' Judgment Day. They're all in their synagogue. Soon you'll hear them start to wail and cry. And, if we're lucky, we'll get to hear the shofar blast."

"Let's hurry to the river!" said the first, Vasili, quickening his pace.

"What's the big rush?" Jaskow chortled.

"I don't know," Vasili muttered uneasily. "The sound of the shofar scares me."

The gang broke into a run. In all the peaceful town, the only sound was the thudding of their feet as they headed downhill to the river.

Shoulder to shoulder, the Jews stood massed in prayer. Their town served as a spiritual center for a number of surrounding villages. Every year, simple Jewish laborers from those villages made the trip to town for Rosh Hashanah, in order to pray with a large gathering of their brethren.

In the house next door to the shul, Bracha Leah lay in bed, in the throes of labor. Her husband, R' Asher Leib, was the *ba'al tokea* in the shul. He stood wrapped in his prayer shawl close to the *bimah*, three shofars resting side by side on the table before him.

One shofar, blackened with age, had been passed down to him by his father, R' Shimshon *"Ba'al Tokea."* His father had produced wondrous blasts from this shofar, but R' Asher Leib had so far been unable to coax out as much as a single sound. The shofar's presence in the shul that day was only symbolic — a token of respect.

It was the second shofar that R' Asher Leib used, year after year. This one was yellow and curved, and he had purchased it for a huge sum from an expert shofar-maker. With this shofar, R' Asher Leib produced marvelous sounds. Hearing the shofar blasts without seeing the blower, one might be excused for thinking that they came directly from Heaven itself.

The third shofar had been a gift from the rabbi. It was a beautiful piece of work, pale in color, with a voice that was thin and delicate. For this reason, R' Asher Leib did not use it regularly. The shofar was present only in case of emergencies — in the event that his usual shofar should suddenly, Heaven forbid, lose its voice.

R' Asher Leib wrapped his *tallis* more securely around himself, closed his eyes tightly, and recited the blessing, *lishmoa kol shofar* — "to hear the voice of the shofar" — with complete concentration.

Then he lifted his shofar to his lips and blew the first *teki'ah*. A mighty sound rolled through the shul, making the very walls tremble. The blast echoed from floor to ceiling, slipped through the shul's walls and windows, and burst outside in a single magnificent note that seemed to shake the entire world.

Bracha Leah, in the house next door, was already in advanced stages of childbirth. She shifted in bed, the midwife beside her, tense with expectation. The sudden shofar blast startled them both. Immediately, the mother-to-be made a last, mighty effort — and her baby was born.

The infant's first wails mingled with the remaining shofar sounds blown by his father, R' Asher Leib, and both were joined by the new mother's soft, exhausted groans.

After the service, when the good news was brought to R' Asher Leib, he went over to the rabbi with glowing eyes. "A son was born to me. He heard the sound of the shofar immediately upon taking his first breath!"

"Is that so?" The rabbi peered at him. "He wanted to hear the shofar?"

Asher Leib was at a loss to understand the rabbi's meaning. "What do you mean, 'wanted'? He was born, and immediately heard!"

The aged rabbi murmured, "'And it shall be on that day that a great shofar will be blown, and the lost ones shall come from the land of Ashur and the rejected ones from the land of Egypt, and they will bow to the L-rd on the Holy Mountain in Yerushalayim.'

"People don't always want to hear the sound of the shofar," the rabbi continued, his eyes piercing R' Asher Leib's with a penetrating stare. "There are those who try to escape its voice ... But the day will come when a great shofar blast will sound, a blast that will be impossible to avoid, and it will bring the most rejected and lost souls back to Yerushalayim."

"Amen," whispered the congregants who were standing around, listening. They knew their rabbi as a holy man, a man through whom the Spirit of Hashem flowed.

"Amen," breathed R' Asher Leib, his eyes streaming with hot tears. The rabbi's words had struck him with a sudden, inexplicable fear. His heart told him that there was meaning behind the words. The rabbi's question had not been an idle one.

"Is that so? He wanted to hear the shofar?"

On *Erev Yom Kippur,* the child was circumcised on the elderly rabbi's knees, and he was named Shimshon, after R' Asher Leib's father, the former *ba'al tokea.* All who were present wished the father success in raising his son to follow in the footsteps of the revered grandfather for whom he had been named, and R' Asher Leib responded to each good wish with a fervent "Amen," as though trying to heap the very essence of blessing on his tiny son's head.

Shimshon soon began to display a sharp and agile mind. His parents were overjoyed when his teachers praised his learning and predicted a bright future for the boy.

"If Shimshon continues to study diligently," more than one teacher told R' Asher Leib, "he has the potential to become a Torah leader for his generation." The proud father's eyes welled up with emotion and gratitude. He hurried home to share the good news with his wife, so that she, too, might rejoice in her child. Ecstatic, Bracha Leah bestowed a great many kisses on her precious only son, born to her after many barren years.

As the High Holy Days approached each year, no one was prouder than little Shimshon. His father was the *ba'al tokea*, second only in the town to the aged rabbi himself. When the time came for his father to blow the shofar, the boy would stand close to him, watching with wide eyes as he tried to learn the secrets of the art. When his father wasn't looking, Shimshon would put the shofar to his own small lips and try to make it "speak." Each time, he failed. He tried again, and again he failed to make even the smallest sound.

The years passed quickly. The elderly rabbi departed this world. R' Asher Leib wanted to live peacefully and reap *nachas* from his only son, but the Enlightenment had come along to shatter the peace of Jewish parents throughout Europe. To his father's grief, Shimshon demonstrated a tendency to embrace the Enlightenment's tenets and to acquire secular knowledge that contradicted the age-old values of the Torah. R' Asher Leib's heart nearly burst with sorrow when he heard that his son had been seen in the company of a group of questionable young men in some of the "Bund's" favorite haunts.

Many parents in his position, whose children had thrown off the yoke of Torah, sat *shivah* and erased the child from their lives. R' Asher

Leib wanted to do the same, but his heart did not permit him to take such a drastic step. "No use burning all the bridges," he told his wife, when she tearfully demanded that they break off relations with their strayed son. "There will always be time to do that, if we choose. And who knows? Perhaps some day he will regret the choices he's made."

"Oh, certainly," Bracha Leah answered bitterly. "You're waiting for Shimshon to do *teshuvah*? A waste of time. If only I'd remained barren! If only I'd never given birth to a son like this ..." And she gave herself up to heartbroken weeping.

Shimshon stood on the other side of the door, listening to his parents talk. What he heard ignited a flame of fury inside him. From that day on, he refused to set foot in his parents' home.

R' Asher Leib was still a robust man, but his hair had turned completely white, like that of a much older person. That year, his shofar-blowing was ragged and broken, as the tears flowed from his eyes to clog the shofar's mouth. From nowhere, a memory popped into his mind: the memory of a newborn child, wailing to the accompaniment of the shofar blast, their voices mingling together and ascending skyward.

"*Teki'ah*," the new, young rabbi — son of the former rabbi — whispered.

The *teki'ah* was ashamed to meet the light of day. Lost in his own grief-stricken world, R' Asher Leib did not hear the rabbi's whisper. How many hopes he had pinned upon his talented Shimshon. His only son — "a Torah leader for his generation" his teachers in yeshivah had predicted. "If he continues in this way, he can become a new R' Akiva Eiger!"

Was there any mockery more cutting?

Only the old rabbi had seen it coming. What was it he had said, that Rosh Hashanah twenty years earlier? "Not everyone wants to hear the sound of the shofar. There are those who try to avoid its voice."

Who knew where Shimshon was at this very moment? No doubt he was idling somewhere with his new friends.

"*Teki'ah*," the rabbi raised his voice slightly, trying to catch R' Asher Leib's eye.

R' Asher Leib sighed deeply. He poured his whole, shattered heart into the shofar, and the shofar seemed to understand that this was no frivolous breath, but something rising up from R' Asher Leib's deepest being — his very lifeblood. Working together with him, the shofar produced a sound to break any heart, and the entire congregation joined in with its own sobbing.

"We've never heard a shofar-blowing like that before," the congregants told each other afterwards. "Those blasts must surely have reached the Heavenly Throne! Even a wall of steel would melt like water from R' Asher Leib's heartbroken blowing."

In the week between Rosh Hashanah and Yom Kippur, Shimshon came to see his father.

"I'm fed up with this dusty hole," he announced, waving a ticket in the air. "I'm going to America! I leave for Odessa tomorrow, and from there I sail to the big city of New York."

"Shimshon!" his father cried, making a quick calculation. "Where will you be for Yom Kippur?"

"Yom Kippur?" Shimshon tried to look as though this trivial detail had slipped his mind. "I'll probably be on the train, headed for Odessa. But — but the conductor is a non-Jew!"

Without a word, R' Asher Leib crumpled and fell to the ground in a dead faint.

When he regained consciousness, he refused to look at his son. Such a son, who had the brazenness to admit that he was planning to desecrate Yom Kippur, had no place in his world.

As the boy was about to leave town however, R' Asher Leib changed his mind and ran to meet his son at the train station.

"Shimshon, my son!" The tears poured down R' Asher Leib's face as he thrust a small, cloth-covered bundle into his son's hands.

"What is this?" Shimshon asked in surprise, turning the bundle over.

"It's better that you don't know that until you arrive in America," his father answered briefly. "I have only one request to make of you. Promise me that you will guard this package from all harm, and that in the fullness of time you will pass it on to your children."

No sooner had the train departed the station than Shimshon unwrapped the bundle curiously.

"Ah, Father's shofar," he whispered, gazing crestfallen at the yellowed shofar. "I thought he might have given me a bit of cash. What use will this ram's horn be to me in America?"

Suddenly furious, he yanked open the window and nearly hurled the shofar through it. But a shred of respect lingered, preventing that rash act. Instead, he re-wrapped the shofar in its cloth covering and stored it away in his luggage.

"Who put the stupid idea in my head to travel to America?" Shimshon asked himself for the thousandth time. He had long regretted the impulsive trip and had been trying to come up with ideas for finding a way back home.

For a full month he had endured the roiling voyage across the Atlantic, terribly seasick like most of his fellow passengers. When the Statue of Liberty appeared before them, the passengers erupted in grateful cheers. But their happiness was short-lived. All the would-be immigrants were herded off the ship like a group of lepers and ushered onto Ellis Island, for fear that they carried the germs of infectious diseases.

Shimshon spent thirty endless days as a virtual prisoner on that island. When he was finally allowed to leave, he had his first close-up look at the gigantic, sprawling city of New York. The teeming streets, the air of excitement and constant motion, took his breath away. Like a dream, all his plans to return to Russia vanished in an instant.

While most of his "Bundist" friends had chosen to immigrate to Palestine, where they were working in the heat of the barren desert and languishing from malaria, Shimshon had opted for America and its golden opportunities. He had been blessed with a fertile mind that included sound business sense, and now he had his chance to put it to use. He did not waste a second. He found himself a tiny apartment in the Jewish section of the city on the Lower East Side, and began to search for work. Sabbath observance, so precious and holy to his fellow Jews, presented no obstacle to his accepting a job. He worked seven days a week, and was commended for his energy and ambition.

That was just the beginning. Shimshon took a loan from his boss and used the money to buy out a failing company. Within a few months he had managed to put the company back on its feet. When he came to his former employer to repay the loan, the other man said, "To be honest, I'd given up on the money. I never thought you would succeed — and so quickly!"

It did not take long for Shimshon to learn the American way of doing business. He went from one success to the next. His competitors whispered bitterly that he must have been born with the Midas touch because everything he touched turned to gold. Following the pattern he had set with his first triumph, Shimshon continued to buy out companies that were on the verge of bankruptcy, and turn them around and set them on a sound financial footing again, in a way that left more experienced businessmen astonished.

In an amazingly short time, "Samson and Sons" had become well known in American business circles as one of its most prosperous shining lights. It owned numerous factories and employed hordes of workers. The banks provided limitless loans for expansion. Successful forays into the stock market doubled the company's money.

In the American lingo of success, Shimshon had "made it."

Sixty years passed.

As the elderly Samson looked over his family, his heart fairly burst with contentment. When, many years back, someone had suggested a date with a Jewish girl, he had seen no reason to reject the idea. Though, deep down, he would not have minded assimilating fully into the lives of his non-Jewish business friends, this was not a rock-hard principle of his. He had ended up marrying the Jewish girl — and found, to his surprise, that both his sons, Jeffrey and Arthur, followed his lead in doing the same when their own times came. Both married girls from Jewish families and raised a fine crop of grandchildren.

On his 80th birthday, Samson sat in his beautiful home, surrounded by his children and grandchildren. Everyone was in good spirits, their laughter floating up to the high ceilings and filling the spacious rooms. Samson watched them happily.

Then he cleared his throat and waited for silence. The family obliged respectfully.

"I am old," he announced without preamble. "No one knows when the day of his death will be. I want to show you something my father gave me a long time ago — a religious object that he passed on to me before I came to America."

Walking slowly, with the aid of a cane, Samson went to his wall safe and turned the knob carefully to unlock the combination. The door of the safe opened wide. Samson drew something out and presented it to his astonished family.

In his hands was a ram's horn, pale gold in color, covered with the dust of ages.

"I was born to the sound of this horn!" Samson said. "It was eighty years ago today, on the first day of the new year."

"But, Grandfather, New Year's Day comes out in the middle of the winter, on January first!" a small granddaughter piped up.

"True. But today is the Jewish New Year. Jewish people have a custom of blowing this horn on this day. They call it a 'shofar.'" He turned to his son, Jeffrey. "Well, Jeffrey, let's see what you can do with it. Your grandfather was a shofar-blower. He was amazing. Let's see if you inherited the skill from him."

Tentatively, Jeffrey took the shofar from him. "This horn is old and dusty," he said. "I can hardly even bear to touch it."

Arthur snatched the shofar away. "There's a synagogue near my home in Queens," he declared. "For the past month, I've been hearing loud sounds every morning. Someone explained that they're made with this kind of horn, and that they're meant to awaken people's hearts."

Arthur raised the shofar to his lips, and the sounds of *teki'ah, she-varim,* and *teru'ah* filled the room.

The blood drained from Samson's face, leaving it white as a sheet. His knees buckled, and he just managed to stagger over to a nearby armchair before collapsing heavily into it.

"You blow just like my father did," he whispered. "The grandfather you're named after. His Jewish name was Asher Leib."

Sixty years of American life were erased in an instant. He was once again in the old *shtetl* that was no more, in his childhood home with his parents — good, serene folk who had worshiped their Creator and had been content with a dry crust of bread to eat. A violent trembling overtook him. It was as though a lightning bolt had lit the landscape, making everything at once terribly clear and terribly painful. In that instant, he knew with absolute certainty, from the depths of his being, that he had wasted his life.

The Jews in that far-off and long-ago *shtetl* had used every minute for Torah and repentance and good deeds. But here in America — everything revolved around the pursuit of money and material ambitions. Where was his father's delicacy of spirit? Everyone here was robotlike, false, and materialistic. "And I am one of them," he thought in anguish. "A fool who thought he was wise. The final page of the calendar of my life will soon be turned ... My mother was right! If only I had never been born, rather than anger my Creator!"

"Shall I blow it again?" Arthur asked gaily. He had been taken aback at his own prowess on the shofar. He had not believed that he would be able to produce the tiniest sound from an instrument he had never handled before in his life. The sounds had been identical to those he had heard this past month, issuing from the synagogue each morning.

At a weak nod from his father, Arthur blew and blew. In all, he blew over one hundred blasts, and perhaps as many as two hundred. And all through them, Samson's shoulders shook as he sobbed into his hands. His sobs mingled with the sounds of the shofar just as they had eighty years earlier. But those had been the wails of a pure, newborn child who had never tasted sin, while today ...

He wept bitterly for a solid hour. His family brought him water to drink and gazed at him, at a loss. These old people tended to get so emotional at the drop of a hat. Arthur kept on blowing the shofar, so engrossed in his newfound skill that he hardly noticed the effect it was having on his father.

"The shofar is yours," Samson said at last, as the echoes of Arthur's final blast rolled away to the four corners of the room. "You deserve it, and it deserves you."

◈

Another ten years passed.

On the kibbutz, a deep afternoon stillness reigned. The kibbutzniks had been up since dawn, toiling in the fields and greenhouses. Now, during the hottest part of the day, they had taken to their beds for a much-needed nap to refresh them for the next round of work.

On a green hill not far from the last kibbutz dwelling, the cowherd tended his cows. He felt peaceful and content. It was a peace he had known from the moment he had decided to forsake the American pursuit of wealth and the "good life" in favor of an Israeli kibbutz.

Martin, or Mordechai, as he was known here, had been considered the least talented among his brothers. They had proved their worth when, with their father's encouragement, they had taken high administrative positions in the huge family business known as "Samson and Sons."

"Martin, how long are you going to live like a dreamer?" his father, Arthur, would ask impatiently whenever he found his son sunk in a reverie in his plush office, chin on one hand and eyes fixed on the horizon. No one understood him — and no one was interested in trying. On the fast track to wealth and success, there was no time for dreams.

Here, among the cows in the meadow, Martin could let his thoughts roam free. For hours at a time he remained absorbed in his reflections, sometimes dipping into a philosophy book he had discovered in the kibbutz library. He would read, and think, and then read some more. The kibbutz members had grown used to the sight of the American volunteer who appeared to be daydreaming from morning to night. He seemed to be a sweet character who would not hurt a fly.

"Hey, Martin, I brought you a package that arrived yesterday at the post office!"

The call roused Martin from the soul-searching thoughts that had lately been occupying him constantly. For some time now, he had become aware of a bottomless hunger which the philosophy books could not satisfy. He had found a small volume one day at the roadside, apparently dropped from some passing car. The volume had the word *Tehillim* stamped on the front cover. Glancing inside, Martin had been thunderstruck at the message of those short, simple sentences.

For the first time, he felt as though a compassionate hand had taken his own and was leading him, the way a mother leads her young son as he struggles to learn to walk.

"Did you hear me?" Gideon, who supervised the kibbutz's dairy farm, waved a small package wrapped in brown paper. "This came for you from America. Looks like your father remembered you," he chuckled.

Martin opened the package, which had the return address of "Samson and Sons" printed in the upper lefthand corner. A piece of stationery fluttered out.

"My dear Martin," Arthur had written. *"In honor of the upcoming Jewish New Year, I've decided to send you the shofar that I received from my father, may he rest in peace. I thought that with your love of philosophy, you'd know better than I what to do with it."*

Martin groped among the wrapping paper until his hands pulled out an inner, cloth-wrapped bundle. A shofar, pale-gold in color and very old, lay inside.

"Hats off to your dad," Gideon exclaimed. "He hit it right on the mark. Today is Rosh Hashanah!"

"What — today?" Martin gasped.

"Yes. What are you getting so excited about? What's Rosh Hashanah to you?"

Martin didn't answer. From the mists of his childhood he drew out a single memory. It had been exactly ten years ago, on the day they had all celebrated his grandfather Samson's eightieth birthday. The scene had been etched into his heart as thought with a chisel. His father had stood blowing a pale-gold ram's horn and producing strange, powerful sounds — while Grandfather, that ruthless businessman who was never seen to shed a tear, had cried like a baby. Martin remembered being frightened. He had turned and buried his face in his mother's side.

And now, here it was, the strange instrument that Grandfather Samson had called a "shofar."

"We blow the shofar today?" he asked Gideon, as he brought the shofar tentatively to his lips.

"That's right. Martin, why are you crying? Martin?"

But Martin didn't hear a thing. A thrill of solemnity ran down his spine as he touched the shofar with his lips. Jewish life — the fruit of hundreds of generations — flowed through his veins and seemed to teach him exactly what to do. He blew the shofar the way his father, Arthur, had blown it ten years before. One long blast, followed by a series of broken sounds. Tears ran down Martin's cheeks as he blew, falling unheeded to the ground. As they did, his assimilated soul melted away, leaving in its place a pure and newborn Jewish one.

Mordechai the Jew ....

He stood blowing and blowing, until his strength was gone. By the time he was done, Gideon was no longer there. Martin-Mordechai felt as though his soul had been washed in clear, cold water. For the first time in his life, he knew that all the questions and doubts that had tormented him throughout his young life had had a purpose — and that purpose had been to bring him here, to this moment. Now he knew exactly what he was supposed to do next, and where tomorrow would bring him.

"And the lost ones shall come from the land of Ashur ... and they will bow to the L-rd on the Holy Mountain in Yerushalayim!"

THEY WILL HEAR FROM AFAR, AND RETURN

OR SIXTY YEARS, R' YISSACHAR DOV FRANK SERVED AS *BA'AL makri* in the old Jewish Quarter shul. It was a large shul, with spacious dimensions and rainbow-curved windows that let the bright Jerusalem sun pour in.

R' Yissachar was one of those special individuals whose piety was even greater than his wisdom. His radiant face and flowing beard seemed to testify to the purity within. As he walked with measured steps from the shul's eastern wall up to the *bimah*, his siddur tucked under his arm, the other men would rise with instinctive respect. His sober expression reminded them that the voice of the shofar would shortly be echoing through the shul.

Usually, it is the shofar itself that draws the worshipers' attention. For a person of feeling, there is nothing more heartbreaking than the shofar blast as it rips through the air. And for a person of halachah, there is nothing more enmeshed in halachic detail than the one hundred prescribed sounds of the shofar. As the congregants stand watching the *ba'al tokea* prepare to blow the shofar, a thrill of anticipation runs through them. And they listen with lowered heads and thoughts of repentance, wiping away a tear perhaps, and checking to make sure that they have heard all one hundred sounds.

In this shul, it was different. It was not that the shofar-blowing itself was trivial in the congregants' eyes — Heaven forbid. It was just that the greatness of "Yissachar the *Ba'al Makri*" overshadowed the *ba'al tokea* and his shofar. It was R' Yissachar's voice that prompted the shofar's sound.

He announced each blast quietly, in a trembling, awe-filled voice that tore at the heart. Eyes glued to his siddur, he would call out "*teki'ah*" amid suppressed tears, "*shevarim*" in a broken voice, and *"teru'ah"* with open weeping, the tears coursing down his cheeks to become trapped in the silver of his beard.

The congregants loved R' Yissachar Frank and would cluster around him to look humbly into his siddur. It was an old siddur and a thick one, its pages yellowed and creased. The siddur had been written 400 years earlier by a great Kabbalist who had been a student of the Arizal. It contained writing in regular Hebrew letters as well as the smaller Rashi script. And the pages containing the shofar-blowing looked like those of no other *machzor*, filled on every side with scribbled secret hints and intentions understood only by the knowledgeable. The men were deeply moved by these incomprehensible signs, which seemed to breathe of higher, secret realms where proponents of good battle mightily with the prosecuting Satan.

Naftali and Yonasan, R' Yissachar's two sons, would *daven* alongside their elderly father and make sure no harm came to him. "Two sons, two worlds," their acquaintances would say of them.

Naftali, the older son, resembled his father down to the last detail. He lived in poverty, learned day and night, observed halachah scrupulously, and was also knowledgeable in the secret Torah. Yonasan, on the other hand, was an experienced and prosperous businessman. While he did not mind picking up a *sefer* now and then, Yonasan was no *talmid chacham*.

R' Yissachar Frank was growing old. For sixty years he had stood and done the calling out for *ba'alei tokea* in the shul in Jerusalem's Old City. Shofar blowers had come and gone, the elderly being replaced by the younger, and still R' Yissacher was the one who stood and called out for them. Now he, too, was getting on in years. The people wondered what would happen after R' Yissacher departed this world. It was not that they wanted to see him go; on the contrary, they loved him. But it is human nature to speculate about another's death much more easily than about one's own.

Which son, they wondered, would take over for the father once he was gone? Naftali or Yonasan?

Naftali was the Torah scholar, but Yonasan had the richer purse and might be able to bribe the *gabbaim* — no difficult feat in a city that saw people dying of hunger every day.

Chaim Zelig, the chief *gabbai*, was of the opinion that Naftali should be appointed the *ba'al makri* after his father's passing; after all, he was a *talmid chacham*. But if he mentioned this to Shmuel David, the second *gabbai*, Shmuel David immediately declared that they should pick Yonasan. Thinking it over, Shmuel David decided that, should the head *gabbai* choose Naftali, he himself would side with Yonasan. And if Chaim Zelig chose Yonasan, Shmuel David would loudly reject such a crass pursuit of money, and would claim that only Naftali, the *bechor*, was worthy of inheriting his father's mantle.

On Friday, *Erev Shabbos Nachamu*, Bracha Liba — wife of R' Yissachar Frank — passed away. The members of Jerusalem's *Chevrah Kaddisha* (Burial Society) hurried as only they know how to hurry, and removed the dead body from the house — and along with it, more than half of R' Yissachar's heart. To live sixty-two years with a person — and what a person! What a life!

The tears welled up endlessly from the deepest part of him, and the heartbroken sighs would not stop. His sons cried along with their father and tried to comfort him.

"Stop it," R' Yissachar sighed. "Your mother died content. I will not."

The brothers sat *shivah* for their mother. As he sat with them, R' Yissachar appeared on the verge of saying something. Each time, however, he pulled back. He kept looking into his old siddur and turning the pages slowly to the place where the shofar-blowing ritual was written. The brothers' hearts thumped loudly as they awaited their father's decision. But, in the end, he said nothing.

On the first *Motza'ei Shabbos* when *Selichos* were said, R' Yissachar Frank led the service. No one present had ever heard him cry as he cried that night, saying, "The soul belongs to You and the body is Your handiwork; have mercy on Your labor." Every heart quailed, and every eye filled with tears, but it was R' Yissachar who wept the most.

Afterward, he returned home and glanced sadly into his old siddur with its many secrets. He climbed into bed, where he recited the *Shema* with great devotion. On the word *echad*, his soul left his body.

❦

The eulogizers cried over R' Yissacher, who had lived 88 good years. But their voices had scarcely faded when the fierce debate began. It started out quietly among the *gabbaim*, and soon escalated to shouts. One said, "Naftali!" and the other declared, "Yonasan!"

The seeds of a full-blown quarrel sprouted in the shul. There were those who sided with one *gabbai* and those who agreed with the other. There were even those who kept switching sides, until the entire shul was caught up in the flames of dispute.

As for the brothers themselves, they stayed out of the fire. Each believed that their father's position belonged to him. And then, one day, Yonasan whispered something in Naftali's ear, and the quarrel was silenced.

Naftali, the *bechor*, was poverty-stricken and his home was bare. As long as they had been alive, his parents had supplied his simple needs. His mother, Bracha Liba, would bring him a bag of flour from time to time, or a box of beans, a large bottle of wine, and the like. But she had passed away just a month before the Angel of Death handed her sons a second tragedy in taking her husband. Naftali thought over Yonasan's proposal. If Naftali would yield the rights to their father's siddur and his position as *ba'al makri*, Yonasan would give him 100 gold napoleons.

One hundred napoleons! Naftali's imagination swam. A single napoleon could feed his family comfortably for a month. A hundred napoleons! A hundred months!

The week of *shivah* passed. It was *Erev Rosh Hashanah,* and still the *gabba'im* — and the rest of the congregation along with them — had not resolved their dispute.

Then the two brothers stepped out of the house of mourning and announced to them all: "We have agreed between us. Yonasan will be the *ba'al makri* and will inherit our father's siddur."

❦

The next day, the first day of Rosh Hashanah, Yonasan stepped up to the *bimah* in his new role as *ba'al makri*. He squinted at the tiny Rashi lettering surrounding the words of the *teki'ah, shevarim, teru'ah*. At one point he called out "*teru'ah, teki'ah*" instead of the other way around; and more than once he mixed up a simple *teki'ah* with *teki'ah gedolah*, until the *ba'al tokea* himself became confused and blew *shevarim* where he should have blown *teru'os* and *teru'os* in place of *teki'os* — throwing in an extra five *teikios gedolos* for good measure!

Pockets of muffled laughter sounded throughout the shul. Under his prayer shawl, Naftali could sense the accusing stares on his back. That morning, before the service, Yonasan had told two or three friends the secret behind his brother's capitulation, warning them not to tell another soul. These "devoted" friends hurried to whisper the secret to others — in strictest confidence, of course. People were calling the 100 napoleons that Yonasan had paid his brother on *Erev Yom Tov* a dirty bribe.

Naftali was shattered. How, he wondered desolately, had he ever agreed to such a plan? He knew that the congregation would never forgive him for his part in making a laughing-stock of what had been so precious and holy. And, as if that were not enough, he and Yonasan had become enemies in the process.

On the spot, Naftali decided to get away — preferably as far away as possible.

Immediately after Succos, Naftali Frank sold his house and all his belongings, took his wife and children, and set sail for America. After thirty-four days at sea, they arrived at the port of New York.

As for Yonasan, he held on to his father's siddur, treating it as a valuable treasure. Every so often, he would take it out and stroke it lovingly. That siddur, and the position of *ba'al makri*, had cost him dearly. He was left without ready cash — money which had often come in handy when trying to tie up a business deal. Without it, he found his opportunities limited. His business did not prosper that year, or the year after.

In the third year, World War I broke out.

England declared war on Turkey. As a result, every English citizen living in Palestine was considered an enemy of the Ottoman Empire. R' Yissachar Frank had moved to Eretz Yisrael from Poland, but had requested and been granted British citizenship at the British Consulate in Jerusalem. His two sons, therefore, were also British subjects — and enemies of the Turks who presently ruled Palestine.

One day in the month of Elul, Yonasan was arrested by Turkish police officers. He was thrown into jail, where he languished for three weeks. Rosh Hashanah came and went while he was in prison, without a *minyan* or a shofar, and Yonasan prayed alone, disjointedly and from memory. On the following day, the Fast of Gedaliah, Yonasan was deported to Egypt together with his family. Of all their possessions, they brought along only a small case containing, among other things, his father's old siddur.

Years of destitution followed for the family. Yonasan and his wife and sons wandered through the gutters of Alexandria, until a wealthy Jew took pity on them. A collector of rare volumes, he agreed to buy the old siddur for one hundred silver coins.

Naftali arrived in America with a respectable bundle of money. With an aching heart, he launched himself into the world of business, and everything he touched was blessed with success. When the first World War broke out, he turned his hand to supplying military needs. But his true love lay with the Torah, and he spent every spare hour learning.

Several years later found Naftali the owner of several factories which manufactured Army uniforms in San Francisco. Naftali was scrupulous in his observance of the mitzvos, and all his factories were closed on Shabbos — a rare phenomenon at that time. Sadly, however, his sons did not hold the same things dear. They did not follow in their father's footsteps. When Naftali grew old, his sons had the factory machines humming seven days a week, much to their father's anguish.

When World War II broke out between Nazi Germany and the rest of Europe, America remained uninvolved at first. But as the years passed and the German military arm reached out to conquer more and more of Europe, the American government became afraid that the conquest would eventually spread to the rest of the world. Then Japan bombed the Navy fleet at Pearl Harbor — and the United States entered the war.

Among those drafted into the army was Oscar (Yissachar) Frank, the youngest of Naftali's sons who had been born in America. He was sent with the American troops to Normandy, France.

Oscar fought valiantly to liberate Italy, where he was severely wounded by German sniper bullets. He was taken to the military hospital at Napoli.

The doctors nearly despaired of his life. The surgery lasted many hours, as they tried to repair his internal injuries. When the operation was over, the chief surgeon said, "We've done everything humanly possible. Now, only He can help." He rolled his eyes skyward.

Oscar lay unconscious for several days. His skin withered until he looked like a person very near death. One of the nurses, knowing that Oscar was Jewish, invited a Jewish rabbi from the town to come and recite *Shema Yisrael* at the dying man's bedside.

Entering Oscar's room, the rabbi's heart twisted at the sight of a young Jewish man who might have been home tasting all of America's pleasures, but who had been thrown instead into the battle against the evil Nazi war machine. The rabbi sat by Oscar's bed and watched for signs of approaching death. He had with him an aged siddur that he had received from his father, a collector of rare old volumes in Alexandria, Egypt. The rabbi turned the pages of the siddur, preparing to read the portions that are said when a soul departs this earth.

Because he did not yet see signs of impending death, the rabbi set himself to wait. Idly, he glanced inside the siddur's front cover. There, in the center of a sketch of the Wailing Wall, were the handwritten words, "Yissachar Frank, Yerushalayim," and a date.

The rabbi's eyes went from the name in the siddur to the name on the patient's chart. His mind reeled with possibilities. Was there a connection between Yissachar Frank and this soldier, Oscar Frank?

Oscar continued to lie unconscious. At last, the rabbi got up, tucked the siddur beneath the patient's head to invoke Heaven's compassion, and left the hospital.

He returned the next day, to find the doctors and nurses exclaiming excitedly.

"A miracle! A great miracle!"

"What miracle?" asked the rabbi.

"That critically injured soldier, Oscar Frank, woke up yesterday and asked for a drink of water."

Entering Oscar's room, the rabbi found him dozing. The same thing happened on the following day. On the third day, however, Oscar Frank was wide awake when the rabbi paid his visit.

"They told me that a Jewish rabbi was here, and I see it's true," Oscar said weakly. "I thought you must have brought the angel Raphael with you."

"Not me," the rabbi answered, smiling. "It was the holy siddur that I placed beneath your head." He reached under the patient's pillow and pulled out the siddur. Then he showed Oscar the name on the inside cover.

Oscar's eyes nearly popped out. "This is the siddur my father told me about. It was because of this siddur that my father traveled to America. Angels must have brought it to you."

"No, I got it from my father, who bought it from a Jewish merchant in Alexandria for a huge sum."

Oscar proceeded to relate to the rabbi the full story of the siddur, as he had heard it from his own father. The rabbi insisted that he keep it. "I give it to you as a gift. Hashem's Hand brought you and me here so that I might return your grandfather's siddur to its rightful owner."

Oscar sighed deeply. "But my father is old now, and frail. What will he do with this siddur? His time has passed."

"And what about you?" the rabbi asked gently. "Are you exempt from following your forefathers' example? Let Yissachar Frank pray from the siddur of his grandfather, Yissachar Frank, *z"l*, and bring peace to his soul."

Three years later, Naftali Frank and his sons traveled to Eretz Yisrael. He wished to visit Yerushalayim, the city where he had been born. To his endless grief, he learned that his old shul in the Jewish Quarter had been one of thirty-two shuls destroyed at the hands of the Arabs after their conquest of the Old City. Naftali wandered slowly through the streets of the city, until he found himself at last in the *Yeshuos Yaakov* shul in the Meah Shearim neighborhood at *Minchah* time.

Several of the men there stared at Naftali as though seeing a ghost. Had R' Yissachar Frank returned to the land of the living? They were looking at a face and bearing that uncannily resembled R' Frank's. A couple of the more daring among them approached Naftali and asked him respectfully whether he was related to the former revered *ba'al makri*.

"He was my father," Naftali answered with deep emotion. At once, he began to recognize the speakers and to put names to their faces: Yankel, Leibel, Nachman. It was all he could do not to collapse with sheer happiness.

"What ever happened to my brother Yonasan?" he asked, when he had recovered somewhat from his first shock.

Yankel and Nachman stared at him without speaking.

"Is Yonasan still alive?" Naftali persisted, beginning to cry. "Tell me the truth."

Sorrowfully, the men related the events of poor Yonasan's life since the brothers had parted. They told him how Yonasan had been deported to Egypt, where he had roamed the streets in poverty and want for years. Finally, some ten years ago, he had managed to return to Eretz Yisrael, destitute and broken. At this very moment, he could be found in the *shteibel* across the street, collecting handouts.

In a flash, Naftali was out the door and crossing over to the other shul. He found an elderly man there, one frail hand outstretched to accept donations. Naftali gazed at the other man's face for a long moment. "It's my brother," he whispered. "It's Yonasan Frank."

Then, with a strength usually reserved for the young, Naftali shouted, "Yonasan!"

Yonasan glanced up — and froze. He began to tremble with shock and fear, as his astonished eyes took in what appeared to be his departed father. It took him a moment to realize that it was his older brother. In the same vigorous bellow, he yelled, "Naftali!" And then the two brothers stumbled into each other's arms and hugged one another fiercely, their tears mingling. And all the men who watched their reunion felt their own hearts turn over and began to cry along with them, tears of emotion and joy.

That Rosh Hashanah, Naftali was asked to serve as the *ba'al makri* in the shul. His brother, Yonasan, stood in a corner and wept like a baby. Afterwards, Naftali went over to him and asked, "Do you want the siddur that you bought from me for 100 napoleons?"

"No! No! I sold it to some Egyptian collector. It was Hashem Who returned it to you," Yonasan said. "I've done enough already." He refused to take the siddur from his brother.

Those congregants who remembered R' Yissachar from the old days cried openly as Naftali officiated as *ba'al makri* that *Yom Tov*. For them, it was almost a form of *techiyas hameisim*. Naftali was now nearly the age his father had been at the end, and they were alike as two drops of water. Sights that they had thought never to see again had returned. And the miracle of the two brothers reuniting and making their peace seemed even greater than that of *techiyas hameisim*.

For nearly forty years, the shofar-blowing had been bereft of the special intentions from R' Yissachar's siddur. For an entire generation, Naftali's heart had been desolate each year at that time.

Now the sons had returned to their rightful place, and all was well once more.

A STRAYED LAMB

THE MOMENT R' MUNISH ATLAS RAISED THE SHOFAR TO HIS lips, he was overwhelmed by an enormous sadness. He had no idea where the strange sorrow came from. With his teeth clamped around the tip of the ram's horn, he began to sway back and forth, trying — unsuccessfully — to shake off the sadness.

The *ba'al makri* standing near him was the shul's aging rabbi, R' Akiva Leiberman. With his eyes glued to his *machzor*, and concentrating on the hidden meanings of each *teki'ah*, R' Akiva did not sense the emotion that had gripped the *ba'al tokea*.

"*Teki'ah*," he intoned.

R' Munish tried to get hold of himself. Once again, he took the tip of the shofar into his mouth. With sweat pouring down his face, he blew into it.

R' Munish was a superb shofar-blower. His fellow worshipers boasted that R' Munish's *teki'ah* was louder and stronger than the mighty whistle that announced the train's arrival in Jerusalem. They said that R' Munish's *teki'ah* would literally shake the walls of the shul, along with the walls of the listeners' hearts. After hearing R' Munish blow the shofar, no man, woman, or child in shul could remain calm. The mighty blasts made everyone tremble with fear. Beneath their prayer shawls or kerchiefs, the men and women would *daven* very earnestly.

For twenty years, R' Munish had served as *ba'al tokea*, and never once had he made a mistake. His shofar-blasts followed the letter of Jewish law, in their order and in their length.

Today, however, was different.

Today, R' Munish blew a mighty breath into the shofar — and not a sound came out. He blew again, and again nothing emerged. He put down the shofar for a brief rest, took a deep breath, wiped the sweat from his brow, and tried again.

After three tries, he finally managed to coax out a *teki'ah* — a weak, pathetic sound that was nothing like the blasts of earlier years. The *shevarim* were feeble and fragmented, while the *teru'ah* was stilted and not pretty to hear.

"What happened to our *ba'al tokea*?" the people asked themselves. "Why is he not managing to blow the way he used to — the shofar-blasts that used to fill us with fear and frighten even the Satan himself? Does he feel unwell today? Is he weak? Or has the sweat that is pouring down his face clogged the shofar's mouth?"

R' Munish tried his best to make his former shofar-music. But the blasts grew weaker instead of stronger, making the children begin to smile behind their hands and amuse themselves and each other by imitating the funny shofar sounds until a stern look from their parents made them stop.

A sudden doubt entered the rabbi's heart. R' Akiva Leiberman wondered whether the tortured blows were halachically acceptable. He wanted to signal for the *ba'al tokea* to hand the shofar over to him. R' Akiva himself was a competent shofar-blower; he was the one who did the job every day in the month of Elul. If R' Munish would give him the shofar, he would see what he could do today, when blowing was not only permissible, but an obligation.

He wanted to signal to R' Munish, but he didn't do it. He hesitated out of respect for R' Munish: He did not wish to embarrass the *ba'al tokea* in front of hundreds of people. At the same time, however, there was the mitzvah of proper shofar-blowing to consider. The rabbi waited for R' Munish to understand on his own what he ought to do.

And at last, after thirty feeble and broken blows, R' Munish did. It was impossible to continue this way. Silently, he handed the shofar to R' Akiva.

R' Akiva was already an elderly man. He was neither the most accomplished shofar-blower, nor the worst. His blasts were not dazzling, but they were halachically kosher. As he blew, R' Akiva was inwardly happy that he had not snatched the honor from R' Munish. Everyone knew that R' Munish was a superb *ba'al tokea* and had been for the past twenty years. Something strange had happened to him today — an extraordinary problem that surely would never happen twice.

On that Rosh Hashanah day, R' Munish had no idea why his blowing had failed. Ten months later, however, he began to have some notion. With anguished heart, he understood why the Satan had ruined his performance on that day. It was meant as a sign of things to come.

Near the end of the summer session at yeshivah, the *mashgiach* phoned R' Munish to ask how his 17-year-old son, Shloimy, was doing.

"Shloimy?" R' Munish asked with sudden fear. "I haven't seen him since the Shabbos before *Rosh Chodesh Tammuz*."

The *mashgiach* gave a confused cough and searched for a way to extricate himself from the conversation. R' Munish, however, would not let him go. He begged the *mashgiach* to explain what lay behind his call.

"Shloimy," the *Mashgiach* said solemnly, "has not been in yeshivah all week." He had told several friends that he had a bad cold, and told others that he had a stomachache. He was going home to rest in bed, on doctor's orders, he said.

Just the day before, the *mashgiach* had learned something new and disturbing. It seemed that Shloimy, before leaving the yeshivah, had confided to yet another friend that neither of the other stories had a word of truth in them. In actuality, he was traveling north to a kibbutz, where he intended to leave the Torah life behind him forever. His friend had believed that Shloimy was joking. It was only now, as the *mashgiach* tried to track the boy down, that things began to look serious.

"I thought maybe you would tell me that it was all nonsense," the *mashgiach* said in a trembling voice. "But since you confirm that your son is not at home this week and never showed up at all, I am very much afraid that it's the last version of the story that is the true one."

A cold sweat broke out on R' Munish's forehead. "What do we do now?"

Their talk went on for some time. When it was over, R' Munish left his house and traveled immediately to the yeshivah, where he met with men who specialize in helping strayed youths return to the fold. Both the *mashgiach* and the *rosh yeshivah* were present at the meeting. Ideas were raised and strategies outlined. Some of the experts said one thing, and others said another. Finally, they concluded with a plan to send a few of their number — articulate young men who knew how to answer questions concerning Jewish faith and philosophy in a non-rejecting way — to meet with Shloimy on the kibbutz. Their aim was not to chastise the boy, but rather to try to prove to him that he was mistaken.

When they set eyes on Shloimy Atlas, they were looking at a stranger. Gone was the yeshivah *bachur* with *tzitzis* hanging out of his pants. In his place stood a youth wearing shorts and a t-shirt, a youth with smoldering eyes.

"Don't call me Shloimy Atlas around here," he warned. "No one knows me by that name."

"What do we call you, then?" one young man asked quickly.

"Dror Yarden."

"Fine. Let it be Dror," the young man said. "Tell me, is it possible to milk cows in the Lower Galilee only by throwing away your *tzitzis*? If learning Torah is hard for you and you crave a life of physical labor, tell us. We can arrange for you to stay at a *shomer Shabbos* settlement."

Shloimy Atlas, a.k.a. Dror Yarden, burst into disdainful laughter. "You are so stupid and naive," he sneered. "You think that I want to be a kibbutznik? Wrong! I have no desire in the world to deal with cows and manure, or with planting and harvesting, for that matter."

"What are you looking for here, then?"

"A place to stay until I get drafted into the army," answered "Dror." As he went on to explain his ambitions, it became clear to his visitors that he had long since become entangled with a group of youths from the far left.

This group might aptly have been named a "Spider Gang." They wove their web for Shloimy Atlas, stalking him the way a spider stalks a hapless fly, spinning its threads until escape becomes impossible. Having captured Shloimy in their net, they were now supplying him with a place to live and money to live on until he landed on his own feet. The day they saw their prey truly captured — the day he believed that all the bridges were completely burned behind him — was the day they would abandon him without a second thought. They would leave him to struggle alone, and would certainly not provide material support to the tune of even a penny.

Anyone who does not know a spider's nature might genuinely believe that it weaves its sweet web out of love for the fly. But the spider, after eating its fill, always leaves the remains of the poor fly clinging to the web for all to see. Only then does it become clear that what seemed like a beautiful friendship was actually nothing but the dance of stalker and prey.

Shloimy, like the fly, had fallen deeply into the spider's trap. His new friends wore pleasant faces and an air of "culture." It was they who had directed him to this kibbutz, as a sort of springboard to a new life of "freedom." But it was a life that held no nourishing water to feed it underneath, but only a pit crawling with snakes and scorpions.

R' Munish waited impatiently for some good news from the activists who had met with his son. He longed for a ray of light to illuminate the darkness that enveloped him from head to toe. But as soon as the young men returned and he saw their faces, the same cloud of sorrow that had covered him on Rosh Hashanah descended again.

Neither R' Munish nor his wife slept much over the next few weeks. They spent the hours of darkness weeping softly over their strayed son. R' Munish would sob until a kind of calm returned. And then, the memories would come.

Shloimy as a newborn baby. "*Mazal tov* to you!" the nurse said, beaming. "You have a beautiful son, healthy and whole." Then the *bris*, when little Shloimy became a full Jew with the King's stamp on his body. Rejoicing, prayers, and good wishes: May this little one grow great in Torah and good deeds!

How many nights had he and his wife lost sleep over their growing boy! They had nursed him through various ailments, both the usual and the not-so-usual, sitting by his bedside for entire nights and placing wet cloths on his burning forehead. What tender words had they whispered to their son on those nights. What sweet songs had they sung. Songs of Torah and *emunah*, songs of holiness and purity.

When Shloimy was old enough, his father had begun to teach him Torah. What love the father had brought to the job; what joy and contentment. And, in due time, they celebrated his bar mitzvah. The party was not spectacular, but heartfelt and modest in the classic Jewish fashion. It had been a thanksgiving feast to their Creator for granting them and their son the privilege of reaching that special milestone.

Night after night, the memories burst over R' Munish on the heels of his tears. What, the poor father wondered, had he done wrong to merit such a punishment?

He wondered, and he wept.

The truth about Shloimy's escape to the kibbutz was kept a dark secret for all of two weeks. Then, in the midst of the summer break, it erupted. Several of his friends found it impossible to guard their tongues another second.

As it happened, when the story reached his shul, R' Munish was still at home. He had been late for the first *minyan* of the day and came to shul just as they were finishing. He entered the shul through a side door and went directly to the deserted women's section to wrap himself in his *tallis* and *tefillin*.

But before he could do more than begin his preparations, he overheard a conversation taking place nearby. The men who had just finished *davening* were discussing something with animation. Through the window connecting the women's section to the rest of the shul, R' Munish could hear them clearly. With a sense of shock, he realized that they were speaking of none other than his own son, Shloimy. Or rather, Shloimy and the rest of his family. The whole story was thoroughly dissected as the men folded up their prayer shawls and put them away.

R' Munish heard every word. For two weeks, he had lived in fear that the awful news would reach other people's ears. Now, the worst had happened.

"What happened, exactly?" asked Yaakov, the *gabbai*.

"Don't you know?" Yirmiyahu answered. "He ran off to some kibbutz, kicking his mother and father right in the face in the process. He doesn't want to have anything more to do with his family."

"Why to a kibbutz?" asked Reuven, a man who enjoyed finding the humor in any situation. "If he has a craving for milking cows, we can accommodate him right here in the neighborhood. We'll bring him his own cow and he can sit and milk her to his heart's content. He can even dress in khaki if he chooses, with boots and a farmer's hat!"

The group broke into laughter.

"But why did he do it?" someone asked. "What was he lacking? He had everything he needed at home."

"That's the whole problem," old R' Shraga said solemnly. "*Vayishman Yeshurun vayivat* — Give a person too much, and he'll rebel."

An innocent conversation between men who had heard shocking news and wanted to understand it. Afterwards, however, when they had dispersed to their homes and R' Munish still stood frozen in the women's section, he heard three other men — longtime neighbors of his — sitting down to analyze the story like dogs gnawing on bones. The conversation quickly turned personal, with the men commenting on R' Munish's *Yiddishkeit* and the kind of home he ran. Once they started looking, they managed to find things to criticize. "Remember the time ..."

R' Munish felt as though someone had taken a hammer and shattered his heart to bits. He could hardly believe what he was hearing. "What fools!" he wanted to scream at those men. "Who do you think you are, to be so smug and self-confident? Remember what *Pirkei Avos* says: 'Do not trust in yourself until the day of your death'! What makes you so sure of your own children? Don't you know that there's an inferno raging in our streets, and it's burning not only the streets but anyone who happens to pass by? Never before has our community been as exposed to outside influences as it has been in recent years. And it's precisely now, when the contrast between our lifestyle and that of the secular world — so devoid of values, except for the dubious one of 'Eat, drink, and be merry, for tomorrow you die!' — is so glaring, that the contamination rears its ugly head, using all the latest technology to spread its humor and song.

"How dare you speak of another person so disparagingly! How can you be so self-assured? Who has guaranteed the future of your own children?"

That was what he wanted to shout with all his might. He felt as though his heart was about to explode with the force of what he was feeling and everything that he longed to say.

And then his heart did explode, in a way. R' Munish fell to the floor unconscious, the victim of a massive heart attack.

All his friends and acquaintances came to see him in the hospital. R' Munish was so broken in spirit that he could hardly speak a word to any of them — especially when his visitors were those members of the early *minyan*.

R' Akiva Leiberman walked into the room. "How are you?" he asked softly.

R' Munish burst into uncontrollable sobs. He cried so hard that the monitors beside his bed began to beep and whistle frantically, bringing a whole medical crew running in. The rabbi was ordered to leave the room at once. It took quite a while for the doctors to stabilize the patient's erratic heartbeat.

R' Akiva waited patiently for the day R' Munish was released from the hospital and sent home. At the first opportunity, the rabbi went to see him. He found R' Munish half-sitting, half-reclining in a deep armchair, his face pale as chalk and his eyes sunken. Quietly, haltingly, he told his story to the rabbi. R' Akiva listened with a sense of growing shock as R' Munish related the conversations that he had overheard from the women's section of the shul.

R' Akiva sat sunk in thought for some time. Then he said, "R' Munish, I've thought it all over. I know that it's terribly painful. It wounds the very soul! But we are not a people who seek revenge. Our glory comes not from destruction, but from doing positive deeds. We have to keep our eyes on the goal, and on that one goal only: that Shloimy return home from the foreign fields into which he has strayed."

Sadly, R' Munish bowed his head in agreement.

"Actually, it's not one goal, but three," the rabbi amended with a smile. "We do want revenge — a sweet revenge, the likes of which you haven't imagined. That is the second request. The third is: Can you blow the shofar for us on Rosh Hashanah?"

The question took R' Munish by surprise. "I — I don't know," he stammered.

"Tell me what you think of this idea," R' Akiva said. Leaning forward, he whispered something in R' Munish's ear.

R' Munish's face lifted as he listened, and a faint smile came to brighten the dark, sad eyes.

On Rosh Hashanah, R' Munish was seated in his usual place in shul, ignoring all the curious glances that were thrown his way. On *Erev Rosh Hashanah,* they had asked him if he would blow the shofar, but he would not reply by so much as a hint. Now, as the time for the *tekios* neared, tension filled the shul.

Would he blow, or not?

Suddenly, a rustle of surprise swept through the shul. A newcomer had walked in. It was a youth, eyes cast down to the floor.

"Shloimy's here!" the people whispered excitedly. "It's Shloimy!"

His hair was long, his yarmulka was small, and his clothing was very different from the kind he used to wear — but it was undoubtedly Shloimy. Or Dror Yarden, as the case might be.

He went up to R' Akiva, who shook his hand warmly and handed him a folded *tallis.* As Shloimy put on the *tallis,* the congregation watched in amazement. What was he planning to do?

The mystery was solved almost at once. Shloimy stood up near the *bimah,* a *machzor* open before him and his father's shofar in his hand. R' Akiva stood to his left, preparing to serve as his *ba'al makri.*

The electricity in the air exploded into pandemonium. On every side, men pounded their *shtenders* and called out angrily. "A secular boy blowing the shofar for us?" "What chutzpah!" "R' Munish has gone too far!"

Several arms reached out to pull Shloimy away from the *bimah* and throw him out together with his shofar.

R' Akiva raised a hand and shouted, "QUIET!"

Like magic, the shul fell instantly silent. Everyone waited respectfully for the old rabbi to speak.

"*Rabbosai,*" R' Akiva said in a trembling voice, "Your complaint is not with R' Munish, but with me. I am the one who asked Shloimy to take his father's place this year."

Tension filled the air as they waited to hear more.

"Shloimy knows how to blow the shofar and can help you all fulfill your obligation," R' Akiva continued. "But anyone who wishes may listen to the shofar-blowing in the shul next door."

With that, he turned back to his *machzor* and began to recite *Lamenatze'ach,* the prayer that precedes the *tekios.*

When his moment came, Shloimy blew with all the strength of his young lungs. The blasts emerged strong enough to shake the walls — but not the listeners' hearts.

The people were angry. Most of the congregation organized themselves after *davening* to hear the hundred shofar blasts a second time, after R' Akiva, R' Munish, and Shloimy had left the shul. They roiled and blustered like a stormy sea. Who had ever heard of such a thing? A young boy living sinfully on a kibbutz, to be the one to rouse the angels that come from the *tekios*? Impossible!

There was, however, one heart that had been touched. A young boy's heart ...

On Yom Kippur, Shloimy returned to *daven* in the shul. His father, R' Munish, did not put in an appearance. On doctor's orders to eat and drink small amounts during the day, he was forced to remain at home. But Shloimy *davened*. He sat beside R' Akiva and prayed intently from the *machzor*, word for word. The sharper-eyed among the congregants claimed that the boy's yarmulka had grown by at least two centimeters since Rosh Hashanah.

The *Ne'ilah* prayer was finished. *Kaddish* was recited. The air was electric with expectancy. Who would blow the shofar?

A mighty blast tore through the shul. It came from the shofar at Shloimy's lips, and climbed quickly up to the heavens. That blast, and its echoes, tore at Shloimy's heart until it crumbled into a thousand pieces.

He blew and blew until there was not a drop of air left in his lungs. The blast grew weaker, and finally died. In its place came the sound of sobbing, no less shattering than the shofar blast that had come before it.

Shloimy Atlas was home.

The city spoke of R' Akiva Leiberman's wisdom for many a long day afterward.

"The wisdom of Shlomo," people exclaimed, again and again. "The old rabbi took the trouble to travel up to the kibbutz in person. He went to Shloimy and said, 'Shloimy, do what you want. Live any way you please. I have just one favor to ask of you: Please do not embarrass your father. He can't blow the shofar this year because of the heart attack he suffered. Come and blow it in his place.'"

A simple request. Shloimy could not refuse. He came to shul on Rosh Hashanah, and returned again on Yom Kippur.

And stayed.

IF I FORGET THEE, ROSH HASHANAH

"**F**LIGHT 423 TO INDIA WILL BE LIFTING OFF IN ONE-HALF hour. Passengers are requested to board at the gate."

The announcement did not arouse any pangs of conscience in Shimon Heligman as he slung his backpack over his shoulders and took a firmer grip on his hand luggage. He was well aware of the day's Hebrew date, but he chose to ignore it. Besides, his airline ticket read "September 13," which held none of the frightening significance of the day's date according to the Jewish calendar, which was 1 Tishrei. Rosh Hashanah!

"My New Year's Day will take place on January 1st," Shimon decided. He had no wish to remember the Jewish New Year. In fact, that was exactly what he was running away from!

How many Rosh Hashanahs had he spent praying alongside his father in the yeshivah at the end of their block? Four, five ... what difference did it make? He remembered the long *tefillos*, the piercing shofar blasts, the *mashgiach's* speech before *Ma'ariv* on the second night. How he had enjoyed all that as an innocent child.

But then he became a teenager and met up with a group of wild kids who were fun to run around with. He met Topaz, a friendly, secular boy from a nearby neighborhood. Topaz had drawn him into places and activities that Shimon had never known before. He had introduced Shimon to new friends and opened doors to exciting pastimes and dark, smoke-filled places that were the very gateway to *gehinnom*. In short, Topaz introduced him to a world where one could do exactly as one pleased. And Shimon had willingly allowed himself to be dragged along.

His parents' pain distressed him — especially his mother's tears. "Shimon, my son, at least put on your *tefillin* and say *Keri'as Shema*. Just two minutes a day. Just that, Shimon — for me!"

So he had done it, for her, though his heart felt as empty as a bottle of beer after he had drunk it down.

"Shimon," his father said to him with anguish in his eyes, "people in the neighborhood are saying, 'Yaakov Heligman's son has turned into a bum.' But that's not what really hurts me. It's the pain of your soul that hurts me!

"I know that you've moved away from everything. But know this, Shimon: There are thirty-six prohibitions that cut a Jew off from his Source, and corresponding to that are thirty-six threads that bring a soul closer to its Source. Please promise me that you will not transgress any of those thirty-six prohibitions. The day will come when you will want to come back. Don't burn your bridges behind you!"

And Shimon had promised his father. He had no idea whether he would be able to keep his promise, but the thought of those thirty-six threads put a great fear into him. While it was true that, right now, he was totally committed to living by his own desires, there was no way of knowing whether someday in the future he might not begin to miss the lifestyle he was throwing away now.

"Ridiculous!" Topaz said, when Shimon broached the idea as they strolled through Jerusalem's Old City before the trip to India. "You'll never want to return to the chains of religion. You've just freed yourself of them and can do anything you want. Why would you ever go back to prison voluntarily?"

"It's not a prison," Shimon argued. "It's just a different lifestyle."

"Call it whatever you want," Topaz had said good-naturedly, and let the subject drop. They wandered into a souvenir shop, where

Topaz bought a necklace as a gift for Shimon. "A souvenir from the friend who opened your eyes," he quipped, hanging the silver chain around Shimon's neck. Dangling from the end of the chain was a medallion with words on it.

"What's that you've put on me?" Shimon demanded, picking up the medallion and reading it. "*Im eshkachech Yerushalayim* — If I forget thee, Jerusalem.' What do I care about Yerushalayim? It's a miracle that you haven't made me wear a necklace saying, 'If I forget thee, Bnei Brak.'"

He wanted to remove the necklace on the spot, but Topaz convinced him to keep it. "Listen, you're about to travel to India. How long will you stay there? Two years? Three? I want you to remember me always."

"'If I forget thee, Topaz,'" Shimon laughed. He let the necklace stay where it was.

He traveled to India together with a group of twenty young men and women. All during the trip, he tried — with a measure of success — to forget the enormity of what he was doing on the *Yom HaDin*, the Day of Judgment. The yeshivah at the end of his block had prepared for this day all month. Elul! He remembered well the tears those yeshivah men had shed as they shouted about "He Who tests hearts on the Day of Judgment." Then the long, silent prayers, whispered with eyes riveted to the letters in one's *machzor*, ears hearing only the sibilant whisperings of one's fellow worshipers and the rustling of turning pages as tear-filled eyes spilled over and dampened them.

But Shimon was determined to forget all that. He carried on animated conversations with his fellow travelers, sang songs with them, and from time to time checked out the view from his airplane window. After a while, someone got out a small, cloth-covered drum and accompanied the increasingly loud singing with a steady beat. Several of the other passengers stood up and shouted at them to be quiet. The young travelers just laughed.

In the yeshivah, the people wept as the *shaliach tzibbur* intoned, "And the angels will hasten, amid fear and trembling, and will call out, 'Here is the Day of Judgment!'" Then the *chazzan* cried, "A person comes from dust and ends in dust ... He is like a shattered vessel ..." The cry reverberated from one end of the vast *beis midrash* to the other, slicing through the worshipers' hearts like a fiery sword.

Shimon lifted a bottle of wine to his lips and finished it off in several long, thirsty gulps.

"This is *yayin nesech*," whispered his near-defunct conscience. To still the tiny voice, Shimon pulled out another bottle. "Leave me alone!" he thought fiercely. "Do you want to take away all my pleasure in this world?"

He was determined to sin and sin, until that tiny voice of conscience would be stilled forever.

He spent the second day of Rosh Hashanah in India. He and his friends booked themselves into a youth hostel and then went out to see the sights and get acquainted with the city. Eretz Yisrael, where Shimon had been born and raised, seemed a million miles away. His mother and father and everything he had once known became, in that single day, no more than a blurred and distant memory. Today was September 14th, and nothing else!

Shimon enjoyed India. From time to time, he would travel to a new part of the country, where he would mingle with the natives, learn their dialect, and wear their clothes. He came to know more about their religion than they knew themselves. His long hair was tied back in a ponytail and three small earrings adorned his left earlobe. He often walked barefoot, swam regularly in the "holy" rivers, and passed many a night in a monastery. As if possessed by a *dybbuk*, he threw himself heart and soul into the worship of foreign gods. It was the best way he knew to stifle the memories that would rise up from time to time, as though from the very depths of his being: memories of Shabbos candles, of his father poring over his *Gemara*, of the *Kosel* stones. To do away with those memories, he would worship every idol under the sun.

Then he heard about the "Silent Monastery."

The monastery, located in the Himalayan Mountains, fired Shimon's imagination and seemed to draw him like a mysteriously powerful magnet. A friend of his who had spent some time there painted a strange and interesting picture of the place. Shimon decided to travel into the mountains at once. Without delay, he purchased an airline ticket to the city closest to the monastery.

When he finally arrived at the place, he saw an old building of stone, surrounded by a tall metal gate and ancient, dusty trees. At first, Shimon was at a loss to find the entrance to the monastery. After a lengthy search, he discovered at last a heavy wooden door. He knocked respectfully, and waited. There was no answer. He tried again. After half an hour's wait, the door was opened by an aged monk with a shaved head. He did not speak, but only gestured angrily, "What do you want?"

"I want to join the monastery," Shimon said.

The monk slammed the door in his face.

Humiliated, Shimon turned to go. Suddenly, the door opened again, and a young, smiling monk emerged. Speaking in English, the monk said, "I am spokesperson for the monastery." He extended a friendly hand. "The monks here have taken a lifetime vow of silence. The gatekeeper could not answer you."

"A lifetime of silence?" Shimon said, stunned.

"Yes. Do you still want to join us?"

The healthier part of him wanted to say, "No." It urged him to run as far as he could get from this oppressive place. Then the restless imp that had been goading him all through India got the better of him once again.

"I'd like very much to be here," he heard himself saying.

"Please," said the young monk. "But you can only start next month. We open the monastery gates just once a month, and new members are accepted only on that day."

Here was another excellent chance to escape. But Shimon was firmly in the grip of his own inner destructiveness. He remained in the vicinity for three more weeks, held fast by an inexplicable stubbornness, as he waited for the happy day when he would be able to bury himself in the society of the silent monks.

It did not take long for bitter reality to puncture Shimon's rosy dream.

Life in the monastery was cold and gray. Speaking even a single syllable was forbidden — except in cross-legged prayer on the hard stone floor, mumbling words that made no sense to him for interminable hours. The monks taught the newcomers how to engage in lengthy meditations and perform rituals in front of a large statue with an unpronounceable name. They fed Shimon and the others rice mixed with a vegetable sauce that looked even worse than it smelled.

Hardest of all, however, was the silence. By nature, Shimon was a lively chatterer. The silence imposed a burden he was not fit to carry.

He tried to comfort himself with the thought that he would soon grow used to this lifestyle. Day after day, however, he felt as though he were being tortured. There was only one thing that relieved the difficult routine. Each day, at noon, the monks would leave the monastery walls to pace decorously around the courtyard for exercise. The walk was more like a prison round than anything else, but it was the only time that a limited number of necessary words were permitted. During this brief exercise period, the monks would hastily discuss important matters.

Not surprisingly, Shimon was the biggest talker in that courtyard. More than once, he was scolded by the monk in charge of the silence. The monk would stomp over to Shimon and clap him roughly on the shoulder. He would speak only five words: "You are talking too much!" The rest of the message was transmitted with a finger to his lips, saying more clearly than any words, "Quiet!"

Shimon would drop his eyes apologetically. A moment later, as the scolding monk moved away, Shimon would eagerly seek out someone else to whom he could talk.

One day, during the noontime walk, he noticed one of the younger monks studying him intently. This was repeated the next day, and the next. Shimon began to feel uncomfortable under the monk's scrutiny — even afraid. Snatches of dark tales that he had heard came back to him now. Tales of midnight murders, of bodies carried out of the monastery walls and burned, with no one on earth the wiser. Shimon began to wonder whether the young monk was planning to add him to the roster of unnamed victims.

When he saw the monk eying him again on the following day's walk, Shimon decided not to hold his tongue any longer. He went directly to the head monk's office and asked to speak to him urgently.

The Silent Monastery, however, had its own way of doing things. Novices had to observe decorum. The head monk was not available except by appointment.

Impatiently, Shimon asked for an appointment, and was told that he could see the head monk in four days' time. They were four days of taut nerves and sleepless nights for Shimon. At last, he found himself facing the head monk across a wooden desk.

"What do you want?" the monk asked.

As briefly as he could, Shimon described the young monk's behavior during their daily walk, and the apprehension it was causing him. The head monk stared at him, and then said, "How long have you been with us?"

"Three months."

"Three months," the aged monk repeated angrily, "and your hair is still long? I will not speak with you until you have shaved your head. You must look just like all the other monks here!"

Indeed, when Shimon had applied for acceptance to the monastery, he had been told that he must shave his head. But he had objected strenuously, saying that he had come for only a short stay and did not want to destroy his looks for a passing episode. Now, however, he had no choice. The head monk had issued an ultimatum. "Shave your head at once, or be severely punished!"

The next morning, Shimon made it his business to find out where the monastery's barber was located. With heavy heart, he went to have his long hair shaved off.

As he entered the barber's room, his knees buckled and he nearly fainted. The barber was none other than the young monk who had been eying him so intently for days! Shimon wanted to run, but his leaden legs refused to move.

At last, he slipped weakly into the barber's chair. This, he felt sure, was the end. One slip of the barber's shaving razor could slash his throat with ease.

The barber hovered over him, a razor in one hand and a pair of scissors in the other. Shimon's heart thumped so hard it hurt. Suddenly, to his astonishment, the barber leaned closer and whispered, in English, "Tell me, are you a Jew?"

"Y-yes." What did the monk want? To be certain that the man he was about to murder was Jewish?

"Me, too," whispered the monk.

"*What?*"

"Don't get excited. I'm a Jew from Israel. Are you from there, too, by any chance?"

"Yes!"

The talk switched immediately to Hebrew. The two nearly broke into a dance, like a pair of long-lost brothers meeting again under the most bizarre and unexpected of circumstances. Who would ever have believed that, just a moment ago, Shimon had been deathly afraid of the monk, whom he had suspected of having murder in his heart?

The monk went on to tell him that he had left Israel ten years earlier, and had since forgotten his birthplace entirely. He had nearly forgotten, too, his Hebrew name, which was Efraim Beit-Halachmi, as well as the fact of his Jewishness. From the moment he had laid eyes on Shimon, however, the early memories had rushed back to the fore.

"It was the medallion you're wearing around your neck that first drew my attention," Efraim confessed. "It reminds me every day of the holy city of Jerusalem. How I long to see the stones of the Western Wall again!"

"It was because of my necklace that you kept staring at me?" Shimon burst into laughter. "And I thought you were plotting to kill me!"

"Would you be prepared to give me that necklace?" Efraim asked, with single-minded persistence.

"No! It's a memento that was given to me by my good friend, Topaz."

"But maybe you'd do it anyway?"

"I'm sorry, but no."

Shimon left the barber a short time later, completely bald. As his hair was being shaved off, something else was happening inside. His dormant conscience had begun to awaken, stinging him with pangs of fearsome regret.

Shimon cried in his bed all that night.

As they paced through the courtyard at noon the following day, Efraim whispered to Shimon, "Come to my room this evening."

In due time, Shimon arrived.

Without preamble, Efraim asked him, "Do you want to leave the monastery?"

"Want to leave?" Shimon almost shouted. Cautiously, he lowered his voice. "I'm dying to leave this prison — to run away and never look back!"

"We can do it tomorrow," Efraim said. "Tomorrow is the one day a month when people come and go. I'm getting ready to leave then."

For Shimon, this seemed like a heaven-sent sign. Efraim's next words, however, sent shock coursing through him with the force of a hammer-blow.

"I have a Hebrew calendar that a friend from Israel sent me," Efraim said. "Do you know what tomorrow's Hebrew date is? It's *Erev Rosh Hashanah!* Tomorrow night is our Jewish New Year. I'm planning to find the nearest synagogue and spend the holiday there."

On Rosh Hashanah he went, and on Rosh Hashanah he returned.

The Rosh Hashanah prayers of those two lost souls in India will never leave Shimon's memory. Today, he is the proud head of a fine Jewish family.

"*HaKadosh Baruch Hu* prepared the cure before the illness," he says, eyes glowing with tremendous joy. He takes the medallion with the words *If I forget thee, Jerusalem* from the wall on which it hangs in a gold frame. As he fingers it, Shimon says, "Poor Topaz never knew what he was doing when he gave me this necklace."

THE SOUND OF THE SHOFAR

"I PROMISE YOU, THEY'LL BE OUT IN A WEEK. I GIVE YOU MY word as a lawyer, and that's something you can depend on. This time, I'm serious. They've crossed the limit. What nerve! I've already spoken to Motti Lakish from the municipality. They've broken a city law regarding the residents' hours of rest. Don't worry, I'm going to throw the book at them and chase them out of here. All the best to you." He hung up.

Attorney Yoram Leiber returned the cell-phone to his pocket. Then he took a long, deep breath that filled his lungs, and exhaled violently. The nerve of those people! It gave him no rest, day or night.

Right here in his neighborhood, opposite his very own house, they were planning to build a shul!

Construction had not yet begun. Had the builder put up a sign saying, "A synagogue will be erected here," Leiber and his neighbors would have had his head on a platter almost before the paint was dry. A shul in their luxury neighborhood in North Tel Aviv? Out of the question!

But the shul's founders had not put up a sign. This is the way it happened.

A few weeks previously, a well-known figure had visited their neighborhood. He was a famous *ba'al teshuvah* and a popular speaker. In the course of a single speech, he managed to capture the hearts of thirty young people, who discovered in themselves an inexplicable and raging spiritual thirst. They had allowed the man to cut off their ponytails and had handed over their earrings, recited the *Shehecheyanu* blessing, and put on *tzitzis*.

Everyone else had been sure it was all a show. Tomorrow, the ponytails would begin to grow again, the *tzitzis* would be relegated to the backs of closets, and the earrings would return to the ears, noses, and even tongues of their former wearers. But today, twenty-seven out of the thirty penitents still remain firm in their desire to change their lives. They even decided to build a shul in their neighborhood — without bothering to ask their elders' opinion on the matter.

In the meantime, the group began to haunt the deserted community youth center. To the dismay of Yoram Leiber and his neighbors, sounds of prayer wafted from the center's windows — the very sounds that he and the others had fled to North Tel Aviv to escape.

Yoram did not believe his ears. Going in person to see for himself, he had found no mirage or hallucination, but a real contingent of the area's finest youth. Avi, Gadi, Rami, Miki and many others — sons of his own closest friends — had hurried to the youth center to attend prayer services.

Yoram felt ready to explode. "A flame has passed through the cedars," he thought fleetingly, quoting from the very Bible he had spurned. He despised the Torah's traditions, and hated all religious symbols. The expression that had leaped to his mind predicted the cedars' doom by the devouring sword of flame. Yoram was determined that this would not happen. He rummaged in his mind for a different expression to describe the situation, and came up with, "Rot and decay are spreading among us."

The words comforted him and made him smile for the first time in hours. Yes, it was all rot and decay, remnants of primitive rituals from earlier times that had no place in modern society. The mere thought of those rituals in his own upscale neighborhood sent his blood pressure soaring.

As he had promised his friends and neighbors, Yoram spared no effort — much of it during his own office hours — to find a legal loophole that would ban the shul from the site. To his fury, the law seemed to fall on the side of the youths. According to the law of the State of Israel, if community members wish to erect a synagogue, the authorities are obligated to let them do so. Twenty-seven young people had requested a shul.

Yoram studied the youth center's documents to see whether the shul would run counter to the founder's wishes. But he learned that there had been no single founder: The community center had been built by the city government. The building had stood abandoned for two years, ever since a larger and more attractive center had been erected on a nearby street. The Tel Aviv municipality had no choice: It was required to provide the young group with a place to pray.

That Friday night, Yoram ground his teeth in chagrin as the melodic strains of *Lechah Dodi* poured from the center's windows. He was angry enough to burst at the seams. Let those black-clad fools emigrate to Brooklyn, where they belonged!

He had a miserable headache already, and it was bound to get worse. If only those confounded *ba'alei teshuvah* would stop singing!

But the "fools" not only kept singing, they sang louder and even more energetically. And one night, Yoram heard a call that shattered the quiet of his living room. More accurately, with his television blaring the room was not exactly quiet, but that was Western culture and therefore acceptable. What he was hearing now was a very different sort of call.

"*Selichos!*"

Selichos?

The wheels in Yoram Leiber's head began to turn. The mere word carried strong religious overtones, but he was not sure what it meant.

He did not have to wait long to find out. Within minutes, Avi, Rami, Gadi and the others came running, large black yarmulkas on their heads and *tzitzis* flying. In the community center, the lights were already blazing and voices were raised in song.

"I will give them something to think about," Yoram fumed to his wife, Reumah. "There is a city ordinance protecting citizens' rest after 11 at night. What time is it?"

"Ten-thirty. Why?" Reumah asked drowsily. Her husband's religious battles held little interest for her.

The *Selichos* services continued, night after night, for a full month (as is the Sephardic custom). The young group of newly-observant Jews worked hand-in-hand with a reputable legal adviser who guided their activities. All of Yoram's scrambling through the law books yielded no results. He quickly saw that the religious group was being guided by a man who knew no less about the law then he himself did. If not for his placid wife, to whom he was able to pour out his venomous feelings from time to time, Yoram would undoubtedly have succumbed to a heart attack or stroke. He swallowed a great many pills for his rocketing blood pressure and spent his free time cursing the religious Jews in the world who would not leave him alone and had come to ruin his own peaceful corner of the globe.

He had run all the way to North Tel Aviv just to escape the religious — and here they were, pursuing him like a shadow.

Yoram had imbibed hatred of religion together with his mother's milk. Ever since he could remember, he had been taught that religious people were the source of all the world's troubles. At first, he had had no idea who those people actually were, as there were none to be seen on the kibbutz on which he had been raised. But his father had been quick to correct that. Every time he saw a picture of ultra-Orthodox people engaged in a demonstration of some kind, he would hasten to explain to his only son, "You see, here are the 'blacks.'"

As a child, this kind of talk had seemed natural. One was supposed to hate the Orthodox, whose extremism caused all kinds of problems. As he grew older, however, Yoram was a little surprised. His father had never spoken with such pathological hatred about the Arabs who threatened their tiny State. He was always quick to find ways to understand or forgive them. It was only the religious Jews who earned his scorn. Yoram became curious to learn the source of his father's deep hatred.

One evening, his parents had a serious talk with him. The talk continued long into the night, and left them all with eyes reddened from weeping.

His father and mother had revealed that Yoram was not their natural son, but an adopted one.

At once, he had asked for details about his birth parents. His parents' reaction had been swift and hard.

"That's why we hate the religious," his father had burst out. "Do you know what they are capable of? We found you in a garbage dumpster — all of one day old!"

"*What?*" Yoram had shrieked in surprise. "That's impossible. Parents don't throw a day-old baby into the garbage!"

"Normal parents don't," his father had replied grimly. "But religious parents who already have twelve children at home — they certainly do throw them away! We found you tossed on top of the rubbish, wrapped in rags and crying weakly. Your mother and I happened to be passing the hospital when we found you. We took you inside and demanded to know who was responsible for this outrage. The hospital conducted an inquiry and informed us that you had been born to ultra-Orthodox parents who already had a dozen or possibly even thirteen children at home. They could not afford to feed another mouth, so they threw you into the dumpster, like a watermelon rind or a piece of dirt."

"Now do you understand why we hate the religious so much?" his mother had asked. "At that moment, your father and I decided to adopt you and to give you everything we could, a wonderful life. But from then on we also despised those creatures who are capable of doing such a thing to their own flesh and blood."

Yoram had sobbed all that night. Shock and confusion left their mark for many days afterward. When the first emotional scars began to heal, Yoram was left with an enduring bitterness. A profound hatred of his birth parents gnawed at him constantly. Later, this personal hatred transformed itself into a generalized hatred of all religious Jews. He loathed the entire ultra-Orthodox community that could allow such horrible people to flourish among them, and wished he could poison the whole lot of them!

Attorney Yoram Leiber planned to stay at an Eilat hotel over the Rosh Hashanah holiday. He had already made reservations for himself and his wife in a luxury suite, and purchased a pair of round-trip airline tickets. He would spend these "High Holy Days" as far away as possible from the gang of fools in the community youth center. Otherwise, he felt, he would go mad from their mournful prayer melodies.

On *Erev Rosh Hashanah,* Yoram and his wife made their way to the small Sdei Dov airport. Reumah had been ready for an hour or more, but Yoram, immersed in a complex legal brief he wanted to finish before he left home, put off their departure first for 10 minutes, then another five, and then five more.

The delay proved his downfall. Their car got stuck in a long traffic jam, and by the time they began to crawl forward again Yoram knew that they had missed their flight. Nonetheless, he continued on to the small airport — only to learn, to his extreme frustration, that the plane had been delayed on the ground for three-quarters of an hour, and had lifted off just two minutes earlier!

"They couldn't wait for us?" he fumed. "Well, they don't know with whom they're dealing. I'll show them. Reumah, we're staying home for the holiday, and the hotel won't see a penny from me. According to paragraph 14 of the relevant law, there is no obligation for a guest to pay a hotel or motel before he benefits from its hospitality."

An airline official tried to calm him. "We are trying to arrange an additional flight," he said. "It would be worth your while to remain here."

"I'm not interested!" Yoram screamed, and returned to the parking lot with his wife trailing behind.

The other latecomers took off on the additional flight about 90 minutes later. Stubborn Yoram Leiber stayed home, nose in a heavy legal textbook.

Out of habit, he strained his ears that night to hear the familiar *Selichos* tunes. Instead, from the hated building came strains of a completely different holiday melody. After the service, he saw streams of young people leave the building with radiant faces. They shook one another's hands warmly and wished each other a blessed new year.

Yoram felt something painful twist in his heart. When had he ever had the chance to stand outside like that and exchange heartfelt good wishes, his face glowing and filled with emotion? What did he have, apart from legal wrangles and courtroom debates?

For that matter, when had he last strolled like that among friends, chatting together in this relaxed fashion? Did he even have any friends?

After a restless night, he woke early the next morning, put on his jogging clothes, and went out for a run. His legs took him past the youth center. He moved determinedly away — only to find himself running back in that direction. This happened again and again. "It's a good thing no one's here to see me," he thought with a wry inner laugh. "I must look like a pendulum on a clock, going back and forth, back and forth."

The shofar blast hit him with shocking suddenness. It made his heart stand still, the way the siren does at wartime.

Without any warning, the sound of the shofar rent the air with a sound he was hearing for the first time in his life. First a long wail, followed by shorter bursts. Yoram began to shake like a leaf in the wind.

He danced about on uncertain feet for a moment, moving as if in a dream. Later, he would describe the sensation as follows: "It was as if an electric shock ran right through me. A powerful current burned my entire body!"

Attorney Yoram Leiber, the sturdy battle-horse who squeezed blood from his opponents in court without mercy, found himself shaken and terrified at the sound of the shofar.

On second thought, it was not an electric current. It was much more than that — something enormously more powerful. The sound wove a spell over him, toppling the defensive wall that Yoram had built on the night his adoptive parents told him of his origins. A day-old infant, tossed onto the garbage-heap!

His legs carried him into the shul. On a conscious level, he wanted to scream at the *ba'alei teshuvah* for disturbing their neighbors' peace with their infernal trumpeting. Secretly, he also wanted to see what the place looked like on the inside.

The shul was filled to capacity. There were many more than twenty-seven people present. Some of them wore festive white clothing. An atmosphere of holy seriousness permeated the room. A few children pointed at Yoram and giggled. He became angry at first, and then blushed in confusion. The children were right: the contrast between the others' holiday garb and his own jogging suit was laughable.

His gaze swept the worshipers, seeking the one who had managed to produce those awesome sounds he had heard. The sheer technique astounded him.

The other men saw him, but did not stare or embarrass him. They let Yoram make his way along the rows of seats until he came to an empty chair and sank into it. He gazed with open curiosity at the instrument that had made the sounds.

"That's a shofar," one of the children told him.

"Shofar? I've never heard that word."

"It's just a ram's horn," the children said, amazed at his ignorance.

No philharmonic orchestra had ever produced such an emotional storm in him. Soon, the "musician" picked up the ram's horn and began to blow it once again. Yoram was nearly swept away by the same powerful feelings he had experienced outside. On the one hand, he was furious at being unable to express his opposition to these rituals and the tremendous noise they made. But, at the same time, with each new shofar blast he felt as though something was melting inside him.

His eyes followed the blower, but he could not see the man's face. A *tallis* covered it almost completely.

Very quietly, Yoram stood up and left the shul.

"They say that this lake is full of crocodiles."

"So what? They say a lot of things."

"And what will you do if you suddenly feel a croc's teeth sinking into your leg? They say it feels like an electric shock."

"Are you trying to scare me? I have some repellant spray with me."

The sounds of revelry might have belonged to children of 10, but they actually belonged to a group of young secular Jews whose average age was 22. They were newly released from army service and had decided to take the almost obligatory trip to the Far East. Yet another group of Israelis who had chosen to abandon a living wellspring to dig in empty pits.

Gabi, Oron, and Tommy were spending some time in Singapore, in Southeast Asia. They had arrived six months before and extensively toured that country, where poverty and wealth existed side by side. The young men tried to learn the local customs as they resolutely ignored a rising tide of emptiness. To divert themselves, they dreamed of traveling on to Tibet and climbing Mount Everest — a dream they all knew would not become a reality. Meanwhile, they killed time with reckless contests and pointless feats of daring. Now, arriving at this small lake, they dived in at once despite the large sign warning of danger in five different languages, along with a picture of a dangerous-looking crocodile that even the youngest child could understand.

"Hey, *chevrah*, are you nuts?"

The three Jewish youths stopped spraying each other with water and looked curiously at the figure that had come running up to the lakeshore.

"*Mazal tov,* we've found another Israeli!" Tommy said with a condescending grin. "Hey, guys, let's get him to come close to the edge and then pull him into the water!"

"He looks religious," Gabi complained. "Do those guys follow us even all the way out here?"

The man did, indeed, look religious. He was young, with a short blond beard and long *tzitzis* hanging down either side of his trousers. In his hand was a small *sefer*. Coming closer to the lake, he called urgently, "Get out of the water! A month ago, an American tourist was devoured right here by a whole school of crocodiles!"

"We're not afraid," Oron said nonchalantly.

"You'd better turn around," the young religious man warned. "Take a look at what's coming at you. Maybe then you'll reconsider."

The three glanced over their shoulders, and began to shriek in panic. A group of large crocodiles was swimming their way at a rapid clip. They were ominously silent, and their eyes were evil.

Spurred by terror, the three young men swam for shore with all possible speed. To their good fortune, the crocodiles had still been far-off when the stranger had spotted them, and the trio managed to clamber ashore and escape at a sprint before the crocodiles reached them.

Five years can pass in a person's life without any experiences that are out of the ordinary — and sometimes, just two or three minutes can leave their mark, changing him forever. The two minutes that it had taken the young adventurers to swim ashore were the second kind. With stunning suddenness, they sensed the profound emptiness of the lives they were leading. They understood the deep feeling of nothingness that had led them into this sort of foolish and dangerous escapade.

"You — you saved our lives," they panted as they stood beside the stranger. "It's as if you were brought here by invitation."

The man shook their sodden hands and said, "I believe that Heaven sent me here to save you. I've been traveling through this area, searching for Jews to come join us in shul on the holiday tomorrow. Local residents mentioned that they had seen three young men jump into the lake. I understood at once that you must be Israelis. Only Sabras jump into a lake after being warned in five languages that doing so is to risk their lives. I see that I was right." He paused. "Who are you?"

They introduced themselves: Gabi, Oron, and Tommy. The stranger then presented himself as Yerucham Shekedi. He told them that he had been staying in the area for several months now, and would soon be organizing a seminar for the many Israelis that passed through Singapore.

"Right now, though, the pressing issue is tomorrow's holiday services at the shul. Will you join us?"

"What holiday is it?" they asked.

By this time, he was accustomed to the ignorance of secular Israeli youth, and did not crack so much as a smile. "Rosh Hashanah," he said simply.

As the three hesitated, Yerucham chuckled, clapped them warmly on the shoulder, and urged, "Come on. Maybe you'll learn something new!"

They came that night, bewildered and unsure of themselves. Uppermost in their minds was escape. But Yerucham and his friends quickly broke the ice and drew in the three secular young men.

That night, the three prayed for the first time in their lives.

The next morning, they came again for the long daytime service. They listened to explanations about the great Day of Judgment, about the shofar-blowing, and the three books that were opened on that day. They were entranced.

In silence, they soaked up Yerucham's explanations. They thought about the significance of what they were hearing, and of the religion that had seemed so oppressive to them when they were growing up. Only today did they understand that they had been raised with lies about their own faith and unfounded hatred of their fellow Jews.

After the day's Torah portion was read, the time came for the shofar to be blown. Oron and Tommy were beside themselves at the sound of the mighty blasts that shook the window panes. As for Gabi, he appeared to be hypnotized. He kept his eyes trained on the shofar without moving, utterly consumed by emotion. Several times, afterwards, he began to walk toward the table on which the shofar lay, and then retreated backward. Yerucham saw, and understood. He picked up the shofar, walked over to Gabi, and placed it in his hands.

Gabi stared at it for a moment, and then brought the shofar to his lips. An earsplitting blast rent the air. He tried again, and the second blast was even mightier than the first.

"He's a born shofar-blower," Yerucham thought. "Who knows how much Jewish talent is buried in the garbage-heaps? They need someone to set them free."

Gabi seemed transfixed by the shofar. Carefully, he imitated the sounds he had heard the *ba'al tokea* produce: the *teki'ah, shevarim,* and *teru'ah.* It was strange to see the secular youth, with his long hair and his earring, lovingly stroke the shofar and succeed in making sounds that might have come from a seasoned *ba'al tokea*.

"Wait till I tell my father," Gabi laughed happily. "He'll never believe it."

Then the laughter died, as he remembered how much his father, attorney Yoram Leiber, despised anything that smelled religious. "Maybe I won't tell him," he thought. "If he saw me in shul here today, listening to the shofar, he would probably have a heart attack on the spot. Actually, I don't much care what he thinks. His rabidly anti-Jewish upbringing was so extreme that I reacted by actually liking religious Jews."

His reflections continued. "Now, here's an interesting thing. This instrument, this shofar as they call it, is drawing me like a magnet and I don't understand why. I'll have to check this out. After the service, I'll talk to Yerucham. He's been signaling that he can't talk until he finishes praying."

On the second day of Rosh Hashanah, Yoram Leiber woke up to find himself filled with curiosity. He must inspect that incredible shofar up close, and learn its secret. He waited until the morning service was over. Listening from outside, he heard the shofar blasts once again; again they moved him, though this time there was no element of surprise. When all the worshipers had gone home, Yoram slipped into the empty building with the stealthiness of a cat going after the cream.

He found the shofar taking pride of place on the table — but, to his surprise, it was not alone. Beside the table sat the "musician" who had blown it. Something about him troubled Yoram. The man sat looking into a big book and swaying gently as he hummed a low tune. Yoram wanted to turn and run. Then the man lifted his eyes and saw him.

"Did you want something?" he asked pleasantly.

"Nothing special," Yoram blurted. "Uh, something interests me about your instrument. What do you call it, a shofar? By the way, what is your name, sir?"

"I am Rabbi Shaul Nahari."

"Nice to meet you. I'm attorney Yoram Leiber. You've probably heard of me; I'm pretty famous in these parts. The religious folk don't like me because I frequently fight them. You're the musician, right?"

"*Musician?* I am the *ba'al tokea.* The shofar is not a musical instrument. It is a holy tool with which we perform a mitzvah."

The rabbi picked up the pale gold shofar and showed it to Yoram. "This is the instrument that the Torah ordered us to blow on Rosh Hashanah, so that the Creator of the world will remember us favorably on the Judgment Day."

This was the longest religious lecture Yoram had permitted himself to hear in his life. The rabbi noticed this, and smiled. "Is this your first time here?" he asked.

"Yes."

"Nice to meet you." The rabbi extended a hand, letting waves of warmth flow out of him and straight into the lawyer's heart. "Do you live in the neighborhood?"

"In the building opposite," said Yoram. "Tell me, how did you learn how to play this so well? Do you practice, and is there special professional training?"

Rabbi Shaul broke into merry laughter. "Professional training? You must be joking!" He shook his head, still chuckling. "No, we are a family of shofar-blowers — seven unbroken generations of experienced *ba'alei tokea.* You might say it's in our blood."

R' Shaul went on to tell Yoram about his father, R' Tzvi Nahari, who had blown the shofar for sixty years before retiring. He described how he himself had been drawn to the shofar even as a young child, and how he had managed to blow it beautifully the very first time he had tried. His father had told him then, "That's how it is in our family. The shofar is an inseparable part of who we are. Everyone in the Nahari family is a *ba'al tokea* from birth. It's the sign of a Nahari son if he knows how to blow the shofar properly."

"I myself," R' Shaul Nahari continued, "am in great demand as a *ba'al tokea*, and I've blown the shofar in many different shuls. I go from one shul to the next. This youth center in your neighborhood is my last stop for today — unless I am summoned again later to blow the shofar for some woman who has just given birth or something of that sort."

"Do you have any brothers or sisters?" Yoram asked. What had come over him? It wasn't like him to invade another person's privacy in this way.

R' Shaul did not seem put out. "I have eleven brothers and sisters, *bli ayin hara*." Then, almost as an afterthought, he added that he had once had a twelfth. "I had a twin brother," he said sadly. "He disappeared from the hospital no more than two hours after birth. The doctors told my mother, 'You had twin boys. One of them is alive and well, but the other died an hour ago. He had serious respiratory problems ... basically, he suffocated for lack of breath.'

"My mother did not believe them. She saw the nurses whispering among themselves constantly, and caught snatches: 'Sara Nahari is naive, like all the Yemenites.' 'She's easygoing.' 'There won't be any scandal.' That was back in the days when the State was new, and when ordinary citizens felt powerless to oppose the governing party. Basically, the government did whatever it pleased. Yemenite children were kidnapped from their parents and handed over to childless couples who wanted to adopt, in exchange for vast sums of money or political favors.

"My mother is elderly now, but she believes to this day that her son was adopted by a childless family, and that he is alive and well today. And she may be right. She cannot forget the baby that was born to her forty-eight years ago, while in the case of one who has died, the person does eventually leave one's mind."

Yoram had to control himself to keep from screaming. "Forty-eight years ago, you said?"

"Yes."

"I am 48 years old." Yoram's face had become pale as chalk. "Interesting ... What is your birthday?"

"The Hebrew date or the secular one?" This secular lawyer probably had no working knowledge of the Hebrew calendar.

"Actually, my family used to celebrate my Hebrew birthday," Yoram Leiber said. "I was born on the 23rd day of Shevat, forty-eight years ago."

R' Shaul froze. "But that's my birthday!"

"In which hospital were you born?" Yoram whispered. He felt as though he were a heartbeat away from fainting.

"Hadassah Hospital, in Jerusalem. In those days, it was on Rechov HaNeviim."

Yoram stared at him. "My adoptive parents found me abandoned in a garbage dumpster in the courtyard of Hadassah Hospital in Jerusalem, on Rechov HaNeviim!"

Their eyes met. With blinding suddenness, Yoram realized what had been subconsciously troubling him about the rabbi all along. Apart from the beard and yarmulka, there was an uncanny resemblance between them ... as though they were identical twins. Was it possible?

His voice grew low and vicious. "Your mother no doubt could not bear the thought of raising a pair of twins, and threw one of them into the rubbish!"

Rabbi Shaul's eyes bulged with anger. Gripping Yoram's hand so hard that it hurt, he said between clenched teeth, "My mother, may she have a long life, grieves to this very day over that thirteenth child of hers, who was taken from her on the pretext that he had died of suffocation. For all these years, the rest of us have urged her to forget the infant she saw only once in her life, and enjoy the dozen other children who are alive and well, thank G-d. And you come along to talk this way? What kind of home were you raised in? Who taught you to hate like that?"

"My adoptive parents," Yoram said, his breathing labored. He put a hand to his pounding head. "I — I'm stunned. I believe they filled me with lies all my life. The fact that they discovered me in a garbage dumpster is about as true as the fact that all religious people are primitive and coarse." He looked up at the rabbi with agonized eyes. "But how will we ever know if I am really that lost son who was stolen from the hospital nursery? There might have been twenty babies born in Hadassah on that day."

A broad smile lit R' Shaul's face. "First of all, I am surprised at you — a successful lawyer like you never once checked his adoption file to verify the story you were told. As a prominent attorney, you must have connections to the right offices where your adoptive parents' lies can be exposed." He handed Yoram the pale gold shofar. "But here is the best proof. If you are a Nahari son, you will know instinctively how to blow this."

Tentatively, Yoram took the shofar. He stared at it, hesitating. R' Shaul clapped him on the shoulder encouragingly. "Go on, give it a try."

Yoram raised the shofar to his lips and blew.

The blast was tentative at first, then gathered strength until it flowed free and loud. Drawing confidence, Yoram blew a second time. This blast belonged to a seasoned *ba'al tokea* — a full-bodied sound that shook the walls. Yoram blew again and again, imitating the broken *shevarim* sounds and then the *teru'ah*, as he had heard R' Shaul produce them. He blew as though he had been a *ba'al tokea* from birth.

Shaken, he lowered the shofar from his lips. "I don't believe it!" he crowed, delighted. "I blew it just like you!"

Rabbi Shaul Nahari threw back his head with joyous laughter. "Yes, you blow exactly like me — because you are a Nahari, exactly like me." He threw his arms around Yoram's neck and hugged him. "Welcome to the family, attorney Yoram Leiber. Maybe it's time to think of a different name ... eh, Mr. Nahari?"

He grinned broadly, and winked at the stunned expression on Yoram's face.

Gabi cradled the shofar tenderly all the way back from shul. Yerucham had given it to him as a gift, and already Gabi cherished it. Every few steps, he stopped to inspect the shofar, and at last he lifted it to his lips and blew into it. Passersby on the Singapore street turned their heads in astonishment, but Gabi ignored them.

He hugged the shofar close, feeling exalted. On his return home, he would mount this shofar in a place of honor in the living room. Let his father say what he would. His mother, Reumah, would probably back him up, and even his father — prominent attorney Yoram Leiber — would not toss the shofar away. After all, his father was always saying that you don't throw things of value into the trash.

Yom Kippur

The Feud

GOLDIE BERMAN WAS THE ONLY CHILD OF ORTHODOX, middle-income parents who lived in a Jewish section of Brooklyn. Outgoing and vivacious, she had a dream she did not hesitate to share with her friends: She yearned to one day become the mother of a large family. The long, silent hours in her own home were oppressive to her, and she dreamed of filling her future life with the shouts and laughter of children.

Nearly every afternoon, after finishing her homework, Goldie would visit a friend's house to enjoy the bustle of a large family and play with her friend's younger siblings. She also volunteered at a child-care center, where the youngsters' games and smiles made up to her, in some measure at least, for what she lacked at home.

In the upper high-school grades Goldie chose courses in early-childhood education. Her teachers declared that, with her love for children, it would only be natural for her to one day open a nursery or play group of her own.

Goldie would laugh. "First let me raise my own twelve babies. That will be my own personal play group." Her eyes grew dreamy. "I'll hug those kids to pieces, I'll take care of them, I'll devote my days and nights to them. I'll give my children everything." A maternal warmth suffused her voice as she wove these dreams about babies yet to be born — babies that would fill her days with laughter, her nights with the usual infant tears, and the deep, satisfying purr of contentment of a baby well fed.

She couldn't wait.

Elchanan Levi never knew his mother and father.

His eyes first opened to a dirty and neglected-looking room with peeling wallpaper: the birthing room at a Bucharest hospital. He opened his eyes and screamed at the cruelty of being torn from his warm home and thrust into a cold, indifferent world. His father had been arrested by the Romanian secret police before Elchanan was born, never to be seen again. This was a common practice in that country: Thousands of people were dragged from their homes, shot, and buried in far-flung forests throughout the country.

Chana Levi, Elchanan's mother, prepared for the birth of her first child with a broken heart — and a terror of what the future held for herself and her helpless infant.

As it turned out, her fear was tragically justified. Just two days after giving birth, the poor mother died of blood poisoning. Elchanan was taken into his uncle's home — his mother's childless brother and his wife — to be raised there.

When he was 10, his uncle and aunt fled with Elchanan to the United States, where they successfully relocated in Brooklyn. The couple continued to raise Elchanan lovingly, giving him a warm Jewish education and unstinting devotion. The boy looked upon his aunt and uncle as the mother and father he had never known.

As a teenager, Elchanan studied at a prestigious New York yeshivah. He threw himself into his learning with tremendous fervor, and his aunt and uncle saw him flourish spiritually before their very eyes.

He did not become a *talmid chacham* overnight. It was a long, arduous process, with gradual change to be seen in him week by week. His uncle and aunt were very proud of him.

By the time he was 21, Elchanan was considered a fine young man and a most desirable marriage partner. Matchmakers came to his uncle suggesting all sorts of fine girls, each one worthy of consideration. But, of all the girls, his aunt favored Goldie Berman.

"She has a reputation for loving children," his aunt said. "Elchanan never had real parents of his own. He is an only child, and so is she. They suit each other. Please G-d, they will have a warm, busy home. Her teachers and friends say wonderful things about Goldie. She will be the mother of a very special family, and a fine homemaker."

Even before the engagement was announced, Goldie shared with her future in-laws her dream of raising twelve children. Delighted, they told her that Elchanan had the same dream. Having been raised without any brothers or sisters, he longed to have a houseful of children. "May Hashem fulfill the words, 'Multiply our offspring and our livelihood like the sand and the stars.' "

Elchanan and Goldie were married in a joyous ceremony, amid dancing and laughter and the abundant good wishes of all their friends.

Maybe Goldie should not have spoken so confidently and openly about the large family she intended to raise. No one knew the reason for Heaven's decree, but the fact remained that, five long years after the wedding, Goldie and Elchanan had not yet been blessed with children.

All their dreams and hopes remained painfully unfulfilled. Goldie and her husband were intensely frustrated and lived in daily anguish. She opened a play group for the neighborhood children and poured all her love into her charges, thankful to the teachers who had urged her to choose this career. Still, her heart overflowed with pain. As for Elchanan, he invested himself completely in his Torah learning. He learned in *kollel* for a good portion of the day, after which he went to the yeshivah and gave a *shiur* to the boys there. His efforts were crowned with success.

At long last, after seven years of barrenness, the Levis' prayers were answered, and they were blessed with a son. Their joy knew no bounds. All their former rosy dreams returned, even more glowing than before. Goldie became the devoted mother she had longed to become, and she poured heart and soul into her only son.

Three years later, they rejoiced again. A daughter was born to them! They were now the parents of two children, a boy and a girl!

From morning to night, Goldie thanked Hashem for her children. Now, more than ever before, she recognized Who conducted the world's business. She might fantasize about a dozen children and prattle to her friends about raising a large family. But it was the compassionate and confident Hand of Hashem that brought new souls into the world. Goldie learned, firsthand, about the tremendous power of prayer.

The Levis raised their son and daughter with total devotion and enthusiasm. The children were their greatest treasure, the answer to their innermost hopes. They raised their only son, Aryeh, with the same energy from the day of his birth until they led him to the *chuppah*. In the same fashion, Goldie devoted herself with care and attention to her daughter, Tamar, giving her a solid and proper upbringing until she turned 18 and marriage proposals began to come in. Tamar, however, was reluctant to undertake the burden of managing a home when she could continue a while longer to enjoy her mother's loving support. "I want to study some more," she demurred. "What's the rush?"

Now that her brother was married, she was the only child remaining at home. Life was pleasant. She had a warm home with wonderful parents whose love and devotion renewed itself each day. Tamar wanted to wait another year or two, and Goldie was reluctant to force her daughter to do anything for which she did not feel ready.

The traffic accident shook the entire Jewish community. Returning home with his wife late one night from a wedding they had attended outside the city, Elchanan lost control of the car and collided with an oncoming truck. In one tragic instant, Aryeh and Tamar Levi became orphaned of both mother and father.

The shock was monumental. For the sister and brother, the whole world seemed to shake on its foundations.

Aryeh's wife and his son, Menashe, aged a year and a half, were a comfort to Aryeh during the dark hours after the *shivah* week. As for Tamar, she began to spend a great deal of time at her brother's home. She visited often, playing with her nephew and trying to find her own consolation in his innocent smiles.

Slowly, an idea dawned in her mind. She must marry and establish her own home. That was the way to put together the pieces of her shattered life.

When she told her brother what was on her mind, he brightened. "That's exactly what Ma wanted. But you didn't agree. You wanted to wait another year or two."

"But that was — before," she said sadly. "Everything is different now."

"We have to think about where to find the money to marry you off," Aryeh thought aloud. "It's easy to talk about making a wedding, but hard to do it."

"I've thought of everything," Tamar said excitedly. "I'll sell the house."

Aryeh's finger wagged in a negative gesture. "Impossible. I am the *bechor*. I inherit a double portion even if I have brothers, and certainly if I just have a sister. According to halachah you have no portion in the inheritance, although I must provide you with support."

Tamar was stunned. "But I need the money so I can get married! You are already settled, *baruch Hashem*. You already have a home of your own."

"And debts of my own, too," her brother said. "When Tati was alive, I didn't know what money was. He bought me the house by getting a bank loan and making a large payment every month. I knew nothing about all that. Only now did I find out that my house is heavily mortgaged. If I don't pay on time, the bank will foreclose on the house."

"What were you planning to do?" Tamar demanded.

"I was going to invite you to live here with us, and rent out our parents' house. I would use the rental money to pay the mortgage."

"And what about me?" Tamar asked, outraged. "Don't I exist? Where are my rights? Where is my portion in the inheritance?"

"That's why I was saying that we have to figure out where to get the money to marry you off," Aryeh said defensively.

This conversation marked the start of a quarrel that grew progressively more serious. Aryeh was a *ben Torah* and a gentle soul by nature who hated controversy of any kind. But his wife stood behind him, urging him to fight for what was rightfully his.

Tamar was cut from a very different cloth than her brother. She could be stubborn, and she knew how to fight when necessary. Over and over, she repeated, "I must have a dowry. There is no one to look after me, except for me!"

Each of them believed that the inheritance belonged to them. The option of dividing the amount was not acceptable to either of them. Aryeh's sense of self-respect would not permit him to drag his own sister to a *din Torah* or arbitration. Bad enough that their beloved parents had died so tragically. Were their children to add to the tragedy by squabbling over the inheritance?

In the end, Aryeh signed away his rights to everything. He did not wish to enter into a legal wrangle with his only sister. But even as he acted in the name of peace, his heart was embittered toward Tamar. His wife, worried about their future, had urged him to keep back at least half of the inheritance, but he saw no possibility of compromise. Growing angrier by the day, she insisted that he sever all connection with his "robber" of a sister.

Aryeh's wife found fertile ground for her demand. Aryeh was already feeling bitter and distressed enough over the whole affair, and his wife did not have to work very hard to get what she wanted.

They broke off all ties with Tamar. There could be no forgiveness for such behavior. They were through!

After Tamar sold her parents' home, word of the inheritance battle and Tamar's iniquity was spread all over town. People looked at her askance, even with anger. Many rebuked her. Some even threatened her. Giving the matter proper deliberation, Tamar took the money and fled from New York. With a painful and difficult fight over the inheritance just behind her, she moved to Eretz Yisrael.

Tamar had an adventurous and energetic spirit. She rented an apartment in Jerusalem and soon became acquainted with several prominent residents of that city, to whom she told the story of the terrible tragedy that had befallen her. But, though she shared the tale of her parents' untimely deaths, not a word crossed her lips about the controversy with her only brother over the inheritance. She was accepted into an excellent seminary, where she enjoyed the protection and support of rabbis and community activists. Not much time elapsed before someone suggested a match for her.

The young man's reputation was sterling: Torah and piety, gentleness and righteousness mingled to form an exceptional personality. The young yeshivah student had grown up in a poor home, and his parents were unable to come up with even five percent of the necessary cash needed to make a wedding and help the young couple set up house. Tamar's prediction — that only the complete inheritance would suffice for her needs — proved true.

She used all the money to purchase an apartment and its furnishings and appliances. All the *chasan*, Shlomo, brought into the marriage was a modest wardrobe and notebooks filled with his Torah insights. These brilliant manuscripts were worthy of being published — if only he had the money to print and distribute them.

Tamar did not invite her brother in Brooklyn to her wedding in Jerusalem. The rift between them was total. It was only a month later that someone dropped the news to Aryeh that his sister was married. Aryeh did not want to hear. The wound was still too fresh, too raw. The only detail he filed away in his mind was the fact that his sister's name was no longer Levi, but Gutberg.

He wished to know nothing else. There could be no forgiveness. They were through!

It was a sultry summer's day in the month of Av years later. During the *bein hazemanim* break between yeshivah semesters, a group of yeshivah students decided to take a hike through the Judean Desert down to Ein Gedi. All of them had heard the warnings about tragic accidents that had taken place on such hikes, and all of the boys chose to ignore them. "We'll say *Tefillas HaDerech* with a lot of *kavanah*," they decided with careless laughter.

They made sure to wear appropriate protective clothing, hiking shoes, and broad-brimmed hats, and they took along ample supplies of water. For emergencies, they even packed flashlights.

"There's nothing to worry about," they told other yeshivah friends who tried to talk them out of the trip. "We're experienced hikers, not irresponsible children. We know the safety rules. We won't follow any unmarked paths, we'll keep in touch with professional guides from the 'Society for the Protection of Nature,' and we're taking along cell-phones."

They climbed to one of the highest points in the Judean Desert, arriving around sunset. The panorama was breathtaking. They saw the Dead Sea, and in the distance the mountains of Edom and Moav. There were hills and valleys of sand and all sorts of interesting formations. With binoculars glued to their eyes, they drank in the view on every side, ending with the kiss of sky and earth at the horizon, dusky blue melting into golden sand.

"The whole hike was worthwhile, just for this view," Menashe said in his American-accented Hebrew, adjusting the binoculars for a better view. As he did so, his foot pressed more firmly into the sandy ridge.

This set off a small avalanche of stones and sand, but Menashe was too engrossed in viewing the scenery to notice it. Suddenly, the ridge broke off completely. A great chunk of earth fell into the abyss below, carrying Menashe along with it. He bounced and rolled among the boulders and sand, the binoculars flying from his hand as he fell faster and faster.

By jumping hastily back, the other boys managed to save themselves. (They had been standing, of course, on an unmarked path.) Only sixty seconds later, the avalanche ended. The peace and quiet of the desert returned. All things considered, it had been a minor avalanche, nothing more. But Menashe was gone.

Shocked and stammering, the boys used their cell-phones to call for help. An army helicopter hovered close to the spot where Menashe had fallen, and its pilot spotted the boy lying unconscious on an outcropping some ten meters down. With special floodlights illuminating the area, Menashe was lifted free and transported to a Jerusalem hospital.

"It's a miracle that his body was caught on those rocks," the paramedics remarked on the way. "If not for that, he would have fallen all the way down."

Menashe lay unconscious in his hospital bed. The medical staff diagnosed a non-lethal trauma to the head, and expected him to regain consciousness any day. They encouraged the patient's friends to sit by his bedside and speak to him, to stimulate the parts of his brain that had not been hurt. His yeshivah friends took turns learning beside Menashe, and told him what was happening at yeshivah: who had become engaged, who had left, and what the *rosh yeshivah* had said in that day's general *shiur*. They read aloud newspaper articles and softly sang songs that they knew Menashe liked.

"Very good," the doctors approved. "Keep it up. He'll wake up soon."

But Menashe lay very still, eyes closed, and did not show even the slightest reaction to anything his friends said. As they watched him lie in deep sleep, attached to his I.V. line and various monitors, his friends began to wonder sadly whether he heard them at all.

Two months passed without any change.

It was *Erev Yom Kippur,* and the new *rosh yeshivah,* R' Shlomo Gutberg, decided to visit Menashe and wish him a *gemar chasimah tovah.* One of the other boys had volunteered to sit by Menashe's bed the next day and recite the Yom Kippur *davening* out loud, word for word. The *rosh yeshivah* had liked that idea, but took it a step further.

"Only one boy? Let's have a whole *minyan* in the room! A *minyan,* a *chazzan,* shofar-blowing at the end of Yom Kippur — the works. Why not? Menashe won't have to miss a thing!"

The doctors gave their consent to the plan.

On *Erev Yom Kippur,* then, R' Gutberg came to the hospital to make sure that all their plans were in place. He found an American man sitting beside Menashe's bed. Behind his glasses, the stranger's eyes dripped tears as he softly recited *Tehillim*.

"*Shalom aleichem*," the *rosh yeshivah* said, shaking the man's hand. "And who are you?"

"I am Menashe's father," the man said, and wiped his eyes.

Taken aback, the *rosh yeshivah* exclaimed, "The boys didn't tell me that you were here in the country! I didn't know."

"Who are you?" Menashe's father asked.

"His *rosh yeshivah*."

Menashe's father explained that he was planning to stay with his son during the nights. "I don't want any *bitul Torah* to come about because of him. That won't increase his merits."

"Very true. We must strive to increase his merits," the *rosh yeshivah* concurred heartily.

The American hesitated. "The *rosh yeshivah* will forgive me," he said, "but I don't recall his name."

"It would be impossible for you to know it," the *rosh yeshivah* explained with a smile. "I was only appointed to the position during Elul, after your son's accident."

"And the name ...?" Menashe's father pressed.

Modestly, the *rosh yeshivah* murmured, "Shlomo."

"Shlomo — what?"

"Gutberg."

A cloud passed over the American's face. "I am familiar with that name. Gutberg is my sister's married name. Don't tell me that you're a relative of mine."

The *rosh yeshivah* raised his eyebrows. "You have a sister by the name of Gutberg?"

"Well ... I did," Menashe's father amended.

"Did she die?"

"I didn't say that! I broke off all family ties with her, that's all."

R' Gutberg was a warm and peace-loving man. "That's not good," he declared. "You must make your peace with your sister. Making up with your sister on *Erev Yom Kippur* can add a great deal of merit to your injured son. As you know, he stands in need of great compassion from Heaven."

Breathing heavily, the father said, "The *rosh yeshivah* is right. I'd like to ask for help in locating my sister. I haven't the slightest idea what she's been up to since leaving New York and getting married here in Eretz Yisrael. Maybe the *rosh yeshivah* knows something about her? After all, Gutberg is not such a common name."

Shlomo Gutberg creased his brow in thought. "I don't know any American woman married to a Gutberg — apart from my own wife, of course. But she has no sisters or brothers. She is an only child. By the way, what was your sister's maiden name?" He caught himself, and smiled, "Ah — Levi, of course. And that's my wife's maiden name as well."

"Levi!" the father shouted in sudden excitement. "You must be my brother-in-law, Tamar's husband!"

"My wife's name is Tamar," R' Gutberg said in confusion. "But she is an only child."

"How do you know that?"

"She has never spoken of any brothers or sisters."

"Were your in-laws killed in a car accident in New York, twenty-two years ago?" the American asked tensely.

R' Gutberg nearly collapsed with shock. "Yes! She always talks about that. I have been to the New York cemetery with her several times, to visit their graves."

"She must have been ashamed of what happened between us. But she does have a brother. *I* am your wife's brother! My name is Aryeh Levi, and I have been your brother-in-law these past twenty years, despite the fact that we have never met. My sister and I quarreled over our parents' inheritance and broke off relations. I have never forgiven her."

His voice had risen several notches as he told his story. Suddenly, he seized the *rosh yeshivah's* sleeve. "Please, do me a favor. Call your wife and ask her to come here now. Let us make up right here, at my son's bedside. Look how much I've been punished because I refused to forgive or know her. My firstborn son is lying unconscious ..." Tearfully, he turned to the boy in the bed. "Menashe, how I wish I could give my life for yours ..." His voice broke as a storm of weeping took over.

R' Shlomo Gutberg held onto the I.V. pole as though for support. "You have never forgiven her?"

"No. But I will forgive her now," Tamar's brother sobbed, "with all my heart."

The *rosh yeshivah's* face darkened with fear and shock, and his fingers trembled like leaves in a strong wind. The words, as they emerged from his throat, were ragged. "You never forgave her? Now I understand!"

Aryeh Levi stopped crying and lifted his head. "What do you understand?"

R' Gutberg spoke emotionally, with visible pain. "Now I know why we have been punished for twenty years — why we have had to suffer childlessness. *Oy, oy*, what I am hearing today! A woman does not reveal to her husband that she has a brother. A brother does not forgive his sister for twenty-two years. Our home has been wracked with such deep pain, an emptiness such as you cannot begin to imagine! And now, a boy has fallen off a cliff and lies unconscious for two months. *Ribbono Shel Olam*, how is it possible for a sin to drag on for twenty-two years? Are we not Your holy people?"

The two men sat and talked for a long time, trying to decide how best to bring Tamar to the hospital, and exactly what to say to her.

"Shall we just put it simply?" R' Gutberg suggested. "Your brother is here, at the hospital, and wants to make up with you?"

They weighed and calculated, until finally the *rosh yeshivah* went home in a taxi. With great emotional turmoil, he told his wife of his shock at discovering her brother, Aryeh, from New York, whose son had been learning in his Jerusalem yeshivah and who had been lying in a coma for the past two months.

Rebbetzin Gutberg broke into prolonged weeping. Twenty-two years of pain poured out of her anguished heart with those tears. She, too, had wondered through the years whether that old quarrel had been the cause of her barrenness. When she had calmed down enough to speak, she agreed to come to the hospital at once.

An hour later, the Gutbergs and Aryeh Levi stood together beside Menashe's bed. The sobbing that took place in that room, even behind closed doors, brought nurses scurrying in to see what was wrong. To their surprise, they found that the E.E.G. machine monitoring Menashe's brain waves showed a sudden elevation in brain activity. As they watched, the patient's eyelids began to flutter rapidly.

"Where is the neurologist?" they called urgently. "Professor Feldman? Professor Feldman, please proceed to room 415 at once!"

The prominent neurologist arrived promptly. After a quick examination of the patient, he rose with a smile. "There has been a marked improvement in Menashe's brain activity. If it continues, I believe that he will wake from his coma within a short period of time."

"Just as the state of unconsciousness between his father and his aunt comes to an end as well," murmured R' Gutberg to the uncomprehending nurses.

"I offer you a blessing, my dear sister and brother-in-law," Aryeh Levi declared, half crying and half laughing. "Next year, with Hashem's help, your state of childlessness will end, too! And your children, like the stars in the sky, will fill your house with boundless joy."

An Unusual Kaddish

THE OLD SHUL IN BOWDON WAS PACKED TO THE RAFTERS. Scores of worshipers stood wrapped in their prayer shawls, waiting. Among them was Bowdon's new rabbi, R' Efraim HaKohen of Vilna, author of the *Sha'ar Efraim*. Soon, the *aron kodesh* would be opened and the words of *Kol Nidrei* would ring out, marking the onset of Yom Kippur, the holiest day of the year.

People were still streaming in, murmuring good wishes to each other in low voices and with somber faces. May it be a year in which Hashem will fulfill all your wishes for the good. Amen!

The ark was opened. A *Sefer Torah* was removed. The men surged forward to kiss the velvet covering that protected the holy scroll. R' Efraim watched the *chazzan* walk up to the *bimah*. Now, he would start reciting the famous opening words: "With the permission of Hashem and of the congregation ..." The air was tense with expectation.

To the rabbi's surprise, different words came out of the *chazzan's* mouth instead. In a sad singsong, he intoned the opening words of *Kaddish:* "*Yisgadal v'yiskadash shemei Rabbah.*"

With the faces of those who share a secret, the congregation answered, "Amen."

When the *Kaddish* was finished, utter silence reigned for a moment. Then, at last, came the emotional cry: "With the permission of Hashem and of the congregation ...!"

The new rabbi was puzzled. He knew of no reason for this strange custom and had encountered it in no other shul. Why recite the *Kaddish* before *Kol Nidrei?*

"It's because of R' Shneur the Apostate," someone whispered to him.

The rabbi was thoroughly astonished now. "R' Shneur the Apostate? How did a person come to earn such a title?"

Later, after the service, R' Sender, the elderly *gabbai*, approached the rabbi. As R' Efraim listened intently, the *gabbai* began to relate the story of R' Shneur the Apostate.

The story took place 500 years earlier, in Bowdon itself. R' Shneur, son of R' Efraim, was one of the town's most respected men. Heaven seemed to have showered him with every good thing. He was a wealthy man, with a house that was the most beautiful in all of Bowdon. His wife was a good woman and his children, Efraim and Avraham, were excellent students. A shrewd businessman, R' Shneur was close to the seat of power and was a frequent guest in the homes of government officials. In this capacity, he acted as a spokesperson for his fellow Jews, both in his own city and in others. He was handsome and charming, respected in his own community and by the surrounding gentiles. His home was a bustling place, with people coming and going at all hours seeking his advice.

Imagine, then, the shock waves that rocked the Jewish community when they heard the staggering news: The respected and respectable R' Shneur had abandoned his wife and family, and married the daughter of a neighboring gentile!

Bowdon was thrown into turmoil. On every streetcorner stood knots of Jews, all heatedly discussing one topic: How in the world, they wondered, could a Jew — especially a Jew in R' Shneur's position — leave his family to marry a non-Jewish girl?

They knew what our Sages have said: "Do not trust yourself until the day you die. Yochanan, the *Kohen Gadol*, served for eighty years and became a Sadducee in the end." But it is human nature to become accustomed to life's usual patterns, and until something extraordinary happens we tend to forget that our holy Torah has anticipated everything under the sun.

After the shock came the anger. Fury against the traitorous R' Shneur swelled rapidly in the town. The humiliation he had heaped upon his good family became not only the family's own business, but that of the entire Jewish community. The more hotheaded among them suggested stoning R' Shnuer, while others thought it a good idea to speak to him, in case perhaps he had begun to realize the enormity of his actions and sought to repent of what he had done.

A delegation was sent to Shneur's new home, where he lived with his gentile wife. To their dismay, they found him far from repentant. The men tried to talk to him. They tried to impress upon him how low he had sunk, betraying his own people and intermarrying among the nations. "Aren't you afraid of being punished? Do you think Heaven will turn a blind eye to your actions?"

Shneur did not answer. Deeply distressed, the delegation left his house. In town, the anger grew hourly. The entire community gathered to discuss the burning question of how to deal with a man who had breached some of the Torah's most severe prohibitions, and brought shame to his people.

It was Reuven the Blacksmith's plan that was adopted in the end. Reuven was getting on in years, and he recalled the way someone who had behaved like Shneur was dealt with in his youth. A group of strong men would drag him in disgrace from his home to the market square, where he would be forced to stand before his entire community. Everyone would spit on him until he was covered with shame from head to toe, the way he had shamed his people. As a crowning indignity, they would cut off his flowing beard.

Because it was wrong to punish someone without due warning, they sent a second delegation to Shneur with the following ultimatum: Either you divorce your non-Jewish wife and return to your family and your people, or we will do such-and-such to you.

The result was not one that the townspeople had anticipated.

Frightened at the ordeal that awaited him, Shneur, together with his new wife, bolted in the night. He fled to a large, distant city where he went immediately to a priest and converted. Shneur, son of R' Efraim, shaved off his long beard and — with the backing of the Church — put his Jewish identity behind him.

The Jews of Bowdon wanted to forget the man who had shamed them all so horribly. It was not long, however, before they found themselves once again discussing the exploits of Shneur the Apostate.

Strange stories began to filter back to Bowdon. Most other Jews who converted bore a strong grudge against their former brethren and looked for every possible way to avenge themselves on the Jews, bearing tales about them to the authorities and worse. Shneur behaved in exactly the opposite fashion. The new religion to which he had fled on his escape from Bowdon was paper-thin in his eyes. He went to church only rarely but socialized much with Jews. Whenever he heard about a Jew in trouble, he rushed to help him without hesitation. He would pay off Jews' loans with his own money. His gentile wife did not hinder these activities. In short, he remained faithful to his people, investing all his energy to help any Jew who needed his assistance.

His new "brothers," the Christians, saw that this new convert was not like all the rest. He did not, as the saying went, spit into the well from which he had drunk. He did not hate his former nation, but rather loved them with all his heart. Seeing this, the Christians hated him and began to persecute him. They chased him out of the neighborhood, forbade him entry to the church, and refused to talk to him. Shneur remained utterly isolated from Jew and Christian alike.

Shneur learned the full meaning of the word "outcast." He was unwelcome in both worlds. With the exception of those he was able to help in some fashion, the Jews regarded him with suspicion, and none could be found with a nice word to say on his behalf. He was disgusting in their eyes. Not only had he abandoned his wife and children, but he had gone to the lengths of marrying a non-Jew. And not only had he married outside the faith, but he had cast aside his faith and embraced a foreign religion. No one was prepared to forgive him.

But Shneur was nothing if not persistent. He was undeterred by the reactions to him, both from the Jews and from the Christians. His efforts on behalf of unfortunate Jews continued. Each time he heard of a Jew who had a case pending with the government or who had been arrested, he went at once to the authorities to speak up on the man's behalf, even resorting to bribery if that was what it took to free the Jew from his plight.

After this had happened several times, word began to spread in the Jewish community: Shneur the Apostate had remained faithful to his people. Gradually, a thawing set in. Little by little, the Jews began to forget their righteous anger. And at last, with time, they became used to him. Their old complaints were buried in the depths of their consciousness and Shneur, to his joy, was accepted as he was.

The main event that propelled Shneur back into the arms of his own people was the blood libel started by Petrik the Talebearer.

Like Shneur, Petrik was an apostate who had converted to Christianity — but there the resemblance ended. Until he was confronted with intense temptation, Shneur had been a good Jew. His surrender to sin had led to his downfall. Petrik, on the other hand, was a bad lot from the start. From the time he knew his own mind, Petrik — or Feivel, as he was originally named — hated his people. The moment he left his parents' home, the thin thread binding him to the faith of his fathers snapped and broke. He converted, proclaiming to the world that he had never been a real Jew. From that day onward he began to persecute the Jews with open hatred. He never lost an opportunity to get a Jew in trouble with the government, and from time to time would supply the authorities with information about Jews who evaded taxes or produced illegal whiskey.

Petrik the Talebearer's latest libel was the classic blood libel: He claimed that, on *Erev Pesach,* a Christian child had been murdered in the basement of Shepsel the *Shochet.* After all, who was more fit to perform that kind of killing than a ritual slaughterer? Immediately, two "witnesses" were found who insisted that they had personally seen Shepsel drag a screaming child through the streets of Bowdon — only to emerge later with a look of murderous satisfaction and a knife dripping blood. The court did not investigate the matter too deeply. In short order, they were prepared to sentence Shepsel to death by hanging.

Before that could happen, there was a commotion at the courtroom door. Shneur the Apostate burst inside, calling urgently to the judges, "Wait a moment! Shepsel is innocent!"

The astonished judges demanded proof. Shneur whispered something into the chief justice's ear. The judge called Petrik to the witness stand.

"What is your profession, Mr. Petrik?"

"What does that have to do with this case?" Petrik asked angrily.

"Answer the question!"

"I tan hides," Petrik muttered.

"And what tools do you use in your work?"

Petrik named several different tools, including wooden scrapers and metal combs.

The judge appeared displeased. "Have you named all the tools of your profession?"

"Yes."

"And how do you cut the hides after you've cured them? With your strong teeth?" the judge snapped sarcastically. "Do you not use knives at all?"

Stammering in confusion, Petrik said, "O-of course I use knives."

"Why, then, did you answer 'Yes' when I asked whether you had listed all your tools?" The judge was clearly beginning to have his doubts about Petrik's honesty. "Is it possible that you were trying to conceal from me the fact that you work with knives?"

Again, Petrik stammered some reply. The judge sent several police officers to check Petrik's workplace. They returned a short time later, faces white as chalk. In the tanner's cellar they had discovered the body of another Christian child who had disappeared from home several days earlier.

The truth came quickly to light: Petrik the Talebearer had himself murdered two Christian children in order to spread blood libels against the Jews in his area. His ultimate aim was to have every Jew in the country deported. It was not long before his sentence was pronounced: Death by hanging!

The episode of Petrik distanced the Christian community even further from Shneur the Apostate. They stepped up their persecution of him — until some extremists plotted an actual attack on his life. Discovering the plot in time, Shneur escaped by the skin of his teeth and found refuge in a safer place.

But the persecution did not stop there. From time to time, they accused him of various crimes, but the talented Shneur always managed to prove himself innocent — which only inflamed his enemies further. They burned down his house, uprooted the trees from his orchards, and plundered his property.

Finally, Shneur was forced to move to a place where no one knew him. He disguised himself and changed his lifestyle. He lived as a hounded and persecuted Jew, mourning secretly over the fragmented life to which his choices had led him.

Shneur the Apostate's two sons, Efraim and Avraham, were both pious young men. When their father had left home, they did not follow him but remained true to their faith. In its first anger at their father, the community had distanced itself from the sons, too. The sons, however, continued observing the mitzvos until everyone saw that they were faithful to their people. From that point on, the members of the community began to respect them as before.

When the time came to call them up to the Torah, however, a question was raised: By what name does one call the sons of an apostate? Could they say, "*Ya'amod R' Efraim ben R' Shneur,*" when Shneur had converted to Christianity?

They brought the question to the *gaon* R' Naftali Hertz, rabbi of Bowdon. He hesitated over his answer for a long time. On the one hand, there was the opinion brought forth in the *Sefer Chassidim* and by the author of the *Terumas HaDeshen*, who ruled that an apostate's name must not be used when calling someone up to the Torah, but rather his own name alone. Weighed against this was the fact that Shneur's two sons were good men who had done nothing wrong. Moreover, the father himself, who had heaped this shame on their heads, regretted his conversion and was being hounded by the very Christians whose religion he had taken on.

R' Naftali knew that R' Shneur had long wished to return to his native faith, which he had forsaken in a moment of weakness. But the law of the land placed a Jew who converted and then returned to Judaism under sentence of death. Shneur was afraid — with good reason — that talebearers would run to the local priests to inform them that he had abandoned the cross.

R' Naftali Hertz brought the question to two Torah giants of the generation: the Maharam of Padua and R' Aharon HaLevi, author of the *Zekan Aharon,* of Kushta. The two ruled that the sons *could* be called up to the Torah by their father's name. Though R' Yehudah HaChassid and R' Yisrael Isserlin had offered an opposite opinion, the Maharam of Padua declared that, according to all reports, "the father of said sons — though living among Christians — is a man who seeks to benefit his people, far and near. Therefore, his intention is borne out by his actions; namely, that he is a remorseful and G-d-fearing man. And this is what I have heard from faithful witnesses."

Most of Shneur the Apostate's remaining years were difficult ones, filled with physical and emotional suffering. He was punished both by Heaven and by man, always moving from place to place to escape the wrath of his Christian enemies. They sought revenge for his gall in helping Jews after he had converted. Such a thing was unheard of!

It was only in his old age that Shneur found a measure of peace. His gentile wife died, and his Christian neighbors forgot about him when he grew elderly. Shneur gathered up his courage and went back to spend the rest of his days in Bowdon.

When his end grew near, Shneur asked his neighbors to carry him, on his bed, to the town's big shul. It was *Erev Yom Kippur,* just before the setting of the sun would mark the start of the Holy Day. As the apostate was carried into the shul, utter silence fell. Shneur's bed was set down in the center of the shul, and he began to speak.

"My good people, I wish to confess before all of you, and before G-d. I sinned, I erred, I transgressed. My sin is too great to be borne. But the gates of repentance are never closed, and I have spent my life thinking about repentance. My actions will speak for me: I spent my entire fortune to help Jews in their times of trouble. I beg of you to pray before the compassionate G-d for the elevation of my sinning soul, so that He may forgive a sinner like myself. And I also ask that, each year before *Kol Nidrei,* you say a *Kaddish* for the elevation of the soul of Shneur, son of R' Efraim."

After speaking these words, Shneur closed his eyes and cried out "*Shema Yisrael, Hashem Elokeinu, Hashem Echad!*" in a mighty voice. On the word "*Echad,*" his soul passed out of his body.

The awe-stricken congregation, on the advice of their rabbi and community leader, undertook to fulfill the dying man's last request. From that year forward, the city of Bowdon maintained the custom, every *Erev Yom Kippur,* of reciting *Kaddish* before *Kol Nidrei* for the soul of the apostate who had died in a state of complete *teshuvah.*

R' Efraim HaKohen had an additional custom. Each year, before *Kol Nidrei,* he would learn the first *perek* of *Maseches Yoma,* which begins, "Seven days before *Yom HaKippurim,*" the first letter of which is also that of the name "Shneur."

How awesome is the power of *teshuvah*!

Succos

THE "WONDER SUCCAH"

"MAY WE COME IN AND SEE THE SUCCAH?"

A group of children stood shyly at the entrance, hoping to get a chance to view the wonderful Levi family succah. There were other children still inside, filling their eyes with the succah's beauty. The group outside was forced to wait until they were done; and the next bunch of young sightseers would do the same. The Levi succah was undoubtedly the most beautiful in the neighborhood, and quite possibly in the whole city. It drew children like a magnet, along with their parents and casual passersby.

Benzion Levi was a carpenter by profession. He had inherited his love of woodworking from his father, Yaakov Levi, a well-known master in his field. Many of the cabinets, tables, and other fine furniture in the area's homes had been fashioned by Yaakov's hands.

"Ah, Levi's handiwork," his satisfied customers would say. "It's furniture that will last for generations!"

Every table was solid as a rock. A chair was a chair, not a wobbly contraption on four legs that threatened to topple like a drunkard after only a year or two. But it was not the soundness of the furniture that was its crowning glory, but its extraordinary loveliness. Each piece that passed through Yaakov's hands was crafted and polished to perfection — the work of a true professional.

And yet, with all his accomplishments, Yaakov's proudest creation was his succah. He poured his soul into the building of that succah. The original creation took him several months, and the result was a stunning piece of work.

"I devote so much time and attention to things that are used in the fleeting, everyday world," he would say when questioned about the inordinate effort he put into building his succah. "How much more — infinitely more! — should I invest in the mitzvah of succah. The succah is built completely for Heaven's sake — a paradigm of *Gan Eden* in this world!"

And when the succah was finally finished, everyone agreed: There was none like it. From its foundation to its cap of *s'chach*, the succah was a thing of beauty and a feast for the eyes.

If Yaakov Levi was a professional at crafting wood, his son Benzion added a touch that exceeded even his father's fine work. Benzion was not only a carpenter, he was also an artist. In addition, he also possessed rare mechanical ability. In Yaakov Levi's succah, the wood itself had been decorative. Benzion went a step further. He painted all the boards white, after which he painted breathtaking pictures on them — pictures of the Patriarchs, the Twelve Tribes, the *Akeidas Yitzchak*, and Yaakov's dream. Pictures of the Israelites going down to Egypt, of the splitting of the Red Sea and the war with Amalek, the *Mishkan* in the wilderness, and the wondrous *Beis HaMikdash*.

Then, to top it all off, the press of a button set springs into action, bringing to light a breathtaking set of woodcarvings. These included various shuls, as well as a Polish town, complete with water carriers and woodchoppers, *beis midrash* and market square ... But no sooner had the viewer recovered from this stunning display than the sound of whirring gears reached his ears. A small coach, harnessed to wooden horses, rolled out. Then a tiny wooden puppet popped the cork on a bottle, poured out some wine, and wished the visitor a hearty *"L'chaim!"*

The fresh foliage decorating the succah was wonderful, cascading down with lush, green beauty. Small glass jars presented the seven species with which Eretz Yisrael was blessed. Alongside the more extraordinary items were the usual glittery chains and decorations all through the succah, arranged with the same precision and attention to detail as everything else.

Yaakov Levi's succah won the title of "Wonder Succah" in his city. Even when others tried to compete with him in creating stunning succahs, none were a match for the Levi succah. It retained its special charm, a beauty that seemed almost unearthly.

Benzion merited something that his father had not. Yaakov had only one son. Benzion, on the other hand, merited seven sons, who grew up to afford him tremendous *nachas* in his old age. When he sat at the head of his table in the succah, surrounded by his sons and numerous grandsons, he felt like a king. As the boys sang the holiday melodies in their sweet young voices, Benzion's heart filled with joy — and thanksgiving to the One Who had granted him the great privilege of living to see his sons' sons seated at his table.

When Yaakov Levi departed this world, Benzion, as his only son, inherited the "Wonder Succah." During the course of his own lifetime, Benzion added a great many details and decorative touches of his own. It was a pleasure to watch him at work. Benzion would sit on a chair atop a tall table, with his two oldest sons, Chaim Simchah and Nachum — then teenagers — standing on the table on either side of him to help him in his work. The younger children helped support their father's chair and handed him the tools he needed. People from all over the neighborhood gathered to watch the work in progress. Over the years, Benzion expanded the succah until it was twice its original size. In addition, he modernized the old succah with innovative and up-to-date effects to dazzle the eye.

Chaim Simchah and Nachum were loyal brothers and also the best of friends. Only twelve months separated their birthdays, and as the years passed, this interval seemed to shrink in significance, until they seemed almost like twins. At the same time, as they grew up, the differences between them became more pronounced.

Nachum, the younger one, had inherited all his father's talents: his woodworking skill, his artistry, and his mechanical ability. With time, he began to make his own contributions to the wonderful family succah.

Chaim Simchah, on the other hand, inherited none of his father's gifts. People said that he had two left hands, and that nothing he touched ever amounted to anything. But Chaim Simchah excelled in his studies at yeshivah; after he married, he found a comfortable niche for himself as a teacher. He was hired by a prestigious Talmud Torah to teach the eighth grade, and soon earned a reputation as an outstanding educator. After just a few years in the classroom, his summer vacations were constantly interrupted by parents begging him to accept their sons into his class for the following year. Word was out that his students were first-choice candidates at high-school yeshivahs throughout the country.

"How many students can I teach? One hundred? Two?" Chaim Simchah would protest when forced to turn away many disappointed parents — among them some of his own closest friends. Not all these parents were willing to forgive his refusal.

As for Nachum, he worked alongside his father in the carpentry business. With his talent and energy, he soon helped develop the family firm into a force to be reckoned with. Most of his younger brothers found their livelihood with "Benzion and Sons, Fine Furniture."

Once a year, on Succos, the entire Levi clan got together in the amazing succah. During the long, noisy family meals, no one was happier than Benzion himself, who was so grateful to have merited such joy in his old age.

It was during these holiday meals that the differences between the brothers was most obvious. All through the weeks leading up to *Yom Tov*, the younger brothers toiled to bring the succah to perfection. At the meal, they sat back and enjoyed the fruits of their labor. But when it came time for *divrei Torah*, they all fell silent. Every eye turned to the eldest son, Chaim Simchah, the *talmid chacham* of the family.

"Chaim Simchah, stand up and speak to us!" the father would fondly order his *bechor*. Pride in his learned son, and humbleness in his presence, was clear in Benzion's every syllable. Hearing it, the younger brothers would feel a twinge of jealousy and shame. They suddenly sensed that all the appreciation their father expressed toward them all during the year was not a thousandth of the respect he felt toward his eldest son.

But these moments quickly passed. As soon as Chaim Simchah concluded his talk, which was filled with short, thoughtful anecdotes of current interest and interesting tidbits of *gematria,* the brothers would burst into song, and the distressing undercurrents were forgotten as though they had never existed.

And then came the day when old Benzion, the father, passed away. The crowds of people who came to visit the mourning sons were quick to notice that the mourners were not sitting *shivah* together. While six of them sat in their father's home, the seventh, Chaim Simchah, had chosen to sit in his own home, alone.

How, the people wondered, had this situation come about?

The curious began to investigate, and they soon brought to light the reason. It seemed that a huge quarrel had erupted among the brothers, even before their father was buried. Benzion Levi had left a detailed will, signed and notarized, describing how he wished his property to be divided. There was only one item which Benzion seemed to have overlooked. He made no provision at all for the famous Levi succah, neither its physical parts nor the beautiful decorations and mechanical wonders.

Chaim Simchah declared that the entire succah belonged to him. As the *bechor*, he was halachically entitled to inherit twice the amount of his other brothers. He was willing to forego material property. "All I want is the spiritual property — that is, the succah!"

Nachum stood up and announced that, on the contrary, it should all go to *him*. Let Chaim Simchah take his double share of their father's property, as mandated by the halachah — but he must not touch the succah. "For years, the planks of the old succah have been crumbling and falling apart, and the mechanical decorations are growing rusty and broken. If I hadn't fixed them all professionally, it would be a rusted junk heap by now, and the wood would be a pile of splinters." He turned to his older brother. "Your position, Chaim Simchah, would not be acceptable to any court. I have invested thirty years in protecting and improving the succah, to save it from the ravages of time — while you haven't raised so much as a finger on its behalf. Where do you get the nerve to expect it all to come to you?"

In the end, Chaim Simchah rose in a fury. Before their father was even laid to rest, the brothers were engulfed in the flames of controversy. The five younger Levi brothers stood solidly behind Nachum and against Chaim Simchah. All the old, forgotten pangs of jealousy came rushing back — the envy and hatred of the uneducated for the *talmid chacham*.

The family's friends were stunned at this turn of events. They tried in every way they knew to restore peace among the brothers. Illustrious rabbis were summoned to shuttle back and forth between them, talking privately with both Nachum and Chaim Simchah. They suggested all sorts of ways that the brothers might compromise. But all their efforts were in vain.

An imp of foolish jealousy goaded the brothers on, sowing ever more controversy and hatred. Each of them grew terribly stubborn, saying, "It's all or nothing!"

One rabbi, a close friend of Chaim Simchah's, tried to talk sense into him. "Nachum is the mechanical genius, the woodworking professional," he said. "If he is unwilling to give up the succah, I can understand that. But you, Chaim Simchah, are a man of the book, a man of the spirit. Why do you care about a pile of painted boards?"

"You don't understand," Chaim Simchah said stiffly. "Do you think I crave painted boards and toys on springs? Those are children's playthings. But that succah is holy — a holy of holies! Apart from me, who will speak words of Torah in the succah?

"If the succah should fall into my brother's hands, what do you think will be its fate? My brothers are ignorant of *Tanach* and Mishnah, and let's not even mention the Talmud. What will those holy succah walls hear? Empty talk, lightheadedness, gossip, and foolish laughter."

People were divided on the issue. Some said, "Benzion was a smart man. He knew the succah would lead to controversy; that was why he refused to mention it in his will."

Others declared, "No, he was a stupid man. Had he set down clearly who he wanted to inherit the succah, no quarrel would have broken out in the first place!"

In the same vein, they were of two minds about the brothers' positions. Some sided with Chaim Simchah, the *bechor*. "He is the oldest, and he is also a *talmid chacham*. It is fitting that the succah belong to him."

Others, however, backed Nachum: "Had he not repaired and maintained the succah all through the years with his own golden hands, it would long ago have turned into a heap of rubbish."

A few of the parents who had been turned away by Chaim Simchah when they had asked to have their sons join his class found a way to exact payment now for what they felt was a personal slight. In various secret and subtle ways, they poured oil on the flames of the controversy, until the whole town was caught up in it. Everywhere, people stood and debated the merits of "The Case of the Quarrelsome Succah."

"What a pity that the holy mitzvah known as *Succas Shalom* — the Succah of Peace — should have turned into a succah of war!" pious people sighed privately. But they could not change reality. A high wall had sprung up overnight between the two brothers, with Chaim Simchah standing firmly on one side, and Nachum just as solidly on the other.

Benzion Levi had died at the height of winter. It was still a long way before another Succos would be upon them, and the quarrel subsided for a while. However, as the holiday approached, tensions rose again. Everyone waited anxiously to see how the matter would be settled.

To general disappointment, the famous succah did not go up at all that year. The beautiful wooden boards sat forlorn in Benzion's old attic. A local rabbi had come up with a compromise proposal that had been, at first, acceptable to all: Chaim Simchah would get the succah for the first two years, after which the succah would rotate from brother to brother during the years to come. At the last moment, however, some troublemakers stirred up the brothers and incited them to refuse the compromise solution.

The following year, Chaim Simchah quietly took the succah boards with the intention of building it on his own property, as the rabbi had suggested. Gossipers immediately carried the tale to the other brothers. Nachum, his five younger brothers, and their sons stood in front of Chaim Simchah's house shouting their disapproval to anyone who would listen. The neighbors milled around, each voicing his own opinion. Distressed and embarrassed, Chaim Simchah did not even cut open the ropes tying the bundles of planks together. Instead, he sadly built the same old succah that he had put up all the years before.

For six long years, the famous succah boards and decorations sat dusty and neglected in Chaim Simchah's attic. As each Succos drew near, he wanted to take the boards out and erect the succah in his yard. But each time, he thought of his brothers and nephews screaming abuse at him outside his windows, and didn't dare.

The news spread with shocking suddenness through the city: Nachum had fallen gravely ill with a rare disease.

Expert doctors were called in, and though the situation looked bleak, they did not give up hope. They recommended surgery at the hands of a renowned British surgeon. "The chances are small," they admitted, "but this surgeon has managed to save the lives of several people who suffered from the same condition."

As is the way of the world, the skilled surgeon refused to lift a finger to help until his fee was assured. In order to raise the necessary sum, Nachum and his brothers would be forced to sell their thriving business and empty their bank accounts.

Chaim Simchah was in a quandary. His heart flinched painfully at the news of his brother's illness, and he felt a powerful remorse over their long quarrel. But his sense of self-respect did not let him run to Nachum's house to visit him on his sickbed. Desperately, he sought a way out of his quandary.

That evening, as he scanned the daily newspaper, his eye was caught by an ad:

"Sales corporation seeking Judaica items." A public auction was scheduled in seven days' time.

His heart in his mouth, Chaim Simchah dialed the company's number and cautiously asked whether they would be interested in buying an old and very fine succah. When the manager learned just which succah they were talking about, he leaped at the offer.

One week later, the succah was sold for a staggering sum. Swallowing hard, Chaim Simchah went to Nachum's house that night and handed over the entire sum, down to the last penny. The sum would cover the operation and all its attendant expenses, with some money left over.

The succah was bought by the authorized agent of Mr. Lehman, of Florida, an elderly and childless multi-millionaire who spent the month of Tishrei in Israel most years. On the day after Yom Kippur, Mr. Lehman hired a team of workers to erect the special succah he had recently purchased.

As the workers untied the ropes that held the planks together, a dusty envelope fluttered down to the ground. One of the men saw it, and brought the envelope to Mr. Lehman.

"What's this?" the rich man asked in surprise. He tore open the envelope. Inside was a folded page. Mr. Lehman smoothed the paper and slowly read what it said.

> *To my dear sons,*
>
> *I am old now, and I fear that I will no longer be with you to celebrate next year's Succos. Know this, my sons! The succah is known the world over as "Succas Shalom — the Succah of Peace." Should you have a falling-out because of this wonderful succah, you will undermine*

the very foundation of this mitzvah. Such a succah cannot survive, as there is no such thing in the world as a "Succah of War."

Therefore, I am leaving behind no instructions about who gets the succah. Whatever I may instruct in the matter, I know that you will harbor a grudge against one another in your hearts. Therefore, rather than fall into controversy, you had best sell the succah to a stranger.

Your father,
Benzion Levi.

Through his agent, Mr. Lehman uncovered the circumstances leading up to his buying the succah. And so it came about that on the first night of *Chol HaMoed*, the entire, reunited Levi clan joined Mr. Lehman in a *Simchas Beis HaShoevah* celebration in his new succah. *Their* succah ....

"What can I say?" Nachum Levi sighed, one hand reaching up to touch the fresh bandage at the side of his head, the only sign remaining of his illness. With his other hand he lovingly clasped that of his older brother. "Had we only allowed Chaim Simchah to build the succah that first year, he would have found our father's letter and we would now be sitting in a "Succah of Peace." And all the painful memories would not be here to plague us."

Chaim Simchah did not answer. Instead, he closed his eyes and began to speak words of Torah on the verse, "And His Succah shall be in Shalem, and His dwelling-place in Zion."

"Let Nachum come *shalem* — whole and healthy — to the *succas shalom*, to his dwelling-place in Zion," he finished. "And *baruch Hashem* that we have merited this day!"

Mr. Lehman was deeply moved. "Please let me add a word," he requested. He looked around the table at the seven Levi brothers. "It seems to me that I will not be running counter to your father's wishes if I invite you all here each year, to celebrate in my succah. Your father's wish has been fulfilled; now the buyer may do as he pleases!

"This succah, as I see it, will stand forever as a succah of peace!"

A PROMISE IS A PROMISE

R'SHMUEL WAS AN EMINENTLY RESPECTED MAN IN JERUSALEM. He possessed every desirable quality: He was learned in Torah, intelligent, rich, handsome, and revered.

He guarded his self-respect zealously. When a fellow citizen called him by the nickname "Shmiel," he refused to turn his head or respond. "My name is Shmuel," he would say stiffly. "I don't know any 'Shmiel'!" Having enjoyed a good livelihood all his life, R' Shmuel never had to ask for any man's help.

There were two personal traditions to which R' Shmuel clung. First, on Yom Kippur, he made sure he was the one called up for the *aliyah* of "*Maftir Yonah.*" And, second, on Simchas Torah each year he would buy the rights to be the *Chasan Torah*. He paid serious sums for both of these honors. Respecting the tradition, neither the *gabbaim* nor the other members of the congregation placed any obstacle in R' Shmuel's way. On Yom Kippur, *Maftir Yonah* was sold to him as a matter of course, and on Simchas Torah the main negotiations surrounded only the *Chasan Bereishis* honor; no one interfered with R' Shmuel's "right" to purchase the honor of being *Chasan Torah*.

R' Shmuel had one son named Dovid, whom everyone called by the nickname "Dudy." The son was exactly the opposite of his father in every way. Where R' Shmuel stood tall and handsome, Dudy was sallow-faced and narrow-shouldered, with a wispy beard, like that of a goat, adorning his chin. Success followed R' Shmuel everywhere, while Dudy failed in everything he tried.

When R' Shmuel lay on his deathbed, he gave the following instructions to his son:

"I have had two good things in my life. One is that I never asked for help from my fellow man. The second is that I always bought the rights to *Maftir Yonah* and *Chasan Torah*. I absolve you of *Maftir Yonah*, as it is very expensive. But I do not absolve you of *Chasan Torah*. Give me your word now that you will be sure to guard my traditions!"

Dudy faithfully promised his dying father that he would do as he wished. With the last of his strength, R' Shmuel murmured, "Remember, Dudy, my son, *Chasan Torah* every year ... Remember, Dudy, not to need people for anything. Remember, my son, *Chasan Torah* ... Remember!"

With those words, R' Shmuel's soul left his body.

The promises Dudy made to his father came back to haunt him almost at once.

R' Shmuel had been a man of means, but Dudy himself did not fall into that category. His father's dying wish precluded Dudy from accepting charity, and this proved a great hardship to him and his family. All the city's poor were helped by a *tzedakah* fund, but now Dudy could no longer benefit from it.

Shaindel, his wife, was incredulous. "How can this be? Shall we all die of starvation? Take money from the charity fund and feed your children!"

But Dudy refused. "When my father was on his deathbed, I gave him my word. I won't go back on it!"

Though Shaindel pleaded and coaxed in every way she knew, her husband remained adamant. Dudy could be very stubborn — and he had promised. Then Shaindel grew angry. She said harsh things to her husband, about himself and about his father, who had made his son accept foolish decrees that stemmed from neither wisdom nor good sense, but from an irrational feeling of pride. Because of them, Dudy was condemning his whole family to suffering.

"What kind of inheritance did your father leave you, so that you and your family do not die of hunger?" she asked pointedly.

Dudy was silent. He had no answer. But immediately after that, he began to search for a job with which to provide sustenance for his hungry wife and children.

Nobody wanted to hire him. Dudy was known as a man who ruined everything he touched. Once, Dudy went to the *Chevrah Kaddisha* (the Burial Society) to ask for work. Out of pity, the managers agreed to let him bury the bodies. "After all, he can't harm the dead!" they reasoned.

But at his very first burial, Dudy's hands trembled so much that instead of lowering the body carefully into the grave, he let it drop all at once, to crash into the hole with a thud. To Dudy's shock, the "corpse" began to cry out and to flail its arms and legs. The man was still alive!

Dudy was fired that very day.

So Dudy was rejected both by the living and by the dead, unable to support his family or provide them with enough for even one meal. His children went hungry, until Shaindel got wise and began to secretly accept money from the *tzedakah* fund to feed her sons and daughters.

For the first few years after R' Shmuel's passing, Dudy managed to hold onto his father's other tradition — buying the rights to *Chasan Torah*. The shul's *gabbaim*, more afraid of the dead than the living, did not dare arouse the wrath of R' Shmuel in Heaven and sold the rights to *Chasan Torah* to R' Shmuel's son for mere pennies.

Each year, on Simchas Torah, Dudy would give a big *Kiddush* in his home after *davening*, amid his crumbling furniture and peeling walls. As they enjoyed the cakes and *kugels* and *schnapps*, the other shul members would wonder where the money had come from for the repast. They did not have any idea of the lengths to which Dudy had gone to make that *Kiddush*.

Before Succos, Dudy had gone down to the valley and collected *aravos*. Heaping them into sacks, he dragged them to the market still wet and fresh, where he sold them all. With part of the money, he bought *lulavim* that were disqualified for use, and used pieces of the *lulavim* to make *koishalach*, or rings to bind *lulavim*. Selling these in turn, he used the profits to buy kosher *lulavim*, which he then sold in the marketplace. In this way, he managed to make small amounts of profit, which he laboriously collected, penny by penny. He was able to celebrate the holiday properly, without disobeying his father's order. Not only that, but he was able, too, to buy the *Chasan Torah* honor and to throw a lavish *Kiddush* for his shul, like respectable people everywhere.

Shaindel disapproved of all of this, because Dudy did not do it for his family but rather for the rights to *Chasan Torah*. All the rest of the year he remained the same as ever, going through the world with eyes that were open but not seeing a thing — like the glass eyes that doctors gave people who were incurably blind. Not that Dudy was actually blind, Heaven forbid, but since the world considered him inept, he went along and justified their opinion of him.

One year, between Yom Kippur and Succos, a wealthy man by the name of Ludwig Berlinski visited Eretz Yisrael. His arrival was greeted with tremendous excitement, because he was one of the leading philanthropists who helped support Jerusalem's poor. A man with a heart as soft as butter, Mr. Berlinski wrote checks from his home in Holland and sent them to Jerusalem every month. He couldn't bear to see another human being in pain or want.

On this visit, too, he did not come empty-handed. Word quickly spread throughout the city that he had brought a large sum of money to be distributed to the needy. A great many people began to swarm out to visit their benefactor.

Mr. Berlinski was staying as a guest in the home of *Rabbiner* Horowitz, one of Jerusalem's rabbis. Visitors lined up to see him from morning until night. No sooner had one man left than another came in to take his place. The philanthropist sat at a table with two great bowls before him, each filled to the brim with gold and silver coins. He did not count them out too carefully, nor did he ask too many questions about why a person had come and what his needs were. The only thing he demanded was that no one come to him twice. Upon entering, the visitor was carefully scrutinized through the rich man's monocle. Then, with a satisfied nod, he would dip into one of his bowls and, with a happy heart, press coins upon the supplicator.

Shaindel was after her husband, Dudy, not to be foolish this time, but to go to *Rabbiner* Horowitz's house like all the others. "If everyone is getting, you should get, too!"

"No," Dudy said stubbornly. "My father ordered me on his deathbed not to take charity."

"What kind of charity is this?" she protested shrilly. "Ludwig Berlinski does not check a person's income. With my own eyes, I've seen respectable homeowners going to see him, people who do not lack butter or milk or meat, summer or winter! Those people took money from his bowls. Are you richer than they?"

Her words were persuasive. Indeed, what sense did it make for him to refuse to take money from a man who did not care how much he gave or to whom, as long as the person lived in the holy city of Jerusalem?

Dudy got up and prepared to go see Ludwig Berlinski. Suddenly, his father's image rose up before him, as he had looked lying ill and near death. "Remember, Dudy, remember …"

"No!" Dudy cried, turning back to his wife. "I can't. My father forbade me. I can't do it."

Shaindel covered her face and burst into bitter tears. As for Dudy, he made his escape from the house as soon as he possibly could.

Dudy walked out into the street with a drawn face. What, after all, could he do? He had given his father his word. There was no way he could fight with his father's soul!

Then, as he stood thinking, a germ of an idea sprouted in his mind.

Dudy hurried to the home of *Rabbiner* Horowitz. He climbed the flight of stone steps to the second story and, heart pounding, knocked on the door.

From inside, Ludwig Berlinski's pleasant voice called out, "You can come in!"

Dudy opened the door. He was in the famous room at last. There stood the rich philanthropist, and there was the table with its two great bowls. Ludwig gazed at him through his monocle. "No, he hasn't been here before," he mumbled to himself. He reached into a bowl for some money.

Dudy grew pale. In a weak voice, he said, "No, Mr. Berlinski, no."

Not understanding, Ludwig reached into the bowl with his second hand as well, and came up with two big handfuls of coins. And still, Dudy murmured, "No, I can't."

"Then what do you want?" the rich man asked with some impatience. "Shall I give you four handfuls?"

"What I want is — a loan," Dudy blurted. "You see, my father, may he rest in peace, instructed me on his deathbed not to take charity from anyone. But I could take a loan. I'll return it all, Mr. Berlinski, I give you my word." His voice trailed off. Dudy felt close to fainting.

Berlinksi measured the other man with a level but curious gaze. "And what else did your father tell you?" he asked sarcastically.

Dudy, missing the sarcasm, thought he really wanted to know. Shyly, he stammered, "M-my father ordered me, just a minute before he died, to be the *Chasan Torah* every year for the rest of my life."

"Is that so?" Berlinski shrugged. "If you want a donation, take as much as you want. I don't give loans."

Once again, Dudy grew pale. Silently, he turned his back and slunk out of the house.

As he did each year, Dudy celebrated Succos with the profits from *aravos* he picked in the valley. Impatiently, he waited for Simchas Torah, when he would be able to buy the *aliyah* as the *Chasan Torah*.

In shul, the merry *hakafos* lasted many hours. This year the dancing was especially lively in honor of their illustrious guest, Mr. Ludwig Berlinski.

When the seventh round of dancing was finally completed, the *gabbaim* stood up and began to sell the *aliyos*. When they reached *Chasan Torah*, they called out quietly, "One franc." (The French franc was in use as legal tender in those days.) As usual, they waited for Dudy to call out as he always did, "Two francs," with which the transaction would be concluded.

Dudy duly called out, "Two francs!" The *gabbai* stood up to announce, "Going twice, going three times …" But a new voice arose from the eastern wall. "Four francs!"

Surprised, every head turned to that side of the shul to see who had intruded on Dudy's longstanding tradition. They saw that it was none other than Ludwig Berlinski himself, noting all the staring faces turned his way and not understanding why. Earlier, he had informed the *gabbaim* that he did not want any sort of honor in shul. Apparently, he had changed his mind. He was challenging Dudy's "right" to *Chasan Torah!*

Dudy nearly slid to the floor. He had to outbid four francs? Where in the world would he get the money? It was only with the greatest difficulty that he managed to scrape together the two francs each year. But more?

"Five francs," he called in a shaky voice. This year, he decided, he would work at stripping carcasses in the marketplace if he had to.

"Six francs," the wealthy man said, holding up six fingers.

The *gabbaim* hurried over to the eastern wall and whispered something to Mr. Berlinski. But he only shook his head angrily; he was not afraid of departed souls.

Dudy leaped to his feet as though bitten by a snake. "Seven!" he screamed. Heaven alone knew where he would find seven francs. He could feed his wife and children for months on that sum!

From the eastern wall: "Ten!"

Dudy felt as though his bones had turned to water. Through his closed eyes, he saw his father's face, as he lay on his deathbed, and heard his father's voice whispering, "Remember, my son, remember …"

In a near-whisper, Dudy countered, "Eleven!"

The *gabbaim* raced back to the eastern wall, but again, the philanthropist's response was negative. "I didn't know his father," Berlinski snapped. "I am buying this with my own money." He raised his voice. "Twenty!"

Again, Dudy saw his father, R' Shmuel, and his face seemed to be glowing like a flame. R' Shmuel's voice whispered, "Dudy, my son, remember. *Chasan Torah …*"

Gathering his strength, Dudy cried, "Twenty-one!" His lips were dry as paper.

Ludwig Berlinski stood to his full height, and called loudly, "One hundred and twenty!"

Dudy collapsed on the floor in a dead faint.

They laid him out on a bench and bathed his forehead with vinegar. They held aromatic salts under his nose. Dudy breathed heavily, and then — with some difficulty — managed at last to open his eyes.

A voice rang out: *"Amod, amod, amod, R' Dovid ben R' Shmuel, Chasan Torah!"* ("Stand up, stand up, stand up, R' Dovid, son of R' Shmuel, *Chasan Torah!*")

Dudy shook his head, wondering if he was dreaming. What was going on?

The wealthy Mr. Berlinski, having bought the *aliyah* for one hundred twenty francs, had instructed the *gabbai* to honor Dudy with *Chasan Torah!*

And what of the *Kiddush*?

The *Kiddush* after shul that day was held in Dudy's house as usual — but paid for, from start to finish, by the great benefactor, Ludwig Berlinski.

As the guests ate their fill of the delicacies, they talked incessantly of the rich man's goodness. It seemed that Berlinski had decided to open an office in Jerusalem, and had appointed Dudy as its "manager"! A steady job, at a steady salary!

And so, Dudy the inept, Dudy the failure, was given a new nickname. Overnight, he became known to one and all as "R' Dovid, *Chasan Torah.*"

A BOY NAMED ILYA

AS THE PLANE LIFTED INTO THE DARK SKIES OVER KISHINEV, capital city of Moldova, Ilya Tomashin gazed out the window and tried to find his father. He knew that this was foolish. When a plane has lifted high enough to turn the city lights into distant twinkling stars, there is not the remotest chance of seeing a person on the ground, or even spotting the car in which he was driving home to his large, now empty house.

A cold pit of desolation settled over Ilya. His emotional ties to his father were very strong, and the fact that his father was a gentile and his mother was Jewish had never meant much to him. The fact, however, had come to have very serious, practical consequences in the boy's life. His mother had decided to leave Moldova and move to Israel, taking her only — and Jewish — son along with her. Her husband, a devout Christian, had opted to remain behind in Kishinev.

His father would keep himself busy with his work, Ilya knew. Dr. Yuri Tomashin was a famous musician who spent all his days immersed in notes and melodies. But at night, when he returned home to his big, lonely house, what would he do then? He would sit and stare sadly at the walls. Maybe he would look to a few glasses of vodka for comfort, but Ilya didn't think so. His father wasn't a drinker.

"Hey, Ilya." There was a friendly thump on his shoulder. "Why are you so sad?"

In the narrow aisle between the seats stood his good friend, Michael Shapiro. He, too, was moving to Israel along with his mother, leaving his father behind. But Michael's father wasn't left alone. His two daughters would be there to alleviate his loneliness.

"I'm not sad," Ilya growled. "I just feel like jumping out of this plane."

"Is that any way to talk?" Ilya's mother, Tanya, demanded from her seat beside him.

"I wanted to stay in Russia," Ilya mumbled. "What do we have in Israel?"

"We are Jews," Tanya said simply. "Russia is our birthplace, but it is not our land. We are going to Eretz Yisrael."

Michael removed himself prudently from the discussion and returned to his own seat. Things were much clearer in the Shapiro family. Mrs. Shapiro had introduced a Jewish atmosphere into the home several years before, so that when she announced one day that she was moving to Israel, her son had reacted enthusiastically.

The Tomashins' situation was very different. Ilya winced at the memory of the endless heated arguments between his mother, his father, and himself. In the end, Tanya Tomashin had her way. She was moving to Israel, and she was taking her son along with her. But Ilya did not want to go, and he made no secret of his feelings.

On their arrival in Israel, they passed fairly quickly through the various levels of bureaucracy. At the end of just three months, they found themselves settled in an apartment in a southern neighborhood of Jerusalem, the capital city of Israel.

From his earliest days, Ilya had been a gifted child. By the time he turned 13, his friends called him "Professor." He read — or rather, devoured — everything he could lay his hands on. He seemed to learn everything and to know everything there was to know. Ilya's extraordinarily high intelligence was something of a challenge to his teachers, more than one of whom felt a bit irritated by this talented student with such wide-ranging knowledge. He sometimes asked questions to which they had no answers, or else contradicted things that they taught, basing his opinion on current literature that exploded old ideas. He befuddled his Russian teachers with the latest thoughts on quantum mechanics and astronomical discoveries, subjects covered in just two of the thirty scientific journals to which he subscribed.

Yuri Tomashin was, of course, very proud of his son. He was certain that Ilya would bring great honor to Russia in the years to come, as a world-renowned scientist. Then Tanya burst his bubble of dreams by taking their gifted son off to Israel. Yuri consoled himself with the thought that Ilya would not want to stay there, and would surely return to his native Russia.

He knew his son well.

From his first moment in Israel, Ilya was bitter. He did not identify with the people he saw all around him, and certainly not with his immediate neighbors, working-class people who seemed to trail light-years behind him. His mother practically had to drag him to school by force. As she had planned ahead of time, Tanya enrolled him in a state-run religious school. She wanted Ilya to learn a little about Judaism and the Torah.

But Ilya had no interest at all in learning about these things. In class, he adopted a provocative attitude, asking heretical questions that threw his classmates into turmoil and enraged his teachers. After one such episode too many, Ilya was asked to leave the school.

To Ilya's satisfaction, but his mother's sorrow, he was next enrolled in a secular school that interested him far more. But here, too, he found no peace. All he really wanted was to return to Kishinev. He made sure not to become too fond of anything in his new home.

Tanya had nearly given up hope. If things were to continue in this negative way, the day would not be far off when Ilya would be celebrating his victory by returning to his gentile father in Russia, where the boy would live out the rest of his life in the most un-Jewish way possible.

One day in early summer, as she sat in her steaming kitchen reading the Russian newspaper, her eye suddenly caught sight of an ad. It had been placed there by an organization that called itself *"Achicha Yisrael — Your Jewish Brother."*

"Come to our summer camp!" invited the advertisement. The camp, it seemed, was for Russian children, aged 13 and 14. "Play and hike and see the country by day," the ad said. "And, at night, enjoy thoughtful philosophical discussions around the campfire."

The ad interested Tanya. She wanted to know more about the camp it described. Wasting no time, she phoned the number listed. As she had thought, the ad had been placed by a religious organization for Russian immigrants — a group whose entire purpose was to help families exactly like her own.

To Tanya's joy, Ilya agreed to register for camp. Apparently, even a kid who feels as if he's suffocating needs the fun and freedom offered by summer camp. For two weeks he lived with a group of boys his own age, swimming in a pool and at the beach, hiking up to the Golan Heights, visiting wadis and waterfalls, climbing Mount Hermon, boating on the Kinneret, and being dragged unwillingly to the gravesite of Rabbi Shimon bar Yochai at Meron. He rappelled in the mountains of the Judean desert and Ein Gedi and made his perspiring way up the snake-path at Masada. He was happy and light-hearted, and open to listening.

At night, as the ad had promised, the campers sat in a circle around a blazing campfire, roasting small potatoes and talking of metaphysical subjects. The counselors made sure always to direct the discussions into thoughtful channels and away from idle chatter. Many of the boys took no part in the heated debates; after a long day in the outdoors, they had no energy left for philosophy. Ilya was one of the few exceptions. All day long, he waited impatiently for the nightly talks, if only in order to demonstrate his intellectual superiority. He was a sworn atheist, a fervent supporter of a modern scientific viewpoint that left no room for G-d. The counselors were well-trained to debate with boys such as this — but even they were unprepared for as tough a nut as Ilya.

Yoshi, the head counselor, was the only one who refused to give up on Ilya. His fellow counselors wanted to throw the boy out of camp, or at the very least make him stop taking part in their campfire discussions. The questions Ilya asked were never openly provocative. On the contrary, he would ask as though from an earnest desire to learn, to understand. But from time to time, as though by the way, he would throw in a statement that ran counter to everything the counselors were trying to accomplish.

"An hour and a half of work goes up in smoke in one second," Arkady complained. Arkady was an experienced counselor who had successfully helped scores and even hundreds of Russian youths find their way to practicing Judaism. "One of Ilya's comments leads to a whole wave of heretical thinking. He's setting us all back — years back, to the rule of an atheistic Soviet government. It is impossible to work this way!"

"Impossible?" asked Yoshi. "But to throw Ilya out and take away the only chance of saving his soul *is* possible?"

He let Ilya stay, although no one and nothing succeeded in making even the smallest crack in the gifted boy's armor of disbelief.

"He's like a sealed box," the counselors declared. "There's nothing to be done with him. A pity to waste our energy."

Yoshi disagreed. Though he secretly thought there was much to what they said, he decided to let Ilya remain in camp. It was true that Ilya's comments undid hours of the counselors' patient work; but until and unless he had proof that Ilya was deliberately setting out to sabotage that work, Yoshi would not throw him out.

Yoshi was making plans that included Ilya. The holidays were fast approaching, and he intended to contact the boy and invite him to be his guest for all of Tishrei.

Ilya, too, was making plans. He held several secret phone conversations with his father, Dr. Yuri Tomashin. The two hoped to reunite in Kishinev immediately after the holidays.

It was an afternoon in mid-Elul when the phone rang. Ilya was surprised to hear Yoshi's voice at the other end. In the intervening month, he had forgotten all about the summer camp.

"I'd like to meet with you," Yoshi said, getting right to the point.

Ilya, who did not have many friends — most of his time was spent with his books and computer games — agreed. A visit with Yoshi promised a fine mental challenge.

Yoshi came over to Ilya's house that evening. After some small talk, he arrived at the purpose of his visit.

"To stay with you for a whole month?" Ilya echoed with wide eyes. "I'll be bored out of my mind!"

"You won't be bored for a second," Yoshi promised. "And besides, as a young intellectual, you owe it to yourself. Come on — stay with us for the holidays, experience it all close-up, and listen to the ideas that lie behind every custom and practice. Afterwards, you can decide whether this lifestyle appeals to you. If not, no one will force his beliefs on you."

Tanya made a big show of objecting to the plan. She knew that the slightest show of enthusiasm would make Ilya suspect that they were trying to make him religious. So she played the game, putting up a great resistance to his leaving for a month.

Ilya consented to go.

Yoshi wanted to show Ilya true Judaism at its best. Together, they stayed at a well-known yeshivah, beginning with *Selichos* on *Erev Rosh Hashanah.*

When the *chazzan* cried out in tears, "Please let me use every appropriate *middah* to supplicate before You, my King!" Yoshi glanced sideways at Ilya to see how the words were affecting him. Perhaps he might be reached through his heart, if not through his mind.

Ilya stood uninterestedly. It was clear that the *chazzan's* emotional prayers did not touch him in the least.

Hundreds of yeshivah students cried out with a single voice, "Do not fling us from You, and do not take Your Holy Spirit from us!" The words reverberated through the *beis midrash* like a storming sea. This, Yoshi thought, would melt a stone.

To his consternation, he saw Ilya peek at his watch.

"Well, Rosh Hashanah is coming up," Yoshi consoled himself. "The long *tefillos*, the shofar-blowing, the *mussar* talks … *B'ezras Hashem*, we will get through to him yet."

Two and a half weeks later, Yoshi sadly decided that the experiment had failed. Any more time he invested in Ilya would be wasted time.

The Rosh Hashanah service had the power to lift mountains, but it did not budge Ilya. He listened impassively to the call of the shofar, and despite all of Yoshi's learned explanations, Ilya did not stop referring to the shofar as an "old-fashioned instrument; there are much better versions these days!"

It all passed like a dream: the Ten Days of Repentance, *kapparos, Erev Yom Kippur,* the last meal before the fast.

Yoshi was able to point to one success along the way: Ilya agreed to fast on Yom Kippur. "Just in order to study, from a purely scientific point of view, the effects of twenty-five hours of continuous fasting on the human body," Ilya explained.

Yoshi hoped that the fast would crumble Ilya's stony heart at last.

But, on *Motza'ei Yom Kippur,* he knew that this hope, too, had been in vain. Ilya fell on the food and drink with gusto, remarking to the discouraged Yoshi, "This unusual day has a powerful psychological aspect. A very interesting experience — but it hasn't made any particular impression on me."

But Yoshi would not give up. Ilya remained as his guest, helping him build a large succah in the yard. Together they went to the *shuk* to buy the *arba minim*: beautiful *esrogim* and long, graceful *lulavim*, three-leaved *hadasim* and perfect *aravos*. Yoshi made sure to accompany every purchase with a detailed and — to his mind — inspirational explanation.

On Succos itself, Ilya sat with Yoshi and his family in the big succah. There were many other guests as well, some of them newly observant Russian Jews whom Yoshi had introduced to the Jewish lifestyle through the *Achicha Yisrael* network. During the course of the meal, Yoshi asked each of them to tell his personal story. Ilya listened with interest, but never stopped inserting a contrary viewpoint. Even Yoshi's patience was wearing thin.

During *Chol HaMoed* they went to a *Simchas Beis HaShoevah* celebration, visiting no fewer than five scenes of public dancing set to lively and professional music. Ilya enjoyed the music, "even though it's loud, Levantine, and monotonous." He even joined the circle of dancers once or twice. But he remained untouched.

As Simchas Torah drew near, Yoshi took inventory. He had nothing more to offer Ilya, apart from the dancing with the Torah during the *hakafos*. Ilya had already experienced joyous Jewish dancing and had emerged spiritually unchanged. And on *Chol HaMoed* there had at least been the advantage of a good band; in shul on Simchas Torah even that would be lacking.

It had been a waste of time, Yoshi had to admit to himself at last. Let Ilya bask in his atheism, if he so chose.

His guest, privately, felt the same way. Given a choice, he would have bolted for home early. It was only politeness that kept him from doing so.

Yoshi heard himself asking, "Ilya, are you planning to stay for Simchas Torah?"

"Do you want me to?" Ilya countered quickly.

Yoshi roused himself. "Yes — I do want you to. Very much so. And you know what? We're going to travel to a big yeshivah in Bnei Brak, where you'll see a thousand yeshivah boys dancing with all their might for hours on end, holding Torah scrolls in their arms. I'm sure that you'll enjoy seeing it, even if only from an anthropological point of view. After all," he said sarcastically, "studying primitive tribes in the jungle can be interesting."

Yoshi had been unable to refrain from delivering this final sting to the guest who had angered and frustrated him for weeks.

On Hoshana Rabbah night, Yoshi and Ilya learned *Gemara* together all night long — "Just," Ilya assured his host, "for the intellectual challenge." They traveled to the *Kosel HaMa'aravi* for *Shacharis*, though Yoshi no longer expected any results as far as his stubborn guest was concerned.

That afternoon, they stood in line at the Central Bus Station carrying small overnight bags and waiting for the bus to Bnei Brak. Yoshi had arranged for them to sleep in the yeshivah dormitory. A last, forlorn hope kindled inside him: "Who knows? Maybe Simchas Torah with a thousand other boys will crack open his sealed heart."

The bus seemed very late in coming. Yoshi fretted, "It seems to me that we may have missed the last bus."

"What do you mean, 'last'?" Ilya mocked. "I can get to Bnei Brak tonight, in a taxi, or hitching a ride."

Yoshi was too tired to get angry anymore.

After a long wait, Yoshi's fears were confirmed. No more buses were running out of Jerusalem that day.

A small group of people had been waiting along with them. "There are some taxis over there," one of them suggested.

They trooped over to the taxi stand, which was located at one side of the Central Bus Station. One driver agreed to take them to Bnei Brak — for an exorbitant price. "The holiday will be starting soon. I'll have to stay in Bnei Brak all day. Pay me for that."

Yoshi looked at his wristwatch. There remained but an hour and a quarter before the holiday would begin. Under normal circumstances he would never have dreamed of leaving the city at such an hour. Now, however, he gambled everything on one last throw of the dice. This would be his last chance with Ilya.

Along with four other passengers, they climbed into the taxi. Even before it had rounded the first bend in the highway out of Jerusalem, both Yoshi and Ilya had fallen into an exhausted sleep.

They awoke in some confusion when the taxi suddenly stopped.

"The engine had to choose this minute to break down," the driver fumed. "It's a miracle that I managed to pull over onto the shoulder of the road. I don't know what to do now."

They were halfway between Jerusalem and Tel Aviv. Six passengers and the driver stood at a loss at the side of the highway. Several passing cars stopped, but each had room to take on only one extra person. In this way, the four other taxi passengers sped off. But Yoshi and Ilya, who refused to be parted, were left with no alternative means of reaching their destination.

"What do we do?" Yoshi asked in perplexity. "Celebrate Simchas Torah on the Jerusalem-Tel Aviv highway?"

"Don't despair," the driver counseled. "My sister lives in a small settlement that's not a very far walk from here."

A spark of hope flared in Yoshi's heart. "Is it a religious settlement?"

"Of course," the driver said. "I know I don't look like anything special, but believe me, my sister is very religious. She'll be happy if we come to her. She loves having guests. She always says to me, 'When Hashem loves someone, He sends him a guest!'"

"Can we come even without an invitation?" Ilya wanted to understand.

"To my sister? You can walk in day or night," the driver answered proudly. "You've never met such a hospitable person! You won't believe it until you've seen it with your own eyes."

They began the walk to the *moshav*. As the sun sank lower and lower in the west, Yoshi kept consulting his watch in growing panic.

"Why do you keep doing that?" Ilya teased.

"If you recall," Yoshi said, "when I took you to *Selichos* on *Erev Rosh Hashanah,* it was you who checked your watch every other minute."

"What's the connection?"

Yoshi smiled. "We were both doing it for the same reason. You wanted to know when the 'torture' of *Selichos* would be over. I want to know when my own torture will end. I also want to make sure I am not transgressing the holiday."

"If the sun sets before we get there, what will you do?" Ilya wanted to know.

The sinking sun painted Yoshi's face with its golden rays. "I will stay right here until the holiday is over!"

"*What?*" Ilya was stunned. "You'd stay here all night, and all day tomorrow?"

"Yes."

Ilya shook his head, bemused. "But why? All you have to do is stick out your hand. Someone will give you a ride."

"Ilya, my friend," Yoshi explained patiently, "if Hashem does not permit it, I can't stick out my hand to any passing car."

"We're here," the driver broke in excitedly. "Here's the *moshav!*"

A couple of hundred yards brought them to the doorstep of the driver's sister. It was three minutes to sunset.

They were received warmly, as the driver had promised they would be. Their hostess apologized endlessly for the fact that the only foods she had to offer them over the holiday were Middle-Eastern dishes. Had she known they were coming, she would have prepared a feast of Russian delicacies.

But the food was not their main interest today. Foremost were the *hakafos*. Though he didn't expect much from the settlement's small shul, Yoshi was overjoyed not to have to spend the holiday on the shoulder of the highway.

There were no thousand boys in this place to dance the night away. There were not even twenty. The congregation of the shul consisted of several dozen adult men and a handful of boys. Yoshi joined in the dancing, grasping a *Sefer Torah* in both arms and throwing all his energy into expressing his joy and thanksgiving to Hashem, Who has separated the Jewish people from the nations of the world and given us the Torah. Yoshi did not forget to add a personal note of gratitude for not having been abandoned on the roadside for the holiday.

To his suprise, Ilya also joined the small circle of dancers. For the first time since they had met, Yoshi sensed a certain human warmth emanating from the boy. Ilya clutched the heavy Torah scroll with great care, afraid lest it slip out of his fingers. When it was time for him to hand the *Sefer Torah* over to someone else, he followed it with his eyes before joining in the circle of dancers, just like one of the gang.

"Maybe a miracle will happen today," Yoshi thought, rubbing his eyes.

But the following night, when they rode home to Jerusalem in the driver's brother-in-law's car, Ilya seemed remote and preoccupied. He hardly spoke a word to Yoshi.

"It was just an isolated episode — a fleeting feeling that left no mark," Yoshi decided sadly.

Ilya went home. He broke off contact, and Yoshi did not hear from him again. Once, he picked up the phone and dialed the boy's number, but almost immediately regretted the call. In tears, Tanya told him that Ilya had left Israel immediately after the holidays and returned to his father in Kishinev.

It was over. All his efforts had been in vain. All of it, from their first meeting to the last, simple *hakafos* in the settlement on Simchas Torah.

Six years passed.

It was a cold Chanukah night in Jerusalem when the phone rang. Yoshi's son picked it up.

"Someone named Ilya Tomashin wants to talk to you, Abba," the boy called.

Astonished, Yoshi took the receiver from his son's hand. "Hello?"

"Hello, Yoshi." The voice belonged to a grown man. Ilya had once had a boy's voice, but six long years had passed since then.

"Where are you calling from?" Yoshi asked politely.

"From Moscow. I wanted you to be the first to know: I've just become engaged. I'll be getting married soon."

"Mazal tov!" Yoshi congratulated him. Then, cautiously, he asked, "Is your bride Jewish?"

"Yoshi, what's the matter with you?" Ilya cried joyfully. "Not only is she Jewish, but she's mitzvah-observant. We're planning to get married in Israel!"

Yoshi was stunned. With difficulty he managed to blurt out, "How's that?"

"Thanks to you, I became religious."

"*What?* You — religious?" Yoshi shouted in disbelief.

"Did you think I was made of concrete?" Ilya chuckled. "Every single minute that you invested in me reaped its fruit. From the yeshivah boys praying on *Selichos* night, to our *davening* at the *Kosel* on Hoshana Rabbah morning."

Yoshi tried to say something, but a golf ball seemed to be stuck in his throat.

"I'll explain," Ilya said. "You made one mistake. You tried to fight an ideological war with me, to force me to surrender, to give up my ideas. You didn't understand that I'm made of different material. As long as you tried to subdue me — I fought back. I acted indifferent, cold, even rebellious. But inside, the things I saw and heard went straight to my soul. That month of Tishrei dug a tunnel for me — a tunnel to freedom.

"But I didn't know that then. Right after the holidays I bolted back to Russia, to my father. From time to time, the *tefillos* and the other things would come back to me. What I missed most of all were those warm *hakafos* in that simple settlement. *That* was no presentation you had prepared for me. You had arranged for a grand show, a thousand boys in a big yeshivah. But it was the small *hakafos* that got to me. When I saw how those simple *moshavniks* looked at the *Sefer Torah,* something melted in my heart. It was not possible for such people to feel that way about a plain piece of parchment.

"I went to yeshivah in Moscow because I wanted to find out what was written on those parchments that could make those people light up with such happiness. I began to learn Torah. At first, it was the intellectual challenge that attracted me, but after a while I began to feel that the words were speaking directly to my soul."

"And what about your father?" Yoshi asked quietly.

Ilya laughed out loud. "You mean my learning partner, Dr. Yuri Tomashin? The Torah's logic enchanted him even more than it did me. He converted to Judaism two months ago and will be moving to Israel with me. You see, it's the custom for both parents to lead their son to his *chuppah*."

THE OLD-NEW SUCCAH

I. A BUBBLING VOLCANO

TUVIA ZIMMERING RETURNED HOME FROM THE PARENT-teacher conference knowing that it would not be an easy night. "I'm going to show Gedalia, my 'jewel' of a son, a thing or two!" he fumed.

Gedalia, 11 years old, had seen his grades plummet for some time now, but had somehow managed to convince his parents that all was well. Tuvia, his father, had been very busy with his work and not watchful enough over his son.

"I'm afraid that Gedalia has been behaving in a very disruptive manner in class," his rebbi had said tonight. "In fact, I'd go so far as to call his behavior 'wild.' He sets a bad example for the class and leads his friends into trouble." There was a possibility, the rebbi had concluded gravely, be — in simplest terms — thrown out of t

Tuvia Zimmering was a fundamentally g to support his family and also set aside r

Torah. But he had one great fault, a fault which overshadowed his many good qualities. It was a character flaw that many knew about, and that some had mentioned to him in calm moments.

Tuvia had an awful temper.

Not just a bad temper, but a flaming one. When Tuvia became angry, smoke seemed to pour from him. The *Gemara's* comparison of an angry man to one who worships false idols seemed apt when Tuvia lost control; he was like a person worshiping a furious god. First he would become completely red in the face, resembling a bubbling volcano about to erupt. And Tuvia always did erupt.

He would shout so loud he would grow hoarse. His shouts would shake the walls of his home and echo throughout the apartment building, startling the neighbors. "Ah, Tuvia's angry again," they would say sadly. "Tuvia's out of control." They knew the pattern well.

As he neared his house, Tuvia's blood began to boil more quickly. He felt ready to explode.

"Take it easy," he whispered to himself. "Try and talk to Gedalia calmly. Listen to what he has to say. Maybe he has an explanation."

"I'll give him an explanation!" seethed the angry part of him, poised and ready to go on the rampage. "What he needs is a good beating!"

And a beating was what Gedalia got that night. Tuvia wrenched his son out of bed and very quickly threw the apartment into turmoil. For the first few minutes, he did try to hear the boy out, to see what he had to say for himself. But not for long. His hand soon whipped out and smacked Gedalia — hard. Once, twice, three times ....

After a while, his anger took on a life of its own. Each strike poured more fuel on the flames of his fury and took it to new heights. For Tuvia, there was no "red line" beyond which it was dangerous to go. For Tuvia at that blindly raging moment, all of existence was a red line.

II. A "MAN OF PRINCIPLE"

Gedalia was indeed a wild boy — but his nature was genuinely sensitive. His uncontrolled behavior came from a lack of understanding and an inability to express himself. Tuvia, his father, never suspected how sensitive his son truly was. He never had a heart-to-heart talk with him to get to know him up close, on the inside. Had he bothered to sit down and talk with Gedalia, he would have discovered that his son had been gifted with a rich inner life and unusual artistic abilities.

But Gedalia was the kind of boy that is now labeled "hyperactive." He was unable to concentrate on his schoolwork for more than five minutes at a time. He was not lazy, nor were his academic skills especially weak. He was simply suffering from a severe inability to focus.

Had his father taken the time to speak with him, to think about him, to consult with experts and get advice about him, he would have learned that this was a problem that had a solution. But Tuvia spoke first and foremost with his hands. It was his fingers that did his thinking for him, and the imprint of those striking fingers was all too often left on Gedalia's cheeks.

The results were terrible. Gedalia's schoolwork plunged further and further. Father and son were engaged in a vicious cycle: As long as Gedalia continued to disrupt his class in *cheder,* his father continued to beat him. And the more his father beat him, the less Gedalia was able to learn.

The boy was thrown out of one school after another, like some kind of bouncing ball. Gedalia's level of learning at the age of 13 was hardly better than that of an 8-year-old. He could not spell and could barely read. As for his handwriting, that was a riddle few were able to unravel.

As the boy's bar mitzvah approached, a school adviser urged Tuvia to make his son a nice party and not to hold back on the celebration as a punishment for his poor schoolwork; the adviser warned that this could only complicate Gedalia's situation further.

"Good," Tuvia said, nodding in agreement. "That's what I thought, too." That very day, he booked a large catering hall for the bar mitzvah.

Just two days later, however, Tuvia was furious at his son again. He discovered that Gedalia had not yet learned a single paragraph about the laws of *tefillin,* even though his father had arranged for someone to learn with him. As if this were not enough, Tuvia further discovered that his "talented" son had taken apart their new computer in order to see how it worked, but could not put it back together again. The computer technician who was summoned to their home declared that the machine was now no more than a pile of junk.

In his rage, Tuvia ran to the phone and, on the spot, canceled his booking with the hall and caterer. He did not calm down until he had screamed at his son, "I promise you that I will not make a bar mitzvah celebration at all, just a *seudas mitzvah* for ten people. That's all!"

Tuvia kept his promise. He fought heroically against his wife, his friends, and his pleading son. He fought, and emerged triumphant from the battle. In his mind's eye, he imagined people whispering about him: "A man of principles." "A wonderful educator!"

Had he known what people were actually saying about him, he would have exploded. The words "principles" and "educator" were not among those chosen to describe him at all. Harsh things were said about his raging temper. The words "angry" and "Tuvia" seemed almost synonymous.

And Gedalia grew worse and worse. He hardly learned at all. Accepted into a yeshivah specifically designed for poor students, he did not even distinguish himself there. At the age of 15, he could express himself with a very weak vocabulary, most of it slang. During the month of Elul, he found a job with a man who sold *lulavim* and *esrogim*. While his classmates back at yeshivah were making special efforts in their learning and spiritual growth in anticipation of the upcoming High Holy Days, Gedalia was busy arranging *lulavim,* counting *esrogim,* and checking that his *hadasim* were properly triple-leafed. He became an expert in the laws of the Four Species, especially on the most practical level. Out of a pile of *lulavim,* he could unerringly put his finger on the best of the lot.

In his spare time, he would go out back behind the store and create colorful chains to be sold as succah decorations. One day, he happened upon a paintbrush. With his own money he bought a set of watercolors and tried his hand at painting. To the complete astonishment of R' Zerachia Shinbaum, owner of the business, Gedalia proved to be an excellent artist. He had been born with a wonderful artistic ability that no one had ever stumbled upon — until now.

R' Zerachia encouraged the boy to paint whenever he had a free minute, and he greatly enjoyed the results. Using plain white sheets of paper, Gedalia breathed color and life into them, painting pictures of people, cars, animals, and more.

But as Elul advanced, there was less and less time for painting. R' Zerachia's shop was filled with customers from morning to night, and Gedalia was kept busy running constantly back and forth between the shop and the storage room. His sensitive hands plucked *hadasim* and checked *esrogim*. The customers praised him for his skill and gentleness. For the first time, Gedalia felt the satisfaction he had never felt at home. He had plenty of freedom here for his hyperactivity. Gedalia's visits to his parents' home were reduced to a few hours at night for sleep — and, even so, he would often leave home in the morning with his cheeks burning from his father's slaps. Tuvia was not at all pleased with the way Gedalia was "wasting his time," heaping embarrassment on his parents and not learning at all. Gedalia promised to use his spare time, when the store was empty of customers, to learn *Mishnayos*. But when those rare moments came, he ran instead to his paints and brushes.

Day by day, his artistic efforts grew more beautiful and expressive. His human faces began to look much more realistic, as did the animal pictures he copied from a succah poster with the words, "Be daring as a leopard." His colors were delicate and expressive. His leopards looked real enough to frighten anyone, and the eagles soared in the blue sky with outstretched wings that one could almost touch.

III. HONIGMAN'S CELLAR

Meyer Honigman never wanted to set foot in Poland again.

From the day he had been miraculously saved, at the age of 14, from a Nazi concentration camp, the trauma had never left him. He wished never to return to that blood-soaked land. He could not forget the way his Polish neighbors had betrayed him and his fellow Jews, slaughtering as many Jews as had their own enemies, the Germans. The Poles would ferret Jews out of their hiding places and hand them over to the Nazi S.S., beaming with pleasure when the Jews were carted off to the death camps. The words *"yemach shemam"* ("may their names be erased!") were frequently on Meyer's lips — referring as much to the Poles as to the Nazis themselves.

"There is no forgiveness," he would declare. "The Poles are the lowest and most despicable race on the face of the earth. No other nation has been the cause of our slaughter as they have. We lived among them for a thousand years, and for a thousand years they shed our blood."

Anyone who had delved into the history books knew that this was not exactly the truth. There had been peaceful years in Poland as well as bloody ones. Yet no one tried to argue with him. Meyer Honigman lived with his rage, with his urge to destroy and avenge himself. Of all his family, he was the only survivor. The Honigman clan had populated an entire Polish town, and now there was no one left but Meyer.

After the war he moved to Eretz Yisrael, where he had the privilege of marrying and starting a family. Two sons and a daughter were born to him and his wife, and there was no prouder father than Meyer. Honigman was once again a name to be reckoned with.

When Poland was opened up to tourists, Meyer was adamant in refusing to even listen to suggestions that he go back for a visit. "Travel back there? To the place where every bit of earth is saturated with Jewish blood?"

His friends would argue, "One must reconcile with reality, Meyer. Do you think we're going there on a pleasure trip? We are going to pray at our fathers' graves, at the graves of *tzaddikim,* to relive our most glorious moments."

Meyer would counter, "I will never forget our traitorous neighbors, Wadislaw Kozloski and his wife, Yanina. My father paid them 200 rubles to protect us. They took the money and made their promises. Two days later, my father was transported to Auschwitz. The Kozloskis chased me out of the cellar where I was hiding, straight into the arms of a German unit that was searching for hidden Jews like me. In reward, the Nazis gave them four long strings of sausage. I saw it with my own eyes. Traitors! Murderers!"

Meyer never tired of describing the cellar from which he had been chased. "My parents' cellar was not a tiny space. It was large, and it ran underneath the entire length of the house. My mother used to store her potatoes there all winter, as well as apples, carrots, and beets. The cellar was like a refrigeration room. It kept the vegetables fresh all winter long, until Pesach. When they chased me out, I had two loaves of bread with me, and plenty of potatoes. I could have held out for months, if not for those foul murderers."

"What else was in the cellar?" his young grandson asked, entranced by Meyer's descriptions. In his childish imagination he saw himself playing in that wonderful place, perhaps hide-and-seek with his friends, where no one would be able to find him. Imagine, a cellar as big as a whole house! A room that you entered through a ladder from a trapdoor in the kitchen floor!

"What else was there?" Meyer echoed. Sadness filled his eyes as painful memories rose up in him. He remembered well what else there had been, but he didn't want to talk about it. Pleasant childhood memories were stored there — a childhood that had been brutally torn from him. The wound was still too fresh.

"We kept our succah boards there," he said, his voice cracking a little as he spoke.

"Boards? Saba, did you keep your succah there so the snow wouldn't ruin the wood?"

"Yes, my little genius," Meyer said, stroking the little boy's cheek. "All year round the succah stayed in the cellar, leaning against one wall. On *Motza'ei Yom Kippur,* after he drank a hot cup of coffee and ate a piece of my mother's good homemade cake, my father would open the green trapdoor in the kitchen floor and go down the twenty-three steps into the dark cellar. He would hold a large kerosene lantern to light his way. My older brother and I would follow him, step by step. We felt so important: We were going to help our father build the succah! The next morning, we would cut branches for *s'chach* from the two trees that grew near our gate." Meyer sighed. "Ah, those were the days."

His eyes had grown damp as he relived the memories. He remembered those succah walls. They had been made out of no ordinary lumber, but from painted boards. Pictures had been painted on them by an artist's hand — his own grandfather's hands. But it had been a well-known secret that Grandfather had drawn only the fruit: the apples, pomegranates, and grapes. Most of the work had been done by his neighbor and dear friend, stunning pictures in a variety of colors marching across the smooth boards.

The memories became too much for Meyer. The tears spilled over and poured down his cheeks. He fell silent, one hand still lovingly caressing his small grandson's cheek. The boy looked up at him with big eyes as he shared in his grandfather's silence.

IV. TO REVIVE THE PAST

"What wisdom will not achieve, time will." Thus went the old adage, and it applied very nicely to Meyer Honigman. After ten stubborn years, the walls of his resistance began to crack. Yet another of his friends was making the trip to Poland; yet another brother-in-law brought back snapshots and impressions from graves of *tzaddikim* and forgotten vistas. Meyer was able to identify most of them with ease. They were, after all, the vistas of his childhood. A person does not forget the scenery of his youth, even if his native land later stuck a knife in his innocent back.

Meyer took stock of his life. He was no longer young. Perhaps he would lie down to sleep one night and not wake again, as happens to many old people. He suddenly longed, one more time, to see his hometown.

He wanted to see his parents' house. Perhaps it had not been destroyed. It might still be standing in its old place, and he could return there to relive moments from his childhood. Of course, he would also visit the graves of holy men and pray there. But he knew one thing for certain: He was not going to visit the death camps. That was out of the question!

With a heavy heart, he went to the Ministry of the Interior to obtain passports and visas for himself and his oldest son, Yossi. From the day he had moved to Israel he had never once left the country. Now he planned to join a group of chassidim who were arranging a summer trip to the burial places of dozens of *tzaddikim* throughout Poland.

The short flight to Europe passed, for Meyer, amid a welter of deep thoughts. He had been chased from this place as an unwanted citizen. He was returning to it today, after more than fifty years, with pride and dignity.

A taxi picked them up at the Warsaw airport and drove straight to Meyer's hometown. The trip was four hours in a northerly direction. As they drew closer, Meyer's heart started to pound painfully in his chest. He began to recognize the scenery around him. And then, he was there.

Time had made its inroads in the dusty Polish streets, but some of the old buildings still stood. Bathed in sweat, Meyer gripped his son's hand tightly. "I'm afraid I won't be able to stand this," he whispered, his face ashen.

The taxi drove slowly through the town. Meyer peered through the window. Where was it? Had his parents' home been destroyed?

Suddenly, he burst into a hoarse shout. "There it is! The house! It's there!"

The taxi stopped. Meyer and Yossi climbed out and walked quickly to the front gate. Meyer was very pale and trembling from head to toe. He recognized the path leading to the front door, and the two trees beside it. And there was the old chicken coop, just as he remembered it. It was as though the intervening fifty-five years had never been.

The house itself looked the way it always had: a simple cottage, only older. A second look revealed a new wing tacked onto the back of the house.

With an uncertain hand, Meyer knocked on the front door. His questing eyes found two tiny nail-holes in the door, where the plaque reading "Yosef Honigman, Accountant" had once been affixed. Now on the door, in a red-lettered sign, was the family name, "Kozloski."

The blood rushed to his head. So those murderers had been thieves as well! They had stolen his pretty house. And why not? They themselves had lived in a miserable hovel. Why not steal the Honigman place? That was why they had turned him over to the Germans, after all — so that there would remain no heir to make trouble for them.

V. SHALL THE MURDERER ALSO INHERIT?

The door opened. In the doorway stood a black-haired farmer, in his mid 40's. Though Meyer had never seen him before, he nearly fainted at the sight of the man: He was a carbon copy of Wadislaw Kozloski. This, then, must be his son.

A flicker of surprise and wariness crossed the man's face, then disappeared. Impassively, he regarded the two Jews.

"Who are you?" Meyer asked the farmer.

"My name is Josef Kozloski. And who are you?" The man had begun his answer hesitantly, but ended on an aggressive note.

"Are you the son of Wadislaw Kozloski?" Meyer pressed, ignoring the farmer's question.

Josef nodded his head, eyes narrowing in suspicion. "What do you want from me?" he demanded.

"I am Honigman. My family lived in this house before the Germans invaded Poland." It was all Meyer could do to utter those words — so deeply imbedded in his being that they seemed almost a part of his bloodstream — without collapsing.

"I was born in this house," Josef snapped back. "I never heard the name Honigman."

Meyer turned an angry red. "You thief! Do you see this?" He pointed at the small indentation where the *mezuzah* had been nailed to the side of the door. "This is the classic sign of a Jewish home. This is where we lived. If you want, I could give you a hundred other signs, all through the house. I could tell you the number of steps in the staircase, the number of windows, and about the trapdoor in the middle of the kitchen, with twenty-three steps leading down to the cellar."

Josef's eyes bulged as he cried, "What do you want?" Then, in a fearful whisper, he added, "My mother and father always told me that the Jews are like evil spirits. If you kill them, they rise up again."

The conversation continued a while longer before Josef Kozloski gave his grudging permission for the Honigmans to enter the house. Meyer gave his word that he had no intention of trying to evict Josef from his home.

Meyer walked slowly from room to room. He sobbed like a baby when he stood in his parents' bedroom, where he had taken his own first breaths. (Josef, too, had been born in this room. But what a difference there was between them! Meyer was the son of the homeowners, while Josef was the son of house thieves.) He pointed to the corner where his crib had stood. This was where his mother would bend over to lift him onto her shoulder, singing soft lullabies. It was from this room that he had left home to attend R' Zelig's *cheder* for the first time. Here was where the first part of his childhood had taken place.

In the dining room, Meyer's eyes misted over once more. Where was the long table where the family would eat their Shabbos and holiday feasts? Where was his father's old *shtender,* at which he had pored over hundreds of pages of *Gemara*?

Yossi Honigman began to be anxious about his father's health. "Let's leave now, Abba," he whispered. But Meyer was stubborn. He wanted to see the cellar. At his request, Josef found a flashlight and they descended the twenty-three steps into the cool, dank room that ran the length of the house.

Piles of onions, beets, and turnips greeted them. The cellar, after all these years, had not changed in its basic purpose as a refrigeration and storage center. Restlessly, Meyer's eyes darted from side to side. At last, they settled on the far wall.

He nearly fainted. There, leaning against the wall as they had always leaned, were the walls of his family's old succah!

VI. A SUCCAH MAKES ALIYAH

Josef was more than willing to let Meyer Honigman have the old succah boards. He had never bothered to figure out what that ancient lumber was for. In the cool, dry cellar, they had been beautifully preserved, and Kozloski was thrilled to learn that they were all that his Jewish visitors wanted.

Meyer hummed a happy tune as they drove toward the airport with the boards. Now he understood why Heaven had directed his steps back to Poland. It was a case of redeeming prisoners: rescuing these succah boards from a gentile's household. The remainder of his stay in Poland had passed like a dream. Nothing seemed as real to him as those precious old succah boards, so bound up in loving memories.

He encountered some difficulty at the airport with the strange cargo he insisted on bringing along. Yossi Honigman kept his head. He phoned several known Jewish activists, bribed senior bureaucrats, and managed the affair to his father's satisfaction. The boards were permitted aboard the plane with them and stowed in the cargo hold. Destination: Eretz Yisrael.

"Succos is in two months," Meyer said happily to his son, seated beside him in the plane. "I want to incorporate these old boards into my succah at home."

"A wonderful idea, Abba," Yossi said soothingly, still concerned about his father's health. It wouldn't do for him to become too excited.

"But there is a problem," Meyer went on. "I had a look at the pictures on the boards. Their colors are nearly completely faded by now. There were such beautiful pictures of the Seven Species and other fruits. Two of the walls had pictures of animals, taken from the words of R' Yehudah ben Teima. Those are nearly erased now. I must have them redone."

Intent on calming his father, Yossi was ready to agree to anything. "Don't worry, Abba. We'll look for a good artist when we get home, and ask him to touch up the original drawings."

The stewardesses came around serving the evening meal, but Meyer had no appetite. He was too impatient to eat. All he could think about were the newfound succah boards.

"No!" he exclaimed determinedly. "We can't take just any artist. We need someone with a delicate touch, with a sensitive spirit, an artist who will repaint every line of every picture with gentleness and sensitivity. Every board, I recall, had a line drawn across the top as a kind of border. That line has disappeared as the wood shrank with time. We must replace those lines the way they once appeared."

"Not a problem, Abba," Yossi laughed. "Even I can draw lines."

Meyer became angry. "You don't understand. They were no ordinary lines. They were fine lines, delicate lines, made by the gentlest hand. Only that kind of hand will be able to draw them properly again."

"Let's *daven* for help," Yossi said, quick to placate his father. "Hashem will guide us to the right person for the job."

VII. IN ZERACHIA SHINBAUM'S SHOP

Rosh Hashanah had come and gone. Meyer Honigman was growing very anxious. He had not yet found the right man to repaint his precious succah boards. Dozens of artists applied for the job, as Meyer was offering a handsome fee to the one who would restore the old wood to its original beauty. But he was a very critical man. In each artist, he found some flaw. None of them seemed to be just the person he was looking for.

During the Ten Days of Repentance, Meyer and Yossi went to Jerusalem to buy a *lulav* and *esrog,* as was their custom each year. On his old, frail legs, Meyer went from store to store in search of the items he wanted. His critical sense would not permit him to buy an *esrog* that was not as nearly perfect as he could find, its color an aesthetic blend of yellow and green and its *pitom* riding proudly, like a victory flag. His chosen *esrog* always looked more like an object created by a craftsman than anything grown on a tree.

In one shop, he stood surrounded by other customers, carefully inspecting the blade of a nice-looking *lulav.* A neighbor back home had advised him to visit Zerachia Shinbaum's shop, where he was sure to find something he liked.

His neighbor hadn't been wrong. Meyer found everything he wanted here. The *esrogim* he inspected were beautiful and unblemished, the *lulavim* straight and tall as soldiers standing at attention. R' Zerachia's young assistant, a boy of about 15, helped Meyer select the items that would allow him to leave the shop completely satisfied. Meyer paid in cash. He was about to walk out, his purchases under his arm, when R' Zerachia called from the other side of the store, "Gedalia, did you show him that special *esrog* that I hid in the back yard?"

A second later, Meyer and Yossi Honigman were following Gedalia to the yard. Gedalia did not make them wait long. He went unhesitatingly over to a box and pulled out an *esrog.* His careful hand held it delicately over its bed of flax. Yossi Honigman was impressed with such expert handling at such a young age.

"What do you say?" Gedalia asked proudly. "Have you ever seen such an *esrog?"*

But Meyer was not looking at the *esrog.* He was staring at the pictures that decorated every corner of the back yard and peeked out from among the cartons of *lulavim* and crates of *esrogim.*

"Who painted these wonderful things?" he asked emotionally.

Bashful, Gedalia inclined his head. "I did."

Meyer jumped as though an electric current had charged through him. "I'm going to talk to your boss," he said, already turning to go back into the shop. "I'm going to ask him if he can free you up for a day or two!"

VIII. GEDALIA THE ARTIST

R' Zerachia agreed to give up his assistant for two days or more. A deep strain of compassion had led him to encourage Gedalia to paint his pictures in order to calm the boy's frustrated spirit and give an outlet to his creative energies. Now he was very happy that the unfortunate boy had at last found someone who knew how to appreciate his talents.

Gedalia threw himself heart and soul into the restoration of Meyer Honigman's succah boards. The work was not easy. The wood was flaking in several places, and worms had left their marks as well. Gedalia scraped and glued, sawed and hammered. Once he had repaired the succah walls themselves, he began to repaint the pictures, under Meyer's constant supervision.

Under Gedalia's skillful hands, the pictures came alive. He breathed life into the lion and the leopard, the deer and the eagle, and he carefully repainted the fruit. He also re-inked the lettering of the prayer said upon entering the succah and the names of the *Ushpizin.* Finally, Gedalia delicately reclaimed the fine line that framed each board. Everything was restored to its original hue, as it had first appeared in Poland some seventy years earlier.

"What did I tell you?" Meyer crowed with delight, showing the repainted boards to his son. "Look how delicately he painted the border. Those lines proclaim, 'Here is where the succah ends!'" His eyes swept the finished product with deep satisfaction. "From beginning to end, a work of art!"

When the old boards from Poland were added to Meyer's succah, the result was breathtaking. He invited all his neighbors in to view the stunning effect.

As for Gedalia, he felt proud of himself for the first time in his life. During *Chol HaMoed,* he begged his father to come with him to see the work he had done on the Honigman succah. Tuvia was inclined to dismiss the whole matter. "I have no interest in succah boards!"

Gedalia hung his head, disheartened.

His wife, overhearing their talk, summoned Tuvia to another room. "Stop torturing the child," she demanded. "Go with him; don't you see how he's been pleading with you!"

And so, unwillingly, Tuvia went with his son to Meyer Honigman's neighborhood. When he saw the succah and its paintings, something stirred deep inside him. He devoured the pictures with his eyes. Finally, he said in a low voice, "I once saw a succah like this. These pictures are familiar to me."

Meyer jumped up as though he had been bitten by a scorpion. "Impossible! There is no succah exactly like this in the world!"

Tuvia stood still a long time, staring at the pictures. On the way home, he seemed a changed man. He spoke gently to Gedalia, as though they were old friends. The moment he walked through his own front door, he leaped at a cabinet and pulled out an old photograph album. Flipping rapidly through its pages, Tuvia suddenly stopped. "Gedalia! Come see! Here are your pictures!"

Tentatively, Gedalia came closer. He looked at the small, black-and-white photographs and saw a succah standing in a courtyard, surrounded by men wearing prayer shawls and *shtreimels*. Ensuing pictures displayed the succah's interior. Gedalia froze. "You're right, Abba. Those are my pictures! My pictures!"

Taking the album with them, they retraced their steps to the Honigman house. They found Meyer entertaining some important members of the community in his succah.

"You said that there is no other succah like this one," Tuvia said, waving the album triumphantly in front of Meyer's face. "Take a look at this!"

Meyer left his guests for a moment. Placing his glasses over his eyes, he studied the pictures and said, "Well, what are you getting so excited about? These are pictures of our succah, back in Poland."

"That's *your* succah?" Tuvia shrieked.

"Of course. This man with the *shtreimel,* holding the *esrog* box, is my father, may he rest in peace — R' Yosef Honigman. And the man standing next to him wearing the *tallis* is his neighbor and good friend, R' Gedalia Zimmering, the artist who painted most of the pictures in the succah. They were good neighbors." Meyer paused. "By the way, how did you get hold of these photographs?"

"How?" Tuvia's voice shook. "Gedalia Zimmering was my grandfather. My father moved to Eretz Yisrael on the advice of his rebbe, and afterwards brought his parents here, too. That's how our family came to be saved from the war — and that's where these snapshots came from!"

He turned. "Gedalia, my son, come here," he said, and his eyes were damp with tears. "You are the one who restored your great-grandfather's paintings — the man whom you are named after. You are a wonderful artist, blessed with talent … and I, like a blind man groping in a tunnel, treated you cruelly. Please forgive me, Gedalia. Forgive me."

Gedalia had not been hugged and kissed like that by his father since he had turned 2. As Tuvia held him long and close, sobbing like a baby, Gedalia had the dreamlike feeling that he had just crossed some sort of line, into a world of beauty the likes of which he had never seen before.

SUCCAH IN THE CLOUDS

THE DAY HE SET FOOT ON THE SHORES OF AMERICA, MICHOEL Gottleib knew that his troubles were just beginning.

He had had an inkling even before that. As he and his wife had sat at home in Lublin debating whether or not to move to America, Michoel had complained: "America? A nation of empty-headed folk, a people far from Torah and the fear of Heaven. How can a Jew like myself, a chassid, move to such a spiritual wasteland? What will become of our children's education?"

But he knew that none of his arguments would help.

Michoel's poverty was no secret. All his neighbors and acquaintances were well aware of the destitution in which he lived. They knew that he was a man of many crafts but few blessings. More than one of his friends had tried, in vain, to rescue him from his difficult situation.

Michoel had the habit of lingering long over the third Shabbos meal. "What do you want?" he would jokingly ask his eleven children, all dressed in rags. "When I sing 'HaMavdil' and ask that my 'children and money multiply like sand,' Heaven answers, 'Money? You're asking for money? Others have already asked ahead of you — bankers and businessmen who hurry to leave the Shabbos behind. But you have plenty of 'children.'"

He stroked his youngsters' heads lovingly. "And what better treasure could there possibly be?" he would add softly.

Michoel was a good-natured man with a pleasant sense of humor. For his part, he was willing to make do with a crust of bread and a bit of potato soup. But his wife, Hinda, had not been blessed with Michoel's easygoing temperament. Poverty etched deep, bitter lines in her face. She was always complaining angrily. Though Michoel tried his best to keep her satisfied and content, nothing helped. Every so often, she would rail at him: "I've never met anyone less successful! All your friends are working and earning nice salaries. They are supporting their wives, as they undertook to do under the *chuppah*. Only you, Michoel, are satisfied with living on a dry crust of bread!"

After such a berating, Michoel would usually try his hand at some new profession. But, generally, it was in vain.

He had already served as a tailor's apprentice, baker's assistant, lumberjack's helper, postman, barber, and real-estate agent. "*Shlemazel*," his friends called him pityingly, while others added as a postscript, "No money will ever stick to his hands."

For years, Hinda endured her lot. From time to time, when she couldn't stand it any longer, she would burst into a tirade of complaints to her husband. But a moment later, her conscience would trouble her and Hinda would calm down as quickly as she grew angry. She would tell herself, "You wicked woman! Is Michoel denying you bread on purpose? Is he to blame if he was born under an unlucky star?"

She would scold herself thus for a long time, until tears of remorse rolled down her cheeks. When he returned home in the evening, she would beg his forgiveness for hurting his feelings. With his good nature, Michoel always forgave her, and harmony was restored to their home ... until the next time.

Their lives went on in this way for years. It looked as though Michoel's luck was never going to change.

Then Chana Baila, Hinda's younger sister, who also suffered from poverty and want, moved to America together with her husband and children. For several months there was no word from them. Hinda began to fear that her sister and the whole family had drowned in the depths of the great Atlantic. And then, half a year after Chana Baila's departure, a letter from her arrived in Lublin.

That letter was nothing but a brief notice that they had arrived safely at their destination. It was another four months before a second letter came — this one filled with bitterness. America's glittering promise looked very different from up close. They had, it seemed, merely exchanged a cow for a donkey. Living in a cramped basement apartment in Chicago, the family was suffering from hunger just as they had back in Poland.

But Yosef, Chana Baila's husband, was an energetic man. From morning to night he worked in a nearby laundry, with such devotion that he attracted his boss's attention. Half a year later, a third letter from Chana Baila arrived: Good news! Yosef had been promoted several times, until he was now the owner's assistant. Then, just a month ago, the gentile owner had suddenly died — leaving Yosef himself the laundry's new owner!

"How much longer are you going to starve in Poland?" Chana Baila wrote. "Come here to Chicago. Michoel will have steady work in the laundry. Yosef, my husband, has a tradition of letting people work for him even if they aren't too successful. He won't let his own brother-in-law and children die of hunger!"

From that day forward, Michoel found himself engulfed in a storm called "America." Armed with resolve, and dazzled by the prospects her sister had held out in her letter, Hinda was determined not to let another day pass without plans for a better future.

"Steady work is waiting for you in America, and you want to sit here in poverty?" Hinda argued forcefully. "Impossible!"

When it all became too much for him, Michoel fled to the *beis midrash*. But Hinda was not about to let this opportunity slip by. She went to all her husband's friends and got them to talk to Michoel, too.

"Why don't you want to go?" they urged. "America seems far preferable to Lublin for you. Your brother-in-law is prepared to offer you a job at his place, so you won't have to work on the holy Shabbos. What could be better?"

When there seemed to be no escape, Michoel said with a deep sigh, "I'll go ask the rebbe."

He knew that his rebbe, R' Yehuda Leib Alter of Ger, author of the *Sefas Emes,* found America disgusting. They said that a chassid once came to the rebbe to ask if he should move to America. The rebbe threw open a window, pointed at a body of water flowing in the distance, and asked, "And why don't you ask if you should throw yourself into the river?"

But when Michoel came to his rebbe, the response was far different. The rebbe heartily shook Michoel's hand and showered him with blessings for success.

"But, rebbe!" Michoel cried. "Does the rebbe agree that I should go to America, that unclean place? What will become of my *Yiddishkeit,* and my children's education?"

"I am not worried about you," replied the Sefas Emes, with a compassionate look. "If you will cling fast to your *chassidus,* America will be all right for you.

"But only," the rebbe added, "on one condition. Promise me that you and your children after you will never shave off your beards. No scissors or shaver shall pass over your faces. If you keep that, no harm will come to your *Yiddishkeit!*"

A large group of friends and well-wishers accompanied Michoel, Hinda, and their children to the railway station. There was a vast emotional gap between Michoel and his wife. While Michoel looked gloomy and withdrawn, his wife was jubilant. So were the children.

Michoel's friends comforted and blessed him over and over. "May it be Heaven's will that you become a very rich man. Just don't forget us!" And Michoel blessed them in return, saying, "How fortunate you are to be staying here in pure, Jewish surroundings. Woe is me, that I have been sentenced to exile in an impure place."

In this way, they parted in peace. Michoel and his family climbed aboard the train, while their friends returned home. They looked forward eagerly to receiving word of the travelers' fortune in the golden land of America.

For the first few days, Michoel and Hinda felt as though they were living in a dream. Hinda was intoxicated, but not from any wine. All her dreams were about to come true. From the moment she spotted her sister and brother-in-law waiting to meet them, her happiness knew no bounds. She liked everything she saw in America. Chicago stretched out before her like an endless wonderland. She listened with pleasure to the traffic outside and enjoyed the bustle of the many people in the streets, each hurrying to his own particular destination. Everything she had heard back in Lublin about the city's fabulous skyscrapers was nothing compared to the reality.

Michoel was living through a very different kind of dream. Everything he had heard about America the unclean was now spread out before his eyes. From the moment Yosef and Chana Baila met them, he was filled with anger.

"Are you Yosef?" he demanded of the clean-shaven man standing before him. "What happened to the beautiful beard you had when you left Lublin?"

"First of all, I'm *not* Yosef," his brother-in-law informed him. "Around here, I'm known as 'Joe.'"

"Joe?" Michoel barely managed to utter the syllable. "You mean to say… *Joe?*"

"Joe!" his brother-in-law repeated, laughing heartily. "It's short for Joseph. Over here, you can't keep your old name. No one will want to know a person with a name like that. I'm called Joe, and I promise you that I have remained as faithful a Jew as I've ever been!"

"That," Michoel muttered, "remains to be seen."

"You can't be called Michoel," Joe continued, ignoring the remark. "Michael — Mike for short — will be your name from now on. And you'll have to cut off your beard with a pair of scissors. You'll be considered a pathetic creature if you walk around with such a beard. No cultured person will want to know you."

"Heaven forbid!" Michoel said forcefully. He turned to his family. "I am not prepared to give up even a tiny bit of what we've brought with us from Lublin. We will keep our names proudly. We will not deviate an inch!"

⌒∞⌒

Michoel and his family rented an apartment on the 6th floor of a tall building in the city. At first, they felt as though they were sitting among the clouds. The children were afraid to look out of the window for fear of becoming dizzy.

Day by day, however, they grew used to their new living quarters. And, finally, they came to feel as comfortable as though they had lived there all their lives. Craning their necks, they would try to see all the way up to the top of the building, the 10th floor.

It was an interesting change even for Michoel. At first, he let himself enjoy his new life. Soon enough, however, his pleasure faded.

"There is no kosher porch here!" he exclaimed one afternoon.

"A kosher porch?" Hinda repeated. She had been glad to see that her stubborn husband was finally beginning to take to life in America. Now, he not only wanted a pleasant apartment, but also a porch? And what in the world was a "kosher" porch?

"Hinda!" Michoel shook his head disbelievingly. "Our porch is completely covered by the one above it. I want a porch that stands open to the sky."

"And what's so bad about a covered porch?" his wife asked. "We don't even know yet what we'll have to eat tomorrow, and you want an open porch? And why do we need a porch at all? Most of the year is rainy. People don't have the habit of sitting out on their porches much."

"I need a kosher porch," Michoel explained slowly, "for a succah."

"Ah! It's the thought of Succos that's bothering you. No problem. Don't worry," his wife consoled him. "It's only Sivan now. There's still plenty of time before the holiday. Maybe you can build the succah on the sidewalk downstairs?"

"This is not quiet Lublin," Michoel said, with a bitter laugh. "If I build on the sidewalk down on Edison Street, some punks will come by and knock it down in the middle of our first meal!"

With a heavy heart, Michoel paced through the apartment. His thoughts took a doleful turn, dwelling on all the problems facing his family. For one thing, would they really have to climb six flights of stairs every Shabbos? And what about Succos?

He was filled with a powerful longing for Lublin, his beloved hometown. He missed his good friends. He wanted to cry, but he remembered that he was a chassid who lived by the credo, "Serve Hashem with joy!" Instead, he picked up a *Tehillim,* found a quiet corner and pored over the *sefer,* shedding hot tears of supplication and hope.

Michoel did not want to take his wife's advice and wait until Tishrei to worry about a succah. As soon as he had learned the laundry business, he turned his thoughts to the precious mitzvah that was uppermost in his mind. "If we wait until Tishrei, we'll be left without a succah," he explained to his brother-in-law, who asked what his rush was.

In the evenings, upon his return home from a hard day's work, Michoel would descend to the yard of the huge apartment building, searching for an empty spot on which he might build his succah. But he was constantly disappointed. If he found a small, kosher area, it turned out that it belonged to some gentile family who had no intention of letting Michoel use it for his strange purposes, not even if he

paid them. Finally, he found a small area he thought he could use —
only to raise his eyes and find that it was located under the spreading
branches of a large tree.

In this way, several weeks passed. Michoel was near the point of
despair, when he was suddenly struck by inspiration.

The roof!

The idea was brilliant in its simplicity. The building had a broad
roof which belonged to all its tenants. Thinking it over, the idea
seemed far-fetched at first. How would his children climb the additional four flights of stairs to the roof? But nothing could deter him.
The next day, he climbed up onto the roof.

The roof resembled a poor village of ancient times, a place where
poverty and clutter existed side by side. Most of the space was taken
up by various structures that had long ago been erected by tenants,
and which had decayed and rusted with the years. There was a maze
of chimneys as far as the eye could see, as well as abandoned crates
and cartons. Michoel's heart quailed at the sight. Was this place
unusable, too?

He looked around, and suddenly, in a secluded corner of the roof,
he saw a kosher spot. It was only four square cubits in all, but it was
an empty area with no chimney or other structure on it. It would be
difficult to put up a succah in that corner because of the piles of
garbage that had accumulated there. It would take several workers to
dig out the mess and clear the small space. Well, that was no problem:
He and his sons would do the work.

First, though, he must put up the succah walls, to claim the spot
as his own.

That very day, he visited a local carpenter and bought a number
of thin wooden boards. Telling his older sons that it was a mitzvah, he
enlisted their help in carrying the boards onto the elevator of their
building. Then, up on the roof, he set up the boards and commenced
hammering them together in his little space.

The noise brought many tenants up to the roof to see what was
going on. They clustered around Michoel and his sons like bees
around honey. A short time later, a severe-looking man appeared and
said something to him in English.

Michoel as yet spoke only a few words of English. But, as far as he was able to understand, he was being told — to his dismay — that the roof was not a free-for-all. The building had an owner, a man who lived in the building itself. That owner was waiting to see Michoel right now. He wanted an explanation.

"Well, Mr. Gottleib," the owner said, settling comfortably back in his armchair, "they tell me that you've snuck onto the roof and are building a wooden room up there."

Michoel's head felt heavy. How to explain to a non-Jew what the mitzvah of succah was all about? A "wooden room" — what a way to describe a mitzvah that Hashem Himself had commanded!

"Please, sir," he said in his broken English. "The roof is empty. I checked it carefully. I am not bothering anybody. Why would you mind if I live in my little 'wooden room' for eight days, and then immediately take it apart?"

The owner made a rapid calculation. He lived by the motto, "Don't give away for free anything for which you can charge money." He shook his head. "Eight days? Rent-free? I can't permit that!"

Michoel stood up, his face white and pinched in his distress. On shaky legs he began to make his way to the door. Then he stopped. He had an idea. He turned around quickly, his face lighting up.

"What if I buy that piece of the roof from you?"

The owner stared at him out of eyes encased in folds of fat. The Jew looked quite excited. He could take advantage of this. He must be sure and suck this bone very dry.

"You want to buy a piece of the roof?" The man took out a small notepad and began to scribble on it. "Mind you, it would have to be a final sale. You can't come running back to me after eight days and say you want to cancel our agreement." He continued to jot down figures. Then he looked up at Michoel. "Pay me $500, and that piece of the roof is yours."

Michoel was thunderstruck. "Five hundred dollars for a few square cubits of space? At that price, I could buy half an apartment!"

"Five hundred dollars, or no deal."

Seeing no alternative, Michoel borrowed the sum from his brother-in-law. By doing so, he gave up half his salary every month for many years to come.

The contract was signed the next day, properly sealed and notarized. The building's owner had brought in a competent lawyer to make sure there were no loopholes for Michoel to wriggle through later.

"That corner of the roof is now yours!" Laughing inwardly, the owner shook Michoel's hand. "Go build whatever you want on it."

Perspiration poured off Michoel's face as he and his sons worked to remove years of trash from their spot. As he labored, he sang snatches of holiday songs. *"Vesamachta bechagecha ... ay, ay, ay, vehayisa ach same'ach!"*

Suddenly, he broke off. He stared, eyes bulging. "What's this?"

One of the old bundles he was clearing away had burst open — to reveal a pile of pearls and gems that winked in the bright sun. Michoel rubbed his eyes. "Am I dreaming?" he whispered.

"Father, look what I found!" his oldest son cried joyfully. He ran over to his father, cupping pieces of gold jewelry in both hands.

To Michoel's amazement, the neglected corner held an incredible fortune in jewels!

The news spread as though carried on the wind. Soon most of the building's tenants were aware of Michoel's marvelous find.

"Mr. Gottleib," the building's owner cried, puffing and panting as he abandoned his comfortable armchair and ran up to the roof. "The treasure is mine! You bought only the rights to use the roof."

"Shall we take the case to the police?" Michoel suggested. "As an honest citizen, I think that we must hand the treasure over completely into the hands of the law."

Reluctantly, the owner agreed. He looked ready to burst into tears.

For the next two months, the treasure sat in a vault at a local police station while an investigation was launched. It turned out that the loot had been hidden by a gang of robbers that had operated in the area twenty years before. The jewels had long been forgotten, and no one had put in a claim for them. By law, they were to be returned to the man who had found them.

"Look here," the lawyer said, waving the contract of sale in the building-owner's face. "What does it say?"

In small letters, buried amid the rest of the legal jargon, were the words, "This corner of the roof, along with all its contents, is sold in its totality to Michoel Gottleib!"

Purim

DO NOT SHED BLOOD
ON PURIM!

TWO WEEKS BEFORE PURIM, R' YIRMI ABELES BEGAN TO FEEL A slight constriction in his throat, as he did every year at that time. A whole decade had come and gone, but still, each year, he felt the same pain inside — the pain of a fresh memory.

"So maybe you'll go make up with him?"

And why not? R' Yirmi clapped himself on the side of the head in frustration. "But what I said was not wrong. It was Purim, wasn't it? Why can't I say what every other yeshivah *bachur* in the world can say on Purim? The essence of the day is an atonement! Everything is permitted on Purim. The day is dependent on you, and you are forgiven for everything done that day."

His thoughts carried him back to that Purim, ten years ago. If only the day had never been! But, to his everlasting sorrow, not only had the day happened, but it hung now around his neck like a heavy mill-stone that he could never put down.

He had been a youth then. Two and a half years earlier, he had enrolled in the famous Terumas HaDeshen Yeshivah. A natural brilliance, accompanied by good character and unwavering diligence, had given Yirmi Abeles a fine reputation in the yeshivah. After the first year, there was not a student at Terumas HaDeshen who didn't know his name, though there were four hundred of them attending the yeshivah. After the second year, everyone was sure that Yirmi would end up a *rosh yeshivah's* son-in-law someday.

Yirmi had another talent. When the time was right, he was excellent at clowning around. Back at his *yeshivah ketanah,* all the boys had clustered around him admiringly when the Purim season came. He was an expert at imitations and a master of words and double-entendres. With a single perfect turn of a phrase, he knew how to deliver a stinging blow. More than one *maggid shiur* at his former yeshivah could testify personally to Yirmi's talents in this direction. But Yirmi was always careful not to overstep the boundaries of good taste. He made sure always to coat the sharp edge of his sting with a layer of sweet honey.

Until Terumas HaDeshen.

During his first year there, Yirmi came down with a case of hepatitis at the beginning of Adar. His friends — having heard about his special talents — hoped that he would recover in time for Purim. They waited impatiently for the Purim party that the yeshivah held every year.

But hepatitis has its own timetable. By Purim, Yirmi was scarcely able to stand on his feet. He had no thought or energy left over for the Purim party at the home of a *maggid shiur.*

His second Purim at the yeshivah, however, found Yirmi hale and healthy. In truth, he would not have minded putting an end to his career as a Purim clown. What had been acceptable in *yeshivah ketanah* would not sit as well with more mature yeshivah *bachurim.*

"Who needs it?" he asked his friends, when they came to remind him that Purim was fast approaching.

"Yirmi! Come on! We're looking forward to hearing you!"

It was impossible to disappoint his friends ... or, in this case, his entire yeshivah. Everyone was waiting for his performance. They looked forward to his sword-sharp word plays, his lightning flashes of wit, his barbs and imitations.

When it came down to it, his friends did not have to coax him too much. The coals of frivolity had not yet been extinguished in Yirmi. He began to prepare for Purim in earnest.

He found plenty of material to work with in R' Tuvia Epstein, the yeshivah's *mashgiach.*

When R' Tuvia spoke, he tended to use elaborate hand gestures, and his voice alternated from a deep bass to a shrill falsetto. He stammered badly when excited by a *shmooze,* sometimes liberally spraying his neighbors in his frenzy. Every third word he uttered was, "That's *moireidik* (awesome)!" To top it all off, he was extremely nearsighted and wore glasses that were almost comically thick.

R' Tuvia was not overly popular among the boys, because he was very strict about their being punctual for *davening* and learning. Flexibility was not his strong point. "Poke fun at R' Tuvia," Yirmi's friends begged.

Yirmi was hesitant. His relations with the *mashgiach* were good. R' Tuvia had never had cause to complain about him. "Leave him alone," his conscience advised.

But it was impossible to pass up such easy prey. The other *maggidei shiur* were sadly lacking in the kinds of laughable characteristics that made R' Tuvia such a promising target.

From the day Terumas HaDeshen was founded, the boys had never laughed as hard as they did that Purim. Yirmi had prepared a "*shmooze*" using the best of his abilities. On Purim night, the boys gathered in R' Tuvia Epstein's house — over R' Tuvia's objections.

"Why suddenly make a party at my house?" he protested. "You always go to one of the *maggidei shiur.* I'm not interested in your kind of 'fun.'"

"R' Tuvia, let's have it at your place just for a change," urged Shimshon Halevi, one of Yirmi's friends at the yeshivah. "You've been left out of things all these years. Don't worry, it will be a party you'll never forget. Yirmi has prepared a fine piece of 'Purim Torah,' complete with *Gemara* and *Rishonim.* You'll enjoy every word of it!"

The *mashgiach* relented. On Purim night, the boys streamed into his house. After a few Purim songs and more than a few drinks, Yirmi began his "*shmooze.*"

He had prepared a solid talk, liberally but tastefully sprinkled with humorous references. The wine he had drunk, however, went to his head and removed the brakes on his tongue. As he rambled on recklessly, R' Tuvia's face grew paler and paler. Yirmi showed everyone just how talented a mimic he was. He portrayed a living caricature of the *mashgiach.* No quirk or mannerism escaped his notice — or his performance.

The other boys rolled with laughter as Yirmi let the spray fly from his mouth and waved his arms in windmill fashion, intoning repeatedly, "Hey, it's just *moiredik!*" He even dredged up a mannerism or two that R' Tuvia had already dropped, at the urging of his family. In short, Yirmi outdid himself that Purim night.

While the boys were "on the floor" — some of them literally — with laughter, R' Tuvia felt as though the last drop of blood was draining out of his body. Yirmi Abeles had embarrassed him in front of his own wife and children, who had looked forward to a merry party and had received instead a cruel show in which their husband and father was the sacrificial lamb.

R' Tuvia had not achieved his position in the yeshivah for nothing. He bit his lip and bent his head in submission. Later, he managed to grapple with the challenge and came to view his shame as an atonement from Heaven. But this state of mind took several days to achieve. Meanwhile, the insult he had suffered burned in his heart like a glowing coal.

For some time afterward, R' Tuvia did not show his face in the yeshivah. He felt that he had held an important position in the students' lives — a position, and an image, which were destroyed by Yirmi Abeles's mockery. He waited for an apology.

As for the students, they never dreamed that their *mashgiach* had been wounded to such depths. It had just been Purim fun, hadn't it? It was only when two weeks had passed without R' Tuvia saying even once, "It's *moiredik!*", and when they saw him wipe his mouth repeatedly during one of the *rosh yeshivah's* talks, that they began to realize that Yirmi's performance had taken its toll. But even so, it did not enter their minds that an apology was called for. It never occurred to Yirmi, either.

Two years later, Yirmi married the daughter of the *rosh yeshivah* of Yeshivas Toras HaBayis. This came as no surprise to anyone. He was one of Terumas HaDeshen's five top students, the epitome of a successful yeshivah *bachur.*

But Yirmi was not yet destined for peace and contentment.

No one knew why, but the marriage of this talented young man and the *rosh yeshivah's* daughter lasted only a short time. Yirmi divorced his wife with a bitter heart, and began to look for another to take her place and bring him happiness. After two long years of loneliness and misery, he remarried. Yirmi's joy knew no bounds. He launched himself back into life with vigor, learning and teaching and spreading Torah with wondrous energy and talent.

Four years passed without bringing the blessing of children to Yirmi and his wife. He visited all the Torah leaders of his time, receiving an outpouring of blessings from each of them. He and his wife went to see renowned doctors. As another Purim came near, doubt gnawed at Yirmi's heart.

"Who knows? Perhaps I am being punished for that unfortunate Purim, and that mocking '*shmooze*' at R' Tuvia Epstein's house."

If that was the case, Yirmi realized uncomfortably, it was up to him to beg the man's forgiveness.

Immediately, a new thought came along to counter the first. "You are such a worrywart! That Purim talk was no different from a million others. R' Tuvia has probably forgotten the whole thing by now. And, if you hadn't had all these problems in your personal life, you would have forgotten it yourself."

In this way, he pushed the matter from his mind. But his home was empty and his wife was sad. From time to time, he would hear her sighing bitterly.

Several more years passed. As each Purim approached, Yirmi would recall that old incident. Each time, he would debate inwardly about the need to apologize to R' Tuvia. And each time, he would end by rejecting the idea. He, Yirmi Abeles, was a respected *maggid shiur.* He delivered wonderful *mussar* talks to his adoring students. Should he abase himself before the *mashgiach* like a boy of 16? Never!

R' Yirmi was still a young man, not yet 30. Most men his age have not yet begun to acquire the mannerisms that come with advancing years. Certainly not men like him, who had once stood on the other side of the fence and made a laughing mockery of every quirk he saw.

But years of pain and distress had left their mark. R' Yirmi had developed several mannerisms of which he was not even aware. They would cross his face like a passing cloud when, in the midst of delivering a *shiur,* he remembered the empty house waiting for him at the end of the day. Or when he attended the seventh *bris* of an old yeshivah friend. R' Yirmi's students were like young people everywhere: They saw everything. Nothing escaped their notice. Every one of their rebbi's mannerisms was recorded on a mental slate, to be retrieved at a later date.

Purim was coming around once more. The boys wanted to have their annual party at their rebbi's house — and R' Yirmi agreed enthusiastically. "I have nothing to be afraid of," he told himself. "And I'd like my wife to see how much my students admire and respect me."

On the big day, the students arrived in droves. R' Yirmi let the wine flow freely. He himself delivered a few pungent witticisms that made the boys laugh uproariously. "Rebbi's really with it," they whispered in surprise. But — tradition is tradition. It was time for the yearly "Purim Torah."

One of the students stood up to give the speech, imitating R' Yirmi's own manner in his classroom. As the talk progressed, R' Yirmi began to blink nervously, hoping that his wife was not in the room. His students were showing him in a light in which he had never seen himself before. He had not known that he habitually made such grotesque and laughable gestures. The blood drained from his face. He wanted to scream, "Stop it right now!" at the top of his voice. But nothing, not even a dry cough, would leave his throat. And then he saw his wife, sitting and watching the show with wide eyes.

She smiled politely, and even laughed once or twice, as is becoming on Purim. But R' Yirmi could tell that his value was rapidly lowering in her estimation. While it is possible to poke gentle fun at human weaknesses, his drunken students had crossed the line and had left good manners behind. They were intent on raising laughs by making a complete mockery of their teacher, on this one day of the year when they could do so with impunity.

The evening was over at last. The students' merry voices echoed in the stairwell as they took their leave. When an irate neighbor came out to complain about the noise — it was, after all, 3 a.m. — they cheerfully offered him a cigar. One yeshivah *bachur* flourished a raffle book and asked if the neighbor was interested in donating to the yeshivah. Laughter followed the boys down the street as they wound their slow way back to the dorm.

In R' Yirmi's house, all was still. His wife did not say a word. He himself felt his face burning even now. Suddenly, with awful clarity, he remembered the wonderful Purim talk he had given in his own day, in R' Tuvia Epstein's house. He had shamed his *mashgiach* in the same way as he himself had been shamed tonight — in front of his own family.

In that moment, R' Yirmi understood what he had done. No false pride stepped in to rescue him this time. "I sinned, and I must beg his forgiveness."

The next day, Purim, found R' Yirmi at his former *mashgiach's* door, a basket of *mishloach manos* tucked under one arm. He laid the basket down on a table and asked to speak to R' Tuvia, alone.

As soon as the door of R' Tuvia's small study had closed behind them, R' Yirmi all but fell to the floor in his contrition. Weeping bitterly, he begged R' Tuvia's forgiveness for that long-ago Purim. In a choked voice he described his life since then and pleaded with the *mashgiach* to hear and accept the words, "Forgive me."

R' Tuvia was astonished. He admitted that he had been deeply wounded by the unexpected mockery that Purim night, so contrary to the respect with which the students had always treated him.

"But I forgave you after a few days," he reported candidly. "All of you."

This news grieved R' Yirmi profoundly. If it was true that R' Tuvia had already forgiven him, then his case was bleak indeed. He would never be delivered from his childlessness.

R' Tuvia thought for several moments. "You're right," he said at last. "Maybe my forgiveness back then was not completely honest. I will think it all through again. I will relive the incident, and will not leave it alone until I feel that I have truly forgiven you with all my heart!"

A month passed — a month of agony for R' Yirmi. Then R' Tuvia Epstein summoned him to his home.

"I have checked and re-checked myself, day after day," he said. "And finally, yesterday, I reached the state where I felt I could forgive you wholeheartedly!"

Exactly one year later, R' Yirmi Abeles honored R' Tuvia Epstein with the position of *sandak* at his first son's *bris* — the child born to R' Yirmi and his wife after eleven years of marriage. It was the happiest day of R' Yirmi's life. And thereafter, before Purim each year, he would drum into his students' ears:

"It is forbidden to shed blood on Purim! A rebbi's blood is not water. They are people, just like you. They can be hurt and insulted on Purim just as on any other day of the year. Take care how you poke fun, boys. Take good care!"

WATER FROM A STONE

MY NAME IS MOSHE KRAUSZ. ONE DAY A YEAR, HOWEVER, my name changes into "Moshe Rabbeinu," and I'll explain why.

I learn in Yeshivas Yemin Torah, a fairly well-known place in Bnei Brak. All year long I'm an ordinary yeshivah *bachur*. But once a year, as Purim draws near, I turn into the "life" of the yeshivah. It was I who initiated the founding of the "T.T." — which, in case you're not aware, stands for "*Tomchei Torah*." Each year, on Purim, groups of us boys make the rounds of people's homes and offer them the privilege of giving *tzedakah*.

We travel in an open pickup truck, dressed in gorilla costumes. Equipped with huge megaphones, with lively music tapes, and with tremendous energy, we set out in the direction of Gush Dan and return in the evening with a nice bundle. The money, I might mention, is used to pay the tuition, room, board, and all other needs of yeshivah boys from poor homes. It supports these *bachurim* discreetly and respectfully, without embarrassing anyone.

For five years in a row, we visited a certain rich man's house — I'll call him R' Itzik Wasserfeld — at noon. R' Itzik lives in a beautiful villa somewhere in Gush Dan. He inherited his wealth from his father, R' Aharon Wasserfeld, who helped support many Torah institutions and passed away about ten years ago. To everyone's dismay, his son followed in his father's footsteps only in that first year. During the mourning period for his father, Itzik Wasserfeld donated generously to all the Torah institutions his father had helped. After that year, he became tight-fisted.

But there's no saying "no" on Purim! We had had a tradition of visiting R' Aharon during the Purim *seudah,* when he would always write us a large check. Once a year, therefore, we came to help his son Itzik break his bad habit of stinginess.

The story I want to tell happened two years ago, on Purim. We came to the Wasserfeld villa at around three in the afternoon, as we did every year. An expensive car stood parked in front of the house, gleaming in the sun. "He inherited that from his father," someone had told us. "But that cheapskate hardly ever drives it. Gas is expensive."

We found Itzik Wasserfeld seated at the head of his table, surrounded by his wife, children, and sons- and daughters-in-law. The meal was frugal, as always, and had been the subject of much humor among us after other visits. We gathered around R' Itzik, seven lively yeshivah boys filled with energy and alcohol. We grabbed his hands and danced with him in a circle. The song, dance, and gaiety created their own dynamic, leading the rich man to write us a respectable check — albeit with trembling hands. It was always I who had the honor of pulling out his checkbook and handing him a pen before he could change his mind. For two weeks afterwards I would walk around feeling important: I had extracted water from a stone! That was why my friends called me "Moshe Rabbeinu."

On our way to the next stop, we would exchange joking comments about the man's incredible stinginess.

"Moshe," one of my pals said, thumping me on the back. "You mustn't eat or drink anything dairy for the next six hours. That money is meat — a chunk of human flesh!"

"No," another friend disagreed. "It's not just a chunk of Wasserfeld's flesh. A full half of his heart came along with that check!"

Once, in an especially sentimental mood, R' Itzik added on the bottom of his check, "With all my heart." We couldn't stop laughing about his choice of words.

The expression "to take water from a stone" was an apt one. Itzik was hard as stone, and giving away his money was like giving away his very soul. "How is it possible?" we would ask one another every year. "A beautiful house filled with the finest furniture — and a meal like that! How do the two fit into the same lifestyle?"

People in the know had a simple explanation: Itzik had inherited the house and furniture from his father. He himself did not enjoy spending a penny more than absolutely necessary.

But he gave to us. One day each year. For five years running.

That was our tradition.

I remember that sixth Purim the way one remembers a nightmare. For various scheduling reasons, we were running early and arrived at Itzik Wasserfeld's house at 1 p.m. The table was not yet set for the *seudah* and was graced only by a few small bowls of sweets and dried fruits. "Probably sent to them as *mishloach manos* by friends and neighbors," we whispered to one another amid many knowing winks. "Would *they* ever set out food for guests on their own?"

We found R' Itzik himself in the beautiful living room, wearing a light robe. At the sight of us, his face lit up. "You came early today?" I was on the point of returning some merry answer when my eye fell on Itzik's two sons, whom we had never before seen at the Purim *seudah*. I immediately recognized the older, a boy of about 14, at once. The blood drained from my face and I must have turned white as a sheet.

I haven't told you that my parents are well-known *ba'alei chesed* in Bnei Brak. Every Thursday night, they distribute Shabbos packages to scores of needy families. Generally, these packages are brought to the family's front door. However, in the case where the recipients are extremely embarrassed about being seen taking charity, we arrange for a meeting place, usually in some shul, where we hand over the food on Thursday nights. Sometimes we hand over more than just food, providing money or some other necessity. To those in dire need, we offer a regular weekly stipend.

And who do you think is the lad who receives the largest of these stipends each week? None other than the son of Itzik Wasserfeld! Until that day, I had only known him by his first name, Avraham. I had not wanted to ask for more.

Avraham grew very pale, too. I saw from Itzik's face that he had grasped the entire situation. His mouth opened like that of a fish, but not a word emerged. He broke out into a cold sweat. My friends, witnessing the unspoken drama, knew instinctively that it had something to do with our host's incredible stinginess. The silence was louder than a thousand shouting voices.

Itzik tried to signal to me not to say anything. I grew confused. At first, I thought that the rich man was just a miserly *shnorrer*. Then, all at once, I understood that the wealthy Itzik Wasserfeld was simply a pitiable beggar: a beggar dressing up as a rich man. Each Purim, we had been accusing him falsely on two counts.

I also understood now why Avraham always looked especially woebegone after Purim each year. I had always thought that it was because Pesach was coming and expenses were mounting. Now I knew the real reason.

I clapped my hands together and began to herd my startled group toward the door. "Out, guys!" I called urgently. Itzik stood with a sad, supplicating look in his eye, as though pleading with me not to give away his secret. It was as if he were saying, "My honored image is all I have left. Don't take that away from me."

But, as I said, I was very confused, and my friends' curiosity was pressing. I practically dragged them outside onto the large green lawn, where I whispered the truth about Itzik Wasserfeld.

They were stunned, and hardly knew how to react. For five years we had been squeezing the man's lifeblood for a good cause. We had been taking money from a man who needed charity himself, and then poking fun at him afterwards.

Too late, Itzik raced out after us. "Please come inside," he invited in a broken voice.

We went in. We stood beside the table adorned with a few bottles and some dried fruits and chocolates, but it was all without meaning. I don't think that even the solemn atmosphere before *Kol Nidrei* on Yom Kippur can be compared to those difficult moments. For the first time, I grasped the true sense of the words, "*Yom Kippurim,* a day like Purim." All of us yearn for moments of soaring elevation in our lives. Instead, we were standing face-to-face with an awesome regret that would never leave us.

Suddenly, Itzik burst into heaving sobs. The tears flowed as though from a bottomless well.

"I have no desire to live any longer," he cried. "My father, may he rest in peace, knew before he died that he was lost. He warned me, 'Itzik, guard the family's honor at all costs. Don't let us become objects of pity. The worst thing in life is to be a pathetic creature whom others pity.' I had heard this same refrain on my father's lips ever since I was a little boy.

"My wife was forced to send our son, Avraham, to receive the Shabbos packages every Thursday. For the first few years, they did it behind my back. When I learned the truth, I was furious. But my wife explained that, without that weekly bundle of food, we would starve. Or, worse yet, I'd be forced to become a beggar on the streets.

"For years, I've been spinning uselessly, like a windmill that achieves nothing. My beautiful car, parked outside? I inherited that from my father. I drive it out once in two weeks or so, so that no one will suspect. So that no one will pity me."

We stood like dummies, hearts pounding in our chests. Itzik studied us with eyes that were still damp with tears. "Now you know everything," he said. "I am exposed. I have nothing left!" The last words were screamed in pain. His wife came running to bring him a glass of cold water, but Itzik didn't even see her. "I am laid bare," he moaned, a frightening froth on his lips. "Have you ever thought of the meaning of the words, 'Blessed is He who clothes the naked'?"

We felt at that moment that he was close to losing his mind, or fainting, or both. Itzik went on, "Don't peel my disguise away. When a man's mask is peeled away in public, he is liable to die that very instant from the shame." He stared at us with wild, sorrowing eyes. "You have stripped me bare. I'm dying! I'm dying!"

With that, his eyes rolled up in his head, and he collapsed to the floor.

There are no words to describe the way we felt. If you had said that we wished we could die on the spot along with Itzik, you would not have been exaggerating. How had we unknowingly turned into murderers?

But it seemed that Itzik wasn't quite dead. Some of the more cool-headed among us grabbed a bottle of cognac and poured it over our host's head. They chafed his wrists and did mouth-to-mouth resuscitation — anything to revive him. And, a few minutes later, Itzik did revive. His eyes opened, but when he remembered what had just happened his head lolled back and he was on the point of fainting a second time.

At long last, my mind began to work again. I was struck by inspiration.

"Boys," I said to my friends, my voice loud and solemn. "I hereby swear all of us to silence. Itzik's secret will not be revealed by anyone here in this room!" I tested each boy with my eyes, and they all agreed. They hardly had a choice in the matter: This was a clear case of *pikuach nefesh*. Itzik's life hung in the balance.

"But the *rosh yeshivah* will ask where my check is," Itzik lamented.

"No problem," one of the group said. "Give me a check as usual, the way you do every year. I'll make sure it's covered."

Itzik protested. "I don't want that. I don't want to be a pathetic creature."

I rose to the occasion. Once again, "Moshe Rabbeinu" found a way to get water from a stone. "You know what?" I said. "For five years you have donated money to us each Purim. How did you manage to cover that? However you managed it, do it again this year." It was the same old game, making Itzik feel important.

So Itzik Wasserfeld wrote us a large check. This time, his hands did not shake at all, and tears of happiness stood bright in his eyes.

We had downed our last drinks and were ready to go, when there was a sudden eruption of blessings among us. Spontaneously, they welled up from the depths of our hearts, directed at poor Itzik.

"Hashem is joining in our blessings," we declared. "May you really grow rich!"

"Amen," echoed through the room. Utterly drained, we left the beautiful house at last. Itzik watched us from the window, eyes beaming with love. "Wonderful boys!" he exclaimed to his wife, loud enough for us to hear. Our hearts melted. All those other years, as he had watched us go, he felt more anger than fondness. And we, outside, had joked around at the "miser's" expense, little knowing that we had just squeezed out of him the small amount of cash that he didn't have!

A few days after Purim, a big businessman approached Itzik with a proposal that Itzik join his business as a partner. No one dreamed that it had been my own father who had arranged the visit. The businessman was a relative of ours.

In the past, Itzik always rejected such proposals with a shuttered face, as though it were beneath his dignity to accept. The true reason, of course, was that he did not have two spare pennies to invest in a business venture.

He tried to reject this proposal, too, but my cousin wouldn't hear of it. "The money? You can give it later. There's no rush. Everyone knows you're a wealthy man."

The venture was a success. Maybe it succeeded because my cousin knows how to run a business; maybe it was because of all the blessings we had heaped on Itzik's head. My cousin gradually moved aside and let Itzik take more control. For the first time in years, Itzik began to make money. A few months later, the business was prospering even more. Though Itzik had not yet grown wealthy, he had a steady salary, and that was something.

Three days ago, before Purim, Itzik called me up.

"Will you come this year?" he asked hopefully.

"What a question!" I answered.

We came with all our equipment: the megaphones, the music, the gorilla costumes. We filled the street with song and laughter. Itzik was waiting for us outside, on the beautiful lawn.

In his hand was a check, written from the very depths of his grateful heart.

THE STRIPED PAJAMAS

THE HOUSE WAS ALIVE WITH THE SWEET AROMA OF BAKING. A tray of fragrant, hot *hamantaschen,* some filled with poppy, others with date spread, had just been removed from the oven and was resting on the countertop to cool off before being liberally sprinkled with powdered sugar.

Zevulun Warshavski dragged himself to the small table in his room. The approaching holiday lightened his heart and filled it with memories of Purims past, dispelling for a moment the cobwebs of old age and his tedious daily routine. It had been the good smells that had taken him from his bed. He wanted to bite into a fresh, hot *haman-tasch* — but he knew that it would never happen. His son, Menachem, would not permit him to eat sweets; Zevulun's blood sugar was already too high. Last year, they had not watched him carefully enough and he had eaten his fill of Purim goodies. Afterwards, he had spent two weeks in the hospital, as the medical staff struggled to control the rampaging blood sugar that threatened his life.

This year, they would watch him like hawks. Especially Menachem, his only son, in whose house he had been living these past seven years since the death of Zevulun's beloved wife.

Menachem, in his father's opinion, was a genuine *tzaddik*. A man who learns in *kollel* and lives in poverty, whose apartment's sleeping area consists of no more than two bedrooms and an enclosed porch for himself, his wife, and seven children — and still, he manages to find room (especially in his heart) for his widowed father. Is such a man not a *tzaddik?*

Menachem Warshavski himself, had anyone asked him, would have resisted being placed into this category. "I'm just an average *kollelnik*," he would have said with his modest smile. "I only hope to fulfill my obligations. Do I get more credit for observing the mitzvah of *kibbud av?*"

In this way, they all lived together, the elderly grandfather and his son's family: ten Warshavski souls crammed into a tiny apartment of 44 square meters. It was stifling by any standard. Menachem and Penina Warshavski were raising their children to have outstanding *middos* — and besides, they loved their *zaydie*. The children had long ago learned to be satisfied with little. Still, 44 square meters, divided by ten, leaves just four-and-a-half meters per person. That is very crowded, indeed. Which only reflects even more gloriously on the Warshavski children.

Menachem made every effort to make his father's presence in the apartment as easy for everyone as possible. He sent his two oldest sons away to yeshivah, where they could sleep in a dormitory. This freed up some space for the others. Everyone appreciated it, though no one said so out loud.

Zevulun sat at the table in his room, which doubled as an enclosed porch. From his vantage point, he could see the other rooms in the apartment. If only he could take part in all the excitement and bustle before Purim ... but that was only a dream. His old legs were not what they used to be, nor were his hands. Actually, nothing was the same as it had once been. Old age, Zevulun sighed. Old age ...

The front door opened. Srulik, his oldest grandson, walked in with a big, happy, "Hi!" His sisters and brothers looked up, happy, too, that Srulik was home from yeshivah. Tami, at 3 years old, the youngest of the family, seized her big brother's hand and held onto it as though afraid someone would steal him away.

"Srulik," she asked in her piping voice, "did you hit Haman yet?"

Srulik's smile widened. "In two days, on Purim night, I promise you that I'll hit Haman with all my might!"

"Will he cry?"

"He'll cry very hard."

"Good!" Tami crowed. With a merry little caper, she sang, "Srulik's going to hit Haman!"

Listening from his porch, Zevulun smiled. "Srulik!" he called hoarsely. "Come here a minute and say hello to your *zaydie*!"

Srulik entered with a big smile and shook his grandfather's hand. "How are you, *Zaydie*?"

"*Baruch Hashem,*" the old man sighed. "All my friends my own age are already covered with dirt. Should I not say '*Baruch Hashem*'?"

Srulik lingered to chat with his grandfather for a few minutes, but it was easy to see that the boy was in a great hurry. He had run home on his lunch break to get his costume for Purim, and had to be back in time for his "*seder.*"

"What do you need a costume for?" asked Srulik's sister, two years younger than he. "Aren't you getting too old for that?"

"We go around collecting money on Purim for the yeshivah's *chasan* fund," Srulik explained. "We dress up in costumes and cover our faces with masks. Do you want everyone to know that your brother is a *shnorrer*? It could hurt your *shidduch* chances in a few years!"

He climbed into the tiny attic, to return a few moments later with a carton. "*Imma*, these are all the costumes, right?"

Penina Warshavski squinted across from the kitchen, tired from all the hard work leading up to Purim. "It seems to me that that's the box. I'm not sure."

Srulik opened the box and pulled out a pair of strange-looking pajamas, very old, with blue and white stripes. The white areas were filled with words in ink.

"What does this say?" He brought the pajamas closer to his eyes. "What funny pajamas. Who dressed up in these old things?"

In his room, Zevulun's eyes suddenly widened. He followed Srulik's actions with close attention. The others had clustered around their big brother and were tugging at the pajamas from every side, clamoring, "What are those? Whose are those? Let me see!"

A shout burst from the old man's throat. "Don't touch them! Leave those pajamas alone!"

Startled, the children drew back. They had never seen their grandfather this angry before. His eyes were blazing and his whole body was trembling. Pale and shaken, Srulik let the pajamas fall from his hands. His reward was another furious shout from his grandfather: "You're throwing them onto the *floor?*"

In a twinkling, the room was emptied. As the children fled, Penina bent, retrieved the pajamas, and folded them carefully. She replaced them in their box. "Srulik didn't do it on purpose," she said gently to Zevulun. "We have two similar boxes in the attic. One of them has Purim costumes and the other is filled with old clothes. He didn't know that."

The old man's inner storm began to abate. As a measure of calm returned, Zevulun asked his daughter-in-law in a whisper, "Was Srulik insulted?"

"I would say that he was — startled," Penina replied. "None of the children are used to seeing you explode like that."

"They're right," the old man said, biting his lips in distress. "I shouldn't have gotten so angry. But you know, those pajamas are my only tangible reminder from … then."

"Perhaps you'd like to tell them why their *Zaydie* has hidden away a pair of pajamas?" She pointed at the knot of children peeking timidly from the doorway.

"You're right. They know nothing at all about that time in my life," Zevulun agreed, stroking his white beard. He motioned to Srulik. "Come here. You asked what those 'funny pajamas' were, and the words and addresses written on them. Are you interested in hearing their history?" He smiled. "By the way, you have to treat them with respect. Those pajamas are older than your father."

"The pajamas are really old!" cried little Yochanan, triggering hysterical laughter. "We have to take them to an old-age home!"

Penina silenced the young boy with a look. Yochanan subsided, and they all drew closer to hear their grandfather's story, the story he had never told them before.

You know your *Zaydie* (Zevulun began) as an old man who lies in bed without strength. But I was once different. I was born eighty-one years ago in Poland, in a small town by the name of Lukoshinska, not far from the Weisel River. To this day, I recall the women going down to the river on sunny days to wash their clothes in the flowing water. How we children used to laugh when our mother, pulling our trousers out of the river, would find a pretty little fish inside — a fish which made it to our next Shabbos table.

As a child, I attended the local *cheder*. I was a wild boy. Together with my good friend, Motka Blumenthal, I'd get into all sorts of trouble. (Zevulun winked at his small grandchildren.)

When we grew a little older, Motka and I became caught up in the alien winds that were blowing through our town. We left yeshivah to join the *HaPoel* movement. We believed in the Socialist ideal with all our hearts. After a year and a half of training, we both moved to Palestine. That was in 1938, just before the outbreak of World War II, when the gates of Europe slammed shut. We traveled on a shaky old boat together with hundreds of young people who wanted to build up the ancient Land of Israel. Motka and I did not want to be separated, so we went together to one of the kibbutzim in the Jezreel Valley. But the day was not long in coming when both of us decided that Socialism was a fundamentally flawed system. Beneath the superficial idealism lay a great many unhealthy drives, including hatred and envy and greed.

We made a sharp turn and joined the *Irgun HaTzeva'i HaLeumi*, popularly known as *Etzel*. Together with our fellow members, we fought actively against the British who ruled Palestine at the time. I personally took part in the attack against British intelligence headquarters in Jaffa, while good friends of mine participated in the bombing of the King David Hotel.

That bombing was calculated to break the British ruling spirit — the "mandate." The King David contained the central British governing bodies: the main British army headquarters as well as the government's central administrative offices. My fellow *Etzel* members, disguised as Arabs, planted 350 kilograms of explosives in milk jugs. A short time later, a mighty explosion rocked the southwest corner of the building — all eight floors of it. That whole section of the hotel collapsed. Unfortunately, a number of Jews who had worked for the British or for the hotel were killed together with the British soldiers.

But we were still not satisfied. Motke Blumenthal and I, and a few others, became busy acquiring weapons. Under the noses of the British, we bought rifles and bullets, automatic submachine guns and grenades. The money for these purchases was funneled secretly to us through various *Etzel* channels.

And then, one sale went wrong.

The note was passed to me as I sat in the barber's chair, having my hair cut. The message was curt and innocent-sounding. *"A man will be coming for 100 kilograms of onions at 2 a.m. tonight."*

For the initiated, however, the message read entirely differently. It told me that I was to bring money to a late-night meeting for the purchase of 100 belts of bullets for an automatic weapon. That was a hefty purchase. Motke and I came to the meeting equipped with a couple of baby carriages for carting away our booty. At 2 o'clock precisely, we sat and waited for the liaison man who was said to have brought the "goods" over from Czechoslovakia a few days earlier.

We were tense; as wound up as springs. The street was dark and deserted. There were no streetlights then as there are today. We sat over our baby carriages, pretending to soothe imaginary babies, and waited. Anyone passing by would have thought we were crazy — two young men sitting with carriages in the middle of a dark, cold Jerusalem street in the dead of night.

Suddenly, Motke said, "You know what? I'm afraid this may be a trap."

I glanced at him in confusion. "A trap? What do you mean?"

"I have a bad feeling about this," he said, gnawing at his nails. "I've never felt this way before."

"So what do you think we should do? Run?"

Motke hesitated. "Maybe."

"Coward," I taunted. "Go, if you want. I'm staying."

Motke was taken aback by my reaction. After a brief consideration, he said, "Let's hide the money."

"What for?"

He analyzed the situation lucidly. "If this is a legitimate deal, then when the man comes with the goods we can simply get the money out and give it to him. But if it's a trap, at least we'll have the money waiting when we get out of jail."

To my ears, he sounded panicky as a rabbit. But there was no real reason to object to his proposal. We looked around. A small basement window stood just above ground level. Motke said, "I know that basement. It belonged to a shoemaker who passed away. No one's there now."

We tried the ancient door. Motke was right: It wasn't locked. In total darkness, we descended the steps to the basement. Feeling our way with our outstretched hands, we managed to "see" what the room contained. There was a bed with a thin, straw mattress, a small table and two chairs, and a shelf containing a great many jars and boxes, most filled with the various nails the shoemaker had used in his work. Motke found an empty box and had the idea of placing the money inside it. We carefully put the money-filled box behind the jars of nails.

As we were leaving, I thought over what we had just done, and was not pleased. Back on the street, by our baby buggies, I snapped in irritation at my friend, "What do we do if this was all just a figment of your imagination? When the seller comes, we'll have to go back into that pitch-dark basement and feel our way to the box with the money."

"You're right," Motke said. "But I feel calmer now."

"You're howling mad, that's what — and I'm a fool to let myself be dragged into your insanity," I retorted. I couldn't understand why I had yielded to his crazy suggestion.

Even before the echo of my words faded, the sudden bright glare of flashlights blinded us. Instinctively, I squeezed my eyes shut to shield them from the light.

"Hands up!" someone shouted. And I knew, with deep chagrin, that Motke's intuition had been right on the mark. We had fallen into a trap.

We were surrounded by British soldiers, all of them carrying rifles. Brandishing their weapons, they conducted a thorough search of our persons, from head to toe. Then they dragged us to a main street, where we were loaded onto a waiting jeep and taken in the dead of night to the Russian Compound prison.

We stayed in jail a full month, awaiting our trial. The British tried to break our spirits and get us to reveal details about our underground operation, but we kept our lips firmly sealed. When the month was up, we went to trial. We were accused of belonging to a terrorist organization, convicted, and sentenced to ten years in jail.

They took us to the Akko Prison. We were in total despair. Akko had the most secure prison in the country. Its walls were made of stones a meter thick, and on one side lay the sea. There was no escape.

We were brought to Akko on *Chol HaMoed Pesach,* brokenhearted and depressed. A few days later, however, we got word that the *Etzel*

was planning a daring jailbreak. Over the next week, small packages of explosives were smuggled into that most secure of prisons. We members of the group who were in jail, totaling forty in all — some of us in for long prison terms, others sentenced to death — were let in on the secret. We even knew the date of the planned attack: Sunday, the 14th day of Iyar.

In preparation for the breakout, we were also given bundles of civilian clothing. When we would escape and put some distance between ourselves and the prison, we were to remove our striped prison "pajamas" and put on the civilian clothes instead, to make the search for us more difficult.

On *Motza'ei Shabbos,* the night before the big day, we were so excited and nervous that it was impossible to sleep. Tomorrow, we knew, we would need to be as alert as could be — but sleep would not come. We were wide awake. In our small cell, there was a certain fear in the air as well. Who would live through the jailbreak, and who would, Heaven forbid, die? Would we succeed in making good our escape, or be captured in the attempt?

At last, we found a way to occupy those suspenseful hours of the night. We had pens and ink with us, and we began passing these from hand to hand, with each prisoner scribbling some parting words on each other's pajamas. On mine, Motka wrote, *"To my dear Zevulun Warshavski, I will never forget you. Mordechai Blumenthal."* I wrote something similar on his.

"Here it is!" Srulik said excitedly, pointing out a place on the old prison uniform to his mother and siblings. They gazed in awe at the faded words on the old striped pajamas.

Penina Warshavski took the pajamas and inspected them with interest. With difficulty, she made out the name "Zevulun," and then, letter by letter, the name "Warshavski."

"If you'll be patient, I'm nearly at the end of my story," Zevulun mock-scolded them. His enthralled family settled back to hear the rest.

Etzel forces arrived in Akko the next day, in two groups. The first group set up roadblocks on all roads leading to the prison, while the second ran ahead to blow a hole in the prison wall. At the same time, we prisoners used the explosives that had been smuggled in to us to create another hole in the steel prison gates. Through this we made our escape, forty members of *Etzel* and *Lechi* (another underground organization). Several dozen Arabs — among them some notorious figures — took advantage of the situation to break out as well.

But when we swarmed outside we ran right into British military forces who had hastened to the spot. In the ensuing battle, five *Etzel* members were killed and seven more injured. One of those wounded was my friend, Mordechai "Motke" Blumenthal. A bullet had shattered his left kneecap.

We ran several kilometers in the direction of the highway. A comrade and I were dragging Motke along with us, but we quickly realized that the situation was impossible. At this rate we would put no distance at all between ourselves and our pursuers, and all of us would be captured. Motke begged us to leave him and run for our lives. With no choice, and with heavy hearts, we did as he asked. We knocked on the door of a Jewish home and pleaded with them to take in our injured friend and escaped convict.

Half an hour later, we arrived at the agreed-upon meeting place. A car waited there to spirit us away to Haifa. Or rather, nearly to Haifa. There were British military checkpoints at the city entrance that we naturally wished to avoid. We left the car several kilometers before it reached the city and continued the rest of the way on foot along dirt paths.

Late that night, I wandered the streets of Haifa looking for a place to rest my head. I was nearly at the point of collapse and could think of one thing and one thing only: sleep.

Suddenly, I saw light coming from the window of a building that I recognized as a shul. Coming closer, I heard something I had long ago forgotten: the sweet sounds of Torah learning. The voices drew me. I felt a strange warmth. "It will be good for me here," I thought, and went inside.

Later, I found out that the place was actually a yeshivah. There were about twenty boys inside, learning with enthusiasm from large volumes. As I approached, they looked up and greeted me with big smiles. I didn't understand why they were laughing at me, until I glanced down at myself. Then I understood only too well. Yours truly was still wearing prison pajamas!

I was so tired that I had forgotten all about changing my prison clothes, and had been wandering the streets with "Escaped Convict!" written all over me. It was truly a miracle than no British soldier happened to lay eyes on me that night.

The young men welcomed me warmly. They lent me clothes — a dark suit and hat — so that I would look just like any other yeshivah student in case the place was searched.

I thought I would stay there only a day or two, but they treated me so well there ... and, besides, I had nowhere else to go. I stayed, and somehow found myself slowly returning to my Jewish roots. Once again, I accepted the yoke of the Torah and mitzvos. I became a *ba'al teshuvah*.

About a year after this, the British left Palestine. I was able to come out of hiding then, and my first move was to search for my friend Motke Blumenthal. To my sorrow, I never did find him. I have no idea what happened after we left him that day, or even whether he lived or died. One day, I traveled to Jerusalem and paid a visit to the old shoemaker's cellar where we had hidden the money. The money was no longer there.

I married your grandmother, may she rest in peace, a few years later. Twelve months after that, our only child and your father, Menachem, was born.

Srulik came closer to his grandfather, wearing a winning smile. "*Zaydie,* if you give me permission, those pajamas would make the greatest Purim costume! If you let me wear them, I'll sell your story to the highest bidder!"

Zevulun was inclined to refuse his consent. The prison uniform carried strong sentimental value for him and he was afraid his grandson would not care for the old garment properly. But Srulik's endless pleading wore him down and eventually changed his mind. "Well, if it's for the sake of a mitzvah, I'll agree."

Srulik leaped into the air with sheer joy. Warmly, he embraced his elderly grandfather. "*Zaydie,* you're the greatest! You've made my Purim."

⌒⌒⌒

When Purim day came around, it did not take long for Srulik to discover that his costume was an unquestionable hit.

In every house he entered wearing the striped prison pajamas, he became the focus of attention. He took advantage of this to charge a "fee" — for charity — for telling the spellbinding tale behind the uniform. He couldn't be sure whether it was the special Purim atmosphere or the unusual costume. What he did know was that his *tzedakah* envelope grew fatter after each house he visited.

That afternoon, a friend dragged him along to the Tel HaShomer Hospital to cheer up the bedridden patients whom the Purim spirit would otherwise have passed by.

"This is silly," Srulik protested. "What are sick people going to donate? My meter is ticking. I can't afford to waste the time."

"You're wrong," his friend retorted. "Don't ask, 'What will they give me?' Ask rather, 'What will I give them?' Money isn't everything in life. Come and do a mitzvah, plain and simple!"

Reluctantly, Srulik allowed himself to be persuaded. The two boys went from ward to ward, bringing *mishloach manos* and a merry spirit to the patients' rooms. Smiles lit the sick folks' faces.

"You see," Srulik told them cheerfully, "I'm also wearing pajamas."

Finally, they came to the room of an elderly and solitary patient. A young Filipino with a bored expression sat in the doorway. He asked them what they wanted.

"We just wanted to go in and wish the patient a happy Purim. Maybe we'll also offer him a small drink of cognac, if he's allowed."

"He's sleeping," the attendant said.

They had turned and were leaving when an urgent voice summoned them back. "Hey, you — Mr. Pajamas! Come back here, quick!"

Srulik turned back. The old man who had been dozing a moment earlier was sitting up in bed now, staring at him. "Quick!" he shouted hoarsely.

The Filipino darted into the room to check the wildly fluctuating monitors. "You're not supposed to get excited," he admonished the patient in fairly fluent Hebrew. "Look, your blood pressure's going up. That's dangerous. Don't you remember how ill you felt yesterday?"

Srulik whispered to his friend, "Apparently, the Filipino works for him. We're looking at a rich man."

The patient ignored the Filipino's warning. To Srulik, in the same urgent tone, he ordered, "Tell me what you're wearing." The words had the air of a command.

Inwardly, Srulik was stung. He didn't like being ordered around. However, he tried to maintain a cheerful expression. As politely as he could, he said to the old man, "I've already told the story of this costume many times today. I've sold it for a nice sum to anyone who's willing to give the money to our *hachnasas kallah* fund. If you want to make a donation — please." He glanced significantly around at the private room and the paid attendant.

The patient grew angry. "You religious people — all you're interested in is collecting money for some cause. Okay, okay, I'll give you 100 shekels. Just tell me where you got those pajamas."

Srulik said, "They belong to my grandfather."

"What's his name?" the old man demanded impatiently.

Srulik drew a deep breath. He had not run across such a difficult character in a long time. "His name is Zevulun."

"Zevulun? Could it be — Zevulun Warshavski?" the old man shrieked.

"Yes!" Srulik was astonished.

"He's still alive?"

"Alive and well, *baruch Hashem*."

The patient leaned forward with some difficulty and began to read the words scribbled in faded ink across the prison stripes. "I recognize my writing," he gasped. "Here's my name — Motke Blumenthal."

"*You're* Motke Blumenthal?" Srulik was the one shouting now.

"The very one."

"My grandfather looked all over for you!"

"On the contrary," the old man corrected, the tears swimming in his eyes. "I'm the one who's been searching for him for fifty years now, in every corner of this land. He simply vanished." He peered at Srulik. "Is your grandfather also religious, like you?"

"Very religious."

"Now I understand why I never located him!" Motke exclaimed. "It never occurred to me to look for him in the religious sectors. What did he tell you about that uniform?"

Srulik rendered a succinct account of the tale he had heard two days before. The old man confirmed every detail, and then took up the story where Zevulun had left off.

"Your grandfather left me that day, injured, in a house in Akko. The family made every effort to help me heal, but the wound in my leg was very serious. After several weeks, gangrene set in and the foot had to be amputated."

He yanked the covers off the end of his bed to reveal a shortened leg, the foot missing.

"Bring your grandfather here today!" Motke ordered.

Srulik refused. "No. I have to prepare him first. I'll bring him tomorrow. Then we'll stage a reunion the likes of which the world has never seen!"

"No, bring him tonight!" Motke thundered. "I'm prepared to pay."

"Do you think everything can be bought with money?" Srulik asked stubbornly. "I have to prepare my grandfather carefully, so he won't have too great a shock."

"But you'll surely bring him tomorrow?" Motke insisted, giving in.

Srulik looked with compassion at the elderly man. "Please G-d, I'll bring him."

The reunion took place amid a sea of tears. Zevulun and Motke were nearly beside themselves with emotion. They embraced each other over and over, liberally dampening one another's shoulders with weeping. Only when they had finally managed to attain a measure of calm did they sit back and begin to tell each other the story of their lives.

Motke's story was a sad one. Though he had achieved material success despite his crippled leg — amassing a great deal of wealth and property — he had never married. He was alone, with only a hired Filipino to serve his needs.

"And you?" Motke asked his old friend. "Did you have success in life?"

"Yes," answered Zevulun. "But not with money. As you can see, I changed my lifestyle. I became a mitzvah-observant person the way I had once been, back in Lukoshinska. I married and had one son, who has given me a great deal of *nachas*. But money? Heaven has decreed otherwise. I live together with my son and daughter-in-law and grandchildren in a tiny, two-bedroom apartment." He sighed. "My grandchildren are wonderful and don't complain, but only someone who's been blind from birth could miss the fact that they're feeling suffocated."

Motke gave him a strange glance. "It's time you moved to a bigger place."

"We'd love to," Zevulun said with another sigh. "But my son spends his time studying the Torah. There's not a penny to spare."

"Did you ever go back to look for that money in the shoemaker's basement?" Motke asked suddenly, changing course.

Zevulun smiled. "Ever go back? I came to Jerusalem, sneaked into that basement when no one was looking, and poured the nails out of every one of those containers. But I never found the container with the money. It was gone."

"I took it," Motke confessed.

"*What?*"

"Yes! Right after I got out of the hospital, I went to Jerusalem just as you did, and sneaked into the basement. I found the money — all of it. Not a penny was missing."

"And you used it for your health," Zevulun said, nodding. "Now I understand."

"You don't understand anything," Motke said sharply. "I didn't touch that money. I saved it for you. I sent it to Switzerland with a friend and deposited it into an account in a bank there. I didn't trust the 'Anglo-Palestinian Bank' and was worried about the prying eyes of the British. Later, I used my financial abilities to invest the money for you, and your investment multiplied by thousands of percentage points." He paused before adding momentously, "You have waiting for you, in that Swiss bank account, something like $200,000.

"But — but why did you do it?" Zevulun asked, thunderstruck. "It's just like the story of R' Chanina ben Dosa, who found some eggs one day, and years later returned a whole herd of goats to the man who had lost the eggs!"

"All these years, I believed that the day would come when we would meet again," Motke said with a nostalgic smile. "I've known you for a long time, Zevulun. Even back in Lukoshinska, you never had two cents to rub together. I imagined that would be the case for the rest of your life."

The reuniting of the two old friends changed Zevulun's life in more ways than one. Not only was he able to enjoy the companionship of Motke once again, but the Warshavski family celebrated the following Purim in a much larger and far more comfortable apartment.

BLANK CHECK

R ABBI YOSEF AVISHAI SHEFTER WAS A MAN WHO RESPECTED himself and was no less respected by others. He taught the third-level *shiur* in a boy's yeshivah called Aron Edus. His standing, from both the scholarly and the social standpoints, was high. His students admired him tremendously.

All was fine with Rabbi Shefter ... until one took a peek at his home situation. There, things were more complicated.

Rabbi Shefter had been blessed with a large family that consisted mostly of daughters. His weekly salary managed to cover their simple living expenses, but when his oldest daughter came of marriageable age, the rabbi faced a crisis. He and Shaindel, his rebbetzin, wanted an outstanding boy for their daughter, but unless they were able to provide the young couple with an apartment — or at least three-quarters of the price of one — no one wanted to hear of the match.

Finally, the daughter became engaged to a fine young man from a well-known yeshivah, and R' Shefter managed to find his way out of his problem by the skin of his teeth — and with the help of a group of active young yeshivah men who undertook the mitzvah of raising the money for *hachnasas kallah*. These four wonderful young men ran around day and night, knocking on doors and asking for contributions.

R' Shefter was not happy about this. He himself was a fastidious man who, had he undertaken the job himself, would have died of shame before he had rung his first doorbell. At first, he wouldn't hear of others *"shnorring"* on his behalf. But he was forced to retreat from this position when he realized that he had no choice — except, Heaven forbid, to break the *shidduch*. For his daughter's sake, he agreed to let others do his "dirty work" for him. His heart shed tears of blood while this donation-hunting was going on. His self-image was deeply wounded at the thought that others regarded him as a charity case.

But when he counted the money that the active young men had collected for him, R' Shefter packed away his inflated ego and his high self-image into a large box, to be opened only after his youngest had been safely married off.

When their second daughter became engaged, R' Shefter and his wife waited expectantly for someone to offer help. To their surprise and dismay, no one stepped forward. They found out that they were not unique. Those wonderfully active collectors had not been idle all this time. They were over their heads now with dozens of prior commitments.

R' Shefter found himself forced against the wall. He phoned a few people and ran to keep appointments with five others in their homes. After much pleading and pulling of strings, he found two collectors who agreed to come up with the funds needed to marry off his wonderful second daughter.

Then came the turn of Gila, the third in line. She was an exceptional girl in every way. Inside and out, she exuded a harmony that reached near-perfection. This time, the rabbi intended to make the boy pay for the privilege of marrying his Gila. Where else would a young man find a bride like this — a girl who, at the tender age of 10, already knew the entire Book of Kings by heart, as well as Samuel and all five *Megillos?* Even before she started high school, it was clear that Gila had a brilliant future in teaching. And indeed, when her time came she was chosen over a hundred other graduates to teach in a new girls high school. Gila was well-versed in halachah, especially the laws of Shabbos, and could quote from memory whole portions of the *Michtav MeEliyahu*. She was a repository of information about the biographies of dozens of great Torah luminaries, having read many books that her friends had never even heard of. Gila, in short, was "a catch."

R' Shefter let everyone know that he was in no hurry to marry off this special daughter. Anyone who wanted Gila Shefter would have to pay for such a precious find. His friends tried to dissuade him from this line of talk. In his circumstances, they explained gently, it was unprofitable to take such a stand. If he didn't want his Gila to remain a spinster until her hair turned white, it was up to him to bite the bullet and come up with a dowry, even if that meant the price of an apartment.

R' Shefter refused to listen. His friends' words fell on deaf ears. He wanted all the world to know how special his Gila's qualities were. He was a very proud father.

One year passed, and then another. Gila was already 21, then 22, then 23 ...

When Gila turned 24, her father broke. Far too late, he understood that he had forced his good daughter to wait in vain, and had lost out on the best of the young men on the "*shiduch* market." Though a person's destined mate is announced forty days before her birth, it was possible to ruin destiny with one's own actions.

But even in this difficult hour, R' Shefter refused to look for anything less than the outstanding package he sought in a husband for his daughter. Only in one detail was he ready to compromise: the financial angle. If Gila became engaged to a truly worthy young man, her father was prepared to take on a heavy financial burden — the full price of an apartment for the couple.

When someone suggested a match with Meyer Brinkner, R' Shefter nearly fainted with joy. It was an outstanding match, even better than he had dreamed of. His head spun with the *chasan's* many qualities.

"First of all, he learns in a yeshivah that is considered the best in the city. Second, he is considered a genius even in that yeshivah. Third, his father is R' Kalman Brinkner, a man of great Torah and piety, a halachic genius who has composed important Torah works. Kalman Brinkner is also a talented businessman; everything he touches turns to gold. Therefore, there is a good chance that the other side will agree to pay half the expenses. Fourth, I happen to know the young man, and apart from his brilliance and *yiras Shamayim*, he is simply a terrific person. Nice looking, tall, pleasant, and outgoing." R' Shefter sighed. "If only they'll agree to the match!"

The *shidduch* ran its usual route. Both sides checked the other, assessed information, traveled, met. The young man and woman in question were both agreeable to the match.

Only one problem remained, a problem that had been swept under the rug.

Kalman Brinkner had declared to the matchmaker from the start that, for his special son, he wanted no less than all expenses paid by the girl's side. The *shadchan* tried to argue with him, saying that things were done differently these days. "And besides, you have two booming real estate offices in Tel Aviv and employ eight people. Why not participate at least to the tune of 30 percent of the expenses?"

But Kalman Brinkner refused to listen. "It's not the money, it's the principle of the thing! My Meyer is worth full payment. Whoever is not prepared to pay had better not bother getting involved."

The matchmaker knew Kalman Brinkner well. Brinkner's word was his bond. With him, a principle was a principle. Not wanting to ruin the match at the very start, he mumbled something to R' Shefter about the *chasan's* side demanding that the *kallah's* father pay for most of an apartment. On his part, R' Shefter seized on the word "most," which was vague enough to mean anything from 51 percent to 99 percent. The *shadchan* decided to let nature take its course. When all was said and done and the two sides met to finalize the terms of the engagment — when a *"vort"* was about to be held and the echoes of the shattered plate were already hovering in the air — then stubborn Kalman Brinkner would doubtless compromise. The matchmaker was loathe to stop the galloping match in mid-course.

But he did not see accurately into the future. Had he really known Kalman Brinkner, he would have spared himself a very difficult moment. When the two prospective *mechutanim* finally did meet to discuss terms, they discovered to their shock that a very wide abyss divided them.

Kalman Brinkner sat in R' Shefter's home and stated flatly, "It's either all or nothing."

R' Shefter thought he would explode with shock and rage, at the sheer chutzpah of the other man's demand. Trying to maintain a calm facade, he asked, "Where is the justice here? We both know that you are a rich man. How is it that a rich man is not embarrassed to demand that a man without resources (R' Shefer did not want to use the word 'poor') pay everything, while he himself gives nothing?"

Kalman Brinkner was not listening. He had received an urgent call on his cell-phone about some business-related matter. Ending his call, he turned back to the girl's father and said coldly, "My friend, if you will not or cannot, you are not obligated to enter into this venture. We can part as friends, with nothing lost. If I meet you in the street tomorrow, I will not avoid you. I will nod my head, and even wish you a good day. But if you want my son Meyer as a son-in-law, this is my condition! I want the *kallah's* side — and that does not have to mean you! — to pay all expenses. And by 'all,' I mean 'all' — from A to Z. Nothing less."

As he spoke these last words, Brinkner scraped back his chair as though preparing to leave. Whether he really meant to end the discussion or whether this was a psychological ploy is impossible to know, because at that moment the phone rang. R' Shefter picked it up, to find the matchmaker on the other end of the line.

The *shadchan* had called to find out how things were progressing.

"R' Brinkner is about to leave," R' Shefter informed him in a low voice. He went on to describe the scene that had just taken place between them.

"Put Kalman on the phone," the *shadchan* said hastily. When he was connected to Brinkner, he implored him to remain there just ten more minutes. "I'll grab a taxi and come right over!"

The ten minutes turned into a full hour. "Traffic jams," the matchmaker explained afterwards. While they waited, and trying to distract themselves from the issue at hand, R' Shefter and R' Brinkner began to discuss Torah thoughts. The talk served to place things in proper perspective; each one was reminded of who he was and what was important in life. The atmosphere, so ugly before, changed completely. By the time the matchmaker hurried into the house, all apologies, he found to his surprise that the air in the room was calm and even friendly. The only fight he could discern was a raging debate on a Torah topic, in which the two fathers had taken one side and the *chasan* stood firm in his opposite opinion.

The matchmaker stood transfixed by the scene. But his reaction was no less extreme than that of R' Shefter himself. During the course of their Torah discussion he had seen with his own eyes the depths of his prospective son-in-law's learning. The young man possessed an extraordinary grasp and analytical ability. It would be a vast shame to let such a pearl slip through his fingers, R' Shefter thought, only because of money.

R' Brinkner, too, had mellowed during their talk, and the *shadchan* was able to sway him from his formerly fixed position. He agreed to chip in for the wedding and for the couple's electrical appliances, leaving the apartment and all the rest on R' Shefter's shoulders.

That night, R' Shefter cried and laughed. He cried with joy at the diamond he had merited for his daughter: A true *ben Torah* with a brilliant and aspiring mind. And he laughed a bitter laugh, because he had no idea where in the world he would find even the first thousand shekels of his obligation.

When he thought of what was expected from him, his laughter became almost uncontrollable. It seemed like an enormous joke to him. To his wife, late that night, he painted an imaginary picture of the two of them walking into their daughter's wedding, dressed in beggars' rags. They both laughed until their stomachs hurt.

Laughed, and cried.

A month passed, then two. R' Shefter immersed himself in his learning and his *shiurim* to his students. Never for an instant, however, did he forget what was expected of him by the winter's end. The wedding had been scheduled for the month of Adar, but beyond taking out a huge loan — a loan which he had no idea how he was going to repay — he had done nothing. By the 17th day of Adar, he would be expected to pay a third of the wedding expenses, after dragging his feet so long that his *mechutan* had declared that he would brook no more delays.

Two days before Purim, R' Shefter made a decision. He told his wife, "You know me well, my dear. I am a man with great self-respect, who never dreamed that he would have to turn into a *shnorrer*. But I have no choice. On Purim, anyone who extends his hand for a donation is given something. I will dress up in a costume that will hide my identity and then ask for money at a few addresses that a good friend has supplied me with.

"I promise you," he added hastily, "I won't shame myself by begging in the streets. I will go only to homes where I can expect hundreds of dollars or thousands of shekels. I can't let two days like Purim and Shushan Purim go to waste. Tell the children that I have to go away to perform an urgent mitzvah, and so I won't be able to be with them for the Purim *seudah*, or the rest of the day."

"I don't believe what I'm hearing!" his wife replied. She went to get the thermometer to check whether he was running a fever. But R' Shefter assured her that he was deadly serious. After a stormy argument, in which his wife declared that she absolutely refused her consent to such a scheme, and that it was unheard of for a respected *mag-*

gid shiur to degrade himself in this way, she came to the belated and bitter realization that her husband had already made up his mind. He was not asking her advice, but merely letting her know what he planned to do that Purim.

R' Shefter had been a yeshivah boy once — a merry yeshivah boy blessed with humorous talent and powers of mimicry. He drew on those long-dormant abilities now. In the home of the friend who had given him the addresses, R' Shefter dressed himself in full chassidic regalia, dyed his black beard white, thickened his eyebrows with black pencil, and unfurled the long *peyos* that he usually wore tucked behind his ears. He switched to a different pair of glasses and walked bent over, leaning on a silver-plated walking stick. One of his good friends was amazed to see R' Shefter transform himself, before his very eyes, into a complete stranger. He burst out laughing when R' Shefter spoke in typical Polish-chassidic Yiddish one minute, then broke into a Hungarian dialect in the next.

"I never knew you could be like that!" the friend exclaimed through his laughter. In response, R' Shefter in his new persona showered him with Yiddish blessings.

R' Shefter bade his friend farewell, and set out on his mission.

It is said that the Emperor Napoleon tried his hand at every profession in the world, and claimed afterwards that he managed to turn a profit at each of them. But he enjoyed collecting alms most of all, he said — so much so that he nearly turned professional beggar! The story floated through R' Shefter's mind all that day.

At the first homes he visited Purim night, he felt his face burning beneath his makeup. His breath was ragged and his heart pounded wildly in his chest. Slowly, however, his confidence grew. He made a short, pleasant speech to each homeowner. He offered a pungent *"vort"* here, and a shower of witty, rebbe-like blessings there, throwing in imitations of well-known figures that had whole families rolling with laughter. He was at his best that night. Hearts and wallets opened to him, and he received large donations that would not have shamed even the most veteran collector.

The next day, on Purim morning, R' Shefter's courage was high because no one had recognized him the night before. He visited a rich man who *davened* in his own shul regularly, and the man did not know who he was. "If he only knew to whom he was speaking!" R' Shefter thought fleetingly, as he pocketed a check for 5,000 shekels for *hachnasas kallah*. During the course of that day, he managed to collect a sizeable amount — and he still had the next day, Shushan Purim, to look forward to. He would travel up to Jerusalem and try his hand there.

Suddenly, he had a wild idea. Try as he might, he could not shake it off. His *mechutan*, Kalman Brinkner, had the custom of giving out very large sums for charity on Purim. On that day, his heart was soft as butter. Anyone who managed to convince him that his need was genuine could expect to receive a truly staggering sum.

"I'm going to him," was R' Shefter's second thought. His first had been, "He gives the whole world gifts, but he was willing to squeeze my very lifeblood before he grudgingly agreed to take a little of the burden from my shoulders."

He turned the idea over and over in his mind. The more he thought about it, the better the notion appeared to him. He would go to Brinkner, change his voice in imitation of a well-known Torah leader, and deliver an energetic talk about the great mitzvah of *hachnasas kallah*. In return, he would receive an enormous check, to atone in part for his *mechutan's* obstinacy and his strange "principles."

The sun was close to setting by the time R' Shefter stood at Kalman Brinkner's door.

"This is where 'my' Meyer grew up," he thought happily. This was where Meyer had been raised, where he had been nurtured until he had developed into such an exceptional young man. With Hashem's help, in just two weeks Meyer would stand beneath the *chuppah* to become R' Shefter's son-in-law.

Trembling, he rang the bell. A ding-dong as cheerful as a flock of happy birds met his ears. From inside, he heard a booming chorus of "*Amen, yehei Shemei rabbah ...*" The door opened.

The first thing to hit him was the smell: It was predominantly alcohol, mingled with the aromas of good food. Then he heard voices upraised in *Tefillas Minchah*. As they wound down, some of the boys — Meyer Brinkner's friends — began to sing and dance in the hallway. Seeing the collector standing in the doorway, they shouted an exuberant greeting, seized his hand, and drew him into their circle.

R' Brinkner stood to one side, watching the dancers with a benevolent eye. When R' Shefter grew weary, his host offered him a plateful of *kreplach*, straight from the pot.

R' Shefter did not refuse. He would do whatever his host wanted, as long as he left this place with a check in his pocket.

After he had seen the newcomer drain a glass of wine, Kalman Brinkner said, "Now tell me what brings you here to me."

R' Shefter wanted to say, "*You* bring me here, you stubborn 'man of principle'!" Instead, he thought a moment and then answered with a blatant Hungarian accent, "My *tzoros* bring me here. Believe me, sir, my heart is ready to burst with my troubles. My daughter needs to get married, and I don't have a shekel for her!"

"And what is your *mechutan* giving her?" Brinkner asked with interest.

"My *mechutan*," R' Shefter said, switching to a plaintive Polish accent, "can't give a thing. He has troubles of his own."

"What happened to him?" Brinkner asked playfully. He liked this *shnorrer*. Every sentence out of his mouth belonged to a different community, and he was very entertaining.

"My *mechutan*," the collector said in a Yemenite singsong, "had a terrible accident. He stopped learning in *kollel* and found himself a job, where he lost his ..." his voice trailed away.

"His wallet!" cried a youth in a green turban.

"His head!" supplied another.

R' Shefter silenced them with an upraised hand and returned to his story, this time in the sober chant of a *mashgiach* delivering a *mussar shmooze*: "*Ay, ay, rabbosai!* He went out into the marketplace of life — and lost his heart!"

The atmosphere was merry and well-lubricated with whiskey. Loud laughter rose up all around.

But Kalman Brinkner did not laugh.

He gazed at his guest's trembling fingers, and his face froze for a moment. Then, thoughtfully, he asked, "How much do you need, my Lithuanian-Yemenite friend?"

"I am no Yemenite," R' Shefter admonished, in a Moroccan accent. "Back home in Casablanca, we had a saying: 'If you give ten thousand dollars — very good. If you give more, you will sit with the first tier of *tzaddikim* in Gan Eden!'"

Kalman Brinkner pulled out his checkbook and signed a check. Then, in front of all his astounded guests, he said emotionally — and with a vain effort to imitate R' Shefter's Moroccan accent — "This is my atonement. Write the check for whatever amount you please." He handed the check to R' Shefter.

The silence was loud as thunder. No one could believe what he was hearing and seeing. Dozens of pairs of eyes raked Kalman Brinkner's face. Was this some kind of Purim joke? Surely he was kidding.

But Kalman Brinkner was not joking. He walked the collector to the door, saying, "You can fill out the check at home tomorrow. Write down the exact amount you will need in order to respectably marry off your daughter."

When the guests had departed and the remains of the Purim feast had been cleared away by the house staff, Kalman Brinkner explained his action to his wife.

"Do you understand? A Jew named Kalman Brinkner is sitting on a mountain of money. Hashem has blessed him with everything, with a successful son and with money and property. But he is stubborn. He insists that his poor *mechutan* pay for everything.

"He tried to tell me a number of times, in various different ways and with all sorts of hints and half-sentences, that he is a destitute man — but I did not want to understand. Well, today I had some shock therapy. That collector said that his *mechutan* went out into the 'marketplace of life' and lost not his head, not his wallet, but his heart! Do you hear? He lost his heart! It was like a fist punching my own heart. I felt myself reeling. And then, I suddenly noticed the man's hand.

"You know that I have a knack for noticing small details. Our *mechutan*, R' Yosef Avishai Shefter, has a small, heart-shaped birthmark at the base of his thumb. I noticed it on the night of the *tennaim*, and I saw it again on our guest's hand ... right there, at the base of his thumb.

"He disguised himself well, our *mechutan*. He only overlooked that one tiny detail. I thought to myself then, 'How symbolic. My *mechutan* has two hearts, and I don't even have one!' And then I thought, if our *mechutan*, an eminently respectable man, has reached such a degraded and desperate position that he is forced to these measures of despair, who knows whether Hashem considers me a terribly wicked sinner? I could picture our Heavenly Father asking me, 'R' Shefter, a man great in Torah, needs to shame and abase himself — to shed his lifeblood in public — simply because you were not pleased to give up your precious "principle"?'

"That was when I decided to give him a blank check. He can write in any amount, even the combined expenses of us both, and I won't care."

His wife nodded slowly. "Maybe you should call him up and let him know that you recognized him behind his costume?" she asked. "So that he'll know you're giving him the money with a full heart."

Kalman Brinkner remained deep in thought for several minutes. Then he said quietly, "I don't know if this has the status of a secret gift, since he knows who gave him the money and I know whom I gave it to. But there is still something to be salvaged here — and that's our *mechutan's* self-respect! Let's leave it alone. Let's leave this Purim with a good taste in our mouths."

Pesach

FLOUR FROM HEAVEN

I. THE YEAR OF THE DROUGHT

THAT YEAR, THE PEOPLE WALKED JERUSALEM'S WINDING streets like shadows. All of Eretz Yisrael was suffering, and Jerusalem was suffering most of all. Poverty and want filled the holy city's streets and homes. Everyone was hungry.

Hunger was the norm in any given year. That particular year, however, the suffering was greatly increased. It was a year of drought. Old-timers remembered many a dry winter, but none as dry as this.

Some years, though the winter tarried, by Chanukah the rains had started falling nicely. Other years, both Chanukah and the beginning of Teves passed with no rain, and it was not until the month of Shevat that the first rain clouds appeared in the sky. And sometimes the blessed rains came to fill the wells only in the month of Adar, when people had nearly given up hope.

That year was the worst. The winter was nearly over, and still the skies remained blue and clear. While citizens of Europe, for instance, yearned for such skies, residents of Jerusalem were beginning to loath and fear them. How many times can a person lift his eyes, hoping against hope to glimpse a rain cloud — only to be disappointed once again?

The sky was like metal, and the earth was hard and dry as copper. After a completely dry winter, it was no wonder that the fields did not produce their crops and not a blade of green was to be seen anywhere.

Where would the people find grain?

II. STARVATION

Along with the drought came deprivation. The wheat fields did not sprout, except to produce a few spindly, nearly-empty stalks. This served to raise the price of flour sky-high. At the height of that dry winter, industrious merchants traveled to nearby Syria to the north, which had suffered less from the drought. There they bought large quantities of flour, for which they charged exorbitant prices back home. The price of a single *rotel* (approx. 3 kilograms) of flour was an entire gold *dinar*! Most of Jerusalem's populace subsisted on very small amounts indeed, eating bread made out of the poor-quality flour normally used to feed chickens. This year, the lowly grain had been elevated to royal fare.

As winter's end approached, the same merchants again traveled to Syria. All of Jerusalem waited with bated breath for their return. This time, however, they came back to announce total disappointment. It seemed that the small amount of rain that had fallen in Syria had yielded a meager crop, with nothing left over for sale to foreign countries.

Panic swept the city. As people in serious numbers began to die of starvation, some went out into the fields to munch on any vegetation they could find — the green stuff normally consumed by goats and cattle. If they happened upon a few kernels of wheat that had somehow been overlooked, they rejoiced as if they had unearthed a rare delicacy. When even that could no longer be found, they wandered — hungry — through the streets and marketplaces. More than a few people fainted right where they stood, and some gave up their souls with a sigh on the spot.

Pesach was coming. This represented a problem of truly awesome dimensions. Where could flour be found for matzahs?

In his narrow room, anxiously pondering this problem, sat the *gaon,* R' Yisrael of Shklov, student of the Vilna Gaon and leader of the Ashkenazi community in Jerusalem in those days. His shoulders sagged with the weight of the burden laid upon them, and his face was drawn with worry. All the land, and Jerusalem in particular, was accustomed to trouble. Difficult times had come and gone in R' Yisrael's experience. But never, since the day he had first set foot on the holy soil of Eretz Yisrael, had he seen as difficult a time as this.

He was prepared to dispense with flour that had been carefully watched. He was more than willing to use plain flour. The problem was, even the plainest of flour was not to be had.

A heavy sigh worked its way up from the depths of his heart, as memories of other years filled his mind.

Ah, those had been good days ....

III. MEMORIES

The wagons stood ready beside the Jaffa Gate. R' Yisrael of Shklov and others — rabbis and community leaders — went out merrily to the fields. They were filled with festive good cheer. It was harvest time.

It had been a good winter. Rain had fallen plentifully that year, and the land had yielded bountiful crops.

"Hashem is with you, brave soldiers!" cried the people as they waved their leaders off.

To the west of Jerusalem, about a half-day's trip by wagon, lay a large Arab village. This village was surrounded on all sides by wheat fields. As far as the eye could see stood tall stalks of wheat, wave upon golden wave that gladdened their hearts even from a distance.

"Blessed is He and Blessed is His Name! This year we will have plenty of matzahs," murmured one of the rabbis at the sight of the golden fields. His eyes watered joyfully.

They worked for several days, long, sharp scythes in hand as they cut down the golden sheaves from morning to night. Sack after sack was filled with wheat. "*L'shem matzos mitzvah,*" they declared again and again. "*L'shem matzos mitzvah!*"

When the wagons appeared on the outskirts of Jerusalem, the people came swarming out to greet the conquering heroes. With song and dance the rabbis were escorted into the city, where the precious sacks were wrapped in special cloths for extra protection, then deposited in designated cellars where they would be zealously guarded against moisture.

That was how they made sure they had "*shemurah*" matzahs in a good year.

IV. A FLICKER OF HOPE IN JAFFA

The door opened. Into the room came Simcha, son of R' Yechezkel the water-carrier. In the city, he was known only as "Yechezkel's Simcha." No one knew his family name, or even if he had one. He was a young man who had a hand in every pot. Like a whirlwind, he seemed to be everywhere at once, in the *beis midrash* and the market square, the *mikveh* and the *beis din*. He knew everything and told everything; the city's business was his business.

It was not like Yechezkel's Simcha to stand by with folded hands during a crisis like the one they were experiencing this year. He poked and sniffed and inquired, asked and traveled, going as far as Jaffa in his efforts to find a source of wheat for the upcoming festival.

"Rebbe!" he gasped, bursting into the room. "I found it!"

"What did you find?" asked R' Yisrael. "Have you come to ask me about the laws of *hashavas aveidah* at this difficult time?"

"No, no — just the opposite! I've come on a very important matter. I've found flour!"

R' Yisrael sat up, every nerve alert. "Where?"

"There is flour in Jaffa!" R' Simcha crowed with delight.

"Who owns it?"

"The Jewish community there has a few sacks of flour!"

R' Simcha was nearly beside himself with excitement, so his story emerged in a rather unclear fashion. Still, R' Yisrael managed to grasp the fact that some fifty sacks of Syrian flour were in storage in Jaffa, miraculously untouched during the hungry months just behind them. Of course, the price being demanded for these sacks was exorbitant. The flour merchants were asking no less than two gold *dinars* for every *rotel* of flour.

R' Yisrael's face fell. "R' Simcha, do you think we've suddenly grown wealthy? We can't pay such prices!"

"If we don't hurry, the entire inventory will be sold in the market-place," R' Simcha babbled. "Surely you don't want to leave Jerusalem's Jews without matzahs on Seder night."

"Do you happen to know how much money there is in the com-munity treasury?" R' Yisrael's voice acted like cold water on R' Simcha's exuberance. R' Simcha fell silent, looking at his rebbe with questioning eyes.

"Our treasury is empty," R' Yisrael continued soberly. "There are not even two coins to clank together and make a sound. Where, then, are we to find the money to pay for this flour?"

So we won't be eating matzahs this year? R' Simcha wondered silently. He didn't dare ask the question out loud.

R' Yisrael gazed at the young man with wise eyes. He pointed upward. "We have a venerable Father. I believe that He will not aban-don His children. Hashem's salvation comes as quick as the blink of an eye."

R' Simcha found his voice at last. "Rebbe, forgive me, but I have checked everywhere in the country. Apart from those fifty sacks in Jaffa, there is not even a kernel of wheat to be had in all the land. If the rebbe doesn't believe me, he can ask Jamal Effendi, the big wheat merchant at the Damascus Gate!"

"My dear R' Simcha, are you speaking of natural means? True, in the natural course of events there is no way out. But I was talk-ing about Hashem's salvation. Is there anything too difficult for Him to accomplish?"

R' Simcha was silenced at last. With bowed head, he left the room.

V. DISAPPOINTING MAIL

Several days passed — mad, frenzied days. R' Yisrael did not sit idly by waiting for a miracle. He sent messengers to all sorts of places, and went personally to investigate other possible sources of flour. All efforts were in vain. The messengers came back empty-handed.

Each day, R' Yisrael walked up to the Jaffa Gate to wait impatient-ly for the postal wagon coming from Jaffa, hoping against hope for help from Diaspora Jews abroad. Knowing of the poverty in which the populace of Eretz Yisrael lived, these Jews usually gave generously to help them. "If a large sum of money were to come now, we'd have reason to celebrate," R' Yisrael thought hopefully. "We'd be able to pay even the outrageous sum that the Jaffa merchants are asking."

It was late afternoon. The sun was heading towards the west, painting the city walls a rosy hue, like flames soaring upward. As R' Yisrael cast a last look down the dusty road, he heard the sound of galloping hooves in the distance. Standing on tiptoe, he peered directly into the setting sun, trying to see. At last, the mail wagon had arrived.

"Has anything come for the Community Chest?" he asked with pounding heart.

"Let me see," came the laconic reply. The driver untied his mail sack and glanced inside. "Here is a letter," he said, handing it over. R' Yisrael could not wait another second. With trembling fingers, he opened it on the spot.

The paper nearly fell from his hands.

"To the holy community in Jerusalem," the brief letter read. "For various reasons, we did not manage this year to collect the annual contribution for Pesach. We hope, with Hashem's help, to send the money immediately after the holiday."

VI. CAMELS, CAMELS EVERYWHERE

R' Yisrael returned home, ashen and bowed. He sank into his chair and burst into tears. "From whence will come my help?" he murmured through bitter tears. His hand pulled a small *Tehillim* from his coat pocket. He opened it and began flipping through its pages blindly. Suddenly, his eyes fell on the words, "My help is from the L-rd, Maker of Heaven and earth!"

He was still staring at the words, astounded, when the ringing of bells reached him. The sound was coming from near his window. He got up and looked out.

R' Yisrael was certain that his imagination was playing tricks on him. In front of his house stood a caravan of camels, all loaded with sacks.

Where had the caravan come from? Just an hour ago there had not been a single camel in the entire city. From where had a whole string of them materialized so suddenly?

Before he could begin to unravel the mystery, an old Arab approached him.

"Are you the Jewish *Chacham?* Leader of the Jews in Jerusalem?"

R' Yisrael nodded his head, speechless.

"Do you see my camels? They are loaded down with wheat. I've just come to Jerusalem from the Galil because I know that you Jews need wheat for your holiday. True? You will surely pay me well for my merchandise!"

"We certainly do need wheat for Pesach," R' Yisrael answered. "However, you should be aware that our community treasury is completely empty at the moment." A sigh that was almost a groan escaped him. The Arab heard it.

The old man peered at R' Yisrael compassionately. After a moment's thought, he said, "I will give you the wheat in any case. I am prepared to wait a little while for my money. I know you Jews: You are a G-d-fearing people and speak the truth. Not like my Ishmaelite brothers, who are liars and the sons of liars!"

"How long are you willing to wait for your payment?" R' Yisrael asked, making lightning-swift calculations in his head. If his Diaspora brothers hurried to send the money right after Pesach, the situation was not so terrible.

"Do not worry. I will return on the eve of your holiday — or on the day after the holiday at the latest."

The Arab whistled to his drivers, who began to unload the camels.

The doors of the special Pesach wheat cellars were thrown wide open.

From every corner, Jews began to gather. With disbelieving eyes they watched the proceedings. "Where did those camels come from? Did they fall from Heaven?" someone joked.

"Hey, time is precious. Let's help them," urged another.

All together, they worked to unload the camels, and in a short time nearly all the sacks were wrapped in their special cloths and safely stored in the cellars.

Bustling and noisy, the Jews and Arabs worked together to complete the job. As they labored, the sun sank to the horizon and evening shadows cast their long arms across the city. Soon it would be dark.

The "volunteer" workers ran to *daven Minchah*, while R' Yisrael, who had *davened* earlier in the afternoon, hurried into his house to bring candles so that the workers would have light.

To his utter shock, when he returned to the street there was not a soul to be seen. The Arab, his workers, and his camels had vanished as suddenly as they had come.

VII. THE CASE OF THE DISAPPEARING ARAB

As R' Yisrael surveyed the cellars bulging with wheat, his heart nearly burst with happiness. But when he remembered the Arab, who had disappeared before they had even concluded on the price, anxiety gnawed at him like a worm. Where would they find the money to pay him, and who knew whether he would demand an exorbitant price for goods he knew they could not find anywhere else?

That night, R' Yisrael wrote several letters to the heads of Jewish communities in the Diaspora, relating the entire incident. Those kind-hearted Jews responded in kind and hurried to send money before Pesach. They gave generously. The money sat in R' Yisrael's drawer, waiting for the Arab wheat merchant's return on Pesach eve.

As the holiday neared, word spread throughout the community: The wheat they had received from the Arab would be enough not only for the matzahs they needed, but for the entire upcoming summer season.

On the 14th day of Nissan, as all of Jerusalem flocked to the Western Wall to recite the *Seder Korban Pesach*, the community's leader was nowhere to be seen. R' Yisrael of Shklov was at home, waiting for the Arab merchant to come for his payment, as they had agreed.

The merchant did not come — neither on that day, nor in the days after Pesach. Immediately after the holiday, R' Yisrael sent messengers to the Galil to make inquiries about the wheat merchant. The messengers went from village to village, but no one knew the man to whom they referred.

For a number of years, R' Yisrael guarded that bundle of money in his home, just in case the merchant would return one day to claim it.

When his own death was near, R' Yisrael summoned his son-in-law and ordered him to watch over the money for ten more years, just in case ....

Ten years later, the son-in-law opened the envelope and distributed the money to the poor, for the sake of peace giving to needy Arabs along with the Jews — just as he had been instructed by his father-in-law, leader of the *Yishuv* in Jerusalem, R' Yisrael of Shklov.

THE SECRET GIVER

"**M**AZAL TOV! MAZAL TOV!*"*

The joyful cries echoed through the building. Despite the late hour, the neighbors forgave the disturbance and walked down to the widow Weiss' apartment to congratulate her in her happy hour.

"We're all so happy for you," said her neighbor, R' Shlomo, with genuine feeling. "How wonderful that you have merited to see this day!"

"And what a *simchah*!" Mrs. Rabinowitz chimed in. "How long we've waited for this. *Nu,* may the words come true: 'Let us rejoice like the years of our suffering.' May there be only happiness in your home from now on!"

From the depths of their hearts, the widow Weiss' neighbors rejoiced with her in her good fortune. Tonight, her daughter had become engaged to a fine and talented young man by the name of Yossi Kahan — a young man who, by the looks of it, would go far in life. At least, that was the decidedly voiced opinion of one of the neighbors, Mr. Raanan, who considered himself an expert on human psychology. "Mark my words, I know people. He's a talented and energetic boy. You'll see that I'm right. After so much pain and sorrow, the widow Weiss deserves a little *nachas*."

Five years had passed, but it seemed like only yesterday when the neighbors had heard the heart-rending cries that froze the blood in their veins.

"Yerucham, what's the matter with you? Wake up! You're already late for *davening*. Yerucham, why are you sleeping so much? Yerucham, get up already! *Oy, oy,* he's not moving. He's not waking. HE-E-LP!"

R' Yerucham Weiss, a young man who had not yet reached his 50th year, had served as a *maggid shiur* in a boys yeshivah. That morning, he simply did not wake up.

Every other day, he woke at 6:30 a.m. On that morning, he was still in bed at 8. He did not respond to his wife's frantic calls and remained still as a stone.

Minutes later, the wail of a siren sounded outside. A team of medical rescue personnel jumped out of an ambulance and sprinted toward the apartment like madmen. To their dismay, there was nothing left to do. R' Yerucham had suffered a massive coronary and passed away in his sleep.

The following day and night were etched deeply in the memories of all the neighbors. How they sorrowed for the unfortunate Mrs. Weiss, left suddenly alone like a ship tossing wildly at sea. The young widow was mother to seven children. Assistance was organized immediately. Rabbis were pressed into service and collections taken up.

Thanks to the help she received both from friends and strangers, the widow managed a reasonable recovery. Mostly, it was thanks to the unceasing care of her neighbors, who would not rest until they had seen the family on its feet again. What the neighbors didn't know was that the lion's share of the money collected on the Weiss family's behalf had been gathered — with tremendous energy and with little regard to his own dignity — by the *gaon*, R' Naftali Berger, who threw himself with unusual dedication into the project.

Nobody knew about this neighbor's special effort. Quietly, away from the public eye, R' Naftali Berger took up donations for Mrs. Weiss and her children. After six months of intensive labor, a bank account was opened for the Weisses. The interest from that account kept the family fed for years.

Just as no one (apart from R' Yerachmiel Zigler, who had to be in on the secret because he was the one who administered the fund) knew of R' Naftali Berger's secret gift, no one knew, either, what motivated him.

The reason was very simple. R' Naftali had been R' Yerucham Weiss' closest friend. The two had worked together in the yeshivah, giving the same level *shiur*. R' Naftali gave the *shiur iyun* to the boys in the morning, while R' Yerucham had delivered the *bekius shiur* to the same boys in the afternoon. The two had been true friends of the heart.

R' Naftali knew very clearly that, unless he acted, his friend's widow and children were liable to starve. He knew Mrs. Weiss' parents well: She came from a prestigious family. In his opinion, Mrs. Weiss would prefer to go hungry rather than ask them for a handout. It was for this reason that he had secretly established the account in her name. Withdrawing money from the bank is not a source of embarrassment. No one need hide her head in shame in front of a bank clerk, because the money she is taking is not his to give. No bank teller would ever make Mrs. Weiss feel like a charity case.

Five years passed. R' Naftali was deeply distressed over the plight of his old friend's daughter, who had reached marriageable age some time ago without any good suggestions for a match. Everything fell through because of the question of money.

While the bank account sufficed to keep the family fed and clothed in a respectable fashion from month to month, there was nothing there to serve as a dowry for a needy bride. The amounts being demanded had climbed to insane heights. The widow was beside herself.

Very late one night, R' Naftali came to visit Rabbi Zigler. The hour of the visit surprised the rabbi, but not as much as R' Naftali's purpose in coming.

"You want to undertake the entire obligation? Are you sure?"

"One hundred percent!"

Rabbi Zigler was an accomplished and respected man, yet at this moment he felt he was facing a giant. R' Naftali Berger had come to tell him how to approach this matter. "Tell the widow Weiss that, if a good match is suggested for her daughter, she is not to reject it for lack of money. Let her commit herself to whatever amount is necessary. I will provide the entire amount!"

A month later, the sound of a shattering plate resounded in the hallway of the widow Weiss' building. Then came the emotional cries of "*Mazal tov*!" And R' Naftali Berger's cries were loudest of all.

It was not only the widow Weiss' who had no idea of her benefactor's identity (though he happened to live two floors above her). Not even R' Naftali's own wife knew of the obligation he had undertaken. She did, however, notice that he had seemed troubled and disquieted of late.

R' Naftali was at a loss. Where could he get tens of thousands of dollars? It had been a simple matter to commit himself; it would be far more difficult to fulfill the obligation. He had no idea where to begin putting together the first hundred dollars.

R' Berger was known throughout the city as an outstanding *talmid chacham* who had published well-received works of halachah and taught Torah to many. All the evening hours he had devoted to collecting funds for Mrs. Weiss' account had been — to use an extreme understatement — unpleasant to him. He repeated the words "Save a widow and her orphaned children" so often that they seemed worn out from overuse. In the homes where he was recognized, it was hard to say who was more embarrassed, he or his host. And where he was not known, the shame was sometimes even greater.

"The Weiss' widow and orphans? I gave yesterday."

"I know these stories. You probably made this one up on your way here."

"I think I know you from somewhere. Just a minute, just a minute … Are you that *shnorrer* that comes around every year around Chanukah time? I remember your face."

"Tell me outright that you're collecting for yourself. I don't mind if you're alive. You don't have to turn your wife into a widow for five shekel!"

"What young people today are prepared to do …"

"You look like a healthy young man. Go out and get a job!"

R' Naftali was a sensitive soul. These encounters nearly brought him to tears. It would be better to skin hides in the marketplace, he thought now, than to have to knock on another door and ask for money.

Then, thinking of his friend's widow, he pushed aside the memory of that awful time. He could not stand by with folded hands and do nothing. Once again, he had undertaken a too-heavy burden — and now the day of reckoning was upon him.

What was he to do?

"Matzah bakery seeking workers."

R' Naftali Berger re-read the newspaper ad thoughtfully. *Rosh Chodesh Teves* had just passed, and this year was a leap year with two Adar months. That meant four months of well-paid work ahead of him. If he slaved away for all those months, he could amass a nice amount of money, all of which would be dedicated to the Weiss *kallah*.

That evening, he traveled to the bakery in the northern section of the city, to ascertain the nature of the work and the salary it paid. All afternoon, he had toyed with thoughts of disguise. Perhaps he should dye his beard a different color?

"HaRav HaGaon R' Naftali Berger, well-known *maggid shiur*, has turned into a blue-collar worker in a matzah bakery." In his imagination, he could already hear the whispers behind his back, in the local *mikveh*, and at the shul entrance. Worst of all, what if the news spread to the yeshivah itself? He could not bear having the *roshei yeshivah* and other rebbis know.

To his satisfaction, he discovered that all the other workers apart from himself were young men from lower socio-economic classes. No one recognized him. Not even the bakery's *mashgiach* knew him. When he introduced himself simply as "Berger," not a single eyebrow was raised in surprise. He breathed a sigh of relief.

R' Naftali, who had never done a hard day's physical labor in his life, began to work evenings until late at night in the matzah bakery. At first he did the easier jobs, but when he learned that the workers who were doing the much harder tasks received higher pay, he steeled himself to ask for those jobs as well.

Along with all of this, he was forced to maintain a war of deception at home. At first, he mumbled something about some anonymous learning partner waiting for him in another neighborhood. But when his loyal wife saw how thin and pale he was becoming, she did not leave him alone until he was forced with a heavy heart to share his secret.

Rebbetzin Berger also came from a rabbinical home. She had never heard of such a thing. "A *talmid chacham* like yourself, hiring himself out for such work, and all for a stranger? Who would ever believe such a thing?"

"The widow Weiss is not a stranger!" R' Naftali said defensively. "Her husband was my best friend."

"But look where this has gotten you. You're pale and weak. I was afraid you were coming down with some terrible illness, Heaven forbid. I never dreamed you were doing this kind of work."

"So who's supposed to worry about the orphaned *kallah*?"

"*Baruch Hashem*, the Jewish people are not orphans. You are not responsible for finishing the job." The rebbetzin spoke calmly, but inside she was furious that her husband, whom she had always protected from doing physical work around the house out of respect for his honor, had undertaken such work and harmed his health on behalf of a stranger. He was practically sacrificing his life!

In a later argument, she added a statement that destroyed R' Naftali's peace. "Don't you see that they will return bad for the good you're doing them?"

"What do you mean?" R' Naftali asked.

"That's the way of the world. The greater the favor you do for someone, the greater their ingratitude."

"You mustn't speak that way about a fellow Jew!" R' Naftali said sharply. "Besides, I know Mrs. Weiss and her children. They are good people, noble people. And don't forget the main thing: They have no idea at all who's been collecting money for them. So what you're saying about ingratitude has no bearing here."

"You'll see," his wife said, ending the argument.

The months passed. R' Naftali Berger, who had been accustomed to preparing his *shiur* together with a learning partner in the afternoons, was forced to cancel the arrangement in order to make sure to be at the bakery on time. His preparation for *shiur* had to be squeezed into odd bits of time, a portion of it after lunch and some more very late at night, after he got home from work, exhausted from the hard physical labor.

It wasn't long before the results began to be noticed.

"Rabbi Berger isn't what he used to be," his students whispered to one another. "His *shiurim* have gone down in quality."

"Maybe he's sick," someone suggested. "He's been very pale and listless lately."

"Take a close look at him. Look at his eyes," another boy remarked.

"What's wrong with his eyes?" they asked.

"They look really happy — showing a kind of inner happiness," the boy explained. The others began to look more closely, and they saw at once what he meant. While it was true that R' Berger looked very tired and pale lately, his eyes were filled with a special, secret joy. Where was this coming from?

"Maybe he's really very sick, and is happy because he's getting ready to move on to the World to Come?" someone offered hesitantly. The suggestion was met with waves of laughter. "Why are you laughing?" he asked, bewildered. "I read that very great *tzaddikim* were happy before they died. All their lives they cling to Hashem, and once the time comes when they'll be really close to Him, they're happy!"

The laughter died down. One of the other boys said, "You're exaggerating. The kind of person you're describing would be one of the thirty-six hidden *tzaddikim* of the world. Since when have you decided to turn Rabbi Berger into one of the '*lamed-vavniks*'?"

⌘

"There are no secrets in this world," R' Naftali thought in despair.

That evening, a group of young yeshivah men had burst into the matzah bakery. "We'll be baking matzahs here tomorrow. We've come to *kasher* the bakery."

Hearing the voice, R' Berger darted into the darkest corner he could find. The speaker was none other than R' Giberstein, the rebbi of the second-level *shiur* at his own yeshivah! And he was accompanied by ten of the yeshivah's best boys. They all knew him very well. How would they react to the sight of R' Naftali Berger standing in working clothes by his worktable, side by side with young men who were clearly no *bnei yeshivah*? He was dusty, covered with flour, with a large apron wrapped around his neck and dangling down to his toes.

He tried not to stand out. As much as possible he bent his head, ostensibly to look for something that had fallen to the floor. But these stratagems did not work. There was a moment of stunned silence as R' Giberstein paled and nearly choked in the middle of a sentence. R' Naftali, head down, sensed the penetrating stares and the total astonishment being directed at him.

The group of yeshivah men left without saying a word. R' Naftali's secret had been exposed.

The next morning, R' Fogel, the *rosh yeshivah,* summoned R' Naftali to his office.

"R' Giberstein spoke with me this morning," he began. "Actually, 'spoke' is not the right word. He cried like a baby. 'Who knows what's happened to R' Berger,' he said, 'if he's come to this!'" R' Fogel seemed close to tears himself. "We never knew you were in such dire financial straits. I feel that the yeshivah is responsible. If only you had said something, just a hint, we would have managed a raise in salary."

R' Naftali felt suffocated. Before his eyes rose the image of his dear friend, R' Yerucham Weiss, a student of R' Fogel's from his youth.

Should he reveal his secret? If he did, others might offer their help in assisting the widow, and he would not have to live a double life that was sapping him of his last strength.

In the end, he decided to remain silent. "My *yetzer hara* is not stupid," he thought. "It's urging me, 'Please, tell R' Fogel all about it. He'll doubtless be unable to keep the story to himself and it will spread. Everyone will crown you with the title of *lamed-vavnik*, one of the thirty-six hidden *tzaddikim*, or something similar.'"

He looked up at the *rosh yeshivah*. "I can't."

"What can't you do?" R' Fogel asked in surprise.

"There is a good reason for what I'm doing, and it's not a question of financial hardship. But I'd like to keep it to myself."

R' Fogel's face darkened. "A man has free will. But don't forget that you have an honorable standing here. You must not degrade yourself. Tell me, please, what I am to do tomorrow if they come and tell me that another rebbi in this yeshivah has decided to become a street cleaner on the night shift?"

Tell him already! The thought flitted through R' Naftali's mind. The temptation was great — too great for him to bear. Pressing his lips tightly together, he stood up and left the room in silence. With every step he felt the *rosh yeshivah's* hard gaze on his back. Had it been anyone but R' Berger, R' Fogel would have issued an ultimatum on the spot: Either quit your night job, or leave the yeshivah. But R' Berger was special. He was dedicated and brilliant and there were few like him around.

What had happened to the man?

There was no happier fellow than R' Naftali when, a few days before Pesach, he laid the bundle of money on Rabbi Zigler's table. It was a significant sum. Though he still had a long way to go before he would fulfill his total obligation, he felt a great sense of release and satisfaction at what he had accomplished so far.

Rabbi Zigler measured him with his eyes. "I'm afraid that you've taken too much upon yourself. You're half the man you were last Chanukah."

"It's a perfect diet plan," R' Naftali joked.

The rabbi stared at him, astounded. How strong this *tzaddik* was! A respected rebbi at the yeshivah had turned himself into a common laborer, doing backbreaking work alongside men of inferior education for nearly half a year, and then giving every last penny of his earnings to a widowed neighbor so that she could respectably marry off her daughter!

"A nation of *tzaddikim*," Rabbi Zigler thought. "Who would have believed it?"

Nor would anyone have been able to predict, or believe, what happened next.

The widow Weiss' daughter was duly married to Yossi Kahan, with the secret help of R' Naftali Berger, who had managed in various ways — all of them painful — to come up with the remaining money. Some of it had come to him in the form of a loan, binding him hand and foot to moneylenders.

The young couple settled in a modest apartment in one of the new neighborhoods where prices were cheaper. They lived one floor above Tzvi Berger — R' Naftali Berger's oldest son, who had married a year before them.

It had been R' Naftali himself who had found the apartment for them in his usual quiet way. No one in the Weiss family stopped to wonder where the suggestion had come from to buy that particular, airy apartment with its possibilities for expansion. Preparations for the wedding had occupied them all exclusively.

What had the happy neighbor remarked on the night of the couple's engagement? "He's a talented boy. He'll go far in life."

Yossi Kahan indeed went far — in quarreling with his downstairs neighbors, the Bergers. He quarreled over the exact expansion plans he was making, over the succah porch he was proposing to add on that would cover half the succah space of the Bergers below, and over the eternal noise that emanated from his apartment late into the nights, disturbing the Bergers' rest. When Tzvi Berger, in his characteristically gentle way, tried to bring the noise to Yossi Kahan's attention, Yossi grew angry. "I'm a sensitive fellow, and until now whatever noise I made was unintentional. Now, I'm going to make noise on purpose, just to bother them!"

He kept his word emphatically.

⁓ↄ ᖆↄ

Tzvi Berger had his suspicions about his father's role in helping the Weiss girl reach the *chuppah*. A powerful intuition whispered that his father was the right place to take his problem.

"*Abba*, we can't take it anymore. Yossi Kahan has made our life a *gehinnom!*"

R' Naftali felt as though his heart was about to burst. Truly, *Chazal* have said, "Women were granted an extra measure of intuition." Hadn't his own wife told him, in so many words, "Don't you see, they will return bad for the good you're doing them. The greater the favor, the greater the ingratitude."

Bitterly, he went to see Rabbi Zigler. Perhaps the rabbi would agree to intervene, in the interest of peace.

As the elderly rabbi listened to the terrible story, he was shaken to his depths. He did not calm down until he had drunk several glasses of cold water. Then he settled himself to think over the situation. Finally, he said quietly, "That's the parable. Do you know its interpretation?"

R' Naftali Berger was a very intelligent man, blessed with a quick mind and an agile grasp. But he was at a loss to understand the rabbi's words.

Rabbi Zigler explained. "Your son's story, and your own, are the parable. The interpretation is — Man!

"A man receives everything from his Creator. A healthy body, limbs and sinews, wisdom and intelligence. And what does he do with them? He sins and angers the very One Who made him — the One Who granted him these gifts. He uses the gifts in order to anger the giver!

"You gave Mrs. Weiss' daughter a nice apartment. What is the honored *chasan* doing with that gift? He is quarreling with your own son, hounding him and embarrassing him in front of the other neighbors and whenever their paths cross."

R' Naftali sat transfixed. R' Zigler had shown him the matter in a whole new light. He had never looked at it in this way before.

He roused himself. "But what of my son? Will the *rav* speak to Yossi?"

"No! I believe that there is no need. *HaKadosh Baruch Hu* is long-suffering and patient when we sin toward Him. But the situation is otherwise when the issue is between two people — especially in a case of rank ingratitude, even unintentional. Heaven will not be silent!"

❧

Three years later ....

It happened on *Erev Pesach*. A large bonfire was lit in the neighborhood for the *chametz* burning. Tzvi Berger stood beside the blaze, a bag of *chametz* in his hand. Nearby stood his neighbor, Yossi Kahan, with his 2-year-old son Yerucham beside him gazing with rapt attention at the flames.

Tzvi Berger threw his *lulav* and *chametz* into the fire. Immediately, he opened his siddur and began to recite from it. Then he continued, "*Yehi ratzon milfanecha ... (May it be Your will ...)* Just as I am burning the *chametz* from my home and property," he said, "please burn the *yetzer hara* out of us."

Yossi Kahan turned, his expression gleeful. "True enough. You do need a special prayer to have your *yetzer hara* burned out of you!"

At that moment, a sudden shout went up. "Be careful, little boy! You're going to fall into the fire!"

Little Yerucham Kahan had edged up to the blaze to inspect it from close up. Another moment, and he would topple right into the flames.

"Help!" his father screamed. He himself was frozen in shock, unable to move. The flames began to lick the child's clothes.

Tzvi Berger reacted instantaneously. Without stopping to think, he darted into the fire, grabbed the child, and picked him up. An agonizing pain seared both his legs as he found a white-hot metal bar blocking his way out. With a mighty leap, he jumped over the bar with the boy in his arms.

Young Yerucham emerged from the fire nearly unscathed. But Tzvi Berger required long and intensive treatment for the burns on his legs.

❧

Rabbi Zigler was the one who finally gave away the secret.

"Our Sages have taught us about the greatness of giving secretly," he explained to the widow Weiss. "But that's when we're talking about two human beings. When, however, we have two people on one side who are more than human — a father and son who behave like angels — and on the other a man who hardly deserves the title, we are obligated to open his eyes in order to help him become human."

Yossi Kahan bawled like a baby. "If I had only known!" he sobbed repeatedly. "If I had only known a little bit of the truth!"

Rabbi Zigler regarded him for a long moment. "Now we've laid the groundwork for good neighborly relations," he said enthusiastically. "Are all those matzahs that R' Naftali Berger baked to lead only to quarrels and dissension?"

"No, Rebbi," Yossi Kahan answered in a chastened voice that left no doubt of his sincerity. "From now on, there will be only peace."

And, from then on, there was.

A CHILD'S NOTEBOOK

I. THE BIDDING

THE CIRCLES OF DANCERS OPENED AND CLOSED AS SONG followed lively song. The boys' faces were red with exertion, beads of perspiration dripping steadily from their foreheads. Then came the old, heartwarming tune: *"Baruch Hu Elokeinu she-*

bra'anu lichvodo ..." ("Blessed is our L-rd, Who created us for His glory ..."). The wild dancing switched in tempo. Legs that had been leaping and kicking with youthful animation touched ground again. "V'nasan lanu Toras emes..." ("And gave us a Torah of truth ..."), "Ay, ay, ay ..."

Afterward, when it was time to read the Torah portion, aliyos were sold according to ancient yeshivah tradition — to anyone who could outbid his fellow students with the number of Gemara pages to be learned.

"Five hundred pages for shlishi, going once, going twice," called the gabbai hoarsely.

"Seven hundred!" came a cry. The gabbai looked up to see Meyer Simcha Kugler, one of the older yeshivah bachurim, watching him hopefully. Before the gabbai had the chance to nod his head, there came a second cry: "One thousand!"

Near the aron kodesh, like a marble pillar, stood Chaim Leibowitz. He was among those who sat at the yeshivah's eastern wall. The glance he threw the gabbai was stern, as if to say, "Don't accept any more bids."

Everyone nodded in agreement. Chaim Leibowitz was worthy of receiving shlishi on Simchas Torah. He was nearly 25 years old now.

Then a surprise occurred. "One thousand, five hundred!"

The unexpected call fell on the yeshivah like a bomb. All heads turned to seek the author of that call. To complete 1,500 pages of Gemara, with Rashi and Tosafos (no exceptions or excuses!) between this Simchas Torah and the next was no light matter.

The bidder was none other than Shmulie Tauber. One of the best and brightest of the students, no one doubted that he would fulfill any goal he undertook. Apart from his regular studies in yeshivah, he would learn the 1,500 extra pages, and he would learn them well!

But no one understood what motivated Shmulie, only 22, to compete with veteran Chaim Leibowitz, his senior by three years. As for Chaim, he gave in on that aliyah but continued his bidding. He finally won shishi of that same Torah reading, at the "price" of 1,200 pages.

By the end of the bidding, six outstanding yeshivah *bachurim* were called up to the Torah for the prestigious *aliyos,* which they had purchased for a collective thousands of pages of *Gemara.*

Why the fierce competition?

According to the tradition in Yeshivas Noda B'Yehudah, all those who were called up to the Torah on Simchas Torah were invited to join the *rosh yeshivah, HaGaon* R' Elisha Frankel, at his Seder that Pesach. Furthermore, each of those who sat at R' Frankel's Seder table that year would not be sitting there again the following year — because it was guaranteed that, during the course of that year, he would get married and establish his own Jewish home. He would enjoy the following year's Seder at either the home of his father or his father-in-law.

This was a long-standing tradition in the yeshivah, fixed for twenty years: Whoever was present at the *rosh yeshivah's* Seder would be married during the following twelve months! This was the source of the competition, especially among the older students, to capture an *aliyah* that would win them a place at that coveted Seder table.

R' Elisha made one condition: The *aliyah* must be "bought" at a price of no less than at least 300 pages of *Gemara.*

Thus was born the eager competition. By Simchas Torah afternoon, everyone knew exactly who would be glued to his *shtender* during the coming year, who would be invited to join the *rosh yeshivah* at his Seder table, and who would become engaged and married at some point during the following year.

That was the tradition.

II. SEDER NIGHT

"Good *Yom Tov*." The *rosh yeshivah* and his wife stood at their door to receive their honored guests. Apart from R' Elisha Frankel's children and grandchildren, there were also last-minute additions: poor folk with no home of their own, an old man who had left the nursing home in honor of the holiday ...

And the crown of them all: the six students! Each of these young men had accepted a burden of hundreds of additional pages of *Gemara.*

The house was brilliantly lit with electric lights, but it was clear to all present that there was more than just a physical source to the illumination. It came from a spiritual "current," a light that descended to earth each year on Pesach night, when *HaKadosh Baruch Hu* and His Heavenly Court listen with pleasure to His children happily fulfilling the mitzvah of "*V'higadeta l'vincha*" ("And you shall tell your son").

After *Kiddush,* everyone drank the first of the four cups of wine, washed their hands to eat the *karpas,* and then launched into the recitation of the Haggadah. R' Elisha raised a question about the different forms that the "*Mah Nishtanah*" takes in our Hagaddah, in *Mishnah Pesachim,* and the format of the *Rif* and the *Rosh.* At once, the beautifully-set table erupted in a heated discourse, as Chaim Leibowitz began in his usual energetic fashion to explicate the matter according to the opinions of the *Rishonim* and the *Acharonim.* But Chaim was not the only eager student present. His yeshivah friends had their own contributions to make to the discussion. The peaceful, sparkling house was transformed into a yeshivah *beis midrash.*

None of the family members was taken aback at the uproar. They were well used to this kind of scene, which repeated itself each year. The yeshivah students who attended their Seder were always the "lions" among the boys. The *rosh yeshivah's* sons and sons-in-law, learned men themselves, debated freely with the yeshivah students while the women and other guests waited patiently on the sidelines, glancing through their own Haggadahs until R' Elisha took pity on them, and with a flick of his finger magically brought the stormy session to an end.

These Torah discussions and arguments repeated themselves at various points throughout the Seder, during the meal, and especially afterwards. While the other guests nodded off and dozed soundlessly over their Haggadahs, the *rosh yeshivah* and his students continued their heated debates nearly till morning.

That was the tradition, year after year.

III. KINDERGARTEN QUESTIONS

"I'd like to say a short *vort,* if I may," said Shmulie Tauber, the youngest of the yeshivah group.

"Of course." The *rosh yeshivah* smiled. A *vort* from Shmulie Tauber was always worth hearing.

Blushing, Shmulie pulled out an old-fashioned child's notebook. Reading from the notebook, he asked a question that 5-year-old might have posed, and then offered an answer that would probably have been suggested by a sharp-witted 7-year-old.

Confusion reigned momentarily around the table. Everyone was astonished to hear Shmulie, of fine mind and high caliber of learning, speaking in a way that suddenly peeled fifteen years off his age. But the *rosh yeshivah* was quick to find a deeper meaning in the question and answer, and explained it according to the Maharal of Prague. The discussion caught fire.

Some five minutes later, there was another lull. The group began once again to recite the Haggadah. They came to the words, *"V'she'eno yode'a lishol, at pesach lo"* ("And to he who knows not how to ask, you open [the discussion] for him").

"Can I say a short *vort*?"

It was Shmulie Tauber again. Calmly, he opened his old notebook and read, "Why does it say *'at pesach lo'*? It should have said *'atah'*! To tell us that, in order to teach this kind of son — one who does not yet know how to ask — we must speak pleasantly, the way a compassionate mother speaks."

His five friends from the yeshivah found themselves blushing with embarrassment. They could not believe what they were hearing. Apparently Shmulie was too young. Didn't he understand that, in this house, on this great night, one did not recite this kind of homespun wisdom? Especially not the kind that seemed — well, a little childish?

The *rosh yeshivah's* son-in-law saved the situation by branching into a related topic. Under cover of the others' voices, Meyer Simcha Kugler whispered to Shmulie, "Is anything wrong?"

"No, why?"

"You paid 1,500 pages of *Gemara* in order to offer insights that would do credit to a fourth-grader? At this table, we don't give these little *vorts*! A *bachur* like you has much more to offer. And if you don't, it's better for you not to volunteer anything of your own, but only to add something pertinent to ongoing discussions. For Heaven's sake, please don't embarrass yourself and the rest of us!"

Shmuel stared at him blankly. If Meyer Simcha hadn't been sure before, a moment later he knew that his words had fallen on deaf ears. Once again, Shmulie Tauber pulled out his old notebook. He read something about the initials of the ten plagues: *D'tzach, Adash, B'Achav.* The other *bachurim* nudged one another meaningfully. Obviously, they didn't really know Shmulie that well. Some of them smiled, smiles of pity and condescension.

Chaim Leibowitz could not restrain himself. To his good friend, Yonah Schwartz, he whispered, "Shmulie heard that one from his *cheder* rebbi!"

"But when?" Yonah asked.

"Yesterday, it seems."

Yonah's face creased with silent laughter. It was only with difficulty that he got himself under control.

"Don't laugh; *'es past nisht,'*" Chaim Leibowitz whispered. "Besides, don't forget — he's an orphan. He lost his father at the age of 10. Maybe there's something lacking in his personality because of that."

Shmulie ignored both the surprised looks and the momentous questions being raised and answered all around him. Every time there was a brief lull in the proceedings, he used it to read another little *vort* from his old notebook. So far, he had offered ten of them.

"*Ilu kara lanu es hayam v'lo he'eviranu b'socho b'charavah ... Dayeinu!*" ("Had [Hashem] split the sea and not passed us through on dry land — that would have been enough!") Shmulie looked up. "But wasn't the sea split specifically in order to let us pass?"

"Why, then?" Meyer Simcha asked, deadpan.

"The answer is that the Haggadah wants to tell us that we would have passed through the sea in any case — but through deep mud, not a smooth, easy path. That's why we thank Hashem and say '*Dayeinu'!*"

"There is genius in simplicity," the *rosh yeshivah* said quickly, into the silence. But he was too late.

With the force of an explosion, the laughter burst forth from the other yeshivah students. Though they did not want to laugh on such an occasion, their sense of the ridiculous proved too strong. In the way of laughter, it rose and expanded. The more they tried to choke it back, the stronger it grew, exploding out of them uncontrollably.

Peals of merriment filled the room. The yeshivah boys laughed until they cried. Though some tried to disguise their amusement by coughing hard, the ruse was all too transparent.

Shmulie sat, notebook in hand, biting his lip. There was a strange gleam in his eye.

"Bring the washing bowls," R' Elisha ordered his daughters. "We're ready for the meal."

"But we're not up to the meal yet!" protested the man from the old-age home.

"We will be in a minute." In a rapid murmur, the *rosh yeshivah* finished reciting the Haggadah. Soon everyone was chewing their portions of matzah, faces serious once again. The aftereffect of the unfortunate incident lingered for a while, before other conversation came to replace it.

It was unclear just how long it would take Shmulie to restore his good name among his fellow students after his behavior tonight. But that behavior did not appear to disturb him at all.

IV. THE NOTEBOOK DISAPPEARS

R' Elisha was angry at his star student, Shmulie Tauber. What was the meaning of his silly behavior at the Seder? Why should such an outstanding student, a young man of whom others spoke with respect, turn himself into a laughingstock?

At the end of the meal, the *rosh yeshivah* went out onto the enclosed porch. "I need some fresh air," he said as he apologized to his guests. On his way out, he lightly touched Shmulie's shoulder.

Shmulie took the hint. A moment later, he, too, left for the porch.

"I don't understand," R' Elisha said, trying to speak patiently though his displeasure was noticeable in every word. "Have you decided to bring back the old days of Novaradok tonight, in my house?"

Shmulie paled. "I don't understand," he said, echoing his *rosh yeshivah*.

"The students of Novaradok used to cause themselves to be ridiculed — for instance, by asking for nails in a pharmacy — in an effort to subdue their pride. I am protective of your honor, Shmulie. Why should a brilliant boy like yourself, who is fully capable of developing wonderful new systems of thought, make himself out to be the village idiot? You acted with forethought and planning, using old *vertlach* out of a child's notebook, like a boy in *cheder*."

Shmulie thought a moment, as though debating whether to speak or to remain silent.

"*Nu, nu?*" urged the *rosh yeshivah.*

"It's not my notebook," Shmulie said.

"Whose it is?"

"It was my father's, may he rest in peace. My father, R' Yosef Tauber, would read these *vertlach* every year, out of this notebook. It was a ritual in our house on Seder night. My father passed away when I was 10, and before he died he asked me to continue the tradition each year. 'Wherever you are, and in whatever circumstances, guard this notebook. And every year, on Seder night, say over the *divrei Torah* written inside.'" Shmulie met R' Elisha's eyes. "That's what he commanded me to do. So every year, on Seder night, I read these *vertlach* out of the notebook, even though I know them by heart."

The *rosh yeshivah's* astonishment began to fade. Shmulie's strange behavior could now be seen in an entirely different light. But a new sense of amazement came in to replace the first. "R' Yosef Tauber?" R' Elisha exclaimed. "From what you've told me, your father was an outstanding *talmid chacham.* Why in the world was he so particular about this tradition?" The *rosh yeshivah's* forehead creased in puzzlement. "Give me the notebook for a minute, please."

Shmulie handed it over to R' Elisha.

With avid curiosity, the others were watching them from the dining room. But only Shmulie noticed them. The *rosh yeshivah* was engrossed in the contents of the notebook.

"It's very old," he murmured. "You can see that." He turned the pages with care.

Shmulie didn't understand why the blood drained suddenly from R' Elisha's face, and why the *rosh yeshivah* began to tremble from head to toe. R' Elisha leaned weakly against a wall.

"Tell me, how did your father get this notebook?" he asked tensely. There was a powerful, repressed excitement in his face.

"I don't know. All I know is that it belonged to his younger brother, who was killed in the Holocaust. My father said something about a train," Shmulie said.

"And where was your father from?"

"He was born near Karkov. I don't remember the name of the village."

"Has your family name always been Tauber?"

Shmulie was taken aback. Quietly, he answered, "No. Our original name was Weissman. My grandfather changed it during the war because of the passport he was using to save himself and his family from the Nazis at the last minute."

"And your grandfather, R' Shimon — is he still alive?"

Shaken by the interrogation, Shmulie stammered, "N-no. He passed away just after they moved to Eretz Yisrael."

"That's what I thought." R' Elisha seemed to wake from a trance. Tears collected in the corners of his eyes and dripped slowly down to his beard.

"It's late. Soon we'll have passed the time to eat the *afikoman*," he said. He stepped back into the dining room, with a bewildered Shmulie following behind. As they entered the large dining room, it seemed to the others that the *rosh yeshivah's* shoulders sagged a little. As for Shmulie, he appeared confused. He was trying with all his might to remember whether he had ever mentioned his grandfather's name to the *rosh yeshivah*.

V. "A BRILLIANT QUESTION!"

"Shmulie, perhaps you'd like to share with us a little *vort* from your notebook?"

All those seated around the table were very tired. Suddenly, heads shot up and ears sharpened. Who had decided to poke fun at Shmulie now, to hurt his feelings just when everyone had forgotten all about his earlier, embarrassing behavior?

Then, to their total astonishment, they saw that the speaker had been none other than the *rosh yeshivah* himself!

Softly, R' Elisha repeated his invitation, eyes glowing with an odd light. Everyone turned to Shmulie, who was once again flipping pages in his old notebook. He read aloud, "'My brother, Elisha, asked me: Why were the two songs, *Echad Mi Yode'a* and *Chad Gadya,* placed next to one another in the Haggadah?'"

"A brilliant question!" mocked Chaim Leibowitz. Swiftly, the *rosh yeshivah* turned a gaze on him that pierced like an arrow. Chaim subsided at once.

"And what answer is brought down there?" R' Elisha asked Shmulie pleasantly.

Shmulie read: "'I answered him that the two songs are really one and the same. Our One G-d, in Heaven and earth, will one day take His revenge and slaughter the Angel of Death, who wishes to slaughter the one lamb — that's the Jewish nation, a single lamb among seventy wolves.'"

Nobody laughed.

VI. YUDELE'S SECRET

"I want to tell you a little story," the *rosh yeshivah* said to the table at large. Everyone sat up expectantly, ready for some incredible new insight. The learned R' Elisha wanted to tell a story!

"There were three of us brothers living in a house in Pordgorz, near Karkov," the *rosh yeshivah* began. He and Shmulie Tauber exchanged a fleeting glance. "We were young, and we were wild. We learned in the local *cheder,* my two brothers and I. Yudele was three years younger than I; Yossel was the oldest, already 12 years old. Little Yudele was a handsome child, with lots of authentic Jewish *chen*. On Shabbos, when he was dressed in his little coat and cap, a light seemed to radiate from him. Yudele had round, innocent cheeks framed by his dangling *peyos,* and dark eyes that always shone with intelligence. His smile would warm the stoniest heart. I remember that the gentiles in the area would always speak jealously about the charm and innocence of Jewish children."

R' Elisha's voice broke. Two large tears spurted suddenly from his eyes, to make their slow way down to his silvery beard. After a brief pause, he drew a breath and continued.

"But the important thing was not the 'container,' but rather its contents. Yudele had many talents, along with a will and determination unusual in a child his age. Everyone predicted a bright future for him. No one doubted that, if he continued on his present path, he would end up to be a Torah leader of his generation. Even at the tender age of 7 he was already writing down his original Torah insights. With a stub of pencil he scribbled them on any scrap of paper he could lay his hands on, so that he would not forget the thought that had flashed through his mind at that minute. In those days paper was not in as ample supply as it is today, and it was nearly impossible to get a real notebook.

"How happy Yudele was when, over the course of one whole, long winter, he managed to save up some money, kopek after careful kopek. 'Elisha,' he told me one day, his face shining with pleasure, 'I have enough money to buy a notebook. Now I'll be able to write down, in an orderly way, all the *vertlach* that I've thought up on the Pesach Haggadah!'

"And, indeed, from that day Yudele began to write in earnest. School was out before the holiday, and Yudele sat writing during every free moment. In total seriousness he looked through *sefarim,* spoke to rabbis ... and wrote. Just like a grown man. I remember well R' Gedalia Fisch, a prominent *talmid chacham* who sat near Yudele in shul. He peeked into the boy's notebook and then ran over, with joy, to my father. 'R' Shimon, your Yudele will be great in Torah. He is a truly original thinker. A boy of 7 who can already write like that!'

"That was Pesach of the year 1939. In September, the Nazis invaded Poland, destroying our lives down to the very foundations. I don't know why Heaven chose to let me live, while my pure and holy brother went down in the flames."

R' Elisha stopped again, his throat choked with tears. The rebbetzin, concerned, hurried over with a glass of hot tea. But the *rosh yeshivah* pushed the glass away. "It is forbidden to drink after the *afikoman*. You know that," he said softly. "The taste of the *afikoman* — reminding us of the *korban Pesach* — must linger in our mouths."

He looked around the table and took up the thread of his story once more.

"I will never forget the moment we parted ways. The Nazi soldiers in their crisp uniforms rampaged through the town, gathering all the Jews in the market square. Then they did a 'selection.' My father, my 12-year-old brother Yossel, and I were supposed to be sent to a labor camp. I was a strong and well-developed boy and looked like Yossel's twin. My mother and little Yudele were forced to board the train to Auschwitz. We ran after them until the train station, wanting to say good-bye, for our hearts foretold that we would never see one another again.

"Yudele had something in his hand. With eyes filled with sorrow, he reached out to hand it to me. 'Elisha, this is my notebook, with the *chiddushim* that I wrote down on the Pesach Haggadah. Since then, I wrote down a few more things. I was so looking forward to saying them next year, at the Seder table. But that won't happen now. I'm afraid that they're going to kill us. Look at those Germans' faces — what wickedness, what hate. They're not human beings, but beasts of prey ... I'll be gone without a trace. Please, for the sake of my *neshamah,* remember me each year on Seder night. Say over my *chiddushim* at the table. In that way, you will remember me and help my *neshamah.*'

"The train began to make its chugging sound. A cruel Nazi soldier yanked Yudele away and threw him into the car as if he were a sack of turnips. The notebook fell out of his hand and landed on the ground, between the railroad tracks.

"'Yudele! The notebook!' I screamed. Then my knees buckled and I fainted."

VII. "WE WERE ALL WEISSMAN"

"When I woke, I found myself in a dark cellar filled with potatoes. The cellar was beneath the house of old Marichka, a gentile peasant who had accepted a lot of money from my parents in return for hiding me. As soon as the Nazis had overrun Pordgorz and begun their cruel killings, my father had decided to prepare a place of concealment for us at this old woman's home. He knew her to have a good nature and he trusted her. And my father was right. Marichka proved loyal. She did not give me away to the Nazis, but kept me hidden in her cellar until the end of the war.

"From the day I was dragged from the station and hidden in Marichka's cellar, I lost all contact with my father and my brother, Yossel. As for the notebook, I had no idea what had become of it. After the war, I joined a group of refugees who had somehow, like me, managed to hold onto life. Together, we made our way to Eretz Yisrael. Here I began a new life. I learned in yeshivah and, with Hashem's blessing, married and established a family of my own.

"The pain remained in my heart for many years. Why had it been decreed that I must remain alone? Why had I not been able to fulfill my poor brother's last request? I prayed that the day would come when I would meet my family again, or at least learn what their fate had been. I prayed, too, that Yudele's notebook would reach me somehow. In the depths of my heart, though, I worried that this was a vain hope. The notebook had been lost on train tracks in Poland. How would it ever reach me? Would an angel descend from Heaven and hand it to me?

"But — my prayers have borne fruit! Tonight, I met my brother's son. Very belatedly, I have learned the fate of the rest of my family — and also learned that the precious notebook was not lost after all. I know now that, when I fainted beside the railroad tracks, my brother Yossel was standing nearby. Thinking that I had died, he grabbed the notebook, hiding it quickly from evil Nazi eyes. He would make sure to fulfill poor Yudele's request.

"I know now, too, that Yossel was saved from the Holocaust and managed to reach Eretz Yisrael. He guarded the notebook zealously, and made sure to read Yudele's *vertlach* to his family each year at the Seder table. One of his sons is sitting right here with us.

"The boy who darted onto the train tracks to get the notebook was named Yosef Tauber. More accurately, in those days he was still called Yosef Weissman. Later, for various reasons, he changed his name to Tauber."

R' Elisha clutched the old notebook. With unsteady fingers he managed to turn to the first page, which he held up for the others to see:

"*Chiddushim* and *divrei Torah* on the Pesach Haggadah. Some of which *Hashem Yisbarach* granted me, and a little that I came up with together with my brother, Elisha. Nisan 5699. Yehudah Weissman."

"*What?*" Shmulie almost shouted. "But — but the *rosh yeshivah's* name is Frankel!"

"And wasn't your father called 'Tauber'?" R' Elisha answered shakily. "We were all Weissman. Before I boarded the boat to France, and from there to Eretz Yisrael, they put me together with a family named Frankel. That's when I took on that name. Later, I considered taking back the name 'Weissman,' to make it easier for any surviving family members to find me. But I was already a grown man by then, and I was embarrassed to get up one morning and change my name. I had begun a new life and was afraid that people would look askance at me."

The electric lights had long since gone out. The large dining room was lit only by the small, flickering flames of the long-burning candles. The darkness and the flickering lights imbued the room with mystery.

"Do you see?" the *rosh yeshivah* asked with a sigh. "How blind my eyes were! I didn't remember the notebook, and was angry with Shmulie tonight. At long last, my dream had come true, but I didn't understand. Had I not been afraid of society at the time, I would have changed my name back to the original version. Then a good man by the name of Yosef Tauber might have heard the name Elisha Weissman. We might have met again.

"But that did not happen. My dear brother Yosef passed away when still young, and we did not have the merit of seeing one another again. But his son, my outstanding student, Shmulie — the nephew that I have discovered tonight — is more stubborn than I. Without shame or fear of 'What they'll say,' he preferred to look like a fool as long as he fulfilled his father's wishes. He sat and read the *chiddushim* of a young boy, a child who was plucked in his innocence, having never tasted sin."

R' Elisha wept quietly for a long time, shoulders trembling gently with his sobs. His wife watched him anxiously, fearful for his health. Again she tried to press the glass of tea on him, but the *rosh yeshivah* pushed the glass aside.

"It is forbidden to let the taste of the *korban* leave our mouths. *Ay, ay, ay,* the taste of the sacrifice will stay forever!"

AN ORDINARY YOUNG MAN

I. BELOW AVERAGE

BY THE TIME YOSSI MILEVSKI WAS 16, HIS PARENTS — Menachem and Tirza Milevski, an educated pair — knew that it would not be easy to marry him off.

Yossi was a good boy, pious, sincere, filled with good *middos* and a desire to help others. What he lacked was that sharp edge that characterized a really special *bachur* — the kind of young man who, when his future father-in-law walks out to shul, elicits comments like, "Your son-in-law, what a boy — just brilliant!" The father-in-law would beam with joy and *nachas,* returning home later with the feeling that he had just made the best deal in the world.

As for the future mother-in-law, she would get the same reactions when she went out, and her phone would not stop ringing with enthusiastic compliments about her daughter's brand-new *chasan.* One caller would describe the boy's unending diligence, first glimpsed when he was only 7; the seeds of greatness could be seen in him already then! Another would praise his excellent mind and predict a glowing future in the highest Torah circles. These were the kinds of calls that uplift the heart like the merry chirping of birds outside your window on a spring morning.

But there was no chance, his parents thought sadly, that Yossi's future in-laws, when his time came, were destined to hear even a quarter of these praises. What could be said about Yossi? He was below average in his studies, with weak skills. Even in his childhood it was clear that he was not cut out for greatness. No one would be rushing to spread this wonderful news. The phones would be silent.

A silent phone on the morning after her child becomes engaged is enough to break any mother's heart. The bitter and inescapable truth, in case she hadn't wanted to face it before, was that her future son-in-law was nothing special. She would quietly "eat her heart out" and a few gray hairs might pop out on her head.

Menachem Milevski had been teaching at a Talmud Torah for twenty-five years. He knew students, and he also knew that not all that glitters is gold. Many students resembled his son, Yossi. They had average abilities and lacked the flash of brilliance that teachers like to see. They are not the first to raise their hands in class, letting the more talented learners among them demonstrate their gifts instead. But Menachem Milevski, from long experience, could attest to the fact that, in many cases, it was the average student who often shone forth as the years went on, while the more "brilliant" ones could prove a disappointment.

He hoped and believed that his Yossi would surprise them all one day.

The trouble was that Yossi's *maggid shiur* in yeshivah, his *mashgiach,* and his friends did not think like his father. They did not need hope for the future to help them sleep better at night. For them, it was enough that Yossi was Yossi: a good boy, a nice boy, outgoing, caring. Once in a while, Yossi, too, would catch the fever of diligence and learn scores of *Gemara* pages "in a single breath." Who needed more than that?

Yossi's mother, Mrs. Tirza Milevski, worked for many years as a high-school teacher, and she shared fully in her husband's feelings and concerns. Her own long teaching experience, as well as her feminine sensitivity, helped her to pinpoint the various kinds of students as early as the first week of school. She saw which girls were popular among their friends but lackluster when it came to classroom performance, and who would go far in life despite an externally bland expression. Always, she prayed to the Master of the Universe that, when the time came to help find a wife for her son, she would find a girl who typified the best of what she had seen in her classrooms: a girl who was quiet and gentle, pious and of good character, no frippery-brained "class queen" — someone, in short, who would suit Yossi's abilities (or lack thereof) in every way.

"Don't worry today about tomorrow's troubles," people say. Menachem and Tirza Milevski distracted themselves from their worry about Yossi's future; he was, after all, only 16. First of all, he could still show signs of improvement, and second, why burden themselves now with future worries? Let sorrow or joy come in its own time.

In the meantime, the couple dealt with the present: teaching, earning a living, and raising their children. They seemed to forget their anxiety over Yossi.

But a worm of worry will burrow into the staunchest heart, so that in the still of the night, when sleep won't come, the question comes back to haunt an anxious parent. What will become of Yossi? What will become of him?

II. ANONYMOUS

The years passed like a flitting shadow. Yossi Milevski was now 20 years old. His parents' hopes and dreams had long since shattered on the rock of reality. Twenty years are enough to tell the wheat from the chaff in anyone. Yossi did not, and never would, merit the label "brilliant." On the other hand, he was not called a "weak boy," either. He was not called anything. An average young man, he was neither praised nor censured. There was not much to say about him, either way. Yossi Milevski was just one of the faceless horde — unnoticed, almost anonymous.

His parents explained to the matchmakers that Yossi was simply unlucky. He was able enough, but lacked the confidence and daring spirit that characterized other boys. That was why he was generally so quiet. "But he's gold," Menachem Milevski assured Chaim Mendel the *shadchan.* "Whoever marries him will be the happiest girl in the world, I promise you!"

Chaim Mendel's "practice" generally took him to the homes of *roshei yeshivah, mashgichim, maggidei shiur,* rabbis, and teachers. He dealt with the elite. Why, he wondered, had Menacham Milevski chosen him? Didn't he know that his precious son would never marry a *rosh yeshivah's* daughter? A wise man knows his place. And in order to help every prospective groom know his place, the matchmaker equipped himself with a thick notebook in which he jotted down all the young men's names and vital statistics. In a cryptic code that only he understood, he would categorize each one: his level of learning, his social standing among his peers, his talents and abilities, lineage, financial means, the young man's personal health and his family's health history, and other symbols that helped him cope with the problem of too little time. His system allowed him to size up a prospect at a glance. Next to Yossi Milevski's name, in his private code, Chaim Mendel had summed up the *bachur:* Nothing much. Not for the likes of Chaim Mendel, matchmaker to the stars.

The moment Menachem Milevski left his house, Chaim Mendel — with a sigh of relief — hurried over to the home of the *gaon,* R' Bezalel Kahane, *rosh yeshivah* of Yeshivas Ma'ayanos HaTalmud. He had a brilliant inspiration for a match for the *rosh yeshivah's* outstanding daughter. The boy he had in mind was, naturally, the elite of the elite, someone whose future stood outlined in gold — a future *rosh yeshivah* himself, in the matchmaker's opinion and that of the young man's teachers and friends.

With prospects such as these to work with, was it any wonder that Chaim Mendel had no time to waste on the likes of Yossi Milevski?

III. A YEAR OF SILENCE

A full year passed. Menachem and Tirza laughed bitterly at their old worry about phones ringing in their future *mechutan's* home to tell him the sad truth about his future son-in-law. There were no such phone calls, because the phone did not ring in their own home. Not a single matchmaker rang them up to suggest a prospect for their Yossi. As Menachem Milevski left the house for the Talmud Torah each morning, he would glance at the phone: Maybe today was the day. Maybe someone would call. His wife left some thirty minutes earlier for her own teaching job, and she, too, cast an imploring glance at the phone on her way out: Would the miracle occur today?

After a full day of work, Menachem would return home with a single, burning question: "Did anyone call today?"

Always, the answer was a brief, sad, "No."

It was "No" times 365. A full year of silence.

When the year was behind them, Menachem decided that it was impossible to wait any longer. Yossi was his eldest; after him waited a line of three daughters approaching their own marriageable ages. If the calls were not coming to him, Menachem would go out to them.

He sat down beside the telephone and began to call each of the matchmakers, one by one.

After two weeks of hard telephone work, there was a gleam of light at the end of the tunnel. Someone referred Menachem to a certain woman who made matches solely *"l'shem Shamayim — for the sake of Heaven."* This good woman specialized in boys like Yossi who were mediocre or weak. Wondrous tales were told of her; she seemed to have been blessed with special Heavenly assistance. Just two days after listening to what Menachem had to say about his son, the phone rang for the first time with the longed-for message. Someone was interested in Yossi!

"I have a *shidduch* for your son," the matchmaker said happily. "Someone special. I have just one question first: Will Yossi insist on wearing a *shtreimel* after the wedding?"

Menachem began to stammer. "L-look, we're chassidim, our whole family wears *shtreimels.* Why should Yossi be any different?"

"Heaven forbid!" the woman exclaimed apologetically. "It's just that I have a wonderful girl for him, only her family doesn't wear *shtreimels.* But maybe that won't hold things back."

But it wasn't the question of a *shtreimel* that held back the match. The girl's father, an outstanding *talmid chacham* by the name of R' Meir Nudel, didn't much care whether his son-in-law wore a *shtreimel* or a hat. It wasn't the headgear that determined his preference for a *shidduch,* but the head underneath.

R' Meir learned all week long in a distant town, arriving home only for Shabbos, but he was in daily telephone contact with his wife. Hearing about the proposed match, he phoned Yossi Milevski's *rosh yeshivah* and heard the following rosy portrait: "Yossi is not the biggest scholar in the world, but he knows how to learn and learns with pleasure. He has wonderful *middos* and a heart of gold, and he is pious and gentle." On that basis, R' Meir Nudel gave his consent to let the match move forward. The two mothers met, and very nearly concluded matters. All that was left was the traditional breaking of the plate.

Then — at the very last minute — the whole thing blew up in their faces.

"Even a cat can ruin a match," goes the old folk saying. In this case, it was no cat, but one of Mrs. Nudel's sisters-in-law who did the ruining. Hearing about the prospective *shidduch,* she wasted no time in phoning Mrs. Nudel. "What," she demanded, "has your wonderful talented Ruti done to deserve a weak boy like Yossi Milevski? Yossi learned together with my son in *cheder* for seven years, and he excelled in only one thing: a complete lack of excellence! Is Ruti, Heaven forbid, a cripple? Does she have some sort of defect that I don't know about? Don't you understand that this match is simply unsuitable? Ruti is a talented girl, outstanding in every area, while Yossi Milevski is, to put it plainly, mediocre. What were you thinking?"

Mrs. Nudel, shaken, asked what else her sister-in-law could tell her about Yossi. Straining every brain cell, the other woman came up with whatever tiny grains of memory she could muster — insignificant things when taken in context, but which in this case loomed large as mountains.

Within minutes, the two women had finished off their conversation — and the match.

IV. A BITTER DISAPPOINTMENT

Yossi stayed home. He had been all dressed and ready to travel to Jerusalem for the *vort.* His sisters, too, were dressed in their best and nearly beside themselves with excitement for their brother. Then, out of the blue, came the phone call.

"We want to think about it a little more," Mrs. Nudel said evasively. "Let's not rush into anything." The simple words took all the wind out of the Milevskis' sails.

There were no dramatic heart attacks or fainting spells on the heels of that traumatic phone call. But anyone who has ever experienced a *shidduch* falling through at the last minute will never forget the pain, humiliation, and bitterness.

Ruti, the almost-*kallah,* on the other hand, did not stay home. That outstanding girl did not suffer as much as a single day of "silent telephone." No announcement had been made, no plate had been broken. Ruti's prospects still shone as bright as crystal. Apart from a few isolated individuals, no one knew about the proposed and rejected match. Ruti had not lacked marriage suggestions before Yossi came along, and she lacked none now. Just a day or two later, Chaim Mendel called with a sterling proposal — the son of a certain *gaon,* a *maggid shiur* in an elite yeshivah. The young man in question was himself a serious scholar and was considered an excellent catch for any girl.

Two weeks after the fateful Tuesday when the Milevski family was forced to abandon their trip to Jerusalem, they opened the newspaper to read a festive engagement announcement. The printed words seemed to leap up at them from the page, salting their still-raw hearts with fresh pain.

Wryly, Menachem Milevski told his wife, "*Nu,* is it any wonder they didn't want us? Look who they hooked up with instead. It's a brilliant match, exactly what they wanted. We're not in their league."

What the Milevski family couldn't know was that the day before, just half an hour before the new *shidduch* was made formal in Jerusalem, a certain matchmaker who knew nothing about the events of a couple of weeks earlier suddenly remembered Yossi Milevski and was struck by inspiration: Yossi would do very well for Ruti Nudel. Not being one to waste any time, the *shadchan* had picked up a phone and dialed the Nudel number in Jerusalem — oblivious to the fact that, on that very evening, preparations were in full swing for a *vort.* Ruti's younger sister answered the phone. Because of all the noise and tumult around her, she did not fully grasp what the man at the other end was talking about. Obediently, she jotted down what he told her to write: "Yosef Milevski, 21 years old, as full of good qualities as a pomegranate is with seeds, modest and refined, not brilliant but with a heart of gold. I think it's a match made in Heaven for Ruti."

Carrying the slip of paper with the phone message, the girl ran laughing to her mother. "*Imma,* you won't believe this. Someone just called with a new *shidduch* for Ruti. Here, read this!" She held out the paper.

Mrs. Nudel, in the midst of arranging fine glasses on a tray, read the message. Her hands began to tremble so violently that the tray slipped out of her nervous fingers and crashed to the floor. For an endless moment, her heart stopped beating and her face grew white as chalk. Was this a bad omen?

She brought the note to her husband, who considered its implications. It seemed to him that Heaven was trying to tell him something. The agitated parents closeted themselves in their room for a hurried conference, but could come to no conclusion. Finally, R' Nudel decided to consult with his rebbe. He called for a taxi and sped to the rebbe's house.

R' Nudel was near panic. The *mechutanim* were due to arrive at any minute, along with their outstanding son. He presented the matter to his rebbe in a garbled and hasty manner, telling the tale out of order and leaving out certain details. He had no idea that his subconscious was arranging for him to present the story in a twisted way, stressing the brilliance of the present match and hardly placing any emphasis at all on the value of the Milevski family.

As people say, "It all depends on how you ask." The rebbe heard R' Nudel out, thought a bit, weighed the matter as it had been presented to him, and then urged the father to finalize the current *shidduch.* He blessed R' Meir and wished him much *nachas.*

As R' Meir Nudel left, he thought in distress, "I didn't tell the story well."

V. A SHOCKING TURNAROUND

The engagement period passed like a rose-colored dream. Each day was filled with prayers for future happiness and harmony, searching for a suitable apartment, and shopping for furnishings. At last, the great day arrived. Hundreds of guests were invited to the lavish wedding hall, among them noted rabbis and *roshei yeshivah.* Gifts poured in, dancers whirled in lively circles. It was a night that had everything … and nothing.

Even before the week of *sheva berachos* had ended, the new bride ran back to her parents' home in tears. The city was appalled by the whispers that began to circulate: "The *chasan* beat her!" What had begun with such high hopes and celebration ended in one fell swoop. A year of drawn-out negotiation ended finally in rabbinical court, with a divorce decree. The painful story had come to an end.

VI. IN THE BAKERY

Like everyone else, the Milevski family heard the story, but there was not even a shred of triumph in their manner. They believed with complete faith that matches are decreed in Heaven. Besides, the Milevskis were simply not the type to crow over others' misfortunes, even others who had hurt them. They were quiet, decent people — not the kind of dazzling folk about whom others would ever shout in the town square, but good people nevertheless.

But the telephone in their house persisted in its stubborn silence. Whole days and then whole weeks passed without a suggestion for Yossi. His parents began to seriously consider letting his younger sisters leap ahead of him in the *shidduch* game. Hearing their low-voiced conferences, Yossi's heart constricted with pain. The phone was beginning to ring with suggestions for his sisters! Very soon now, he would be branded with the stamp, "Class B — Inferior Goods," for all to see.

Yossi said nothing at first. Then, when he had recovered somewhat, he said only one word: "Okay." He would not stand in his sisters' way.

Pesach was approaching. For several years, Yossi had been in the habit of working in a matzah factory at this time of year. He had earned a reputation as one of the best workers: His hands were swift and nimble and he was expert in every stage of matzah preparation. Groups of yeshivah boys clamored to work under his tutelage. Everywhere he went, Yossi spread an air of piety and *yiras Shamayim*. Even non-yeshivah youths who came to work in the bakery were impressed and moved by his scrupulousness with halachah and his enthusiasm for the job.

That year, a new group joined the old-timers at the bakery. Yeshivah boys from Jerusalem had heard of this bakery's special standards of *kashrus* and outstanding supervision, producing the best matzahs to be found. They asked for permission to bake 200 kilograms of matzahs there.

"But we especially want Yossi *'HaGomer'* ('the Finisher') to work with our group," they emphasized again and again. Last names were unimportant at this time of year. Yossi was known simply as "Yossi HaGomer."

One evening, they came. They washed their hands and changed their clothes, then air-cleaned their new clothes with powerful blow-dryers. Every worker underwent a scrupulous inspection by the group's leader, R' Meir Nudel, who they said came home only for Shabbos. From Sunday until Friday he learned in a distant yeshivah, almost completely cut off from mundane concerns. There was no one quite like him.

Cries of *"L'shem matzos mitzvah!"* rang out through the bakery. White dust began to fly through the air above the deep bowls, as special water was mixed into the carefully guarded flour. Then a sprint for the tables, where the dough was formed into long, thin rolls, cut into small sections, and passed with lightning swiftness to the next workers in the assembly line.

The group leader passed among the tables, his sharp eyes taking in every detail without overlooking a single crumb. The one who most found favor in R' Meir Nudel's eyes, however, was the "Finisher." Watching Yossi through the bustle and clamor, he reflected that it had been a long time since he had seen a young man like this. The longer he observed the pious and energetic baker, the more he liked him. Yossi was quick and efficient, and extremely careful to observe every halachah pertaining to his holy task. R' Meir saw and approved of the way Yossi quietly supervised every detail of the operation. The young man's manner was pleasant and his face glowed with the joy of the mitzvah. There was a clean, wholesome air about him that pleased R' Meir very much.

A group of children followed Yossi from table to table, eager to learn every step of the process from his own lips. With exemplary patience, he explained: "The first man mixes the water with the flour. The next one kneads the dough with a long stick and prepares a long roll. The cutter then slices small, round sections from the roll and passes them to the boys on the other side of the table. Then the 'starter' begins to roll the small piece of dough into a flat circle and passes it to the 'middleman' who flattens it still further. From there, it reaches me — the 'finisher.' I roll the dough very, very thin, bringing the matzah to the size you're used to seeing on Pesach. Then I pass the matzah over to the 'riddler,' who riddles it with holes and places it on the flat end of the pole to be placed in the oven."

The children buzzed with questions. Yossi answered each one patiently, then went on to describe the tasks of the "baker," who baked the matzahs, and the "cooler" whose job was to quickly cool the steaming matzahs, and then the "packer" who arranged the fresh matzahs in boxes. "Now, *that* is an art — to arrange the matzahs in such a way that they don't break, and so that each box is exactly the proper weight."

After he had satisfied the children's curiosity, Yossi did not waste a moment. He pulled a small *Mishnayos* from his pocket and began to read it with absorption. The other workers stepped outside for some fresh air or a bite to eat before returning to the job. But Yossi did not leave. Curious, R' Meir approached him. Shaking his hand warmly, he remarked, "I notice that you don't go outside."

With a bashful smile, Yossi murmured, "I have plenty of other chances to get fresh air." It occurred to R' Meir Nudel that the young man before him was reluctant to mingle with the others outside, where there would be opportunities for idle talk and even gossip. Yossi stopped learning *Mishnayos* for a moment as he heard himself being summoned to help wash some poles in the oven room. In his haste, he left the small volume behind.

R' Meir picked it up, intensely curious. On the flyleaf he found a small, handwritten note: "I have taken upon myself to learn *Mishnayos* for the elevation of the soul of the childless Chaim Zalman *ben* R' Shaul Leib, until his first *yahrzeit*." Beneath was a list of tractates: *Berachos, Pe'ah, Bikkurim, Demai, Shevi'is, Shabbos, Eruvin,* etc. "Say little and accomplish much" was evidently this young man's motto. He was apparently prepared to learn all six *Sidrei Mishnah* for the sake of a childless man's soul — though no one would ever thank him for it.

A truly fine young man, R' Meir whispered to himself, eyes darting to and fro to make certain that no one had observed him. Had the "finisher" written his name anywhere?

Then he found it. "*Yosef Milevski.*"

"Yossi!" came a shout, accompanied by a vigorous hand-clapping. "Everyone come on, we're starting! Where is Yossi *HaGomer*?"

Yossi Milevski ... the name seemed familiar. From where? R' Meir wondered.

Then, like a bolt out of the blue, he remembered. R' Meir nearly fainted. Was this the young man who had been suggested for his Ruti? White-faced, he found the bakery owner and asked whether "Yossi the Finisher" had learned in such-and-such yeshivah.

The harried baker, racing from room to room, called out over his shoulder, "I don't know yeshivahs, but that boy I do know. I've never had a worker like him. If I had a daughter, I'd grab him for a son-in-law. The woman who marries him will be a happy wife. Such a good heart, such gentleness and refinement, I've never seen in all my life!"

Without knowing it, the baker served as Yossi's matchmaker. His first — and his last.

VII. HAPPY EVER AFTER

Yossi smiled his bashful smile as he sat at his own engagement party, surrounded by his *roshei yeshivah* and those of R' Meir Nudel, his *kallah's* father. The two sets of parents chatted with remarkable friendliness, as though there were no history between them. The friends who had come to join in the celebration sang for hours on end. The fact that the *kallah* was divorced was no secret, but no one commented on it. Only a few of those present knew that this *shidduch* had been near fruition originally, rejected, and now revived.

Yossi's father-in-law did not test his scholarly skills. No one asked the *chasan* to demonstrate his abilities by delivering a learned talk.

After all, he was just an "ordinary young man."

THE PROTECTOR

WHEN NISSAN ROLLED AROUND, YOUNG MENDY WAS as happy as though all the rest of the year had been created just for the sake of this one month. For, had the Jewish calendar not plodded on from day to day and from month to month, how could this marvelous month come to be?

Mendy loved it all — the long vacation from school, the excitement and preparations, and the climax: Seder night. On his last day of school, he ran home, burst through the front door, and shouted, "*Imma*, I'm here!" — as though to announce, "The vacation has started!"

His mother, Sara Zelda, a rather frail woman, would raise her eyes skyward and murmur a prayer of thanks for this dear son of hers, who was ready to shoulder his share of the hard work.

Mendy Schick was not an only child. He shared his Jerusalem home with five brothers. Because they had no sisters to help with the Pesach cleaning, it was all up to them. The brothers did not relish the work. When they were little, the street games outside drew them like magnets, and as older boys their *Gemaras* and learning partners were the lure. Still, it was impossible to abandon their mother to her rags and cleaning fluids. So the boys labored unwillingly at their tasks — with the expected results.

Sara Zelda did not complain. Better for the house to be a little less clean and for her older sons to learn a little more. With a full heart, she consented when they asked permission to leave for the *beis midrash*. After they were gone, she resumed her scrubbing until the skin peeled from her fingers.

But when young Mendy, the fifth son, grew older, things changed.

Mendy was no slouch in the classroom. On the contrary: With his natural ability and diligence he had carved out a place for himself among the class' top three students. But his conscience was just as active as his mind. He could not concentrate on his studies in the *beis midrash* with the image before him of his mother's bleeding hands scouring the big pots. So he chose to remain at home, always at his mother's side with a helping hand, despite her weak remonstrances and her efforts to send him back to the *beis midrash*. Mendy did not let himself be persuaded. He knew that, without obtaining help immediately, his mother would one day collapse under her load.

Besides, he liked the work. The scrubbing and scouring that bothered most boys his age did not daunt him at all. He slaved from morning to night, beating mattresses and airing linens, cleaning books and polishing mirrors. At night, when his exhausted body cried out for sleep, he dragged himself to the *beis midrash*. He did not return home until he had spent two or three hours in sweet Torah study.

"*Abba*," Mendy called, his merry laugh pealing through the room. "Look what I found in a drawer!"

He was holding a folded sheet of paper in which lay a small piece of matzah. A stale, musty smell emanated from the packet.

"Maybe someone once hid the *afikoman* and then forgot all about it?" Mendy speculated, still laughing. "One of my older brothers must have hidden it ten years ago."

He drew back his arm, about to toss the ancient piece of matzah into the trash can that stood in the center of the room, waiting for all the odds and ends being thrown out at this season. His father, R' Chaim Leib, came running. "No, no, don't throw it out!" he shouted. A hand shot out to take the matzah in its paper wrapping from Mendy, an instant before it was due to land in the trash heap.

Mendy grew pale. His father was normally an extremely serene man whose calm was rarely shaken. If he had shouted in such a panic over a piece of old matzah, there must be something more to the story than met the eye.

R' Chaim Leib held the matzah close, kissed it with reverence, and then stood gazing at it with caressing eyes. "*Der heilige matzah* (The holy matzah)," he whispered. "*Der heilige matzah*." Once again, he bestowed a kiss on it.

Mendy could not restrain himself any longer. "*Abba*, that matzah you're holding — what is it? What is its secret?"

Still holding the matzah tightly with a reverent hand, his father began to speak.

R' Yitzchak Isaac Schick was an elderly man when he decided to move to Eretz Yisrael.

Immediately after Pesach, he sold his business and all his property, down to the last worldly good he owned. Because travel was so fraught with difficulty and danger in those days, he went to see his rebbe to ask for his blessing.

Though the rebbe was still young, having been appointed recently to the position upon his father's death, his black hair and beard did not detract from the fire in his eyes or the holiness of his person. He turned those burning eyes on R' Yitzchak Isaac, his old chassid, and exclaimed, "You want to move to Eretz Yisrael? So! Another 'mechutan' with Eretz Yisrael!"

My grandfather, Yitzchak Isaac, stood stunned. He hardly knew how to respond to the rebbe's sharp words.

"I, myself, am nothing, I know," he said humbly. "But I do not travel alone. My wife and children and their families are all coming with me. The children, at least, who have not yet sinned — they, surely, are 'mechutanim' with Eretz Yisrael."

"You are undoubtedly fine Jews," retorted the rebbe. "You are certainly worthy of going to Eretz Yisrael. Moshe Rabbeinu did not merit such a thing, but you do, of course."

R' Yitzchak Isaac's heart began to flutter like a flock of frightened starlings. The blood drained from his face and he nearly fainted to the ground. He had never expected such a response. In his innocence, he had believed the rebbe would merely grant him his blessing and the meeting would be ended.

Could the rebbe possibly be angry that R' Yitzchak Isaac had not consulted with him beforehand, but had rather come here today with a finished plan in hand? Troubled, he stammered weakly, "I — I am sorry that I did not come here to ask the rebbe's advice. In my excitement, I forgot that, in the case of such an exalted mitzvah, one does not decide on his own."

But the rebbe's thoughts did not run in this direction. Fixing the elderly chassid with a piercing stare, he said forcefully, "All roads are dangerous. You must beware."

R' Yitzchak Isaac had hardly had time to absorb this message when the rebbe got up and hurried into an adjoining room. He returned a moment later, carrying a piece of round matzah left over from the Pesach just past.

"This is shemurah (guarded) matzah," the rebbe said. "As long as you know its whereabouts, you will be protected by Heaven — both you and your family after you. Take it. Go in peace and be successful."

Mumbling his farewell, R' Yitzchak Isaac prepared to leave in confusion. Just before he went, the rebbe thumped him warmly on the shoulder. "Do not hesitate," he urged. "Everyone is going to Eretz Yisrael."

✍️

The Schick family sailed for Eretz Yisrael during the month of Iyar, when the skies were clear blue and the wind gentle and mild. The color of the sky was reflected in the waves, which splashed against the ship's hull and sent a fine spray into the air. A strong, salt tang stayed with the travelers throughout the journey.

The sudden storm that sprang up was unexpected. Even the captain, with his long years of experience at sea, was caught unaware by the lightning-swift change in the weather. The wind began to shriek powerfully, while the skies darkened with heavy black clouds. An instant later, rain began to lash the decks, soaking the sailors who struggled to maintain the ship's balance in the face of the ever-strengthening waves.

But their efforts were in vain. The ship's walls began to splinter and crack, issuing frightening squeaks that grew ever louder. The passengers stared at each other first in dismay and then in despair. It seemed clear that the ship would not survive much longer. In a few moments, it would sink to the bottom of the ocean along with everyone on board.

Huddled with the other passengers on the lower deck, prepared to jump into rickety life boats that held out no real hope of survival, the Schick family prayed. R' Yitzchak Isaac recited the *Shema* and whispered the *Viduy.* "Master of the Universe," he said, eyes wet, "I wanted to be buried in Eretz Yisrael, and now I will not even merit that. But if that is Your will, I will accept the decree with love."

The rebbe had been right. Apparently, he had foreseen R' Yitzchak Issac's end at the bottom of the sea, where he would prove to be a nice meal for a passing whale.

Thinking of the rebbe's words, R' Yitzchak Isaac froze. Indeed, the rebbe, in his wisdom, had foreseen this catastrophe! Hadn't he said, "All roads are dangerous"? In the end, though, he had handed over the *shemurah matzah* and blessed him, saying, "Go in peace."

"Everyone is going to Eretz Yisrael," the rebbe had added. Didn't that mean that the whole family would merit a safe arrival in the Promised Land?

Gripping the deck railing with all his strength, R' Yitzchak Isaac stumbled away as quickly as he could on his trembling legs, back down the stairs to the abandoned cabin.

"Stop!" cried a sailor. "Don't go down there. There's flooding. You could drown!"

R' Yitzchak Isaac ignored the warning. Gasping and stumbling, he made his way to his cabin, which was dangerously tilted and already filling with water. He thanked Hashem fervently when he found the packet of matzah on an upper shelf, still dry. Using the last of his failing strength, he took his bundle along with the matzah and made his way back to the lower deck.

"Look what I brought with me!" he gasped to his family. "The *shemurah matzah* is here. We will be saved!"

His children thought their father's fear had caused him to lose his wits entirely. What did a piece of matzah have to do with a storm-tossed ocean?

R' Yitzchak Isaac fumbled through his bag until his fingers met the thin packet of matzah. He drew it out. "See?" he said, waving the matzah in front of the other passengers' stupefied eyes. "I got this from the rebbe, as a token of protection. In its merit, we are all going to come out of this alive!"

"Tell that to the birds," scoffed one. "In a minute we're all going to drown, and the birds will get to eat some tasty matzah crumbs. Don't you hear? The wind is picking up and getting stronger..."

A powerful gust hit R' Yitzchak Isaac and threw him against the railing. The packet of matzah flew out of his hand. For a long moment, the wind kept it hovering over the churning waves.

"The matzah!" he shrieked in anguish. "The matzah is going to land in the water!"

"You will soon be reunited with your precious matzah," the same scoffing passenger told him. "We are all about to drown."

At that moment, the wind died down, and the matzah fell into the sea.

As the matzah touched the water, a new silence fell. The giant waves became subdued, and the wind calmed.

R' Yitzchak Isaac got shakily to his feet. The other passengers stared at him in wonder. Seconds ago, the sea had been held fast in the grip of a storm that had threatened them all with drowning. Now — wonder of wonders! — with the matzah on the water the raging waves had quieted and were docile as lambs.

Stooping, a passenger picked up something from the wet deck. It was the remains of the matzah that had been blown into the water. With considerable awe, he handed it to R' Yitzchak Isaac.

"Hold onto your matzah," he whispered reverently. "It is very powerful. Surely it will protect you and your whole family."

"And, just as that passenger predicted," R' Chaim Leib concluded, "that leftover piece of matzah was carefully guarded by my grandfather, R' Yitzchak Isaac, and his sons after him. But even more than we have watched over it, it has watched over us! For more than sixty years, it has protected our family from water and fire, from sickness and tragedy, from every kind of disaster and epidemic. And you were about to throw it into the garbage!"

Mendy looked with affection at the piece of matzah, blackened and hard but not eroded by time. "How did the matzah come to be in our house?" he asked. "Don't you have a lot of cousins?"

"My father was R' Yitzchak Isaac's oldest son," his father replied. "And I am his *bechor.*"

Replacing the matzah in its paper wrapping, he thrust it deep into the recesses of the drawer, just beneath a small bag containing the golden curls that had been shorn from little Mendy's head at the age of 3.

"Because you're working so hard to clean the house for Pesach and honoring your mother," R' Chaim Leib told his son, "you're the only one who knows the matzah's hiding place. Please, keep it from all harm."

The following year, the matzah disappeared.

The matzah simply vanished from its hiding place, as though the earth had swallowed it. R' Chaim Leib was deeply distressed. Together with Mendy, he searched every drawer, and then the rest of the house. But the matzah was nowhere to be found!

R' Chaim Leib's heart foretold grim tidings. And he was not wrong. It was as though the disappearance of the protective matzah had opened the door to all sorts of destructive powers. Just a few months after the matzah was lost, R' Chaim Leib died a sudden death. Shortly afterwards, his wife, Sara Zelda, became ill in turn. She was hospitalized for a long time. During her absence, the house was like a storm-tossed ship in the heart of a raging sea.

It was wartime in Palestine. Hardly had the echoes of World War II died away when the Holy Land found itself ensnared in the thick of its own deadly struggle. Underground groups formed to combat the British who were in charge of the Palestine Mandate, and these groups drew young people like magnets. Mendy's four older brothers joined the fighters, and gradually dropped every sign of their religious heritage.

Mendy, now 18, was also caught up in the powerful current of the day. A fervent believer that the British should be driven from the land, he did everything in his power to help turn that dream into a reality. Mendy was sure that he could do this and still hold onto his Torah and mitzvah observance. But constant association with the secular youth who formed the membership of those underground organizations had their influence on him. Gradually, he discarded his Yerushalmi dress, his broad-brimmed hat, and black socks. Finally, he abandoned his last symbol of religiosity: He placed his yarmulka in a drawer, to keep as a remembrance.

Only Pinchas, the sixth and youngest son, remained true to his father's teachings. When the War of Independence was over, Sara Zelda licked her wounds. Her two oldest sons had been killed in battle. Her next three sons had abandoned the faith of their youth. Only her youngest, Pinchas, remained to comfort her in her bereavement.

The winter of 1994 found Mendel Schick, attorney-at-law, over his head in legal files that took up the lion's share of his time.

His law offices in Tel Aviv absorbed him from morning to night. Mendel Schick was a vigorous lawyer who was nearing retirement age, but he showed no inclination to leave his work. On the contrary: He was filled with energy and life-loving joy. His partners, some twenty to thirty years younger, could not keep up with Mendel's killing work pace.

And then, suddenly, came the blow.

Mendy's oldest son, Erez, a young lawyer of 40 who lived near his father in the same North Tel Aviv neighborhood, began to feel ill. He was sent for tests, whose results confirmed the doctors' fears. The disease had sent its tentacles throughout his body. Erez's days were numbered.

Mendy Schick did not give up. He went to the most prestigious doctors in the country, seeking a second opinion. Only two of them gave him anything to hope for. "There is a certain hospital in Boston where they could possibly operate. But the chances of recovery are slim."

Mendy and Erez prepared their passports and booked themselves on a flight to Boston. Pesach was fast approaching. Their flight was scheduled for the first day of *Chol HaMoed.*

The ringing of the phone did not arouse Mendy's interest. He tried to ignore it, then finally gave in to the persistent ringing and picked it up. It was his mother, Sara Zelda, on the line.

"She's probably calling to wish me a good *Yom Tov,*" he thought. Despite her 90 years, his mother stubbornly refused to leave her home and move into an old-age facility.

"My Mendy," Sara Zelda murmured. "How are you? My heart tells me that something is not all right with you."

Mendy was silent. No one knew about Erez's sickness — certainly not his elderly mother. Though her mind was as lucid as ever, ripening and deepening with the years like fine old wine, Mendy had not seen fit to tell her the bad news. But her intuition, apparently, was too strong for him!

"Mendy, do you remember once, when you were a young boy, you helped me clean the house for Pesach?" she asked nostalgically. "Maybe you'll come help me again this year?"

Mendy was taken aback. Was his mother's mind fogging up after all? To ask him, a 64-year-old lawyer, to get down on his hands and knees and start scrubbing the house? With his income, he could hire a complete staff of cleaners for her.

"What about Pinchas' children?" he asked. "Can't they help you?"

"I want you to come. Just like in the old days," his mother answered calmly. "And when you finish working, we'll sit together and remember the past."

He came. His mother knew her Mendy well. He had always been drawn to memories of the past, perhaps the more so because he had severed his bonds and moved into the secular camp.

For a full day, he toiled like a young boy. Sara Zelda supervised carefully. As Mendy worked, he was swamped with a kind of homesickness for his vanished youth. He remembered how he used to drag himself to the *beis midrash* at night, using the last of his strength, just for the sweet pleasure of learning a difficult *sugya* and mastering it. Thinking of it now, his heart felt as though a hand were squeezing it.

Toward evening, his mother asked him to wait for nightfall and then check the house for *chametz*. He complied willingly. Stepping outside to a nearby shop, he purchased the requisite candle and feather.

When darkness fell, he donned a black yarmulka, lit the candle, and recited the blessing, "*Al biur chametz.*" Sara Zelda had already distributed ten pieces of bread, carefully wrapped in paper, throughout the rooms of her apartment. Under her eagle eye, Mendy began to search for them.

His nostalgia grew stronger as he opened the old chest of drawers and inspected each drawer. A hundred years of history were in these drawers. He opened the bottom one, checked it cursorily, and was about to close it again; it was late, high time for him to be returning to Tel Aviv. But there were only nine pieces of bread in his bag, and his mother was signaling him that the tenth was hidden in this drawer. Yanking at it with all his might, he pulled the drawer fully out of its slot. It fell to the floor with a crash. Mendy bent to pick it up.

All at once, he froze. In the space behind the drawer, toward the back of the chest, lay two paper packets. Slowly, he pulled them both out. A gasp escaped his lips.

"What happened?" his mother asked in alarm.

Wordlessly, he showed her. One packet contained his long-ago golden curls. And in the other, black-and-white and stale and silent, lay a piece of *shemurah matzah*.

When the tenth piece of bread had been found and collected, it was time to talk. Mendy told his mother everything, about his son's illness and their planned trip to Boston. Sara Zelda urged him force-fully to take the matzah along with him to the United States, citing the matzah's long tradition of guarding and protecting the family. Out of respect for his mother, Mendy did not decline.

Sara Zelda wrapped the matzah in a clean white cloth and placed it in her son's bag, right beside his passport.

The doctors in the Boston hospital sent Erez immediately for a battery of tests and X-rays, the usual procedure before surgery. When the laboratory results came back, the medical staff met with Mendy and Erez and told them something that it had been well worth their long trip to hear.

"The situation isn't as serious as was thought. There are signs that the illness is going into spontaneous remission!"

Erez was checked over and over, to ensure that no mistake had been made. But, in the end, the Boston doctors came to the happy conclusion that the signs of recovery were growing stronger. There was real hope that, with proper treatment, Erez would be restored to good health! He could receive the rest of his treatment back home, in Israel.

"We need to think about the future carefully," Mendy told his son as they flew eastward over the Atlantic. "Both because you've suddenly found out that you *have* a future ... and because this piece of matzah proves that I've been wrong all along, from the day I took off my yarmulka. What was it that the rebbe told my great-grandfather that day? 'As long as you know where it is, the matzah will protect you and your children after you.' He must have been referring to more than just physical protection."

"*Abba*?" his son asked, watching him curiously. "Are you afraid of that piece of matzah?"

"I'm not afraid of the *shemurah matzah*," Mendy replied. He wiped his damp eyes with his handkerchief. "What I am afraid of is the true Protector that stands behind the matzah — the Guardian of Israel!"

Shavuos

RESCUED FROM THE FLAMES

FOR YEARS, R' SHABSI FELDMAN HAD CHERISHED A dream of writing a *Sefer Torah,* but he had not had the wherewithal to do so. Now, at last, his dream had become a reality.

Shabsi was a Holocaust survivor, the only one in his Polish town to escape the Nazi wrath. Upon entering the town, the first thing the Nazis had done was to round up all the Jews, confine them to the large shul, and then set the place on fire. The building had burned to ashes to the accompaniment of the soldiers' evil laughter.

Only Shabsi Feldman remained alive.

As the flames had begun to rise, he dashed over to the *aron kodesh* to try to save the *Sefer Torah* that his grandfather had written. The tongues of flame, licking him on every side, prevented him from achieving his aim. All he managed to rescue was the old wooden *"yad"* (pointer) that his grandfather had carved in honor of the *Sefer Torah.*

It was a large *yad* and especially beautiful. A tiny shofar, an *esrog,* and clusters of grapes adorned the glowing wood. Clutching the *yad* as the flames crackled and roared around him, Shabsi didn't stop to think. He threw open the eastern window and leaped outside. To his good fortune, the Germans had already left the area, or he would surely have been shot on the spot.

For three days, Shabsi hid in a gentile family's barn. Cowering in a haystack, he neither ate nor drank during that entire time, and as a result, he nearly starved to death. Through a string of miracles and wonders, he managed to escape that place and to somehow survive the terrible war years. The *yad* accompanied him wherever he went, wrapped in cloth and securely hidden under his clothes, to protect it from the rigors of the road.

After many adventures and close calls, Shabsi Feldman finally succeeded at last in reaching Eretz Yisrael. He settled in the holy city of Jerusalem and there he established a family of his own. Heaven had pity on him and provided him with a good wife and a pleasant home near a shul in an old Jerusalem neighborhood. Shabsi supported himself and his family by making the boxes for *tefillin*. In time, he achieved a reputation as a fine craftsman who offered reasonable prices, so there was always a long line of customers waiting for his *tefillin* boxes. People would joke that, if a man wanted his son to have *tefillin* with Shabsi Feldman's boxes, he had better order them on the day the boy was born!

Shabsi had golden hands. Had he dedicated longer hours to his craft, he might have grown rich. However, he loved to learn Torah. He would rise for the early *"vasikin" minyan* each morning in the nearby shul, return home for a light breakfast, and then sit down to a morning's work. After four hours at his workbench, he would put aside his tools, rest a short while, have a bite to eat, and make his way to the shul. There he would sit and learn Torah for many hours in partnership with Noach Sofer.

Noach Sofer, like Shabsi, might have grown wealthy from the outstanding *tefillin* and Torah scrolls that he wrote in his beautiful, clear hand. No one in Jerusalem produced work comparable to his. But Noach Sofer, like Shabsi Feldman, loved the Torah with an unquenchable love. The two men learned together in the old shul, page after page, tractate after tractate. They had a regular *seder* to learn *Mishnayos* and another for *Shulchan Aruch,* the weekly Torah portion with its commentaries, *Navi,* and *mussar.*

For years, Shabsi had longed to have a *Sefer Torah* written in memory of his departed relatives — his parents, brothers, sisters, and fellow townspeople who were destroyed by the Nazis on that terrible day. But his good friend and learning partner, Noach Sofer, charged a high fee for his work, and Shabsi simply couldn't afford it. He was silent about his dream, never even mentioning it to Noach. Had Noach known that his friend wanted a *Sefer Torah,* Shabsi was sure he would have reduced his price drastically, something that Shabsi did not want him to do. Noach had many children: There were thirteen mouths to feed at home.

Then, one day, Shabsi was struck by inspiration. Noach Sofer had thirteen children, ten of whom were boys. Ten pairs of *tefillin* boxes, sold to Noach at cost price, in exchange for a reduced-rate *Sefer Torah* — a deal to leave them both satisfied!

Around that same time, the government of Israel signed an agreement with Germany to accept compensation for victims of the war. Shabsi had been vigorously opposed to this, saying that he would never take a penny from the Germans because money could not clean away blood. Now, however, he began to think differently. On the contrary, let the money of that evil empire be used to write a *Sefer Torah* for the elevation of some of its victims' souls. He met with a representative of the German government one day, told his story of horror, loss, and travail, and a few months later began to receive checks in the mail.

He pulled his chair close to Noach Sofer's and told him of his secret wish.

Noach liked the idea at once. He had been concerned about *tefillin* boxes for his ten sons and wanted Shabsi's handiwork. The two drew up a brief contract on a piece of paper. Shabsi committed himself to producing ten pairs of *tefillin* boxes for Noach's sons at cost price, while Noach obligated himself to write a *Sefer Torah* for Shabsi at a very reduced rate.

Shabsi did not want to burden Noach by pressuring him to hurry. Noach wrote the Torah at a leisurely pace, a line here and a column there. *Parashah* added to *parashah* and parchment to parchment, until at the end of five years' time the Torah was ready, perfect and beautiful.

In a moving ceremony, Shabsi donated the *Sefer Torah* to the shul close to his home, dedicated to the elevation of the souls of the holy martyrs. And on the Torah's mantle hung the old wood-carved *yad* that he had rescued from the flames. Many tears coursed down Shabsi's cheeks as he hung that *yad* in place, while in his heart he mourned. The faces of all those he had lost seemed to hover before his eyes.

The years passed, one following another in quick succession. For thirteen years, the members of the shul read often from Shabsi's Torah. The shul's *gabbaim* honored the memory of his loved ones by bringing out the *Sefer Torah* at every opportunity. The Torah was no longer new; the *yad* was looking the worse for wear; Shabsi, the maker of *tefillin* boxes, was no longer young; and one night Noach Sofer closed his eyes and never opened them again. The wonderful learning partnership was broken.

But Shabsi's love of Torah did not wane. He sat alone in the shul now, in the same old corner, and learned in a low voice, with a melody that came from the depths of his heart. His mind was still sharp and his thirst for Torah as strong as ever. He listened to new *divrei Torah* as greedily as a fish which, although immersed in water all its life, still opens its mouth to catch any falling raindrop.

Shabsi still rose very early every morning for the *vasikin minyan*. One day, when it was still dark, he heard suspicious noises coming from the shul. The shul-members' habits were as familiar to him by now as those of his own family. He knew when the shul's doors were unlocked and who was first to arrive each morning. Pricking up his ears, he strained to hear. These were not the sounds of benches being moved by Chaim David, the *maggid shiur* for the morning *kollel,* nor the soft hum of Shmuel Baruch's learning. Checking his watch to make certain, Shabsi saw that it was still too early for either of those men to be in shul. Throwing on his coat, he grabbed a large flashlight and ran to investigate.

He was correct in his suspicions. The shul's door hung open in a strange way, its lock broken and dangling sideways. Bursting inside, Shabsi screamed, "Thieves! I've already called the police!" Running to the window, he shouted as loudly as he could into the quiet street, "There are thieves in the shul! *Help! Thieves!*"

The two men standing beside the *aron kodesh* froze for an instant. For a moment their hands, busy shoving holy objects into large sacks, were stilled. Then they exchanged a quick glance, seized the sacks, and raced for the door. As they passed Shabsi, he bravely shone his flashlight into the face of the first, a large, heavyset man. Furious, the thief grabbed the flashlight out of Shabsi's hand and used it to clout him powerfully on the head. Shabsi fell senseless to the ground. The pair of thieves ran for their lives, taking two Torah scrolls with them. One of them was Shabsi's, with the old wooden *yad* dangling from the handle.

Shabsi's cries had roused the neighborhood from its sleep. They hurried to the shul — too late to stop the thieves. Fearfully, they saw Shabsi's inert form lying on the floor, eyes closed and blood seeping from the wound in his head. As quickly as could be, an ambulance was summoned and he was transferred to the hospital. Word rapidly spread among his family and neighbors that Shabsi was unconscious and that they should pray for his life.

R' Yitzchak Burstein made the most of the time he spent in Russia. When the Iron Curtain had opened, he had traveled to Russia to found a yeshivah to service the city of Kiev and several other towns. Yitzchak was well aware of human nature, and he firmly believed that in order to form a close bond with a student it was necessary to speak his language. Therefore, he spared no effort in mastering the Russian language, until he spoke it as fluently as his own native tongue.

Yitzchak's family continued to live in Jerusalem, waiting eagerly for their father's periodic visits home.

On Lag B'Omer eve, 10-year-old Gadi Burstein had climbed a tall pile of wood to prepare it for that night's bonfire. The pile was unstable. Suddenly, it collapsed, Gadi's feet shot out from under him, and he rolled to the ground, landing on his head. Gadi was borne off to the hospital, unconscious.

Word was sent to his father, R' Yitzchak Burstein, in Russia. He boarded the first plane bound for Israel, and later that day he was sitting at his son's bedside in the Intensive Care Unit, a *Tehillim* in hand. All the way back home, he had wondered fearfully whether his family had said that Gadi was hurt only to soften the blow, and that he would find a much worse tragedy awaiting him when he arrived. To his relief, he found the situation exactly as they had described it. Though he cried bitterly to see his son lying unconscious, he found comfort in his faith and heard with pleasure the doctors' opinions that the injury had not been severe; it was likely that Gadi's condition would continue to improve each day.

Several days later, another unconscious form was brought to the next bed, this one belonging to an elderly man. Yitzchak read the name at the foot of the bed: *Shabsi Feldman*. From Shabsi's son, R' Yisrael Feldman, he heard the story of the thieves who had broken into the shul and nearly crushed Shabsi's skull.

On *Erev Shavuos,* Yitzchak Burstein came to spend the holiday at his son's bedside. His heart constricted painfully as he remembered the year before, the way he and Gadi had spent the entire Shavuos night learning together. On the spot, he decided to do the same tonight. Though Gadi was unconscious, his soul could undoubtedly hear. Also, the doctors urged relatives of patients in comas to speak to them, because in many instances the brain awoke from such talk.

Shabsi's son, R' Yisrael, entered the room before *Yom Tov* began and asked Yitzchak Burstein if he could keep an eye on his father, as no family member would be there that night. "We're organizing a prayer and *Tehillim* rotation on Har Tzion," he explained. "My father, he should live and be well, used to go there every Shavuos night to recite the entire *Sefer Tehillim* near the tomb of David HaMelech who, as you know, passed away on Shavuos. We want to continue his tradition, so that he may merit a full recovery."

Yitzchak Burstein agreed, and asked whether several chapters of the *Tehillim* they would be reciting that night could be dedicated to his son, Gadi. Yisrael consented enthusiastically, adding that they would not only dedicate a few chapters, but a whole *Sefer Tehillim*. "Not only I, but the whole crowd will say the entire *Sefer Tehillim* twice. Once for my father, and once for your dear son."

These words sent a ray of hope and comfort into Yitzchak's downcast heart. The thought that *Tehillim* would be said for his son by King David's tomb on Shavuos night made the long hours that he sat beside Gadi's unconscious form easier to bear. He divided his time between learning *Gemara* and reciting the *Tikkun Leil Shavuos*. Gadi had always loved saying the *Tikkun*. Two years ago, on Shavuos, when just a child of 8, he had managed to say the entire *Tikkun* on *Yom Tov* night, and had been so proud of himself.

Yitzchak didn't know how it happened. Sometime around midnight, his eyes closed and his head drooped as he fell into a light doze. Suddenly, he woke with a start. "What am I doing, sleeping on Shavuos night?" he scolded himself.

Yitzchak noticed two burly fellows who were conversing quietly near him. They were speaking in Russian, and Yitzchak was able to understand every word.

"No one is near the old man's bed," one said.

"But there is that religious Jew beside the boy's bed," the other pointed out.

"Nonsense, he's asleep," the first said impatiently. "I'm turning off the old man's ventilator and getting out of here. In twenty minutes, the machine will go on again automatically. I'm sure he'll be dead by then."

Yitzchak's heart pounded. Was he still asleep, dreaming, or was this really happening?

He moved his head slowly to one side and glanced quickly at the two men. They were dressed in the uniforms of hospital orderlies.

Quickly, Yitzchak began to sway in his seat and to learn in a loud voice, to prove to the pair that he was fully awake. Thoughts swirled through his mind: He must phone Yisrael Feldman and let him know that someone was trying to kill his father. But tonight was *Yom Tov!* But wasn't this a case of *pikuach nefesh?* Anyway, Yisrael Feldman was not at home right now, he was at the tomb of David HaMelech. Should he run over to the guard standing at the hospital entrance? No, that would give those two a chance to carry out their plot. And they just might harm Gadi, too, in revenge.

On impulse, he pressed the "Call" button by Gadi's bed. A nurse came running. "What happened?" she asked, bending concernedly over the boy. If a religious Jew was pressing the buzzer on a holiday, it must mean there was a serious problem.

"It's not about my son," Yitzchak said. "I wanted to find out what those two workers" — he pointed at the pair — "are doing here so late at night."

"I really don't know," the nurse said, clearly taken aback. She approached the two men. "What are you looking for in the middle of the night?"

The pair threw a murderous glance at Yitzchak, mumbled something unclear, and hurried away from the spot at once.

Yitzchak sighed in relief. The danger had passed — for now.

More than thirty people stood at the site marked "King David's Tomb" on Har Tzion, reciting *Tehillim* with fervor. Yisrael Feldman led his extended family in praying for his father's health. He was about to announce that they would be reciting the *Sefer Tehillim* a second time for the speedy recovery of Gadi Burstein, when two Arabs entered the site.

Everyone stared at them in mingled surprise and alarm. What were two Arabs doing here in the middle of the night? They appeared to be searching for someone. Their eyes darted to and fro, returning again and again to Yisrael Feldman. Certain that the pair's intentions were far from pure, several people ran to call in the Israeli soldiers standing guard in the Old City. The Arabs were asked the reason for their presence, and when they did not answer clearly, were requested to leave at once.

Dawn came. The complete *Sefer Tehillim* had been recited twice that night, once for their father and relative, Shabsi Feldman, the other for a stranger, a boy by the name of Gadi Burstein. But then, no Jew is ever truly a stranger. All Jews are brothers.

The family made its way to the Western Wall plaza to pray at dawn along with thousands of other Jews. Yisrael Feldman suddenly saw the two Arabs, waiting in a shadowy corner. Filled with curiosity, he approached them.

The two made no attempt to hide their satisfaction. "Hey, the minute we saw you we knew you were someone we could do business with. You're a man of common sense."

"What do you want?"

They glanced around to make sure they were not overheard. "If you want, we can take you to a room where there are all kinds of good things."

"What kinds of things? What are you talking about?"

They whispered, "There's a storage room, not far from here, maybe a five-minute walk, filled with stolen goods. Only we know where to find it. There are some of your books there — your holy books."

"Holy books?" Yisrael echoed blankly.

"The Torah," one of them said, remembering the word. "Nice Torah scrolls, pretty, worth a lot of money. Do you want to come?"

"Certainly."

"Give us $5,000 and we'll lead you to the room."

Yisrael thought quickly. *Sifrei Torah!* Just a week ago, two *Sifrei Torah* had been stolen from his own neighborhood shul, one of them his father's. Could these be the two Torah scrolls the men were referring to?

"It's a holiday, so I don't have any money with me," he told the men. "After the holiday, let's meet again at King David's tomb. I'll be able to give you the money then."

The pair was disappointed. "You're not interested? We'll go to another Jew!"

"No religious Jew will give you even a shekel today," Yisrael explained. "On our holidays, we are forbidden to handle money."

"All right," they grudgingly agreed. "We meet tomorrow at noon at the tomb. You bring the money."

"I will," Yisrael promised. Silently, he added, "and also the police."

Morning broke over Jerusalem.

Yitzchak Burstein sighed with relief. The difficult night was behind him. From the moment the Russian criminals had left, he had been afraid to leave the Intensive Care room for even a moment, lest the two return and disconnect Shabsi Feldman's breathing apparatus. He longed to go to the *Kosel* now for the *vasikin* service. Casting his eyes over his son, he looked for signs of improvement. But Gadi lay as motionless as before, eyes closed. He looked as though he were sleeping the sleep of the just — a sleep that had lasted eighteen days already.

Still, the doctors who examined him every day believed that he would wake soon. If only they were right.

A choked cough startled him. Glancing at Shabsi Feldman's bed, he was astonished to see that the old man's eyes were open! Shabsi was coughing beneath his oxygen mask. A weak, old man had recovered before a 10-year-old boy! Shabsi had been here only a week, and already he was waking up, while Gadi showed no signs of recovering consciousness. Bitter tears gathered in Yitzchak's eyes.

He wiped them away and scolded himself. "Shame on you!" he thought. "Don't you know that every person has his own fate, his own Divine Providence decreed from Above?"

He approached Shabsi's bed. The elderly man motioned for Yitzchak to remove the mask from his face, but Yitzchak dared not comply on his own. He raced to the nurse's station. "Old Mr. Feldman has woken up!" he announced happily, glad to be able to impart good news.

A nurse came quickly into the room and confirmed it. "Feldman's awake," she alerted the doctor on duty.

Yitzchak left Gadi in the care of a student of his who had volunteered to sit with his son. "Why had a pair of Russians been plotting to kill the old man?" Yitzchak wondered as he made his way slowly home. It seemed a mystery without an answer. The question occupied him all the way to his house.

When he had finished *davening,* Yisrael Feldman headed for the hospital to check on his father. His eyes bulged disbelievingly and his heart leaped nearly out of his chest when he saw the change. His father was awake!

His joyous cries echoed through the Intensive Care Unit, and only the nurse's stern shushing forced him to stop.

Blinking back tears, he leaned over his father. "You know, *Abba,* we said *Tehillim* for you at David HaMelech's tomb all night. See how powerful prayer is? Here you are, awake already!"

Shabsi could not yet speak. A hoarse whisper was all he could manage: "The Torah."

"Of course, this is the day we received the Torah. But, *Abba,* you are not obligated to read from the Torah today."

Shabsi waved his hands frantically. "The Torah, the Torah."

Yisrael knew very well what his father meant. He wanted to know whether his *Sefer Torah* had been among the things stolen from the shul. Yisrael did not want to distress his father, so he continued to play the fool and pretended not to understand Shabsi's meaning.

Shabsi continued to recover. What had happened to him was reminiscent of our Sages' statement that the sick were cured at the time of *Matan Torah.* Within hours, he revived considerably and was functioning well. The doctors said that if the recovery continued to progress, Shabsi would soon be released from the ICU and placed in a regular ward.

Very early the next morning, the two Russian "orderlies" appeared at Shabsi's bedside. "We've come to transfer you to the ward."

Waking groggily from a deep sleep, Shabsi was confused. The pair began to wheel his bed out of the room.

Refreshed from a short nap at home, Yitzchak Burstein had just returned to the hospital for another stint beside his son's bed. The doctor had seen further improvement in Gadi's condition, and had informed Yitzchak optimistically that he could awaken "any time now." Perhaps today would be Gadi's day. Prayer, prayer, and more prayer.

Suddenly, in a panic, he saw the two Russians wheeling Feldman's bed out of the room. They were going to kill the old man! One of them had a syringe in his hand and was bending over Shabsi while the other continued to slowly wheel the bed.

A scream pierced the early-morning quiet. "Help! Murder! They're going to murder him! *He-e-elp!*"

Nurses and orderlies came running from every direction. "What's going on?" they asked in agitation.

Yitzchak pointed to the Russians. "Ask them who they are, if they belong to hospital personnel."

The two "orderlies" began to run. Their pace would not have shamed an Olympic runner, but doctors and nurses and hospital staff blocked their exit on every side.

The police were summoned. It did not take long for them to ascertain that the two Russians were not and had never been employed by the hospital.

Yisrael Feldman, entering the hospital during the height of the commotion, discovered that his father had nearly been murdered in his absence. His father pointed shakily at the burly Russian who had held the syringe. "That's him. That's him!" His eyes bulged with emotion.

"Who is he?" Yisrael asked urgently.

Shabsi waved his arms. "The thief. He stole the Torah."

"Are you sure, *Abba?*"

Shabsi was not feeling well physically, but his mind was clear. "Of course. I shone my flashlight on him. He's the one who hit me on the head."

The police investigation led them to an abandoned storage room on Har Tzion. They brought with them the handcuffed Russian who had struck Shabsi Feldman on the head, and Yisrael Feldman, to whom the Arab pair had tried to sell the stolen goods. Perhaps this was the very place where the Arabs had intended to take him. They, too, had talked about a storage room in the area.

Yisrael quickened his pace until he had outstripped the police and the suspect by some twenty meters. He found the two Arabs he had met on Shavuos night, hiding behind a stone wall. Suspiciously, they demanded, "How did you know where to come?"

Yisrael gestured at the approaching police, and pointed at the handcuffed Russian. "I brought him, too. I don't need you any longer. I can handle this alone."

The Arabs bolted like frightened rabbits.

The police opened the storage room door to find piles of treasure. The criminals, apparently, had made liberal use of this room, filling it with stolen holy artifacts. Yisrael immediately identified the two Torah scrolls that had been stolen from his shul — his father's and another. Having been taken in the most recent theft, the *Sifrei Torah* lay at the top of the pile. The thieves had already changed the look of Shabsi's Torah, having removed its mantle and replaced it with a different one. But for some reason they had neglected to remove the most identifying detail of all —

The one-of-a-kind wooden *yad* was still dangling, clinging to it as though determined never, ever to be lost.

THE CASE OF THE
MISSING TRACTATE

IT WAS 2 A.M. WHEN WE CLOSED OUR *GEMARAS*.

"We'd better get going if we want to reach the *Kosel* in time to *daven* with the *vasikin minyan*," said Eliyahu Reisner, the practical one of our group. It was Shavuos night, twenty-five years ago. We were a group of yeshivah students who learned in the Bayit Vegan section of Jerusalem, and we planned to walk to the *Kosel HaMa'aravi* for *Shacharis*. It was a long walk.

As we trudged through the dark, chilly streets into the face of a rising wind, we were young, idealistic, and happy with life. On our way we burst into song several times, and saw other groups also bound for the Old City. It was a liberating feeling, walking and singing through the dark streets. On such a night, who needed sleep?

The most recent election in Israel had brought Menachem Begin's Likud party to power after twenty-nine years in the opposition. The walls were still plastered with election posters, but none of us paid them the slightest attention. Who cared about politics, on the great night when *HaKadosh Baruch Hu* had chosen us from among all the other nations of the world, and given us His Torah?

After some 40 minutes of steady walking, we suddenly felt thirsty. The discomfort persisted until we came to a large shul where blazing lights and raised voices testified to the many men and boys learning within. One of our group, peeking inside, announced that there were plenty of refreshments. Without further ado, we entered the shul.

We paused inside the doorway, embarrassed. There were the tables laden with coffee, cake, and cold drinks; but we hesitated before partaking of them. An alert *gabbai* approached. Hospitably, he invited to us to help ourselves.

In short order, we had refreshed ourselves with some cake and cold juice. As we prepared to leave, my gaze wandered over the crowded shul. Nearly every person present was learning, though a few were reciting the *Tikkun Leil Shavuos*. My eye fell on an unusual pair poring over *Gemaras* nearby. They seemed completely out of place in this crowd.

One was an elderly man, clean-shaven, his white hair worn long. His fingers boasted more than one gleaming gold ring.

The other was a boy of perhaps 16 or 17, with curly locks reaching nearly to his shoulders. On his head — looking as though it had been placed there only temporarily — was pinned a small knitted yarmulka. The old man's diminutive black yarmulka gave the same impression.

But the strangest thing about the pair was not their appearance. The mass *teshuvah* movement had already begun to sweep the country, making it far from unusual to see all kinds of people taking their first steps toward the religion of their fathers. What drew the eye was their learning. They shared a single large *Gemara*. The old man, who looked as though he would have fit naturally into an executive boardroom, was apparently very much at home with the Talmud. He read from the *Gemara* and explained some complex thought with lively vigor, a finger waving in the air in the time-honored manner of yeshivah boys. He learned like a person who has been in the *beis midrash* all his life, though his appearance strongly contrasted with this impression. As for the youth, he listened attentively to the old man's explanations, breaking in from time to time with a short comment or question of his own.

I moved closer, irresistibly curious.

As I had guessed, they were learning in English. The *Gemara* open in front of them was *Tractate Shabbos*. Listening, I identified the words "*Kafah HaKadosh Baruch Hu aleihem har kegigis*" among the welter of American-accented English. They were learning the *sugya* that deals with the giving of the Torah. As he spoke, the old man seemed seized with a burning enthusiasm. The whole scene moved me deeply, and I watched and listened unabashedly, unmindful of my manners.

One of my friends nudged me in the ribs. "Binyamin, we're in a hurry."

I whispered, "Take a look at that 'unusual' pair. There's a story here. I've got to find out what's behind their learning that way."

"We'll be late for *vasikin*."

"I'll catch up. Don't wait for me," I whispered back impatiently.

My friends lingered another minute or two, but when they saw that I had no intention of budging at the moment, they gave up and left.

Walking up to the pair, I coughed politely. The old man noticed me at once, though the boy remained totally absorbed in what they had been talking about.

"*Gut yontiff,*" the old man greeted me, his face aglow.

I gathered my courage and came close enough to glance into their *Gemara*, as though seeing it for the first time. I told them a brief *vort* on the words, "When Yisrael said *na'aseh* before *nishma*." They listened with interest. Even someone as young and inexperienced as I could see that, while the old man followed what I was saying, the boy did not understand a word. I was not surprised at the boy's reaction, but the old man's did startle me: He, too, looked completely un-Jewish.

I was unable to conquer my curiosity. In Yiddish, I asked them who they were and how they had come to be here.

Laughing heartily, the old man thumped me on the shoulder. "You'll be a journalist yet, young man. You know how to smell out a story. And it's true — there's a good one here!"

"I'd like to hear it," I said eagerly.

The old man pointed to the *Gemara*. "Right now, we're learning. This is the night when the Torah was given. If you want, come see me at the Plaza Hotel after *Yom Tov,* and we'll talk."

I thanked him happily, and stood up. If I ran, I might still catch up with my friends. But the old man motioned for me to come close again. "When I say after *Yom Tov,* I don't mean your *Motza'ei Yom Tov.* I mean what you'd call *Motza'ei Isru Chag.*"

I was taken aback. Had he not remembered to mention this detail, I really would have come to see him on the night after the holiday. "We keep two days of *Yom Tov,*" the old man added, as though in clarification.

I left the shul, sunk in thought. Who could know a Jewish heart? From the looks of him, I would have thought the fellow didn't even keep Shabbos. And here he was, talking about a two-day *Yom Tov!*

On the night *Isru Chag* ended, right after my third *seder* at yeshivah, I hurried onto a bus for the ride to the Plaza Hotel. I found the room without any trouble. The old man was there with the boy; they had been looking through an English translation of a Torah book. The old man shook my hand warmly and introduced himself: "I'm Mr. Samuel Diamond."

"Nice to meet you. I'm Binyamin Kaufwasser."

"Good, good." Mr. Diamond invited me to accompany them down to the lobby. Politely declining, I asked him to get down to business. "I'm really curious," I admitted.

He studied me for a moment with smiling eyes, murmuring something about the impatience of the younger generation. Gesturing at his companion, he said, "He's just like you. Right, Ralph?"

The boy named Ralph made a face and continued to stand at the window, which commanded a sweeping view of the illuminated Old City walls.

Without further ado, the old man began his story.

Seventy-five years ago, in December of 1902, the Diamond family in the Polish city of Zanstochov was blessed with a baby boy whom they named Shmuel. Until he was 12 years old, Shmuel's life was no different from that of any other Jewish child in Poland at the time. Then came the day when one of Poland's foremost *geonim* came to his *Talmud Torah* to test the children. Afterwards, he requested an urgent meeting with Shmuel's father, Reuven Diamond.

Reuven was a simple porter who earned his living hauling closets and tables and bundles on his back. For his sons, however, he sought a different kind of life. He wanted them to be great in Torah. When the *gaon* informed him that his son, Shmuel, was a genuine *iluy* (genius), Reuven's eyes lit up with happiness. And when the *gaon* asked him to send Shmuel away to a fine yeshivah, Reuven did not refuse.

A few months later, Shmuel Diamond went to learn in the town of Zatovska, with the *gaon* R' Kalman Rosenblitt.

This was not a yeshivah like the ones we know of today. It was simply a collection of boys of various ages who thirsted to learn from a certain *rav.* R' Rosenblitt, in addition to his uncanny skill at probing the depths of Torah, was also an outstanding educator. Some thirty students had gathered around him. Shmuel Diamond was the youngest of the group; he celebrated his bar mitzvah in the yeshivah instead of at home in Zanstochov with his parents. His mother and father came to mark the great day with him, shedding tears of joy as young Shmuel delivered a scholarly talk on the subject of *tefillin*.

When he had finished speaking, his *rosh yeshivah* kissed the boy on the forehead and predicted that, if Shmuel persisted diligently with his studies, he would be great in Torah.

Reuven and Sarah Diamond were beside themselves with happiness.

Shmuel Diamond applied himself to his learning for several years, and his future in Torah seemed bright indeed. He seemed to have the potential to become a shining star in the next generation's firmament of Torah leadership.

But the more glowing a person's outlook in this area and the more interest he displays, the stronger the challenges he encounters. Shmuel began to face various tests, particularly with unsuitable friends — friends that he made outside the yeshivah walls. These young men loaned him books antithetical to Torah, works that sowed poisonous seeds in his mind and soul.

Shmuel was very bright. He knew that open rebellion would lose him everything. Therefore, he behaved carefully and awaited his chance. To the outward eye, his *Yiddishkeit* changed not at all. Not a single strand was missing from his curly *peyos*. The customary cap worn by Polish Jews remained on his head as before. He continued to *daven* the way a yeshivah boy should. None of his yeshivah friends suspected a thing.

Shmuel Diamond was a pious Jew on the outside; inside was another story entirely. He continued to learn diligently as he had before, only slipping away at rare intervals — out of sight of his vigilant rebbis and friends — to meet the new friends who were as distant from Torah and *Yiddishkeit* as East is from West. No one in yeshivah had an inkling about these secret meetings.

News of R' Kalman Rosenblitt's sudden illness landed on his students like a thunderbolt. One day he had delivered his *shiur* as usual, building concept upon concept until an entire edifice stood firmly cemented with the mortar of his logic. That evening, he felt unwell and went to bed. His wife ran to the *beis midrash* to obtain the students' help for her ailing husband.

Inexperienced as they were, the boys were ready to do all they could in this crisis. They traveled to a nearby city to bring back a medical specialist. The doctor examined R' Kalman thoroughly and pronounced his diagnosis: "It's his heart." R' Kalman's condition was grave.

In later days, the medical establishment would call what R' Kalman had experienced a "heart attack." But Dr. Flossburg, of the Warsaw Hospital, had not yet heard of this term.

Still, the doctor was able to see how serious the rabbi's condition was. Before he left the house, he warned the students that R' Rosenblitt had only days to live. R' Kalman was not yet 50.

The students refused to admit defeat. Gathering in the *rav's* room, where he lay looking only half-alive, they discussed the situation.

"We have to do something!" cried Chezkel Lodzer, one of the older boys at the yeshivah, through ill-disguised tears. "We can't just sit with our hands folded."

"But what do we do?" demanded Yekusiel Radomsker. "You heard what the doctor said."

"Yes, we all did," Chezkel retorted. "But there are other doctors in the world."

Chanoch Henoch Cracower joined the conversation. "Forget the doctors; they don't know anything. Their job is to diagnose illnesses and collect their fees. We have to go directly to the *Ribbono Shel Olam,* to beg for the rebbi's life. We have to beg for him to be spared for our sake, so that we can learn Torah from him. I heard, in the name of *gedolim,* that when Heaven sees that many people need someone, they judge his fate differently. They take into consideration the fact that he's sorely needed."

"And I heard," Shmuel Diamond put in, "of a great rebbe who was mortally ill, and his chassidim donated years of their own life to him. Everyone gave one year, more or less, and the rebbe recovered completely!"

The moment the words were out of his mouth, he wished he could take them back. He had heard the story as a child at his father's knee. It was part of his history. But now he no longer believed such things.

His friends waxed enthusiastic. Yes! They would each donate years of their own lives to R' Kalman, and he would recover at once. Clustering around their beloved rebbi's bed, they decided to put the plan into operation without delay. Shmuel was asked to be the record keeper. On a large sheet of paper, he wrote his friends' names and their pledges:

"Shimon David HaKohen has donated one year to R' Kalman ben Chaya."

"Yaakov Dov HaLevi has donated one year to R' Kalman ben Chaya."

"Yekusiel Radomsker has donated eighteen months for the recovery of our rebbi."

The page was soon filled. Every boy donated a year, apart from Yekusiel who offered eighteen months of his time without a second thought, and thrifty Naftali Warshawer who volunteered only six months.

Even Shmuel Diamond had donated one year without blinking an eye. In his heart, he scorned the idea that he himself had suggested, and did not believe for a moment that he would actually lose a year of his life because of a verbal commitment.

The boys were about to sign the document when the blankets stirred. R' Kalman made a sign with his hand, and then opened the eyes that had been closed.

The students crowded closer around their rebbi's bed. R' Kalman whispered weakly, "I thank all my beloved students for this precious gift. But I do not agree to accept it under any circumstances!"

In a tearful voice, Chezkel Lodzer asked, "But why not?"

Hoarsely, R' Kalman answered, "I do not want to live on time borrowed from young boys. If you want to do me a favor, undertake to learn the entire *Shas* for the sake of my recovery. Divide up all the tractates and commit yourselves to learn them during the coming year. Maybe, in the merit of your learning, *HaKadosh Baruch Hu* will send me a *refuah sheleimah*."

Quickly, Chezkel turned the page over and wrote on its blank side: "*Tractate Berachos*. I, Yechezkel Shraga ben Shimon, undertake *bli neder* to finish *Tractate Berachos* within the next three months, for the full recovery of R' Kalman ben Chaya."

He turned to Shmuel Diamond. "*Tractate Shabbos?* A genius like you should be able to handle 157 pages without too much trouble."

"Of course," Shmuel answered promptly. "I'll finish within six months." No one sensed that his enthusiasm was artificial, only skin-deep.

"*Tractate Eruvin?*" Chezkel went on, writing busily. "Yankel Levy — Yaakov Dov HaLevi — can you handle that?"

"Yes," Yankel answered at once, privately wondering which was more difficult, donating a year of life or learning *Tractate Eruvin*.

Each of the students committed himself, ensuring that the entire *Shas* would be learned within a specific time period. The paper was filled from top to bottom. Motivated by a fierce desire to see their rebbe get well, the boys agreed to complete all of *Shas* within no more than half a year.

The plan worked.

Dr. Flossburg's bleak prognosis did not materialize. R' Kalman recovered slowly. Two months from the day he had fallen ill, he returned to deliver his *shiur* to his happy students — while they made every effort to use any spare minute to learn the extra tractates they had undertaken for his recovery. At the end of six months, they had completed the entire *Shas*.

Or had they?

All the tractates, from *Berachos* to *Niddah,* were completed. Only one *maseches* was missing, *Tractate Shabbos.*

Shmuel Diamond learned only the first and last sections of that tractate — and those were only for the sake of the talk he had to deliver at the *Siyum HaShas.* While his friends were struggling with all their might to learn their allotted portions, Shmuel would go out to a smaller *beis midrash* that stood empty all day and where, he said, he could learn more easily. He would pass his time there reading his secular books. For safety's sake, he would keep an open *Tractate Shabbos* in plain view on his *shtender* at all times.

But his fears of being caught were groundless. No one knew of his secret activities. He locked the shul doors from the inside, and whenever he heard approaching footsteps he hastily hid his book underneath the open *Gemara,* raising his voice in "learning."

When it came time to make their *siyum,* the boys' faces shone with joy. R' Kalman had suggested a single *siyum* on the last tractate of *Shas,* to include the whole Talmud. But the boys, to give their rebbi more pleasure, chose to make an individual *siyum* on each tractate.

When Chezkel Lodzer finished his brief talk, Shmuel Diamond stood up to deliver his talk on *Tractate Shabbos.* At that moment, R' Kalman suddenly lifted his eyes in a penetrating stare. Shmuel felt as though white-hot pincers were piercing his heart and testing his innards. For a moment he stood confused. Then, collecting his wits, he began to deliver a talk that displayed the best of his ability, dazzling his fellow students with questions and answers that linked the beginning of the tractate with its end, and tying it all up in such a way that his friends murmured, "That Shmuel always was an *iluy,* and he still is one!"

By the time the third *siyum,* on *Tractate Eruvin,* was done, R' Kalman was fatigued. He asked Zelig Mezritcher, who had learned the last *maseches,* to wind up his portion and complete the *Siyum HaShas.*

"Thank you," R' Kalman told his students emotionally. "You boys have restored my life. I have no doubt that my recovery came sooner because of your learning."

Happily, the boys went to wash their hands for the *seudas mitzvah.* R' Kalman exchanged a few words with Chezkel Lodzer, his oldest student. Their conversation was brief, and it took place in private, away from listening ears. Chezkel nodded, and whispered something back.

Though the two tried their best to be discreet, Shmuel Diamond's sharp eyes didn't miss a thing.

∽⌘∾

Three months later, on a Friday, R' Kalman told his family with a satisfied air that today was his 50th birthday. "'In the year of this *Yovel*,'" he quoted, "'each man will return to his plot of land.'" These enigmatic words were accompanied by a meaningful look.

His wife thought that he was merely quoting at random. But the following day, on Shabbos afternoon, after partaking of the Shabbos *cholent*, R' Kalman lay down for a nap and suffered a second heart attack. This time, he didn't recover.

The horrifying news that their rebbi had suddenly passed away struck the students with a mortal blow. They wandered aimlessly outside the house of mourning. All through the rest of that Shabbos they restrained their tears, but when three stars peeped out of the velvet sky, they allowed full vent to their agony and gave voice to heart-rending wails.

Shmuel Diamond cried along with his friends, but as he displayed genuine distress over his rebbi's death, a new thought came to him: Here was his chance to escape! He had revered and respected R' Kalman and in his rebbi's presence had been afraid to openly rebel against his upbringing. But things would be different now.

He cried again at the funeral, but this time he was forced to admit to himself that the tears were false. He could not stop thinking of breaking free. Then, as he returned from Zatovska's small funeral home with the others, a new thought came along to trouble him: Had it been the missing tractate, *Tractate Shabbos*, that had caused R' Kalman to lose his life? Because he, Shmuel, had neglected what he had committed himself to do, because he had not learned what he had pledged to learn, one tractate had been missing to complete the *Shas*.

He chased the disturbing thought from his mind. "What's it to you?" he asked himself fiercely. "You don't really believe that stuff." The seeds of heresy that had taken root in him had swallowed up the faith with which he had been imbued since early childhood.

During the following weeks, he planned his next move carefully. He was already 17 years old, at the peak of his strength. From inertia, his friends continued to learn in the yeshivah for several weeks longer; but without a guiding hand at the helm, the group soon fell apart. The boys dispersed in every direction and entered new yeshivahs. Shmuel, too, left Zatovska — but his destination was not another yeshivah. Neither did he return to his parents' home in Zanstochov.

He found temporary lodgings in a small town on the outskirts of Warsaw. Secretly, he hired himself out as a manual laborer, in order to earn the price of a ship's passage. By the time he turned 18, he found himself standing on deck aboard the *Louisiana,* en route to New York.

Shmuel did not leave the ship the way he had come. When he stepped aboard, he was still dressed in the traditional garb of religious Polish Jewry, his coat long, his *peyos* grown, and a *tefillin* bag tucked under his arm. When he disembarked, he was wearing a short, modern coat, his *peyos* had been shorn, and the *tefillin* bag had sunk to the bottom of the sea. A Jew had entered the port of Danzig, but a complete gentile stepped off the ship at the New York harbor.

Shmuel's first days in the Golden Land were sweet as a dream. In Poland he had behaved like a frightened rabbit, always afraid of being seen — but here, he was free! There was no one to watch him, or judge him. No one to tell him what to do. True, he had nothing to eat and was hungry, but the delirium of freedom satisfied him for now. Sniffing out opportunities, he presently offered himself as a construction worker with a firm called Triboro Buildings. He climbed tall scaffolding without fear. After several weeks, he heard his co-workers discussing a technical difficulty in reaching the next floor, the 57th of the skyscraper they were building. Shmuel — who now called himself Samuel, or Sam for short — asked what was holding up the work.

"We're out of gas," Tony, a thick-muscled Italian explained. "We can't start welding on the next floor."

"Why do you need gas to weld?"

"Hey, I forgot that we're dealing with a 'greener' here," Tony sighed. He went on with a brief explanation of the role that gas played in supplying an energy source for the intense heat needed to solder the giant metal columns. "We're waiting for the big gas equipment to be lifted up here. The crane broke down."

"What an awkward way of doing things!" Sam said in surprise. "Must you have a fire? Isn't there a quicker and more efficient energy source than gas equipment?"

Tony grew angry. "The green guy is asking questions. The egg wants to teach the chicken!"

Sam sat sunk in thought. His gaze flitted over other skyscrapers nearby, most of them already filled with offices and office workers. Sam loved to look at these tall buildings at night, golden rectangles of light towering against the dark horizon. Where in all of primitive Poland was there such a sight to be seen? Over there, in the old country, they were still using kerosene lamps for light, and only in the largest cities was electricity hooked up.

Suddenly, he had a daring idea. Electricity!

"Tell me, Tony," he said, tugging at the Italian's sleeve. "Where can I find the foreman?"

The other man laughed. "You want to quit? You don't have to say a word to anyone. Just get up and go!"

"Tony, could you please just answer me?"

Tony pointed at the workers' elevator, which had discharged a ruddy-faced man in a hard hat. "There he is. Watch out, he's got a temper. We call him 'Kicking Jeff.'"

Sam had never been afraid of a short fuse. He approached the foreman and asked if fire was strictly necessary for soldering. Jeff raked him with a scornful glance. "Kid, go back to work."

"But we can't work because there's no gas," Sam said stubbornly. Then, simply and clearly, he outlined his plan: to use electrical cables

— already in place inside the building — to generate the necessary heat, as it did for the powerful irons and washing machines in commercial laundries. That would, Sam said, eliminate the use of clumsy gas equipment.

Jeff was impatient at first. But when he finally grasped the import of what Sam was suggesting, he nearly fell off the scaffolding. "It's possible to generate heat with electricity," he echoed in astonishment. "I get the idea. You're saying they already use that heat in irons and washing machines? Very true. Why didn't we think of that?"

Sam descended with the foreman. Jeff brought him to the construction company's general manager and let him present his idea.

As he absorbed the essential concept, the manager jumped out of his chair. Sam never went back to the scaffolding. The manager appointed Sam as his personal assistant and, after a short time, when the construction company began to solder exclusively with electrically-generated heat, Sam took out a patent in his own name. He became a special consultant to the firm. The manager thought it a waste of Sam's talents to put him to work at simple manual labor — and, again and again, Sam Diamond proved him right. More than once, the manager happily remarked on the parallel between the name "Diamond" and his valued assistant's worth to the firm.

"Shall I go on, young man?" the old man in the Plaza Hotel inquired. "Or have you grasped the basics already?"

"I want to hear the whole story, please. If it's not too hard for you," I pressed politely. The old man seemed reluctant to continue, and I wanted to know why.

The old man sighed. "I wish I could go back and live my life over. This time, I would have chosen to learn *Tractate Shabbos* while R' Kalman Rosenblitt was still alive."

"What happened after you were promoted at work?" I asked curiously. To hear the old man's sighs, his life in America had not been well spent.

"What happened? A few years later, I took over the manager's job and sat in his seat around the executive conference table at Triboro Buildings. I changed the name to 'Diamond Buildings.' And the firm seemed to be made of diamonds. Whatever I touched turned to gold — or diamonds, as the case may be! Under my leadership, the firm saw a 300-percent growth rate. I built skyscrapers in Los Angeles, in Chicago, in Miami. Where didn't I build?

"During that same period, I married my wife, a Jewish woman — may she rest in peace. Though I was no longer religious, I feared assimilation and clung tight to the slender thread that linked me to the Jewish people. I knew that if I married a non-Jew, my children would not be considered Jewish.

"A year after our marriage, our son was born. We named him Joseph, after my wife's father. But the name we called him was not Joe, but Tom. There were two forces fighting inside me. On the one hand, I wanted to remain a Jew. But, on the other, I tried to imitate the lifestyle of the gentiles around me. That's why I called my son 'Tom.'

"Tom was an only child. It was as if all the blessings in the world were concentrated in that one boy."

"Why do you speak of him in the past tense?" I asked.

A tear trickled down the old man's wrinkled cheek. "Wait, and you'll hear," he said.

Tom was beautiful as an angel. Artist friends of mine begged for a chance to paint his portrait. He was also very bright and unusually talented. My wife and I loved him with more than just an ordinary parent's love — I would say we were sick with love for him! Sometimes, at work, I would start daydreaming about Tom and forget the rest of the world for hours. Tom might have become very spoiled and egotistical, but he had the sweetest nature in the world. An outgoing boy, from the time he was 2 he hardly walked down the street without a few friends trailing after him. He had been blessed with natural leadership qualities, and there was every sign than he would go far in whatever field he chose: politics, statesmanship, or the military.

We chose the military. When Tom finished his education in an expensive college, we sent him to serve in the United States Army. His superiors liked what they saw, and decided that he was best suited to being a fighter pilot. Tom sailed through all the qualifying exams and his basic training. Not only was he sharp-witted and diligent, he was also extraordinarily patient. It was no wonder that he was always surrounded by a crowd of admiring friends. Success seemed to dog his footsteps. When he would return home on his infrequent leaves, the phone never stopped ringing.

After two years of flying fighter jets, Tom got married. Like me, he chose not to break the thread that linked him to his people; he, too, married a Jewish girl. When his son, little Ralph, was born, there was not a prouder grandfather in the world. I showered gifts on my employees at "Diamond Buildings" and doubled their salaries the same week.

The old man's voice broke. "And then came the Saturday I'll never forget. It was sixteen years ago now. On my doorstep stood a serious-faced army officer. I knew at once. Tom had been killed on a training exercise over Greece. I hadn't known that he had been flying intelligence missions with top-secret classification."

Old Mr. Diamond was finding it hard to speak. I felt deeply at a loss, and for a moment I weighed the option of getting up and leaving him in peace. But the boy, Ralph, signaled for me to stay. In a moment, Sam Diamond's melancholy voice filled the air again.

From the moment we heard about our son's death, our lives seemed like a wasteland. All our success, our money, our accomplishments, the praise and stature we had achieved, were like dust beneath our feet. I wandered around the house like a caged lion, and when I finally returned to work at my wife's urging, I was a terror to my workers. We tried going away, but even on a mountain peak in the

Alps or on safari in Africa, we could not forget Tom's smiling face for a moment. We could not be comforted.

Then, one Saturday, an unexpected memory popped into my brain and would not go away: "The missing *Tractate Shabbos*!" R' Kalman Rosenblitt had died on Shabbos, and so had my son, Tom. The missing tractate had exacted payment for the debt!

And that was when I suddenly realized that I was a believer. Forty years of living as a heretic melted in a single moment. I felt G-d's presence clearly and tangibly — and I knew why I had been punished.

I tried to help him along. "The rest is clear enough," I said briskly. "You returned to the old ways. You became mitzvah-observant again."

"Don't jump ahead!" Sam flared. "Patience, my boy. Why are you stopping me? I'm trying to tell you my life story. Hear me out, please."

I fell silent, and Sam went on.

If it hadn't been so sad, it would have been almost funny. Even though I knew that G-d's hand had displayed itself to me, I still did not change my lifestyle even an iota. After a long time, my wife and I began to resume the routines of our normal lives. What gave us the strength to go on was that sweet little baby, our beloved grandson, Ralph — only son of our only son. We wanted to adopt him as our own, but his mother, who had remarried, wanted to keep him with her. We began to see less and less of Ralph. I threw myself into my work and made sure to fill every waking hour with some activity so as not to have time to think about Tom.

My wife was not so fortunate. She found herself unable to forget her grief for even a moment. She faded away and finally departed this life, leaving me truly alone in the world. A few months ago, I decided to visit Israel. I don't know why I never thought of doing that before.

I came to Jerusalem, and my feet carried me to the religious neighborhoods.

I was in a state of shock. The world that I thought had died decades before was thriving before my very eyes! In the streets I saw charming children with curly *peyos,* just like the ones who used to play in those old Polish towns. I couldn't believe what I was seeing. Then I heard a familiar sound. It was the roar of learning, and it was coming from a large building. Moving in a daze, like a sleepwalker, I climbed the stairs and went inside.

For several minutes, I stood just inside the doorway, unable to move or speak. Hundreds of boys were learning energetically — learning the same *Gemara* that I had tossed aside so many years before. Their eyes shone as they debated loudly. I was drawn to them like a magnet. Standing near a pair of learning partners, I saw that they were learning *Tractate Kesubos,* a tractate I had not seen for many a long year. I heard them arguing a point — in English! I knew I'd have no trouble communicating with these two. Without stopping to think, I blurted, "Your friend here is right. If you'll turn seventeen pages ahead, you'll fine his exact *sevarah* in the first *Tosafos* at the top of *amud beis.*"

They fell silent, staring at me with wide eyes. "What did you say?"

I repeated it, and they immediately turned the pages to find the *Tosafos* I had mentioned. I then related to them an original thought on the subject that I had heard from R' Kalman Rosenblitt. I have an excellent memory, but even I had never guessed that entire *shiurim* from the past were indelibly etched in my brain.

Gradually, others began to listen, until we were surrounded by a circle of yeshivah boys. I didn't understand why they were so interested in me: Had I sprouted a pair of horns? Now I know the answer: I looked completely non-Jewish — bareheaded, with rings on my fingers, the last person they would have expected to talk knowledgeably about *Gemara!*

Behind my back, one of the boys pointed me out to his rebbi, and before I knew it I had been invited into the *rosh yeshivah's* office for a chat.

The *rosh yeshivah* listened closely as I explained my background. When I was done he asked me to come back to Israel for another visit at Shavuos time, and to be his guest for the *Yom Tov* meals. I did so, together with my grandson, Ralph, whom I easily managed to persuade to come — despite his mother, who felt she was doing me a big favor in allowing her son to accompany me to Israel.

Sam Diamond smiled beatifically. "I must state here, in total astonishment, that my young grandson shows genuine signs of a true affinity for the Torah and *Yiddishkeit!*"

Ralph, seeing that he was being spoken about, smiled politely. I glanced at him briefly, then kept my eyes riveted to his grandfather.

"Why do you look so surprised?" Sam asked me. "I know it's not exactly your run-of-the-mill life story, but still ..."

I spoke slowly. "It's not every day that you hear a story like this."

"True," old Sam nodded.

We parted in friendship. It was late when I left the hotel. I did not think I would see him again.

The next morning I related the story to my friends at yeshivah around the breakfast table. I didn't expect it to go further, but within hours, there wasn't a person there who had not heard the tale of Sam Diamond's life.

During the midday break, Yossi Himmelfarb, an older student, asked me if the American tourist was still in Israel.

"I don't know," I answered. "I have his phone number at the hotel, if you want to try and find out. Why do you ask?"

Yossi hesitated, as though debating whether or not to share something with me. Finally, he said, "My grandfather learned in Zatovska with R' Kalman Rosenblitt. I'm curious to know whether the two of them learned together."

I went to the phone booth with him and dialed the number. Sam was in his room!

I greeted him warmly, and told him of the latest development before handing the receiver to Yossi Himmelfarb. He introduced himself, then asked, "Do you remember a boy they called Chezkel Lodzer? Do you happen to know what his family name was?"

Sam mumbled something as he strained his memory.

"Could it have been 'Himmelfarb'?" Yossi prompted.

"Yes!" old Sam cried. "Yes, it was! He was named Chezkel Himmelfarb, but in those days we often didn't use people's last names but rather the city or town that they came from. I was called Shmuel Zanstochover and he was called Chezkel Lodzer. That's why I found it hard to recall his last name."

"It's so nice to speak to you!" Yossi said emotionally. "I am Chezkel Lodzer's grandson. My grandfather told me about a friend of his at the yeshivah who left Poland for America. I think my grandfather would be happy to meet an old friend."

Sam shouted, "I don't believe it! You're Chezkel's grandson? I must see him!"

"With pleasure," Yossi's grandfather said a little later, when Yossi phoned him. "I've been waiting for this moment for years. I never thought I'd meet up with Shmuel Zanstochover again."

I'll spare you unnecessary details about the reunion that took place several hours later between two of R' Kalman Rosenblitt's former students. The meeting took place at Chezkel Himmelfarb's home. The most emotional point was when Sam broke down in tears and sobbed to Yossi's grandfather, "R' Kalman Rosenblitt died because of me. It was because of the missing *maseches*!"

R' Chezkel waited for Sam to calm down before answering. "Ease your mind, Shmuel. Do you remember the *Siyum HaShas* that we held in rebbi's honor?"

"Do I remember? What kind of question is that?"

"And do you remember the sharp glance rebbi gave when you started delivering your speech?"

Sam sighed. "How can I forget? That glance has hounded me all through the years."

R' Chezkel Himmelfarb smiled slightly. "Well, R' Kalman was no fool. He smelled something fishy about you and knew that your talk was devoid of real content. That's why he asked me to learn *Tractate Shabbos* in your place. You can put your conscience to rest, Shmuel."

Sam considered this. "I do remember now that I saw the two of you whispering together before the meal." Suddenly, he groaned. "But my son was also killed on a Shabbos!"

"At the time," Chezkel said, "I asked rebbi whether I should let you know the truth — let you know that I had learned *Tractate Shabbos* in your place. I wanted you to know that we knew we couldn't depend on you! But R' Kalman said, 'Absolutely not.' First of all, he didn't want to embarrass you. And second, he would let your conscience trouble you all your life. 'If Shmuel strays from the right path,' rebbi said, 'his conscience will chase after him always.'"

"But according to what you've just told me, it hasn't been my conscience that's been chasing me, but only my imagination!"

"These were R' Kalman's exact words: 'It's better that he doesn't know. Let his imagination hound him all his life,' " R' Chezkel said quietly.

There was a silence, which was soon filled with the harsh sound of Sam's renewed weeping. "But my son was killed on a Shabbos."

"Hashem's ways are mysterious," R' Chezkel murmured. "What do we understand about His taking away a son in order to restore a strayed soul to Him? Maybe it was because you desecrated so many Shabbosos? You did so knowingly and deliberately, despite the fact that you had had the correct upbringing."

At these words, Sam burst into truly heart-rending sobs. In English, he screamed, "Do you have any idea how many Shabbosos I have desecrated?"

Ralph, Sam Diamond's grandson, spoke up for the first time.

"Grandfather, why look at the cup as half-empty? You can also see it as half-full. If Hashem gives me many years of life, I promise you, Grandfather, that I will keep many more Shabbosos than you've desecrated!"

Sam drew a deep, shuddering breath. "You're so young, Ralph. You have no idea of the challenges life will throw at you."

Ralph smiled comfortingly at his grandfather. There was a hint of steel in his voice as he declared, "My rebbis at yeshivah will help me through. And I know that, with Hashem's help, I will succeed!"

This volume is part of
THE ARTSCROLL SERIES®
an ongoing project of
translations, commentaries and expositions
on Scripture, Mishnah, Talmud, Halachah,
liturgy, history, the classic Rabbinic writings,
biographies and thought.

For a brochure of current publications
visit your local Hebrew bookseller
or contact the publisher:

Mesorah Publications, ltd

4401 Second Avenue
Brooklyn, New York 11232
(718) 921-9000
www.artscroll.com